A W... PRO...

AND

HIS DIAMOND BRIDE

BY
LUCY GORDON

Lucy Gordon cut her writing teeth on magazine journalism, interviewing many of the world's most interesting men, including Warren Beatty, Charlton Heston and Sir Roger Moore. She also camped out with lions in Africa, and had many other unusual experiences which have often provided the background for her books. Several years ago, while staying Venice, she met a Venetian who proposed in two days. They have been married ever since. Naturally this has affected her writing, where romantic Italian men tend to feature strongly. Two of her books have won the Romance Writers of America RITA® award.

You can visit her website at www.lucy-gordon.com

A WINTER PROPOSAL

BY
LUCY GORDON

DID YOU PURCHASE THIS BOOK WITHOUT A COVER?
If you did, you should be aware it is **stolen property** as it was reported *unsold and destroyed* by a retailer. Neither the author nor the publisher has received any payment for this book.

All the characters in this book have no existence outside the imagination of the author, and have no relation whatsoever to anyone bearing the same name or names. They are not even distantly inspired by any individual known or unknown to the author, and all the incidents are pure invention.

All Rights Reserved including the right of reproduction in whole or in part in any form. This edition is published by arrangement with Harlequin Enterprises II B.V./S.à.r.l. The text of this publication or any part thereof may not be reproduced or transmitted in any form or by any means, electronic or mechanical, including photocopying, recording, storage in an information retrieval system, or otherwise, without the written permission of the publisher.

This book is sold subject to the condition that it shall not, by way of trade or otherwise, be lent, resold, hired out or otherwise circulated without the prior consent of the publisher in any form of binding or cover other than that in which it is published and without a similar condition including this condition being imposed on the subsequent purchaser.

® and ™ are trademarks owned and used by the trademark owner and/or its licensee. Trademarks marked with ® are registered with the United Kingdom Patent Office and/or the Office for Harmonisation in the Internal Market and in other countries.

First published in Great Britain 2011
Harlequin Mills & Boon Limited,
Eton House, 18-24 Paradise Road, Richmond, Surrey TW9 1SR

© Lucy Gordon 2011

ISBN: 978 0 263 88852 2

23-0111

Harlequin Mills & Boon policy is to use papers that are natural, renewable and recyclable products and made from wood grown in sustainable forests. The logging and manufacturing processes conform to the legal environmental regulations of the country of origin.

Printed and bound in Spain
by Litografia Rosés S.A., Barcelona

Dear Reader,

I must admit to getting a wistful satisfaction from writing about a heroine whose beauty and allure knock men sideways. No hopeless sighing for her. One quirk of her gorgeous mouth, a look from her sultry eyes, and they fall at her feet, begging for her attention. I guess we've all indulged that fantasy at some time.

But the underlying truth is never so simple, as I learned from Pippa, heroine of *A Winter Proposal*. Beneath the surface of the sultry siren is a woman who has been hurt almost beyond bearing, and who has sheltered behind her desirability and her reputation as a good-time girl, determined not to let the world discover her fears.

Those fears include Christmas and mistletoe—both of which bring back suffering she can't bear to recall.

But then she meets Roscoe, a man as damaged as herself, and as skilled at hiding it. Each of them sees through the other's defences to the loving hearts beneath. Harsh and forbidding on the surface, Roscoe discovers depths of tenderness within himself, and uses them to rescue Pippa. Through him she finds that Christmas can once more be a time of joy.

But they are not alone in their struggle. Pippa's beloved grandmother, Dee, has always been a loving presence, offering advice, and standing as a symbol of love's triumph to inspire her to her own happy ending.

Warmest wishes,

Lucy Gordon

CHAPTER ONE

AFTER five years the gravestone was still as clean and well-tended as on the first day, a tribute to somebody's loving care. At the top it read:

MARK ANDREW SELLON,
9th April 1915—7th October 2003
A much loved husband and father

A space had been left below, filled three weeks later by the words:

DEIRDRE SELLON,
18th February 1921—28th October 2003
Beloved wife of the above
Together always

'I remember how you insisted on leaving that space,' Pippa murmured as she tidied away a few weeds. 'Even then you were planning for the day you'd lie beside him. And the pictures too. You had them all ready for your own time.'

A family friend had returned from a trip to Italy and mentioned how Italian gravestones usually contained a picture of the deceased. 'It really makes a difference to know what people looked like,' she'd enthused. 'I'm going to select my picture now.'

'So am I,' Dee had said instantly.

And she had, one for herself and one for her husband, taken when they were still in robust middle age. There, framed by the stone, was Dee, cheerful and ready to cope with anything life threw at her, and there was Mark, still bearing traces of the stunning good looks of his youth, when he'd been a daredevil pilot in the war.

Below them was a third photograph, taken at their sixtieth wedding anniversary party. It showed them standing close together, arms entwined, heads slightly leaning against each other, the very picture of two people who were one at heart.

Less than two months later, he had died. Dee had cherished the photograph, and when, three weeks after that, she had been laid beside him Pippa had insisted on adding it to the headstone.

Finishing with the weeds, she took out the flowers she'd brought with her and laid them carefully at the foot of the stone, murmuring, 'There, just how you like them.'

She rose and moved back, checking that everything looked right, and stood for a moment in the rich glow of the setting sun. A passer-by, happening to glance at her, would have stopped and gazed in wonder.

She was petite, with a slender, elegant figure and an air of confidence that depended on more than mere looks. Nature had given her beauty but also another quality, less easy to define. Her mother called her a saucy little so-and-so. Her father said, 'Watch it, lass. It's dangerous to drive fellers too far.'

Men were divided in expressing their opinion. The more refined simply sighed. The less refined murmured, 'Wow!' The completely unrefined wavered between, 'Get a load of that!' and '*Phwoar!*' Pippa shrugged, smiled and went on her way, happy with any of them.

Superficially, her attractions were easy to explain. The perfect face and body, the curled, honey-coloured hair, clearly luscious and extravagant, even now while it was pinned back in an unconvincing attempt at severity. But there was something else which no one had ever managed to describe: a knowing, amused look in her eyes; not exactly come-hither, but the teasing hint that come-hither might be lurking around the corner. *Something.*

A wooden seat had been placed conveniently nearby and Pippa settled onto it with the air of having come to stay.

'What a day I've had!' she sighed. 'Clients talking their heads off, paperwork up to here.' She indicated the top of her head.

'I blame you,' she told her grandmother, addressing the photograph. 'But for you, I'd never have become a lawyer. But you had to go and leave me that legacy on condition that I trained for a profession.'

'No training, no cash,' Lilian, Pippa's mother had pointed out. 'And she's named me your trustee to make sure you obey orders. I can almost hear her saying, "So get out of that, my girl."'

'That sounds like her,' Pippa had said wryly. 'Mum, what am I going to do?'

'You're going to do what your Gran says because, mark this, wherever she is, she'll be watching.'

'And you were,' Pippa observed now. 'You've always been there, just out of sight, over my shoulder, letting me know what you thought. Perhaps that was his influence.'

From her bag she produced a small toy bear, much of its fur worn away over time. Long ago he'd been won at a fair by Flight Lieutenant Mark Sellon, who'd solemnly presented him to Deirdre Parsons, the girl who later became his bride and lived with him for sixty years. To the last moment she'd treasured her 'Mad Bruin' as she called him.

'Why mad?' Pippa had asked her once.

'After your grandfather.'

'Was he mad?'

'Delightfully mad. Wonderfully, gloriously mad. That's why he was so successful as a fighter pilot. According to other airmen that I spoke to, he just went for everything, hell for leather.'

To the last moment, each had feared to lose the other. In the end Mark had died first, and after that, Dee had treasured the little bear more than ever, finally dying with him pressed against her face, and bequeathing him to Pippa, along with the money.

'I brought him along,' Pippa said, holding Bruin up as though Dee could see him. 'I'm taking good care of him. It's so nice to have him. It's almost like having you.

'I'm sorry it's been so long since my last visit, but it's chaos at work. I used to think solicitors' offices were sedate places, but that was before I joined one. The firm does a certain amount of the "bread and butter stuff", wills, property, that sort of thing. But it's the criminal cases that bring everyone alive. Me too, if I'm honest. David, my boss, says I should go in for criminal law because I've got just the right kind of wicked mind.' She gave a brief chuckle. 'They don't know how true that is.'

She stood for a moment, holding the little bear and smiling fondly at the photos of people she had loved, and still loved. Then she kissed him and replaced him in her bag.

'I've got to go. 'Bye, darling. And you, Grandpa. Don't let her bully you too much. Be firm. I know it's hard after a lifetime of saying, "Yes, dear, no, dear", but try.'

She planted a kiss on the tips of her fingers and laid them against the photograph of her grandparents. Then she stepped back. The movement brought something into the extreme edge of her vision and she turned quickly to see a man watching her. Or it might be more exact to say staring at her with the disapproval of one who couldn't understand such wacky behaviour. Wryly, she supposed she must look a little odd, and wondered how long he'd been there.

He was tall with a lean face that was firm almost to the point of grimness. Fortyish, she thought, but perhaps older with that unyielding look.

She gave him a polite smile and moved off. There was something about him that made her want to escape. She made her way to a place where there were other family graves.

It was strangely pleasant in these surroundings. Although part of a London suburb, the cemetery had a country air, with tall trees in which birds and squirrels made their homes. As the winter day faded, the red sun seemed to be sliding down between the tree trunks, accompanied by soft whistles and scampering among the leaves. Pippa had always enjoyed coming here, for its beauty almost as much as because it was now the home of people she had loved.

Just ahead were Dee's parents, Joe and Helen, their daughter Sylvia and her infant son Joey, and the baby Polly. She had never known any of them, yet she'd been raised in a climate of strong family unity and they were as mysteriously real to her as her living relatives.

She paused for a moment at Sylvia's grave, remembering her mother's words about the likeness. It was a physical likeness, Pippa knew, having seen old snapshots of Great-Aunt Sylvia. As a young woman in the nineteen-thirties she'd been a noted beauty, living an adventurous life, skipping from romance to romance. Everyone thought she would marry the dashing Mark Sellon, but she'd left him to run off with a married man just before the war broke out. He died at Dunkirk and she died in the Blitz.

Something of Sylvia's beauty had reappeared in Pippa. But the real likeness lay elsewhere, in the sparkling eyes and readiness to seek new horizons.

'In the genes,' Lilian had judged, perhaps correctly. 'Born to be a good time girl.'

'Nothing wrong with having a good time,' Pippa had often replied chirpily.

'There is if you don't think of anything else,' Lilian pointed out.

Pippa was indignant. 'I think of plenty else. I work like a slave at my job. It's just that now and then I like to enjoy myself.'

It sounded a rational answer, but they both knew that it was actually no answer at all. Pippa's flirtations were many but superficial. And there was a reason for it, one that few people knew.

Gran Dee had known. She'd been a close-up witness of Pippa's relationship with Jack Sothern, had seen how deeply the young girl was in love with him, how brilliantly happy when they became engaged, how devastated when he'd abandoned her a few weeks before Christmas.

That time still stood out fiercely in Pippa's mind. Jack had left town for a couple of days, which hadn't made her suspicious, as she now realised it should have. Wedding preparations, she'd thought; matters to be settled at work before he was free to go on their honeymoon. The idea of another woman had never crossed her mind.

When he returned she paid an unexpected visit to his apartment, heralding her arrival by singing a Christmas carol outside his door.

'New day, new hope, new life,' she yodelled merrily.

When he opened the door she flew into his arms, hoping to draw him into a kiss, but he moved stiffly away.

Then he dumped her.

For a while she'd been knocked sideways. Instead of the splendid career that should have been hers, she'd taken a job serving in the local supermarket, justifying this by saying that her grandparents, both in their eighties and frail, needed her. For the last two years of their lives she'd lived with them, watching over them, giving them every moment because, as she declared, she had no use for boyfriends.

It was then that the innocent beauty of her face had begun to be haunted with a look of determination so fierce as to be sometimes alarming. It would vanish quickly, driven away by her natural warmth, but it was still there, half hidden in the shadows, ready to return.

'Don't give in to it,' Dee had begged in her last year of life. 'I know you were treated cruelly, but don't become bitter, whatever you do.'

'Gran, honestly, you've got it all wrong. So a man let me down! So what? We rise above that these days!'

Dee had looked unconvinced, so Pippa brightened her smile, hoping to fool her, not very successfully, she knew.

Only after her death had Dee been able to put the situation right with a modest legacy, conditional on Pippa training for a proper career.

Pippa had changed from the quiet girl struggling to recover from heartbreak. Going back out into the world, starting a new life, had brought out a side she hadn't known she had. Her looks won her many admirers, and she'd gone to meet them, arms open but heart closed. Life was fun if you didn't expect too much, and she'd brought that down to a fine art.

'Aunt Sylvia would have been proud of you,' her mother told her, half critical, half admiring. 'Not that I knew her, she died before I was born, but the way she carried on was a family legend and you're heading in the same direction. Look at the way you're dressed!'

'I like to dress properly,' Pippa observed, looking down at

the short skirt that revealed her stunning legs, and the closely cut top that emphasised her delicate curves.

'That's not properly, that's improperly,' Lilian replied.

'They can be the same thing,' Pippa teased. 'Oh, Mum, don't look so shocked. I'm sure Aunt Sylvia would have said exactly that.'

'Very likely, from all I've heard. But you're supposed to be a lawyer.'

'What do you mean, "supposed"? I passed my exams with honours and they were fighting to hire me, so my boss said.'

'And doesn't he mind you floating about his office looking like a sexy siren?' Lilian demanded.

Pippa giggled.

'No, I guess he doesn't,' Lilian conceded. 'Well, I suppose if you've got the exam results to back you up you'll be all right.'

'Oh, yes,' Pippa murmured. 'I'll be all right.'

One man, speaking from the depths of his injured feelings, had called her a tease, but he did her an injustice. She embarked on a relationship in all honesty, always wondering if this one would be different. But it never was. When she backed off it was from fear, not heartlessness. The memory of her misery over Jack was still there in her heart. The time that had passed since had dimmed that misery, but nothing could ever free her from its shadow, and she was never going to let it happen again.

'I reckon you'd have understood that,' she told Sylvia. 'The things I've heard about you—I really wish we could have met. I bet you were fun.'

The thought of that fun made a smile break over her face. Sometimes she seemed to smile as she breathed.

But the smile faded as she turned to leave and saw the man she'd seen before, frowning at her.

Well, I suppose I must look pretty crazy, she thought wryly. *His generation probably thinks you should never smile in a graveyard. But why not, if you're fond of the people you come to see? And I'm very fond of Sylvia, even though we never met. So there!*

Her mood of cheerful defiance lasted until she reached her car, parked just outside the gate. Then it faded into exasperation.

'Oh, no, not again!' she breathed as the engine made futile noises. 'I'll take you to the garage tomorrow, but start just this once, *please*!'

But, deaf to entreaties, it merely whirred again.

'Grr!'

Getting out to look under the bonnet was a formality as she had only the vaguest idea what she was hoping to find. Whatever it was, she didn't find it.

'Grr!'

'Are you in trouble?'

It was him, the man who'd interrupted her pleasant reverie in the graveyard and practically driven her out by his grim disapproval. At least, in her present growling exasperation that was how it seemed to her.

Not that he was looking grim now, merely detached and efficient as he headed towards her and surveyed the car.

'Won't it start?'

'No. But this has happened before, and it usually starts after a while if I'm firm with it.'

His lips quirked slightly. 'How do you get firm with a car? Kick it?'

'Certainly not,' she said with dignity. 'I'm not living in the Dark Ages. I just—tap it a little and it comes right.'

'I've got a better idea. Suppose I tow you to the nearest garage, or have you got a special one where you normally go when this breaks down?'

'My brothers own a garage in Crimea Street,' she said with dignity.

'And do they approve of your "tapping" the car?'

'They don't approve of anything, starting with the fact that I bought it without consulting them. I just loved it on sight. It's got so much personality.'

'It's certainly got that. What it hasn't got is a reliable engine. You say you have brothers in the trade, and they let you buy this thing?'

'They did not "let" me because I didn't ask their permission,' she said indignantly.

'Nor their advice, it seems. I hope they gave you a piece of their minds.'

'They did.'

'So would I if you were my daughter.'

'But I'm not your daughter, I haven't asked for your help and I certainly haven't asked for your interference. Now, if you don't mind, I'd like to leave.'

'How?' he asked simply.

In her annoyance she'd forgotten that she was stranded. She glared.

'It's three miles to Crimea Street,' he pointed out. 'Are you going to walk it? In those heels? Or are you going to call them to rescue you? They'll love that.'

'Yes, and I'll never hear the end of it,' she sighed. 'Ah, well, I don't seem to have any choice.'

'Unless I give you a tow?' Seeing her suspicious look, he said, 'It's a genuine offer. I can't just leave you here.'

'Me being such a poor, helpless damsel in distress, you mean?'

His lips twitched. 'Well, there must be something of the damsel in distress about you, or you wouldn't have bought this ridiculous car.'

'Very funny. Thank you for your offer of help, but I'll manage without it. Good day to you.'

'Come off your high horse. Come to think of it, a horse would probably have served you better than this contraption. I'll fetch my car and connect them.' Starting to move off, he turned to add, 'Don't go away.'

She opened her mouth to reply, had second thoughts and closed it again. It was annoying that she couldn't help laughing at his jibe, but that was the fact. She was still smiling when he returned in an expensive vehicle that made her eyes open wide.

'Oh, wow! Are you sure you want that thing seen with my old jalopy?' she asked.

'I'll try to endure it.' He worked swiftly to connect the cars, then opened his door and indicated for her to get into the passenger seat.

She had to admire the smooth, purring movement of his vehicle, which spoke of expense and loving care, suggesting that this man had an affinity with cars. Since she loved them herself, she could feel some sympathy, even a faint amused appreciation of how she must look to him. He'd implied that she reminded him of a daughter, and she wondered how many daughters he actually had.

'I'm Roscoe Havering, by the way,' he said.

'Pippa Jenson—well, Philippa, actually.'

'Pippa's better: more like you.'

'I'm not even going to ask what is "like me". You have no idea.'

'Cheeky. Very young.'

'I'm not that young.'

'Twenty—twenty-one—' he hazarded.

'Twenty-seven,' she laughed.

It was as well that traffic lights had forced him to halt

because he turned quickly to stare at her in surprise. 'You're not serious.'

'I am.' She gave him a wicked smile. 'Sorry!'

'How can I believe you?' he said, starting up again. 'You look more like a student.'

'No, I'm a solicitor, a staid and serious representative of the law.' She assumed a deep voice. 'Strong men quake at my approach. Some of them flee to hide in the hills.'

He laughed. 'I think I'll get you home first. I won't ask who you work for. Obviously, you have your own practice which is driving everyone else into bankruptcy.'

'No, I'm with Farley & Son.'

She saw his eyebrows rise a little and his mouth twist into a shape that meant, '*Hmm!*'

'Do you know them?'

'Quite well. I've used them in the past. They've got a big reputation. You must be impressive if they've taken you on. Aren't we nearing Crimea Street now?'

'Next one on the left.'

They saw the garage as soon as they turned into the street. The little business that Pippa's great-grandfather, Joe Parsons, had set up ninety years earlier had flourished and grown. It was now three times the size, and her brothers, Brian and Frank, had bought houses on the same street so that they could live close to their work.

They were just preparing to shut up shop when the little convoy rolled into view. At once they came out onto the pavement and stood watching with brotherly irony.

'Again!' Frank declared. 'Why aren't I surprised?'

'Because you're an old stick-in-the-mud,' Pippa informed him, kissing his cheek, then Brian's. 'And clearly you didn't mend it properly. This is Roscoe Havering, who came to my rescue.'

'Good of you,' Brian said, shaking Roscoe's hand. 'Of

course a better idea would have been to dump her in the nearest river, but I dare say that didn't occur to you.'

'Actually, it did,' Roscoe observed. 'But I resisted the temptation.'

The brothers laughed genially. They were both in their forties, heavily built and cheerful.

A few moments under the bonnet was enough to make Frank say, 'This'll take until tomorrow. And look, I'm afraid we can't invite you in. The family's away and we've sort of planned...well...'

'A night on the tiles,' Pippa chuckled. 'You devils! I'll bet Crimea Street is going to rock.'

'You'd better believe it!'

'OK, I'll come back tomorrow.'

'Don't you live here?' Roscoe asked.

'No, I've got my own little place a few miles away.'

'Where exactly?'

She gave him the address in the heart of London.

'I'll take you,' he said. 'Get in.'

Relieved, she did so, first retrieving two heavy bags from the back of her car.

'Thanks,' she said as she clicked the seat belt and slammed the door. 'I've got a heavy night's work ahead of me and I've got to give it everything.'

'No hungry man wanting his supper cooked?'

'Nope. I live alone. Free, independent, no distractions.'

'Except visiting your friends,' he observed.

'They're my brothers—oh, you mean in the graveyard. I suppose you thought I looked very odd.'

'No, you looked as if you were enjoying the company. It was nice.'

'I always did enjoy my grandparents' company. I adored them both. Especially Gran. I loved talking to her, and I guess I just can't stop.'

'Why should you want to?'

'Most people would say because she's dead.'

'But she isn't dead to you, and that's what matters. Besides, I don't think you worry too much about what other people say.'

'Well, I ought to. I'm a lawyer.'

'Ah, yes. Staid and serious.'

She made a comical face. 'I do my best.'

Outwardly, he showed nothing, but inside his expression was wry. Twenty-seven. Was he expected to believe that? Twenty-four, tops. And even that was stretching it. If she really worked for Farley she was probably little more than a pupil, but that was fine. She could still be useful to him.

A plan was forming in his mind. The details had to be fine-tuned but meeting her was like the working out of destiny. Somewhere, a kindly fate had planned this meeting and he was going to make the most of it.

'It's just there,' Pippa said, pointing through the window to a tall, expensive-looking apartment block.

'There doesn't seem anywhere to park,' he groaned.

'No need. Just slow down a little and I'll hop out. Just here where the lights are red.'

She reached for her bags, flashed him a dazzling smile and got out swiftly.

'Thank you,' she called, backing off.

He would have called her to wait but the lights changed and he had to move on.

Pippa hurried into the building and took the elevator to the third floor. Once in her apartment, she tossed the bags away and began to strip off.

'Shower, shower,' she muttered. 'Just let me get under the shower!'

When she was naked she hurried into the bathroom and got under the water, sighing with satisfaction. After relishing the cascade for a few minutes, she got out and dried herself off, thinking of the evening's work that lay ahead. She felt ready for it now.

But then something caught her eye. One of her bags lay open on its side, the contents spilling out, and she could see at once that one vital object was missing.

'Oh, heavens!' she groaned. 'It must have fallen out in his car and he drove off with it.'

The sound of the doorbell revived her hope. *Roscoe Havering. He's found it, brought it back to me. Thank heavens!*

Pulling a large towelling robe around her, she ran to the door. 'I'm so glad to see you—'

Then she stopped, stunned by the sight of the young man who stood there, his air a mixture of pleading and defiance.

'Oh, no,' she breathed. 'You promised not to do this again.'

CHAPTER TWO

FOR most of the journey Roscoe wore a frown. Things were falling into place nicely. Not that this was a surprise. He was an organised man, skilled at controlling his surroundings and making things happen as he wanted, but even he could hardly have arranged matters as neatly as this.

So his frown didn't imply problems, simply that there were still details to be sorted before he'd fixed everything to suit himself, and he was giving that desirable outcome the concentration it deserved.

Now he could see the large, comfortable house that had once been his home. These days it housed only his mother and younger brother Charlie, although Roscoe had kept his room and usually slept there a couple of nights a week to keep a protective eye on both of them. His mother was looking anxiously out of the window and came to the door as soon as she saw him. She was approaching sixty, nervously thin but still with the remnants of good looks.

'Is it all right?' she asked. 'Have you sorted it?'

He kissed her. 'Sorted what?'

'About Charlie. Have you arranged everything?'

For just the briefest moment he tensed, then smiled.

'Mother, it's too soon to arrange everything, but I'm working on it. Don't worry.'

'Oh, but I must worry. He's so frail and vulnerable.'

Luckily she wasn't looking directly at him, or she'd have seen the cynical twist of his mouth. Roscoe had an unsentimental, clear-eyed view of his younger brother. He knew Charlie's volatility, his ramshackle behaviour, his headlong craziness and his selfishness. All these he saw through a filter of brotherly affection, but he never fooled himself. Frail and vulnerable? No way!

But he knew his mother's perception was different and he always avoided hurting her, so he simply said, 'Leave it to me. You know you can trust me.'

'But you will make them drop those stupid charges, won't you? You'll make those horrid people admit that he's innocent.'

'Mother, he's not exactly innocent. He more or less admitted—'

'Oh, but he didn't know what he was saying. He was confused.'

'He's not a child. He's a young man of twenty-four.'

'He's a child in his heart, and he needs his big brother to defend him.'

'I'm doing my best. Just leave it to me.'

'Oh, yes, you always protect him, don't you? You're such a good brother. I don't know what I'd do without you.'

'Well, you don't have to,' he said gently. 'So it's all right.'

'Now come indoors and have your supper.'

'Fine, I'll just get my things.'

But, as he leaned into the car, he froze suddenly.

'Oh, Lord!' he groaned, seizing something from the floor at the back. 'How did that get there?' He straightened up, holding a large envelope. 'It must have fallen out of one of her bags and she rushed off without noticing. Perhaps I can call her.'

He pulled out the contents, all papers, and went through

them looking for her phone number. He didn't find it, but he did notice that these were serious papers. She'd spoken of a heavy night's work ahead, and would probably need them.

'I'm sorry,' he sighed. 'Can you hold supper? I'll be back in an hour.'

He was gone before his mother could complain.

'Jimmy, you promised to leave me alone.' As Pippa spoke she was backing off, one hand clutching the robe across her breast, the other held up defensively. 'We agreed it was over.'

'No, you said it was over,' he protested. 'I never said it. I couldn't say it, feeling the way I do. Oh, Pippa, I miss you so much, if you only knew. But you do know in your heart, don't you? I couldn't be so crazy about you if you didn't feel just a little something for me.'

'I do feel something for you,' she sighed.

'There, I knew it!'

'But it's not what you want. It's mostly pity and a sort of guilt that I let things go so far. Honestly, Jimmy, I didn't mean to. I thought we were just having a good time with no strings. If I'd known you were getting so serious I'd have discouraged you earlier.'

'But you didn't,' the young man pleaded. 'Doesn't that prove you feel something for me?'

'Yes, it means I feel like a kindly aunt, and that's not what you want.'

His face fell and she knew a pang over her heart. He was a nice boy, and he'd appeared on the scene just in time to discourage the one before him. She'd been grateful, and after that they'd shared many a laugh, some dinner engagements and a few kisses.

Then things had got out of hand. He'd grown serious, wanting to take her away for a weekend. Her refusal had increased his ardour. He'd spoken of his respect, and proposed marriage. Her rejection had cast him into despair.

'Couldn't we give it another try?' he begged now. 'You tell me what it is about me that annoys you and I'll be careful never to do that.'

Reluctantly, Pippa decided that only firmness would be any use now.

'When you talk like that it annoys me,' she said. 'When you haunt me, and telephone at all hours, sending me flowers which I don't want, bombarding me with text messages asking what I'm wearing, then I get very annoyed.

'You're a nice boy, Jimmy, but you're not for me. I'm sorry if I led you to believe otherwise. I didn't mean to. Now, please go.'

Something in his eyes made her pull the edges of her robe closer, clutching them firmly. His anguish was being replaced by the determination of a man who would no longer accept no for an answer.

'Please go,' she said, stepping back.

'Not without a kiss. You can grant me that, can't you?'

'I think not. Goodbye.'

Pippa tried to close the door but he forestalled her. Now his breathing was coming heavily, the arms that closed around her were strong, and she was no longer sure she could deal with him.

'Let me go, Jimmy.'

'Not until I'm ready.'

'Did you hear me? I said let me go and I meant it. Stop that. *Jimmy, no!*'

On the journey back to Pippa's apartment Roscoe was frowning again, but this time in confusion. On the one hand there was her appearance—young, dainty, vivacious. On the other hand there were the papers with their plethora of facts and figures that only a skilled, serious mind could understand. He tried to fit the two sides together, and couldn't.

This time he found a parking space and entered the building, going to study the list of residents by the elevator.

'Can I help?' A middle-aged man was passing by.

'I'm looking for Miss Jenson's address.'

'Blimey, another one. They pass through here like an army. Mind you, even she doesn't usually have two in one evening.'

'Indeed,' Roscoe said carefully.

'I tell you, it's pathetic. They come here with their flowers and their gifts, begging her, pleading with her, but it's no use. When she's bored with them she dumps them. I've tried to warn some of them but will they listen? You'd expect a man to have more dignity, wouldn't you?'

'You would indeed,' Roscoe said, still guarding his words.

'But they say she's magic and they can't help themselves.'

'You spoke of two.'

'Yes, the other one hasn't been here long so you'd better go carefully. Good-looking young fellow. Shouldn't think you'd stand a chance. She's got a pick of them, you know. Best of luck, though.'

He passed on out of the front door, leaving Roscoe wondering what he'd wandered into. But what he'd just heard was good news in that it made Pippa likely to be more useful to him, and nothing else mattered. He located the apartment and got into the elevator.

As soon as the doors parted he heard the noise coming from just around the corner, out of sight, a male voice crying out, 'You can't be so cruel—'

Then Pippa's voice. 'Can't I? Get out now or I'll show you how cruel I can be. I'm told I have very sharp knees.'

'But I only—*ow*!'

'Now go. And don't come back.'

Roscoe turned the corner just in time to see the young man stagger back, clutching himself, then collapse to the ground. Through the open door he could see a woman, or perhaps a goddess. She was completely naked, leaving no detail of her glorious figure to the imagination. The hourglass shape, the curved hips, the tiny waist, the breasts slightly too large, although his view of them was partly obscured by her glorious hair, not pinned back now but cascading down in a riot of curls.

After a moment he realised that the vision was Pippa, but not the light-hearted girl he'd met earlier. This was a very angry woman, standing triumphant over her defeated foe who was writhing on the ground. Literally.

The vision vanished at once, not in a puff of smoke but in a hasty movement to make herself decent by pulling on a robe as soon as she saw Roscoe. Only the fury on her face remained.

With the robe safely concealing her, she came to the door and addressed the young man. 'I'm sorry, Jimmy, but I warned you. Don't come back here, ever.'

Jimmy's face was sullen as he hauled himself to his feet, all good nature gone. 'You haven't heard the last of this,' he spat. '*Jezebel!*'

Incredibly, a smile flickered over her beautiful features. 'Oh, come on, you can do better than that. Who was Jezebel, after all? Now, if you'd said Mata Hari I'd have been insulted—or maybe flattered, one of the two.'

'Mata who?'

'Oh, go and look it up!' she said with the exasperation of a schoolmistress. 'But *go*!'

Scowling, he dragged himself to his feet and began to

limp away, but not before turning to Roscoe. 'You've been warned,' he spat. 'She won't treat you any better.'

Roscoe held up the envelope. 'I'm just the delivery man,' he said mildly.

Jimmy flung him a speaking look and limped away. Roscoe waited until he was out of sight before saying, 'I'm sorry to arrive unexpectedly, but you left this in my car.'

She made as if to take the envelope that he held out, but snatched her hand back as the robe fell open.

'I'll take it inside,' he said, moving past her.

She followed him, slamming the front door, hurrying into the bedroom and slamming that door too. Roscoe wondered at her agitation. After all, she'd been the victor, conquering and subduing her foe. He would have given a good deal to know the history behind that scene.

The apartment was what he would have expected, lush and decorative in a way he thought of as ultra-feminine. The furniture was expensive and tastefully chosen and the shelves bore ornaments that suggested a knowledge of antiques.

In one corner of the room was a desk with a computer and various accessories, all of which were the very latest, he noted with approval. It seemed to tell a different story to the rest of her. Ditzy dolly-bird on the one hand, technology expert on the other.

But probably the computer had been installed by her employers. That explained it.

She came whizzing back into the room, dressed in sweater and jeans. They were sturdy and workaday, unglamorous except that they answered all questions about her figure.

'Are you all right?' he asked.

'Certainly I'm all right. Why shouldn't I be?' She sounded a tad defiant.

'Just that he seemed rather overwrought—'

'And he called me Jezebel, implying that I'm a floozie, that's what you meant.'

'That's not what I meant at all.'

Even to herself, Pippa couldn't have explained why she was on edge, except that she liked to stay in control, and being discovered as she had been was definitely not being in control.

'Look, I just came back to return your papers,' he said hastily. 'Don't blame me for finding…well…what I found.' Too late, he saw the quagmire stretching before him.

'And just what do you think you found?' she demanded, folding her arms and looking up into his face. It was hard because he had a good six inches over her but what she lacked in height she made up in fury.

His own temper rose. After all, he'd done her a favour.

'Well, I found a girl who'd been a bit careless, didn't I?'

'Careless?'

'Careless with her own safety. What on earth possessed you to get undressed if you were going to knock him back?'

'Oh, I see. You think I'm a vulgar tease?'

'No, just that you weren't thinking straight—'

'Or maybe you're the one not thinking straight,' she snapped. 'You jump to the conclusion that I stripped off to allure him, and the true explanation never occurs to you. Too simple, I suppose. *He arrived after I had come out of the shower.*'

'Oh, heavens, I should have thought of that. I'm sorry, I—'

'I didn't get undressed for him,' she raged on, barely hearing him. 'I'm not interested in him and so I've told him again and again, but he wouldn't take no for an answer. Just like a man. You're all the same. You all think you're so madly attractive that a woman's no never really means no.'

'I didn't—'

'Conceited, arrogant, bullying, faithless, treacherous—'

'If you'd only—'

'Leave, now!'

'If I could just—'

'No, you can't "just". *Leave!*'

'I understand that—'

'Listen, the last man who came in here wouldn't go when I told him to, and you saw what happened to him.'

'All right,' Roscoe said hastily. 'I really only came to return your property.'

'Thank you, sir, for your consideration,' Pippa responded in a formal voice that was like ice, 'but if you don't leave of your free will you'll do so at *my* will and that—'

'I'm going, I'm going.'

He departed quickly. Whatever the rights and wrongs of the situation, this was no time to argue. For some reason, she was ready to do murder. It was unfair, but there was no understanding women.

From Pippa's window, a curve in the building made the front door visible. She stood there watching until she saw him get into his car. Then she turned and glared at the photograph of her grandparents on the sideboard.

'All right, all right. I behaved terribly. He came to return my things and I was rude to him. I didn't even thank him. Why? *Why?* I don't know why, but I was suddenly furious with him. How dare he see me naked! Yes, I know it wasn't his fault; you don't have to say it. But you should have seen the look on his face when he saw me on display. He didn't know whether to fancy me or despise me, and I could strangle him for it. Grandpa, stop laughing! It's not funny. Well, all right. Maybe just a bit. Oh, to blazes with him!'

Down below, Roscoe took a quick glance up, just in time to see her at the window before she backed off. He sat in his car for a moment, pondering.

He'd gained only a brief glimpse inside her bedroom, just enough to see a double bed and observe that it was neatly made and unused. He'd barely registered this but now it came back to him with all its implications.

So she really had refused him, which meant she was a lady of discrimination and taste as well as beauty and glowering temper. Excellent.

Later that night, before going to bed, he went online and looked up Mata Hari:

Dutch, 1876-1917, exotic dancer, artist's model, circus rider, courtesan, double agent in World War One, executed by firing squad.

Hmm! he thought.

It was a word that occurred to him often in connection with Pippa. With every passing moment he became more convinced that she would fit his plans perfectly.

The two men regarded each other over the desk.

'Not again!' David Farley said in exasperation. 'Didn't he promise to reform last time?'

'And the time before,' Roscoe sighed. 'Charlie's not really a criminal, he just gets carried away by youthful high spirits.'

'That's your mother talking.'

'I'm afraid so.'

'Why can't she face the truth about Charlie?'

'Because she doesn't want to,' Roscoe said bluntly. 'He looks exactly like our father, and since Dad died fifteen years ago she's built everything on Charlie.'

The door opened and Roscoe tensed, but it was only a young woman with a tea tray.

'Thanks,' David Farley said gratefully.

He was a burly man in his late forties with a pleasant face and a kindly, slightly dull manner. He cultivated that dullness, knowing how useful it could be to conceal his powerful mind until the last moment. Now he poured tea with the casual skill of a waiter.

'Has your mother ever come to terms with the fact that your father committed suicide?' he asked carefully.

Roscoe shook his head. 'She won't admit it. The official story was that the car crash was an accident, and we stuck to that to discourage gossip. Now I think she's convinced herself that it really was an accident. A suicide would have been a rejection of her, you see.'

'Of all of you,' David ventured to say. He'd known Roscoe for years, right back to the time he'd been a young man who admired and loved his father. He too had suffered, but David doubted anyone had ever considered this.

Now, much as he'd expected, Roscoe shrugged aside the suggestion that he actually had feelings and hurried to say, 'If I can pull Charlie through this without a disaster I can get him onto the straight and narrow and stop her being hurt.'

'Do you know how often I've heard you say that?' David demanded. 'And it never works because Charlie knows he can always rely on you to rescue him from trouble. Just for once, don't save him. Then he'll learn his lesson.'

'He'll also end up with a criminal record, and my mother will have a broken heart,' Roscoe said harshly. 'Forget it. There has to be a way to deal with this, and I know what it is. It's important to put the right person on the case.'

'I shall naturally deal with this myself—'

'Of course, but you'll need a good assistant. I suggest Miss Philippa Jenson.'

'You know her?'

'I met her yesterday and was much impressed by her qualities,' Roscoe declared in a carefully colourless voice. 'I want you to assign her to Charlie with instructions to give him her full attention.'

'I can give Pippa this case, but I can't take her off other cases. She's much in demand. Don't be fooled by her looks. She's terrifyingly bright and one of the best in the business. She qualified with some of the highest marks that have ever been seen, and several firms were after her. I got her by playing on her sympathies. She did her pupillage here and I managed to persuade her that she owed me something.'

'So she really is qualified? She looks so young.'

'She's twenty-seven and already becoming well known in the profession. This lady is no mere assistant, but a formidable legal brain.'

The last three words affected Roscoe strangely. The world vanished, leaving only a young, perfect female body, glowing with life and vigour, dainty waist, generous breasts partly hidden by the luscious hair that tumbled about them, beautiful face glaring at him with disdain.

A formidable legal brain!

'What...what did you say?' he asked with an effort.

'Are you all right?'

The vision vanished. He was back in the prosaic offices of Farley & Son, facing David Farley across a prosaic desk, drinking a prosaic cup of tea towards the end of a prosaic afternoon.

'I'm fine,' he said quickly. 'I just need to settle things with Miss Jenson. Can I see her?'

'She's in court this afternoon, unless perhaps she's returned. Hang on.' He seized the phone, which had rung. 'Pippa! Speak of the devil! How did it go?... Good...good. So Renton's pleased. You made his enemies sorry they were born, eh? I knew you would. Look, could you hurry back? I've got a new client waiting for you. Apparently you already—'

He checked, alerted by Roscoe's violent shake of the head.

'You're already known to him by repute,' he amended hastily. 'See you in a minute.'

Hanging up, he stared, puzzled. 'Why didn't you want me to say you'd already met?'

'Best not. Start from scratch,' Roscoe said. Inwardly, he was musing about the name Renton, which he'd glimpsed on the papers he delivered last night, plus a mountain of figures.

'So she has a very satisfied client?' he mused.

'One of many. Lee Renton is a big man in the entertainment field, and getting bigger. There were some grim accusations hurled at him by someone who'd hoped to take advantage of him, and failed. Financial stuff, all lies. I knew Pippa would nail it.'

'So her adversary *is* sorry he was born?' Roscoe queried.

'Nasty character, up to every trick. But then, so is she. Great on detail, reads each paper through thoroughly. Nothing escapes her. She'll be here in a moment. The court is just around the corner.'

'Solicitors don't usually appear in court, do they? I thought that was the role of barristers.'

'The old division still exists,' David agreed, nodding, 'but its lines are getting blurred. These days, solicitors can act as advocates more often than in the past, and when they're as good as Miss Jenson we encourage it. You've made a good choice.'

'Yes,' Roscoe murmured. 'I have.'

'Luckily for you, she's a workaholic or she might be reluctant to add to her workload so close to Christmas.'

'Close to Christmas? It's only November.'

'Most people start planning their schedule now so that they can grab some extra days off when the time comes. Pippa does the opposite, comes in earlier, works later. The nearer to Christmas it gets, the more of a workaholic she becomes.

I could understand it if she was alone, but she's got plenty of family. It's as if she's trying to avoid Christmas altogether.'

'You make her sound like Scrooge.'

David grinned. 'Well, I think I really have detected a touch of "Bah! Humbug!" in her manner.'

His phone rang. He answered it and made a face. 'Don't send him in or I'll never get rid of him. I'll come out there.' Rising, he said, 'Stay there and I'll be back in a minute.' He hurried out.

While waiting, Roscoe went to stand by the window, looking down on a part of London that spoke of wealth and manipulation, people in control, sophistication—rather like one aspect of Pippa Jenson. But not all of her, he thought, remembering the unselfconscious way he'd seen her joking with the headstone yesterday.

The door opened. Somebody flew into the room, speaking breathlessly. 'Oh, my, what a day! But it was worth everything to see the look on Blakely's face when I had all the figures—'

She stopped as Roscoe turned from the window.

'Good afternoon, Miss Jenson,' he said.

CHAPTER THREE

FOR a moment Pippa's face was full of shock. 'You,' she murmured.

Then shock was swiftly replaced by a smile. 'So prayers do get answered after all,' she said.

'I'm the answer to your prayers?' he queried. 'Now that I wasn't expecting.'

'Meeting you again is the answer to prayer,' she said. 'It gives me the chance to say thank you, otherwise I'd have had to search for you all over London. You came to my rescue three times last night—towing me to the garage, taking me home, bringing my papers over—and then I was rotten to you. I can't forgive myself.'

'No, that's my job,' he agreed. 'Let's forget it now.'

'That's kinder than I deserve. When I think—'

The door opened. It was David with the man he'd been trying to get rid of, and who was now talking nineteen to the dozen, causing David to make a face of resignation.

'We're in the way,' Roscoe said. 'Let's have a bite to eat. Cavelli's is very good, and it's nearby.'

'Great. I'm famished.'

Cavelli's was a small restaurant over the road, just opening for the early evening. They found a table by the window.

'I'd toast you in champagne,' Roscoe said, 'but I'm driving. What about you?'

'I'm afraid my car's still on the sick list. I came in by taxi.'

'Champagne, then.'

'Not on my own. What I'm really dying for is a cup of tea.'

He placed the order and sat regarding her for a moment. Her hair was pinned back again, as he'd first seen it, but the rich honey colour still had a luxuriant appearance. She was dressed for business in a dark blue trouser suit of decidedly mannish cut. But if she thought for a moment that it masked her vibrant sexual allure, she was deceiving herself, Roscoe thought.

He pulled himself together. This was a time for business. The 'other' Pippa, the one he'd seen last night, must be firmly banished. He did his best to achieve that, but it was hard when all around them people were turning to look at her in admiration.

They toasted each other in hot tea, and Pippa sighed theatrically with relief.

'You don't know what I owe you,' she said. 'Those papers won the case for me. Without them, it would have been a disaster.'

'Yes, you couldn't have made Frank Blakely sorry he was born, which I gather you did.'

She gave a triumphant chuckle. 'I reported the figures, he disputed them, I produced the papers that proved them, he demanded to know how I came by those papers, I said my lips were sealed—'

'That sounds a bit dodgy,' Roscoe said, grinning, pleased.

'Do you mind?' she demanded, mock-offended. 'I am not "a bit dodgy".'

'I beg your pardon—'

'I'm *very* dodgy—when I have to be. It depends on the

client. Some need more dodginess than others. Some don't need any.' She added wickedly, 'They're the boring ones.'

'I see you believe in adjusting to their requirements,' he said appreciatively.

'That's right. Ready for anything.' She chuckled. 'It makes life interesting.'

'Miss Jenson—'

'Please, I think we've passed the point where you could call me Pippa.'

She didn't add, *After the way you saw me*, but she didn't need to.

'Pippa—I'm sorry if I embarrassed you last night. I only wanted to return your property.'

'It wasn't your fault. It was just unlucky that you turned up...well...at that moment.'

'He seemed to feel very strongly about you.'

She sighed. 'He's a nice boy but he can't understand that I don't feel the same way. We went out for a while, had some fun, but there was nothing in it beyond that.'

'Not on your side, but surely his feelings were involved?'

For a moment Roscoe fancied a faint withered look came over Pippa's face.

'And if it had been the other way around, do you think he'd have cared about my feelings?' she asked quietly.

'Perhaps. He seemed to have really strong emotions about you.'

The look vanished so fast he couldn't be sure he'd seen it. 'Life's a merry-go-round.' She shrugged. 'You have to look forward to the ups but always be ready for more downs.'

'So there's nobody special in your life at the moment? Or are there a dozen like him ready to spring out like last night?'

'Possibly. I don't keep count. Look, I just wanted to

apologise for the way I flew at you. After what you did for me, you deserved better. Today was a triumph. I had two job offers as I was leaving the court, and without those papers I'd have got nowhere. So I owe you, big time. I meant what I said. I'd have hunted you down through all London to tell you that.'

'And if I hadn't known exactly where to find you, I'd have hunted you down too. I have a job that only you can do.'

'Are you the client David mentioned?'

'That's right.'

'Ah, I begin to see. You want someone good with figures, right?'

'Among other things,' he said carefully. 'The case I want you to take concerns my younger brother, Charlie. He's not a bad lad, but he's a bit irresponsible and he's got into bad company.'

'How old is he?'

'Twenty-four, and not very mature. If he was anyone else I'd say he needed to be taught a lesson, but that—' he hesitated before finishing stiffly '—that would cause me a certain amount of difficulty.'

'You couldn't afford to be connected with a convict?' she hazarded.

'Something like that.'

'Mr Havering—'

'Call me Roscoe. After all, what you said about me calling you Pippa—well, it works both ways, doesn't it?'

For a moment the naked nymph danced between them and was gone, firmly banished on both sides.

'Roscoe, if I'm to help you I need full information. I can't work in the dark.'

'I'm a stockbroker. I have clients who depend on me, who need to be able to trust me. I can't afford to let anything damage my reputation.'

His voice was harsh, as though he'd retreated behind steel bars. But the next moment the bars collapsed and he said roughly, 'Hell, no! You'd better know the real reason. If anything happens to Charlie, it would break my mother's heart. He's all she lives for, and her health is frail. She's been in a bad way ever since my father died, fifteen years ago. At all costs I want to save her from more suffering.'

He spoke as though the words were tortured from him, and she could only guess what it cost this stockbroker to allow a chink in his confident facade and reveal his emotions. Now she began to like him.

'Why is he in trouble?' she asked gently.

'He went out with his friends, had too much to drink. Some of them broke into a shop at night and got caught. The shopkeeper thinks he was one of them.'

'What does Charlie say?'

'Sometimes he says he wasn't, sometimes he hints he might have been. It's almost as though he didn't know. I don't think he was entirely sober that night.'

Pippa frowned. This sounded more like a teenager than a young man of twenty-four.

'Do you have any other brothers or sisters?' she asked.

'None.'

'Aunts, uncles?'

'None.'

'Wife? Children? Didn't you mention having a daughter?'

'No, I said *if* you were my daughter I'd give you a piece of my mind.'

'Ah, yes.' She smiled. 'I remember.'

'That'll teach me not to judge people on short acquaintance, won't it? Anyway, I have neither wife nor children.'

'So, apart from your mother, you're Charlie's only relative. You must virtually have been his father.'

He grimaced. 'Not a very successful one. I've always been so afraid of making a mess of it that I...made a mess of it.'

Pippa nodded. 'The worst mistakes are sometimes made by people who are desperately trying to avoid mistakes,' she said sympathetically.

Relief settled over him at her understanding.

'Exactly. Long ago, I promised my mother I'd take care of Charlie, make sure he grew up strong and successful, but I seem to have let her down. I can't bear to let her down again.'

It felt strange to hear this powerful man blaming himself for failure. Evidently, there was more to him than had first appeared.

'Does he have a job?'

'He works in my office. He's bright. He's got a terrific memory, and if we can get him safely through this he has a great future.'

'Has he been in trouble with the police before?'

'He's skirted trouble but never actually been charged with anything. This will be his first time in court.'

She wondered what strings he'd had to pull to achieve that, but was too tactful to ask. That could come later.

'Was anyone injured?' she asked.

'Nobody. The shop owner arrived while there were several of them there. They escaped, he gave chase and got close enough to see them just as they reached Charlie. He began yelling at them, which attracted the attention of two policemen coming out of the local station, and they all got arrested.

'The owner insists Charlie was actually in the shop with the others, although I don't see how he can be sure. He must have just seen a few figures in the gloom.'

'What about the others? Haven't they confirmed that he wasn't in the shop?'

'No, but neither do they say he was. They hum and haw

and say they can't remember. They were really drunk, so that might even be true. But the owner insists that he was there and is pressing charges.'

She considered. 'Any damage?'

'None. They managed to trick their way in electronically.'

'So the worst he might face is a fine. But he'd have a criminal record that would make his life difficult in the future.'

'It's the future I'm worried about. They're a bad crowd, and they're not going to stop. It will get worse and worse and he'll end up in jail. I've got to get him away from that bunch.'

'Doesn't he begin to see that they're bad for him if this is the result?'

'Charlie?' Roscoe's voice was scathing. 'He doesn't see the danger. So what if he's convicted for something he didn't do? He'll just pay the fine and laugh his way home. There's a girl in this crowd who's gained a lot of influence over him. Her name's Ginevra. He's dazzled by her, and I think she gets her fun by seeing what she can provoke him into doing.'

Pippa frowned. 'You mean he's infatuated by her. There's not a lot I can do about that.'

'But there is. You can break her hold over him. Instead of being dazzled by her, he could be dazzled by you. He's easily led, and if Ginevra can lead him into danger you could lead him into safety.'

'And suppose I can't get that kind of influence over him?'

'Of course you can. You're beautiful, you've got charm, you can tease him until he doesn't know whether he's coming or going. If you really set your mind to it you can get him under your thumb and make him safe. I know you can do it. I've known you were the perfect person ever since we met and I learned who you worked for.'

So carried away did he become, explaining his plan, that he missed the look of mounting outrage in Pippa's eyes.

'I hope I've misunderstood you,' she said at last. 'You seem to be saying that you want me to be a...well...'

'A mentor.'

'A mentor? That's what you call it?'

'You point the way to the straight and narrow and he follows you because he's under your spell.'

'Ros— Mr Havering, just what kind of a fool do you take me for? I know what you want me to be and it isn't a mentor.'

'A nanny?'

The discovery of what he really expected from her was making her temper boil again. 'Be careful,' she warned him. 'Be very, *very* careful.'

'I may have explained it badly—'

'On the contrary; you've explained it so perfectly that I can follow your exact thought processes. For instance, when did you decide that you wanted me for this job? I'll bet it was last night when you arrived at my home. One look at me and you said to yourself, "She's ideal. Good shape. Handy with her fists and no morals". Admit it. You don't want a lawyer, you want a floozie.'

'No, I want a lawyer, but I can't deny that your looks play a part.'

'So you admit I look like a floozie?'

'I didn't say that,' he said sharply. 'Will you stop interrogating me as if I were a prisoner in the dock?'

'Just demonstrating my legal skills which, according to you, are what you're interested in. Tell the court, Mr Havering, exactly when did Miss Jenson first attract your attention? Was it when she was naked, or several hours earlier when you saw her in the graveyard? You saw her swapping jokes with a headstone and decided she was mad. Naked *and* mad! That's a really impressive legal qualification.'

He took a long breath and replied in a slightly forced manner. 'No, I too sometimes talk to the headstone when I visit my fa— Never mind that. I didn't know we were going to meet. It was pure chance that your—that Miss Jenson's car broke down, we got talking and she told me where she worked. That firm has handled legal work for me before and I was planning to approach them about Charlie. I saw that she would be the ideal person to take his case.'

'You decided at that moment, knowing nothing about her legal skills? But of course those weren't the skills that counted, were they? What mattered was the fact that she was a vulgar little piece—'

'I never—'

'A ditzy blonde with curves in the right places, who could be counted on to seduce your brother—'

'I'm not asking you to—'

'Oh, please, Mr Havering, credit the court with a little common sense. If you'd managed to set them on the road together, that is where it would have led eventually. At the very least, the question would have come up. You don't deny that, do you?'

'No, but—' He stopped, seeing the pit that had opened at his feet.

'But perhaps you were counting on this vulgar, unprincipled young woman to deal with him as effectively as you saw her deal with another man. A good right hook, a well-aimed knee—who needs legal training?'

She stopped, slightly breathless as though she'd been fighting. She couldn't have explained the rising tide of anger that had made her turn on him so fiercely. He wasn't the first client whose attitude had annoyed her, but with the others she'd always managed to control herself. Not this time. There was something in him that sent her temper into a spin.

'I think we've said all we have to say,' she informed him, beginning to gather her things. 'I'm sorry I won't be able to meet your requirements, but I'm a lawyer, not an escort girl.'

'Please—'

'Naturally, I shan't be charging you for this consultation. Kindly let me pass.'

He had her trapped against the wall and could have barred her exit. Instead, he rose and stood aside. His face was unreadable but for the bleakness in his eyes. Despite her fury, she had a guilty feeling of having kicked someone who was down, but she suppressed it and stormed out.

Just around the corner was a small square with fountains, pigeons and wooden seats. She sat down, breathing out heavily and wondering at herself.

Fool! she told herself. *You should just have laughed at him, taken the job, knocked some sense into the lad, then screwed every penny out of Havering. What came over you?*

That was the question she couldn't answer, and it troubled her.

Taking out her cellphone, she called David.

'Hi, I've been hoping to hear from you,' he said cheerfully. 'Wait until you've heard my news. The phone's been ringing off the hook with people wanting you and nobody but you. You made a big impression in court today, producing those figures like a magician taking a rabbit from the hat. Working for Roscoe Havering will do you even more good. Everyone knows he employs only the best.'

'Tell me some more about him,' Pippa said cautiously.

'Hasn't he told you about himself?'

'Only that he's a stockbroker. I—want to get him in perspective.'

'He doesn't boast about what a major player he is, that's true. But in the financial world Roscoe Havering is a name that pulls people up short. They jump to do what he wants—well, I expect you've found that out already. What he doesn't readily talk about is how he built that business up from collapse. It was his father's firm, and when William Havering committed suicide it smashed Roscoe.'

'Suicide?'

'He didn't tell you that?'

'No, he just said his father had died and his mother never really recovered.'

'There was a car crash. Officially, it was an accident, but in fact William killed himself because his life's work was going bust. Roscoe worked for his father. He'd seen the financial mess they were in and tried to help, but there was little he could do. Secretly, I think he blames himself. He thinks if he'd done more he might have prevented the disaster—used his influence to pull William back from the brink. It's nonsense, of course. He was only twenty-four, little more than a beginner. There was nothing he could have done.

'After William's death he managed to save the business and build it into a massive success, but it changed him, not really for the better. His ruthless side took over, but I suppose it had to. You won't find him easy. What he wants, he wants, and he doesn't take no for an answer.'

'But do you realise what it is that he wants?' Pippa demanded. 'Am I supposed to seduce this boy, because you know what you can do with that idea.'

'No, of course not,' David said hurriedly, 'but let's be honest, you've had every man here yearning for you. You'll know how to get this lad's attention.'

'I'm not sure—'

'You haven't turned him down?' David sounded alarmed.

'I'm thinking about it,' Pippa said cautiously.

What are you talking about? raged her inner voice. *Just tell him you've already said no.*

'Pippa, please do this, for the firm's sake. Roscoe brings us a lot of work and, between you and me, he owns our office building. He's not a man I want to offend.'

David was a good boss and a kind man. He'd taught her well, while keeping his yearning admiration for her beauty behind respectable barriers.

'I'll get back to you,' she said.

She was thoughtful as she walked back to Cavelli's, trying to reconcile the contradictions that danced in her mind. She'd perceived Roscoe Havering as an older man, certainly in his forties, but if David's facts were correct he was only thirty-nine.

It was his demeanour that had misled her, she realised. Physically, he was still youngish, with dark brown hair that showed no hint of grey or thinning. His face was lean, not precisely handsome but intelligent and interesting. It might even have been charming but for a mysterious look of heaviness.

Heaviness. That was it. He seemed worn down by dead weights that he'd carried so long they were part of him. They aged him cruelly, but not permanently. Sometimes she'd surprised a gleam of humour in his eyes that hinted at another man, one it might be intriguing to know.

She quickened her steps, suddenly eager to talk to him again, wondering if he would still be there. He might have walked out. Or perhaps he was calling David to complain about her.

But as soon as she went in she saw him sitting where she'd left him, staring into space, seemingly full of silent sadness. Her heart was touched, despite her efforts to prevent it.

Control, warned her inner voice. Stay impartial. His outrageous request must be considered objectively.

How?

She approached quietly and pulled out a chair facing him. He looked up in surprise.

'I'm sorry I stormed out like that,' she said. 'Sometimes I get into a temper. Shocking loss of objectivity, especially in a lawyer. A wise man wouldn't want to employ me.'

'There's such a thing as being too wise,' Roscoe said gently. 'I'm sorry, too. I never meant to offend you. I expressed myself badly, and you were naturally upset.'

'You didn't express yourself badly. You laid out your requirements for your employee, making yourself plain on all counts, so that I'd understand everything before committing myself. That was very proper.'

He winced. 'I wish you wouldn't talk like that.'

'I'm merely trying to be professional.' She gave a wry smile. 'It's just not very nice to have people thinking I'm a tart. It's even worse when that's my chief qualification for a job.'

'I never said that,' he disclaimed hurriedly. 'Nor did I mean it. But you do seem to have the ability to love 'em and leave 'em.'

'Oh, I believe in leaving 'em. I just manage without the love 'em bit.'

'That's what I want. You can cope with Charlie better than a more naive girl would. You could handle him, keep him in order, make him see things your way. What's funny?' Her sudden chuckle had disconcerted him.

'You are,' she said. 'You're making such a mess of this. What you really want is a heartless woman who can take care of herself, and you're tying yourself in knots trying to say so without actually saying the words. No, no—' she held up a hand to silence his denial '—we've covered that ground. Let it go.'

'Will you help me?' he asked slowly.

'If I can, but things may not work out as you plan. You've

assumed that he'll take one look at me and collapse with adoration. Suppose he doesn't?'

'I think that would be a really new experience for you,' he said, trying to sound casual.

'Not at all. The world is full of men who are indifferent to my charms.'

'You just haven't met them yet.'

'I've met plenty.'

'Splendid! Then you'll know what to do. Just use whatever methods you normally use to overcome their resistance.'

Her lips twitched. 'I could take that as another insult.'

'Yes, you could—if you were determined to.'

'What does that mean?'

'I means that I've realised that you can twist everything I say into an insult, and you do it whenever it suits you. So now I'm fighting back.'

'How?'

'By refusing to let you bully me,' he said firmly. 'I am *not* going to cower and watch every word in case you misunderstand. You don't actually misunderstand anything. You know I don't really mean to insult you, so don't try to score points off me. I don't want you to seduce Charlie. I want you to beguile him, make his head spin until he'll follow your lead. You'll do a good job and I'll respect you for it. And if we fight, we fight openly. Agreed?'

There was a definite no-nonsense tone to his voice, making it clear that he meant every word. He was putting his foot down, asserting himself, warning her not to mess with him—all the powerful, dominant things that she had instinctively associated with him.

And yet—and yet—

Far back in his eyes, that look was there again—a gleam that might have been conspiratorial humour.

Or perhaps not.

After a moment Pippa held out her hand to him. 'Agreed.'

They shook. She took out a notebook and spoke formally. 'I need to know as much about the gang he's running around with as you can tell me.'

'They're all young people who seem to live on the edge of the law. They don't even have proper addresses. They squat, which means they move on a lot as they get caught. I don't know for a fact that they steal, but they don't have any regular source of income. Charlie definitely gives Ginevra money. They live from hand to mouth, which he finds exciting. Here. That's the two of them together.'

From an inner pocket he took out a photograph that seemed to have been taken in a crowded room, probably a squat. In the centre, a young couple lay back in each other's arms.

'He keeps that as a treasured souvenir,' Roscoe observed curtly. 'I wanted you to see it, so I stole it from him.'

'Good for you,' Pippa murmured. Studying the picture, she felt a rising tide of excitement. 'Yes, now I begin to understand. She's up to her old tricks.'

'You know her?' Roscoe demanded, startled.

'Yes, and her name's not Ginevra, it's Biddy Felsom. I suppose she thought the new name sounded more glamorous. Her hobby is teasing the lads to do daft things to win her favour. She's done a lot of damage in her time. What's the matter?'

The question was surprised from her by the sight of Roscoe's face, filled with shock and dismay as he stared over her shoulder. The next moment she heard, above her head, the petulant voice of a young man.

'So there you are, Roscoe. Hiding from me, I suppose. You must have known I'd be over here as soon as I found out what you were up to.'

'Charlie—'

'Well, you can forget it, do you hear? I know exactly the

kind of creep you'll want to hire for me, all settled and respectable. Let's be respectable, whatever else happens. No way. I'll find my own lawyer—someone who understands the world and lives in the present. *Ow!*'

He hopped back, wincing as Pippa's chair was pushed out hard against his leg.

'I'm so sorry. I didn't mean that to happen,' she said untruthfully.

Gazing up at him, she knew he had a grandstand view of her face and the generous curves of her breasts, with just one button of the sedate blouse undone. Now the smile, soft and warm, dawning slowly, suggesting that she'd been pleasantly amazed at the attractions of the young man looking down at her.

'Hello,' she said.

CHAPTER FOUR

CHARLIE drew a long, slow breath, visibly stunned. This was useful, Pippa thought, bringing a professional mind to bear on the situation, because it gave her the chance to study him.

He was certainly handsome. His face was slightly fuller than his brother's, just enough to give it a vivacious quality that was alluring. His mouth was attractively curved, and she guessed that many a girl had sighed hopelessly for him. He was too boyish to attract her, but he seemed pleasant.

'Hello,' he murmured, distracted. Then he recovered his poise and seated himself next to Pippa. 'Look, I'm sorry. I'm only mad at him.' He indicated Roscoe.

'He must be an absolutely terrible person,' she said sympathetically.

'He is. Definitely.'

'And now he wants to force his choice of lawyer on you—someone middle-aged and ignorant of the modern world, who won't understand you. Oh, yes, and *respectable*. Shocking!'

She couldn't meet Roscoe's eye. He was leaning back, regarding her performance with wry appreciation.

'By the way, I'm Charlie Havering,' the young man said, holding out a hand.

'I'm Pippa Jenson,' she said, taking it. 'And I'm your lawyer.'

Charlie grinned. 'Yeah, right!'

'Seriously. I'm a solicitor. I work for Farley & Son.'

'But you can't be,' Charlie protested. 'You don't look at all respectable.'

'Watch your manners, Charlie,' Roscoe said. 'This is a highly qualified lady you're talking to.'

'I can see that,' Charlie said, taking her hand. '*Very* highly qualified.'

Roscoe caught his breath as he found himself surrounded by double entendres. 'I only meant,' he said carefully, 'that she's a professional—no, not like that—'

He swore inwardly as he realised what Pippa could make of this, but she surprised him, bursting out laughing. Laughter possessed her utterly, making her rock back and forth while peals of merriment danced up from her and Charlie regarded her with delight. In fact Roscoe realised that everyone in the place was smiling at her, as though just by being there she brightened the day.

She reached across the table and took Roscoe's hand. 'Oh, shut up,' she told him, still laughing, 'You make it worse with every word.'

'I don't mean to. I was considering your feelings,' he said stiffly, withdrawing his hand.

'Heavens, we're way past that. Enough. It's finished.'

'As you wish. But Charlie, behave yourself.'

'Why, when I'm talking to the most gorgeous girl I've ever met? *Hey!*'

One moment he was leaning close in a seductive conspiracy. The next, he was bouncing with agitation at something he'd seen.

'It's him,' he yelped, leaping to his feet. 'Just let me get to him.'

Across the restaurant, a long-haired young man turned in alarm, then vanished between some curtains, closely followed by Charlie.

'What was that?' Pippa said, looking around.

'A man who owes him money,' Roscoe observed. 'One of many.'

'So that's your brother. He'll be an interesting client. Yes, I think I'll accept his case.'

It was on the tip of Roscoe's tongue to tell her to forget it because he'd changed his mind. But he controlled the impulse, as he controlled so many impulses in his life, and sat in tense silence, a prey to opposing feelings. On the surface, things were working out exactly as he'd wanted. The smile she'd given Charlie was perfect for the purpose, and it had had the desired effect. His brother had been transfixed, just as Roscoe had meant him to be. So, what more did he want?

He didn't know. All he knew for certain was that he hated it.

'Pippa,' he said edgily, 'I must be honest, I think you're going about this the wrong way.'

'What?' She stared at him. 'I'm doing what you said you wanted.'

'Yes, but I had in mind something a little more—' He hesitated, made cautious by the look in her eyes.

'A little more what?' she asked in a voice that was softly dangerous.

'More subtle,' he said desperately.

'Mr Havering, are you telling me how to do my job?'

'I wouldn't dare.'

'Really? I'm not sure of that. Perhaps we should have discussed this before now, so that you could tell me exactly how a woman goes about beguiling a man? After all, I know so little about the subject, don't I? How stupid of me not to have taken lessons from you! Why don't you instruct me now so that I'll know which boxes to tick?'

'All right,' he said quickly. 'Of course you know more than I do about this.'

'Which I thought was why you hired me. Anyway, I'm not doing well, since his attention was so easily distracted. One hint of an unpaid debt and he's off. Hmm! Perhaps I should review my strategy.'

'I feel sure your strategy is quite up to the challenge.'

'It's the first time a man has walked away from me when I was trying to mesmerise him. I could feel quite insulted by that.'

'You're having a bad day for insults, aren't you?'

'Between you and him, yes.'

'Then I may as well add to my crimes by pointing out that he didn't walk away from you, he ran away at full speed. Perhaps I've hired the wrong person.'

'You could be right. Desperate measures are called for. I must lure my prey into a net from which he cannot escape.'

'Always assuming that he returns at all,' Roscoe pointed out. 'You may have to go after him.'

'Please!' She appeared horrified. 'I never "go after" a man. They come after me.'

'Always?' he asked, eyes narrowed.

'If I want them to. Sometimes I don't bother.' Thoroughly enjoying his discomfiture, she smiled. 'And never mind condemning me as a hussy, because that's exactly what you hired me for.'

'Is there any point in my defending myself?' he growled.

'None whatever,' she assured him.

She was curious to know what he would say next, but Charlie spoiled things by reappearing, cursing because his prey had escaped.

'Did he owe you very much?' Pippa asked, turning from Roscoe with reluctance.

'A few thousand.'

'Perhaps we can recover it by legal action,' she suggested.

'Ah...no,' he said awkwardly. 'It's a bit...well...'

'All right, let's leave it,' she said quickly. 'The sooner we get down to business, the better.'

'Yes, we must have a long talk over dinner,' Charlie said. 'The Diamond is the best place in town. Come on, let's go.'

'First you ask Miss Jenson if she is free,' Roscoe said firmly. 'If she is, then you ask if she can endure an evening with us.'

'*Us?* Ah, well—I didn't actually mean that you should come with—'

'I know exactly what you meant, and you can forget that idea. Miss Jenson, could you put up with the two of us for a few more hours?'

'I'll do my best,' she said solemnly. 'We have serious matters to discuss.'

'I agree, so we can forget The Diamond,' Roscoe said, taking out his cellphone and dialling. 'Hello, Mother? Yes, it's me. We're on our way home and we have a guest. I've found a first-rate lawyer for Charlie, so roll out the red carpet for her. Fine. See you soon.' He ended the call.

Charlie, who had been spluttering fruitlessly, now found his voice. 'What about how I feel?' he demanded.

'The Diamond is no place for a serious discussion.'

'And doesn't Pippa get a say?'

'Miss Jenson has already done us the honour of agreeing to dine with us. Since this is a business meeting, I'm sure she feels that the venue is irrelevant.'

'Certainly,' Pippa said in her briskest tone. 'I have no opinion either way.'

'You're going to just let him walk over you?' Charlie demanded.

Pippa couldn't resist. Giving Roscoe a cheeky sideways

look, she leaned towards Charlie and said, 'It can't be helped. In my job you get used to clients who want to rule the roost.' She added conspiratorially, 'There are ways of dealing with them.'

The young man choked with laughter, jerking his head towards Roscoe. 'Think you can get him on the ropes?'

'Think I can't?'

She was watching Roscoe for his reaction. There was none. His eyes were on her but his face revealed nothing. Clearly, the notion of tussling with her, whether physically or emotionally, caused him no excitement.

'Just promise that I can be there to see you crush him beneath your heel,' Charlie implored.

'When you two have finished,' Roscoe said in a bored voice.

'Just a little innocent fun,' Charlie protested.

'Sorry, I don't do fun.' Roscoe's voice was so withering that Pippa threw him another quick glance. For a moment his face was tight, hard, older.

'That's right, he doesn't,' Charlie said.

'OK, I'm here,' said a voice overhead.

Charlie groaned, then bounced up as he recognised the man who owed him money, now holding out an envelope.

'I only ran to get this,' he said. 'I always meant to repay you.' He dropped the envelope and fled. The reason became obvious a moment later.

'There's only half here,' Charlie yelped. 'Hey, come back!' He resumed the pursuit.

Alone again, Roscoe and Pippa eyed each other, suspicion on one side, defiance on the other.

'How am I doing?' she asked.

'You've certainly got his attention. I'd give a lot to know what he's thinking.'

'He believes what he wants to believe,' she said with a

small flash of anger. '*Men always do*. Didn't you know that? I know it. And so does any woman who's ever had a man in her life.'

'And when a woman knows it she makes use of it?'

'She does if she has any sense of self-preservation. And may I remind you again, Mr Havering, that I'm doing what you hired me to do? You're paying for my skills, but you don't get to dictate what skills I use or how I use them.'

'Don't I?'

'No, because if you try I'll simply step aside and let Charlie see you pulling my strings.'

He drew a sharp breath. 'You really know how to fight dirty.'

'Have you only just realised that?'

He regarded her. 'I think I have.'

'Good, then we understand each other. Now he's coming back. Smile at me so that he'll know that all is well between us.'

'I wonder if that day will ever come,' he said softly.

But the next moment he was smiling as she'd suggested, even talking pleasantly, loud enough for Charlie to hear. 'My mother's housekeeper is an expert cook. I promise that you'll enjoy tonight's meal, Miss Havering.'

'Pippa,' she said. 'After all, we're fighting on the same side.'

His eyes warned her not to push her luck, but he only inclined his head before rising and saying, 'I'll get the car. Be waiting for me outside and don't take too long.'

She longed to salute him ironically and say, *Yes sir, no sir. I obey, sir.* But he was gone before she had the chance.

'That's his way,' Charlie said, correctly interpreting her seething. 'People give up arguing. You will too.'

'Will I? I wonder. Did you catch up with that man?'

'No, he escaped again. But at least I got some of the money.

And now we're alone, can I tell you that you are the most beautiful creature I've ever met?'

'No, you can't tell me that,' she said. 'For one thing, I already know and, for another, your brother wouldn't approve.'

'Oh, forget him. What does he have to do with us?'

Pippa frowned. 'He's protecting you. Don't you owe him some kind of consideration?'

'Why? He's only thinking of himself. The good name of Havering must be defended at all costs. The truth is, he cares for nobody.'

'And nobody cares for him?' she murmured slowly.

Charlie shrugged. 'Who knows? He doesn't let anyone inside.'

It sounded so convincing, but suddenly there was the whispered memory of Roscoe saying, 'If anything happens to Charlie, it would break my mother's heart... At all costs I want to save her from more suffering.'

This wasn't a man who cared nothing for anyone. He might care so much that he only admitted it under stress.

Or perhaps Charlie was right. Which of the two was the real man? Impossible to say. Unless...

Suddenly the waiter hurried up to them, almost stuttering in his agitation. 'He's in the car...says he told you to be out there waiting for him. He's good 'n mad.'

They ran outside to where Roscoe's car was by the kerb, engine running. When they had tumbled into the back seat, Pippa said politely, 'I'm really sorry,' but Roscoe only grunted, his eyes on the traffic as he edged his way into the flow. She supposed she couldn't blame him.

Their destination was an expensive London suburb, full of large detached houses standing in luxurious gardens. A woman was waiting by the gate, smiling and waving at the sight of them. She was thin and frail-looking, and Pippa recalled Roscoe saying that she'd been in a bad way ever since his father's death, fifteen years earlier.

But her face was brilliant with joy as Charlie got out of the car and she could hug him. He handed Pippa out and she found herself being scrutinised by two bright eyes before Angela Havering thrust out a hand declaring that she was *so* glad to meet her.

Roscoe drove the car away.

'He has to park at the back,' Charlie explained. 'He'll join us in a minute.'

'Come inside,' Angela said, taking her hand. 'I want to know all about you, and how you're going to save my dear boy.'

She drew Pippa into the house, a lavishly elegant establishment, clearly furnished and tended by someone who'd brought housekeeping to a fine art, with the cash to do it.

In the kitchen they found Nora, a cheerful, middle-aged woman in a large apron, presiding over a variety of dishes.

'I hope I didn't make your life difficult, coming unexpectedly,' Pippa said as they were introduced.

'There's plenty to eat,' Angela said. 'It's always been one of my husband's maxims that a successful house has food ready all the time.'

Pippa smiled, but she had a strange, edgy feeling. Angela spoke almost as if her husband were still alive.

Nora poured wine and Angela handed them each a glass and raised hers in salute.

'Welcome to our home,' she said to Pippa. 'I'm sure you're going to make everything all right.'

It was a charming scene, but it would have been more charming, Pippa thought, if she'd waited for Roscoe to join them. It was a tiny point, but it troubled her.

From the kitchen window, she had a view of the back garden, with a large garage at the far end. As she watched,

Roscoe came out of a side door of the garage and began walking to the house.

'Here he is,' she said, pointing.

'Oh, good. I was afraid he'd keep us waiting. Honestly, he can be so inconsiderate.'

Over supper, Angela was on edge, constantly turning an anxious expression on Charlie, then a frowning gaze at Roscoe, as though silently criticising him for something. To Pippa, it seemed as though she'd given all her love to one son and barely registered the existence of the other.

Of course, she argued with herself, Charlie was a vulnerable boy threatened with disaster, while Roscoe was a powerful man, well able to take care of himself. But still…

Charlie's cellphone rang. He went out into the hall to speak to the caller and, as soon as he'd gone, Angela clasped Pippa's hand.

'You see how he is, how he needs to be cared for.'

'And he's lucky to have a brother who cares for him,' Pippa couldn't resist saying.

'Oh, yes, of course there's Roscoe. He does his best, but when I think of what might happen to my darling…maybe prison…'

'He won't go to prison,' Pippa said at once. 'It's a first offence, nothing was stolen and nobody was hurt. A fine, and perhaps some community service is the worst that will happen.'

'But he'll have a criminal record.'

'Yes, and that's why we're working so hard to defend him.'

'Oh, if only my husband were here,' Angela wailed. 'William would know what to do. He always does.'

Roscoe's eyes met Pippa's and a little shake of his head warned her to say nothing. She nodded, feeling all at sea, glad to keep quiet.

'But you've got me to help, Mother,' Roscoe reminded her.

'Oh, yes, and you do your best, but it's not the same, is it?'

'No, it's not the same,' Roscoe said quietly.

'If only he hadn't gone away. He should be here now that we need him so much.'

Again, she might have been speaking of a living man, and Pippa wondered uneasily just how much she lived in the real world.

As she spoke, Angela fiddled constantly was a ring on her left hand. It was an engagement ring, with an awesome central diamond, surrounded by smaller diamonds.

'That's my engagement ring,' Angela said, seeing her glance. 'It was much too expensive and William couldn't really afford it in those days, but he said that nothing was too much for me. All these years later, I still have it to remind me that his love never died.' Her voice shook.

Pippa was uncertain where to look. Angela's determination to thrust her emotion on everyone was difficult to cope with, even without knowing that it was misplaced.

Charlie returned after a moment, bearing a cup of tea which he set before his mother.

'Why, darling, how kind of you to think of me!' She turned to Roscoe. 'Isn't Charlie a wonderful son?'

'The best,' Roscoe agreed kindly. 'Now, drink up, and have plenty of sugar because that always does you good.'

'Here,' Charlie said, spooning sugar madly into the cup. His mother beamed at him.

So the spoilt child got all the credit, Pippa thought, while Roscoe, who was genuinely working hard to ease her troubles, was barely noticed.

Then she reproved herself for being over-emotional. Roscoe was only doing what was sensible, supporting his mother and Charlie so that the family should not disintegrate. The idea that he might be saddened by being relegated to the shadows of Angela's affection was too sentimental for words. And if there was one thing Roscoe was not, it was sentimental.

And neither was she, she reminded herself.

Nonetheless, she couldn't help warming to him for his generosity and patience.

A little later Angela went away into the kitchen, and she seized the chance to tell Charlie about Ginevra. He was reluctant to believe the worst, but Pippa was firm, saying, 'I don't want you to contact her unless I say so. Give me your word.'

'All right, maybe I was a bit mad but she made my head spin.'

'Well, it's time to stop spinning. Mr Havering, do you have a computer here that I could use?'

'It's upstairs,' Roscoe said. 'I'll show you.'

'Beware,' Charlie warned. 'He's taking you up to his bedroom, a place where no sensible woman goes.'

'Cut it out,' Roscoe advised him wearily. 'Miss Jenson, I hope you know you have absolutely nothing to fear from me.'

'That's not very flattering,' Charlie protested illogically.

'Unflattering but sensible and businesslike,' Pippa said. 'Mr Havering, let me return the compliment by declaring that I too am entirely free from temptation. Now, shall we go?'

'I'll come too,' Charlie declared. 'To protect you.'

'I need no protection,' she declared firmly. 'Ask your brother how I deal with troublesome men.'

Charlie's eyes widened. 'Hey, he didn't—?'

'No, I didn't,' Roscoe said, exasperated. 'But I witnessed the fate of someone who did. Take it from me, you wouldn't like it. Stay here and look after Mother.'

Roscoe's room was much as she would have expected—full of straight lines, plain, unadorned, unrevealing. The bed was narrow and looked hard, the wallpaper was pale grey, without pattern. There was a television, modest, neat, efficient; a set where a man would watch the news. A monk could have lived in this room.

But his real home was an apartment elsewhere, she reminded herself. She wondered if that was any different, and doubted it.

But then she saw something that made her stare and gasp with delight.

'Wow!' she breathed. 'How about that? Let me look at it. Can you just—? Yes, that's right. Oh, it's the most beautiful thing I've ever—yes—yes—yes—' Her hands were clasped in sheer ecstasy, her voice full of joy, her eyes glowing with blissful satisfaction.

Roscoe regarded her, fascinated. It wasn't his first sight of a beautiful woman in transports—in his arms, sometimes in his bed.

But this one was looking at his computer.

A touch of the switch had caused the machine to flower into glorious life, making her watch, riveted, as one state-of-the-art accessory after another leapt into the spotlight.

'Oh, goodness,' she breathed. 'Why haven't I ever—? I've never even heard of some of these.'

'One of my clients owns a firm that makes software and computer peripherals,' Roscoe said. 'He's at the cutting edge and I get everything ahead of the game. I'll tell him you're interested and I'm sure he'll fix you up.'

'Oh, yes, *please*! And look at the size of that screen, the biggest I've ever seen.'

'You should try one,' Roscoe said. 'It's useful for having multiple documents open at once.'

'Ah, yes,' she murmured. 'Useful. How do I go online?'

He touched a switch and in a moment she'd connected with her work computer, entered the password and brought up a list of documents. A few more clicks brought Ginevra's face to the screen just as Charlie entered the room.

'Hey, that's her!' he exclaimed. Then he stared at the caption. 'But who's Biddy Felsom?'

'She is,' Pippa said. 'Known to the police as a small-time offender and pain in the neck. She enjoys getting stupid boys to do things they shouldn't, pulling their strings, like she pulled yours.'

'Well, she's history,' Charlie said. 'I know that you'll save me from her.'

'Good. Now it's time I was going home,' Pippa observed.

'I'll drive you,' Roscoe said.

'No you won't, I will,' Charlie was quick to say.

'Neither of you will,' Pippa said. 'Mr Havering, will you call me a taxi?'

'I'll drive you,' Charlie insisted.

'Shut up!' his brother said impatiently. 'Can't you see she's had enough of the pair of us tonight? Miss Jenson, I suggest that the next meeting should be at my office. My secretary will call you to fix a time.'

'Certainly,' she said in her most efficient tone.

'I know you can rescue me,' Charlie said. 'We'll do it together because I'm going to take your advice in *everything*.'

He said the last word with a breathless sincerity that made her regard him wryly. His eyes twinkled back at her and they laughed together.

Angela came in and demanded to know what was happening. Charlie proclaimed his faith in Pippa, which made his mother embrace her.

Roscoe took no part in this. He was calling the taxi.

Just before it arrived, Charlie came to stand before her. 'There's something I've just got to know,' he breathed.

'I'll tell you if I can,' she promised. 'What is it?'

'This,' he said, putting a hand behind her head and whipping out the clip in her hair, letting her glorious locks flow free.

'I've wanted to do that ever since we met,' he said.

'Then you should be ashamed of yourself,' Roscoe growled. 'That's no way to treat a lady.'

'Pippa's not offended,' Charlie pleaded. 'Are you?'

'No, I'm not offended, but right this minute I feel like your nursemaid. I think you should call me Nanny.'

'Not in a million years,' he said fervently.

She gave a crow of laughter. 'Well, my taxi seems to be here, so I'm leaving now. I'll see you soon.'

Charlie and Angela came with her to the gate, but Roscoe stayed back, declaring curtly that he had work to do. At the last minute he pushed a scrap of paper into Pippa's hand and turned away to climb the stairs.

As the taxi drew away she strained to read what was on the paper, mystified by Roscoe. When her hair flowed free she'd caught a glimpse of his face, full of shock as though he'd been stunned. But that made no sense. He'd seen her hair the night before. There was nothing to surprise him. Yet a man who'd been punched in the stomach might have looked like that.

Now he was giving her secret notes, and she wondered if his stern facade had melted long enough for him to send her a personal message. Could he be reacting to her as a man to a woman? She found herself hoping so. There was something about him that made her want to know more. In another moment she would find out...

Then she passed under a street lamp long enough to see what he'd written to her.

It was the address of his client's computer firm.

CHAPTER FIVE

NEXT morning Roscoe's secretary called and they set up the appointment at his office for the following day. An hour later Charlie came on the line, wanting to see her that night. Since there was still much she needed to discover she reluctantly agreed to let him take her to The Diamond, although a nightclub wasn't the place she would have chosen.

She supposed she should notify Roscoe, but she stopped her hand on the way to the phone. He was just a tad too controlling for her taste, and yielding to it would only make him worse. She would make a report afterwards.

That evening she dressed carefully, choosing a fairly sedate black satin gown with a long hem and modest neck. She'd beguiled Charlie enough to secure his attention, but she had no wish to entice him further.

Downstairs, he had a car waiting, complete with chauffeur.

'I hired it for the evening,' he said, getting in beside her. 'I don't want to drive, I want to concentrate on you, now I have you all to myself.'

'That's lovely,' she said. 'Just you, me and my notebook.'

'Notebook?'

'Well, this is a professional consultation, isn't it? You're going to fill me in on any aspects of the case that were overlooked before.'

He grimaced.

At The Diamond she had to admit that he was a skilled host, recommending dishes from the elaborate menu, knowing which wine to order. He seemed in a chirpy mood, but at last she looked up to find his face pervaded by a wry, almost hangdog look.

'I guess you were right about Ginevra,' he said. 'I tried to call her. I know you told me not to, but I had to try.'

'What happened?'

'She hung up. I can't believe I was taken in so easily. But at least now I've got you. You're my friend, aren't you? Really my friend, not just because Roscoe has hired your legal skills?'

'Roscoe does a lot for you,' she reminded him.

'I know I should be grateful to him. He's always looked after me, but…but he does too much, so that sometimes I feel I don't know who I really am. What would I do if I was left to myself? Stupid things, probably.'

'Why don't you tell me about it?'

Once Charlie started to talk, it all came tumbling out—the years of growing up in the shadow of tragedy, the crushing awareness that he was all his mother lived for, the feeling that he could never be free.

'My dad killed himself,' he said sombrely, 'but Roscoe won't allow it to be mentioned, especially to Mum. That's his way. "Do this, Charlie, don't do that. Join the firm, Charlie—"'

'Did he make you join his firm?'

'He suggested it, and what Roscoe "suggests" tends to happen.'

'Couldn't you have held out against him?'

'I suppose. Actually, I feel a bit guilty about Roscoe. I get mad at him, but I do know the truth.'

'Which is?'

'That he's always had the rough end of the stick. I think Mum blames him for Dad's death, not openly but she says things like, "If only he hadn't been so tired that day, he might not have crashed." And she says other things—so that I just know she thinks Roscoe wasn't pulling his weight.'

'Do you believe that?'

'No, not now I'm in the firm and know a bit about how it works. Roscoe was the same age I am now, still learning the business, and there was only so much he could have done. And I've talked to people who were there at that time and they all say there was a big crash coming, and nobody could believe "that kid" could avoid it.'

'"That kid,"' she murmured. 'It's hard to see him like that.'

'I know, but that's how they thought of him back then. And they were all astounded when he got them through. I respect him—you have to—but I can see what it made him. Sometimes I feel guilty. He saved the rest of us but it damaged him terribly, and Mum just blames him because…well…'

'Maybe she needs someone to blame,' Pippa suggested gently.

'Something like that. And it's so unfair that I feel sorry for him. Hey, don't tell him I said that. He'd murder me!'

'And then he'd murder *me*,' she agreed. 'Promise.' She laid a finger over her lips.

'The reason I don't deal with Roscoe very well is that I'm always in two minds about him. I admire him to bits for what he's achieved in the firm, and the way he puts up with Mum's behaviour without complaining.'

'Does he mind about her very much?'

'Oh, yes. He doesn't say anything but I see his face sometimes, and it hurts him.'

'Have you tried talking to him about it?'

'Yes, and I've been slapped down. He shuts it away inside

himself, and I resent that. He's been a good brother to me, but he won't let me be a good brother to him. That's what I was saying; one moment I admire him and sympathise with him. The next moment I want to thump him for being a tyrant. I'm afraid his tyrant side outweighs the other one by about ten to one.'

'If you weren't a stockbroker, what would you have liked to do?' she asked.

'I don't know. Something colourful where I didn't have to wear a formal suit.' He gave a comical sigh. 'I guess I'm just a lost cause.'

She smiled, feeling as sympathetic as she would have done with a younger brother. Beneath the frivolous boy, she could detect the makings of a generous, thoughtful man with, strangely, a lot in common with his brother. Charlie wasn't the weakling she'd first thought. He had much inner strength. It was just a different kind of strength from Roscoe.

'You're not a lost cause,' she said, reaching over the table and laying her hands on his shoulders. '*I* say you're not, and what I say goes.'

He grinned. 'Now you sound just like Roscoe.'

'Well, I *am* like Roscoe.' Briefly, she enclosed his face between her hands. 'He's not the only one who can give orders, and my orders to you are to cheer up because I'm going to make things all right.'

She dropped her hands but gave him a comforting sisterly smile.

'D'you know, I really believe you can,' he mused. 'I think you could take on even Roscoe and win.'

'Well, somewhere in this world there has to be someone who can crush him beneath her heels.'

'His fiancée couldn't.'

'His fiancée?' Pippa echoed, startled. Since learning that

Roscoe lived alone, she had somehow never connected him with romantic entanglements.

'It was a few years back. Her name was Verity and she was terribly "suitable". She worked in the firm, and Roscoe used to say that she knew as much about finance as he did.'

'I dare say she'd need to,' Pippa said, nodding.

'Right. It makes you wonder what they talked about when they were alone. The latest exchange rate? What the Dow-Jones index was doing?'

'What did she look like?'

'Pretty enough, but I think it was chiefly her mental qualities he admired.'

'Charlie, a man doesn't ask a woman to marry him because of her mental qualities.'

'Roscoe isn't like other men. Beauty passes him by.'

'Then why did you warn me against going up to his room yesterday?'

'I was only joking. I knew he had no interest in you that way. Don't you remember? He said so himself.'

'Yes,' she murmured. 'He did, didn't he?'

After that, she relapsed into thought.

Another bottle of wine was served and Charlie drank deeply, making Pippa glad he wasn't driving.

'Was he very much in love with her?' she asked.

'I don't know. Like I said, he doesn't talk about his feelings. He wanted her in his way. The rest of us look at a beautiful woman and think *Wow!* Roscoe thinks, *Will she do me credit?* I don't think he's ever thought *Wow!* in his life.'

Oh, yes, he has, she thought, gazing silently into her glass.

Noticing nothing, Charlie continued, 'She could be relied on to know what was important—money, propriety, making the world bow down before you. And she'd give him intelligent children who would eventually go into the business. What more could he want?'

'Surely you're being unfair?'

'Well, losing her didn't seem to break his heart. He didn't even tell us at the time. One day I mentioned that we hadn't seen her for a while and then he said they'd broken up weeks ago. Any normal man would drown his sorrows in the pub with his mates, but not him. He just fired her and she ceased to exist.'

'He actually fired her?' Pippa was startled.

'Well, he said she'd left the firm, but I reckon he made her understand that she'd better leave.'

She felt as though someone had struck her over the heart, which was surely absurd? From the start, she'd sensed that Roscoe was a harsh, controlling man, indifferent to the feelings of others as long as his rule was unchallenged. So why should she care if her worst opinion was confirmed?

Because she'd also thought she saw another side to him—warmer, more human. And because Charlie himself had spoken of that softer side. But the moment had passed. Charlie had switched back from the sympathetic brother to the rebellious kid, and in doing so he'd changed the light on Roscoe who was now, once more, the tyrant.

She knew a glimmer of sadness, but suppressed it. Much better to be realistic.

It was time for the cabaret. Dancers skipped across the stage, a crooner crooned, a comedian strutted his stuff. She thought him fairly amusing but Charlie was more critical.

'His performance was a mess,' he said as the space was cleared for dancing. 'Listen.'

To her surprise, he rattled through the last joke, word perfect and superbly timed. Then he went back and repeated an earlier part of the act, also exactly right, as far as she could judge.

'I'm impressed,' she said. 'I've never come across such a memory.'

He shrugged. 'It convinced Roscoe that I was bright enough to be a stockbroker, so you might say it ruined my life.'

He made a comical face. She smiled back, meaning to console rather than beguile him. But the next moment her face lit up and she cried out in pleasure, 'Lee Renton, you devious so-and-so! How lovely to see you.'

A large man in his forties was bearing down on them, hands extended. He was attractive, and would have been even more so if he could manage to lose some weight.

'"Devious so-and-so!"' he mocked. 'Is that any way to address your favourite client?'

'That's not what I say to my favourite client. To him, I say, "Sir, how generous of you to double the bill!"'

Lee roared with laughter before saying, 'Actually, I'll gladly pay twice the bill after what you did for me.' He seemed to notice Charlie for the first time. 'I'm Lee Renton. Any friend of Pippa's is a friend of mine.' He pumped Charlie's hand and sat down without waiting to be invited.

'I did a court appearance for Lee the other day,' Pippa told Charlie. 'It went fairly well.'

'Don't act modest,' Lee protested. 'You're the tops and you know it.'

'Meaning that I saved you some money?'

'What else?' he asked innocently.

'What are you doing here?'

'My firm provided the entertainment here tonight, and I'll probably buy the place. I'll call you about that.' He blew her a kiss. 'You look ravishing, queen of my heart.'

'Oh, stop your nonsense!'

'Do you say that as a woman or as the lawyer who recently handled my divorce?'

'I say it as the lawyer who'll probably draw up your next pre-nuptial agreement.'

He bellowed with laughter. A passing waiter caught Charlie's attention and he turned, giving Renton a chance to lower his voice and say, 'Quite a performer, your companion—I overheard him retelling those jokes and he was a sight better than the original comedian. Does he do it professionally?'

'No, he's a stockbroker.'

'You're having a laugh.'

'Really. He's actually a client and we were discussing his case.'

'Yeah, right. This is just the perfect place for it. All right, I'm going. I have work to do. Stockbroker, eh?' He thumped Charlie on the shoulder and departed.

Charlie frowned, turning back from the waiter. 'Lee Renton? I've heard that name somewhere.'

'He's very big in entertainment. He buys things, he promotes, he owns a television studio.'

'*That* Lee Renton? Wow! I wish I'd known.'

He looked around, managing to spot Lee in the distance, deep in conversation with a man whom he overwhelmed by flinging an arm around his shoulders and sweeping him off until they both vanished in the crowd.

The waiter brought more wine and he drank it thoughtfully. 'Do you know him well?'

'Well enough. I'll introduce you another time.'

He drained his glass. 'Come on, let's dance.'

He was a natural dancer, and together they went enjoyably mad. The other dancers backed off to watch them, and when they finished the crowd applauded.

Charlie's eyes were brilliant, his cheeks flushed, and Pippa guessed she must look much the same. In a moment of crazy delight, he put his hands on either side of her face, just as she had briefly done to him at the table. But when he tried to kiss her she fended him off.

'That's enough,' she said when she could speak. 'Bad boy!'

'Sorry, ma'am!' He assumed a clowning expression of penitence.

'We're going back to the table and you're going to behave,' she said firmly.

Then she saw Roscoe.

He was sitting at a table on the edge of the dance floor, regarding her with his head slightly tilted and an unreadable expression on his face. Beside him sat a woman of great beauty in a low-cut evening gown of gold satin, with flaming red hair. Pippa saw her lean towards him, touching his hand gently so that he turned back to her, all attention, as though everyone else had ceased to exist.

'What's up?' Charlie asked, turning. '*What?* Damn him!'

He hurried her to the table, muttering, 'Let's hope he doesn't see us. What's he doing here?'

'Who's that with him?'

'I don't know. Never seen her.'

'Did you tell him you were coming?'

'No way!'

'Then perhaps it's just bad luck.'

'Not with Roscoe. I've heard him say that the man who relies on luck is a fool.'

'Yes, in stockbroking—'

'In everything. He never does anything by chance. He's a control freak.'

Pippa had no answer. She, whose presence here was a result of Roscoe's commands, knew better than anyone that Charlie was right. She shivered.

Now she could see Roscoe leading the woman into the

dance. The band was playing a smoochy tune and they moved slowly, locked in a close embrace. Pippa shifted her seat so that she had her back to them and began to chatter brightly about nothing. Words came out of her mouth but her mind was on the dance floor, picturing the movements that she'd avoided seeing with her eyes.

At last the music ended and Charlie groaned, 'Oh, no, he's coming over.'

Roscoe and his partner were bearing down on them. Without waiting to be invited, they sat at the table.

'Fancy seeing you here!' Roscoe exclaimed in a voice of such cheerful surprise that Pippa's suspicions were confirmed. This was no accidental meeting.

He introduced everyone, giving the woman's name as Teresa Blaketon. Charlie was immediately on his best behaviour in the presence of beauty, Pippa was amused to notice.

'I think we should dance,' Roscoe said, rising.

It would have been satisfying to ignore the hand he held out so imperiously, but that was hardly an option now, so she let him draw her to her feet and lead her back to the floor, where a waltz had just begun. She decided that there was nothing for it but to endure his putting an arm about her and drawing her close.

But he didn't. Taking her right hand in his left, he laid his right hand on the side of her waist and proceeded to dance with nearly a foot of air between them. It was polite, formal and Pippa knew she should have been glad. Yet, remembering how close he'd held his lady friend, she felt that this was practically a snub.

'I'm glad to see that you're taking your duties seriously,' he said. 'For you to spend an evening with Charlie is more than I'd hoped for.'

'Don't worry, it'll appear on the bill,' she said cheerfully. 'And, as it's my own time, I'll charge extra. Triple at least.'

'Don't I get a discount for the meal he bought you, and the first class champagne?'

'Certainly not. I drank that champagne out of courtesy.'

'I see you know how to cost every minute,' he said softly.

'Of course. As a man of finance, you should appreciate that.'

'There are some things outside my experience.'

'That I simply don't believe,' she said defiantly, raising her head to meet his eyes.

He was looking down on her with a fixed gaze that made her suddenly glad her dress was high and unrevealing. Yet she had the disconcerting sense that he could see right through the material. Even Charlie hadn't looked like that, and for a moment she trembled.

'You flatter me,' he said. 'The truth is, I'm mystified by you. When I think I understand you, you do the opposite to what I was expecting.'

'Just like the financial markets,' she observed saucily. 'You manage well enough with them.'

'Sooner or later, the financial markets always revert to type. With you, I'm not so sure.'

'Perhaps that's because you don't really know what my type is. Or you think you know, and you're mistaken.'

'No—' he shook his head '—I'm not arrogant enough to think I know.'

'Then let me tell you, I'm devoted to my job and to nothing else. I promised to get to know Charlie and "beguile" him, but I couldn't have done that in an office. It was necessary to work "above and beyond the call of duty."'

'And how is your case going?'

'Fairly well. He's seen through Ginevra.'

'And if you can persuade him to grow up, he's all set for a serious career.'

'You mean in the firm with you? Suppose that isn't what he wants?'

'He'll thank me in the end, when he's a successful man and he realises I helped to guide him that way.'

'Perhaps you should stop guiding him and let him find his own path.'

'Into a police cell, you mean?'

That silenced her.

After a moment he said, 'Why are you frowning?'

'I'm just wondering about your methods.'

'I don't know what you mean.'

'You don't really expect me to believe this is coincidence, do you? You knew Charlie was going to be here.'

'I see. I'm supposed to have every room bugged, and to bribe half the staff to bring me information. Shame on you, Pippa.'

She blushed, feeling foolish for her wild fantasies.

'I suppose I might be the evil spy of your imagination, if I needed to be,' he said in a considering tone, 'but when my brother conducts every phone call at the top of his voice I simply don't need to be. I happened to be passing his office when he booked the table.'

'And you made immediate arrangements to put him under surveillance. Or me.'

'I made immediate arrangements to have an enjoyable night out.'

'Teresa must have been surprised to be summoned at the last minute.'

'Teresa is a lovely woman, and she enjoys nightclubs. It gives her a chance to display her beauty, which, you must admit, is exceptional.'

It was on the tip of her tongue to ask if he'd hired his companion as he'd hired her, but her courage failed her. Besides, the memory of how he and Teresa had practically embraced as they danced, was all the answer she needed. It seemed to underline his sedate demeanour with herself.

She wasn't used to that. Men usually seized the opportunity to make contact with her body. One who behaved like a Victorian clergyman was unusual. Interesting.

Annoying.

The floor was getting crowded. Dancers jostled each other until suddenly one of them stumbled, crashing into Pippa, driving her forward against Roscoe, cancelling the distance he'd kept so determinedly between them. Taken by surprise, she had no time to erect barriers that might have saved her from the sudden intense awareness of his body—lithe, hard, powerful.

It was too late now. Something had made her doubly aware of her own body, singing with new life as it pressed up to his, and the sensation seemed to invade her totally—endless, unforgettable. Shocking.

She tried to summon up the strength to break the embrace, but he did it for her, pushing her away with a resolution that only just avoided being discourteous.

'We'd better return to the table,' he said.

Then he was walking off without a backward look, giving her no choice but to follow. Which *was* discourteous. She might have been irritated if she hadn't had an inkling of what was troubling him. She too needed time to think about what had just happened; time to deny it.

Charlie had reached the point of talking nonsense and Teresa looked relieved to see them.

'How did you get here?' Roscoe said, placing a hand on his brother's shoulder with a gentleness that contradicted the roughness in his voice.

'I hired Harry and his car. He's waiting for us.'

'Good. He can take you home while I take Pippa.'

'Hey, Pippa's with me—'

'And the less she sees of you in this state the better. Waiter!'

In a few minutes he'd settled everything—Charlie's bill as well as his own. They escorted Charlie out to the side road where the chauffeur was waiting. Teresa helped to settle him in the back seat, which gave Pippa the chance to mutter to Roscoe, 'I'll take a taxi home.'

'You will not.'

'But I don't want to be a gooseberry,' she said frantically. 'You and she...I mean...'

'I know exactly what you mean and kindly allow me to make my own decisions.'

'Like you make everyone else's?' she snapped.

'I won't pretend not to understand that, but you can't have known my brother a whole two days without realising that he's vulnerable. I don't want people to see him like this. Do you?'

'No,' she said. 'Just let me say goodnight to him.'

But Charlie was dead to the world and she stood back while Harry drove off with him. Watching Roscoe get into the driving seat of his car, she realised that she'd seen him drink only tonic water, and after several hours in a nightclub he was stone cold sober and completely in control.

Which was typical of him, she thought crossly.

Teresa didn't seem annoyed at having Pippa foisted on her when she would no doubt have preferred to be alone with Roscoe. As they sat together in the back she chatted merrily, mostly about Charlie, whose company she had enjoyed, especially as he had entertained her by running through some routines by another more talented comedian he'd recently seen perform.

'He's really good,' she recalled.

'You shouldn't encourage him,' Roscoe said over his shoulder. 'He's a sight too fond of playing whatever part he thinks people want.'

'Which will surely be useful in a stockbroker,' Pippa observed. 'He must need various personalities, depending on whether he's buying shares or selling them, manipulating the market, or manipulating people. With any luck, he'll be almost as good at that as you.'

Teresa rocked with laughter. The back of Roscoe's head was stiff and unrevealing.

Outside her apartment block, he got out and held open the door for her, a chivalrous gesture that also gave him the chance to fix her with a cool, appraising stare. She returned it in full measure.

'I hope your evening was enjoyable, Miss Jenson.'

'I hope yours was informative, Mr Havering.'

'More than I could have imagined, thank you.'

'Then all is well. Goodnight.'

Once in her apartment with the door safely shut behind her, Pippa tossed her bag aside, threw herself into a chair and kicked off her shoes, breathing out hard and long.

'Phew! What an evening! Get him! More informative than he could have imagined. I'll bet it was! Hello, Gran! Don't mind me. I'm good 'n mad.'

She was addressing the photograph that she kept on the sideboard, showing the wedding of Grandmother Dee and Grandfather Mark. Dee had once confided to her that there had been complications about that wedding.

'I was pregnant,' she'd said, 'and that was scandalous in nineteen forty-three. You had to get married to stay respectable, and I wondered if he was only marrying me because he had to.'

'And was he?' Pippa had wanted to know.

Dee had smiled mysteriously. 'Let's say he had his own reasons, but it was a while before I discovered what they were. On our wedding day I still couldn't quite believe in his love.'

Yet the young Dee in the picture was beaming happily, and in Pippa's present mood it all looked delightfully uncomplicated.

'Fancy having to be married before you could make love,' she mused.

In her mind she saw Roscoe dancing with Teresa, holding her in an embrace that spoke of passion deferred, but not for long. Right this minute they were on their way to her home, or perhaps to his, where he would sweep her into the bedroom and remove her clothes without wasting a moment.

She knew the kind of lover he would be: no-nonsense, not lingering over preliminaries, but proceeding straight to the purpose, as he did with everything. As well as pleasuring his woman efficiently, he would instruct her as to his own needs, with everything done to the highest standards. Afterwards, Teresa would know she'd received attention from an expert.

For a while Pippa's annoyance enabled her to indulge these cynical thoughts, but another memory insisted on intruding—his care for his mother, his patience, his kindness to her. All these spoke of a different man, with a gentle heart that he showed rarely. Was that gentleness also present in the lover?

'And why am I bothering?' she asked aloud. 'Honestly, Gran, I think you had it better in your day.'

Dee's smiling face as she nestled against her new husband seemed to say that she was right.

Pippa sighed and went to bed.

The night that followed was the strangest she'd ever known. Worn out, she had expected to sleep like a log, but the world was fractured. Two men wandered through her dreams—one gentle, protective and kind, the other a harsh authoritarian who gave his orders and assumed instant obedience. Both men were Roscoe Havering.

In this other world he danced with her, holding her close, not briefly but possessively, as though claiming her for ever. Unable to resist, she yielded, resting against him with a joy that felt like coming home. But then she awoke to find her flesh singing but herself alone.

In a fury, she threw something across the room. It was time to face facts. Roscoe had appeared at The Diamond the night before in order to study her and see if she was doing her job as a hired fancy woman. Whatever gloss he tried to put on it, that was the truth. Curse him!

Unable to lie still, she rose and began to pace the room, muttering desperately. 'All right, so I felt something. Not *here*—' she laid a hand quickly over her heart '—no, not there, but—' she looked down at her marvellous body '—just about everywhere else. Only for a moment. And he needn't think I'm giving in to it. I've done with that stuff for ever. So that's settled. Now I need to get some more sleep.'

CHAPTER SIX

When Pippa finally awoke it was to the memory of the appointment at Roscoe's office that morning.

'Oh, no,' she groaned. 'I'm not going!'

But she knew she was. The professional Miss Jenson didn't tamely back off. She got out of bed, showered in cold water for maximum alertness and ate a hearty breakfast, calculated to enhance energy and efficiency. The fact that she was inwardly fuming was of no interest to anyone else. Certainly not Roscoe Havering.

Now that the first hint of winter snow was in the air, she chose her attire for warmth: severe suit, long coat, flat shoes. With a face free of make-up and her hair scraped firmly back, she decided that she looked just right: a lawyer, not a fancy piece, whatever a man with no manners might think.

She put in a hard morning's work at her office, then David looked in for a quick word.

'Off to see Roscoe? Good. You've probably learned all about him by now.'

'The odd detail,' she said, assiduously hunting for something inside her desk.

'Then you'll have heard that there's nobody in the business with a higher reputation. His speciality is discretionary dealing.'

Pippa knew that some brokers simply followed their

clients' instructions, but did not give advice. Others would give advice, but not make final decisions. Most demanding of all was discretionary dealing, where the broker ascertained the clients' long-term objectives, and then had authority to make decisions without further consultation. Only the best and most trusted brokers could do this, and it came as no surprise to know that Roscoe Havering was one of them.

'A lot of brokers came out of the recession looking bad,' David told her. 'Not him. If anything, his trade has doubled because clients have flocked to him, disillusioned with the others. Plus there are rumours of a link-up with the Vanlen Corporation that would make Havering one of the richest and most powerful men in the financial world.'

Pippa mulled this over on the journey to Threadneedle Street, in the financial heart of London. Now the snow had properly started and, as she stepped out of the taxi, she pulled her coat tight, relieved that she would get her car back tomorrow.

Roscoe's office was located in a historic building, converted to modern day requirements. Dark deeds had occurred there centuries ago. Dead bodies had once been discovered in the cellar, one of which was a man known personally to the reigning monarch of the time. But only the building's outside reflected the dramatic past. Inside, all was corporate efficiency, bland colours and straight lines.

But I'll bet there are still plenty of dark deeds, Pippa reflected as she hurried into the elevator. *Just a different kind.*

She was curious to see how well Roscoe's establishment reflected the man, and it was no surprise to discover that he was on the top floor, with a view down on the world. As expected, she found the atmosphere subdued, even slightly haughty.

The receptionist showed her to a seat. 'I'm afraid there'll

be a slight delay,' she said. 'Mr Vanlen just walked in without warning. He's going to Los Angeles for some big international gathering, and he's annoyed because Mr Havering won't go too. But Mr Havering says those meetings are all talk and no substance, and he won't budge. Vanlen did a quick detour on his way to the airport, so at least he can't stay long.' She made a wry face. 'He never seems to think that other people might be busy.'

'I know the type,' Pippa said with feeling.

From behind a door she could hear a voice raised in argument. 'We can't waste time. This is a big deal for both of us. When everything's signed we're going to be the kings, and you want that as much as I do… What's that? The hell with keeping my voice down! Let them know that they've got to be afraid of you, that's what I say. It's where half the pleasure lies.'

The secretary groaned. 'You hear him. That's how Vanlen thinks. Heaven help us all when that tie-up goes through. Mr Havering's a tyrant now but when he—'

She stopped as Vanlen's voice was raised again. 'I can't believe you're really not coming to Los Angeles. Surely that's—?'

'I'd better go in,' the secretary said hastily. 'Mr Havering is fed up with that subject.'

She hurried over and knocked on Roscoe's door, opening it just in time for Pippa to hear him saying harshly, 'I'm not going and that's final. I don't have the time. Anyway, the conference starts tomorrow and I'd never change my mind at this late date.'

Too right, she thought. Anyone who tried to divert Roscoe from the course that suited him was in for a nasty surprise.

'Hey! It's you!' The delighted voice came from Charlie who'd just appeared, his eyes shining at the sight of her.

'Thanks heavens you're here!' he exclaimed, coming to sit beside her. 'This place is doing my head in!'

'I gather great things are afoot,' she said.

'You mean Vanlen? Oh, yes! We're going to be the greatest. No one will be able to touch us or compete with us, and then Roscoe will have everything he wants.'

'Nobody has everything they want,' she protested.

'That depends what they actually do want,' Charlie pointed out. 'If you keep your wants down to very few, it would be quite easy.'

'And what are his wants?' she asked curiously.

'Him up there, you down here saying, "I obey, I obey!"'

He said the last words in a mechanical voice of such fine comical effect that she couldn't help laughing.

'You ought to have gone on the stage,' she said.

'Yes, I used to think that might be nice, to stand up there in the spotlight, with the audience in the palm of my hand, knowing they were hanging on my every word.'

'Which means you've got a lot in common with Roscoe after all,' she pointed out.

'Yes, I suppose I do. But I want to make them laugh and love me. He wants to make them cower and fear him. And, like I said, when he's teamed up with Vanlen, he'll have everything he wants in the world.'

She was temped to agree, but illogically her sense of justice came to Roscoe's defence. 'Aren't you being a bit unfair? What about the "other Roscoe" you told me about at The Diamond—the nicer one, with feelings?'

'You imagined that.'

'No, I didn't. I remember every word you said.'

'All right, that Roscoe exists too, but only rarely. You'll be dealing with the strong one, so never drop your guard.'

'Careful, Charlie, I don't think you know him as well as you think you do.'

He eyed her shrewdly. 'So he's still exerting his charm over you, is he? He can do that, if he thinks it's worth it. But beware the day when you're no further use to him.'

This was probably good advice, she realised. She was about to ask Charlie to tell her more but he'd already tossed the subject aside to concentrate on something that interested him more.

'Wow! Get you!' he said, his eyes caressing her from head to toe. 'I know what you're doing with that severe look,' he went on. 'But it doesn't work. You're still gorgeous. Aren't you going to take that coat off?'

It was hot in the building and she was glad to let him ease the thick garment from her shoulders. But he took advantage of the situation to slip an arm around her waist, so that she edged away, muttering, 'Not here!'

'Here, there and everywhere,' he persisted. 'There's nobody else around.'

He managed to get both arms around her, resisting her attempts to escape. She groaned, exasperated by the silly boy who couldn't understand that this wasn't the time or the place.

'Someone's coming,' she said frantically. 'Charlie, stop that.'

He was reaching up to free her hair, sending it cascading in joyous beauty around her shoulders. He'd done this before, but that time had been in the privacy of his own home, with only his family there. Now it was in front of Roscoe's door as it opened and a man emerged.

He was thin, with a face that was so pleasant and humorous that at first she couldn't believe this was the man she'd overheard. But his grinding voice was the same, asking, 'Am I interrupting something?'

'Yes,' Charlie said defensively. 'You certainly are.'

'Sorry.' Vanlen held up his hands and backed off.

His glance at Pippa was appreciative and his look said all too plainly that he was a man of the world in these matters. She had met this attitude before and dealt with it too efficiently to be offended now, but she could cheerfully have throttled Charlie. Vanlen departed just as Roscoe appeared in the doorway, his eyes frosty as he regarded his brother.

'Is this fellow bothering you, Miss Jenson?' he demanded. 'If so, say the word and I'll defenestrate him.'

'You will not,' Charlie said, hastily getting behind a chair.

Pippa tried not to choke with laughter, and failed.

'It means throw you out of the window,' she assured Charlie.

'Oh. Are you sure that's all?'

'Quite sure. Stop worrying.'

He returned to her side, addressing Roscoe belligerently. 'I was just telling *Miss Jenson* that it's no use her trying to hide beneath dull clothes. She's still gorgeous beyond belief. Or perhaps you don't think so.'

'I think Miss Jenson looks acceptably professional,' Roscoe said in an indifferent voice. 'Which is exactly what I'd expect of her.'

Cheek! she thought.

He seemed strained and she wondered how long he had dallied in Teresa's bed, and how much had she exhausted him. But he showed her courteously into his office and enquired politely after her car.

'It took some time for my brothers to find the spare part it needed,' she said, 'but they finally managed it, and I'm getting the car back tomorrow.'

She and Charlie sat facing the desk, behind which Roscoe surveyed them from a position of authority, which was how, Pippa guessed, he felt most comfortable.

He pressed a buzzer and spoke to his secretary. 'We don't want to be disturbed.'

'Ah—no!' Charlie squealed. 'I'm waiting for a call. I've told my secretary to fetch me.'

'Then we'd better hurry,' Roscoe said ironically. 'We mustn't keep the betting shop waiting.'

'I got a hot tip,' Charlie explained. 'If it comes in, it'll get me out of trouble on a lot of fronts.'

'I don't know why I bother to teach you about stocks and shares,' Roscoe groaned. 'You're only happy making ridiculous bets.'

'But surely buying stocks and shares is a kind of betting?' Pippa observed innocently.

Charlie gave a muffled choke of laughter. Roscoe's glance told her that he didn't appreciate that remark.

'All right,' she said hastily. 'Let's get on. I've been reviewing the matter and it seems to me—'

The discussion became serious. Pippa put forward her most professional aspect, but all the time she had a strange feeling that it was a mask. There was an uneasy tension in the air, not between herself and Charlie, but between herself and the man who'd held her at a distance last night while burning her with his eyes, a man who eyed her with suppressed hostility, who challenged her every movement.

'I've told the police I wasn't in that shop,' Charlie complained. 'They just say, "Come on, now. Why not just admit it?"'

'They also keep saying things like, "We know what you lads are like,"' Roscoe said. 'As though they were all exactly the same. What's the matter?'

Charlie had suddenly started coughing, but he recovered in a moment. 'Nothing, nothing,' he said with the sudden urgent air of someone who wanted to change the subject. 'Now, where were we?'

He plunged back into serious discussion, talking so sensibly that Pippa's suspicions were aroused. Only one thing could make Charlie sensible, and that was the need to divert attention. She became sunk in thought and had to be recalled by Roscoe, who was staring at her in astonishment.

'Just let me catch up with my notes,' she said hastily. 'Ah, yes, here—'

She got no further. The door was flung open with a crash and a wild voice said, 'I've got to talk to you.'

Turning, she saw a man of about forty with a haggard face and dishevelled hair. His eyes were bloodshot and he seemed on the verge of collapse.

'Mr Franton, I gave orders that you were not to be admitted,' Roscoe said in a hard voice.

'I know. I've been trying to see you for days, but I can't get in. If I could just talk to you, make you understand—'

'But I do understand,' Roscoe interrupted him coldly. 'You deceived me and a lot of other people, and you very nearly involved this firm in a scandal from which it might never have recovered. I've always made it clear that insider trading is something I wouldn't tolerate.'

Pippa understood. Insider trading meant making a profit by the use of privileged information. If a business was on the verge of bankruptcy but only a few people knew, those people would be sorely tempted to sell their shares while they were still worth something, saving themselves financially while others were ruined. It could even happen that the sudden surge in sales precipitated a collapse that might otherwise have been avoided.

In a stockbroking firm such inside knowledge was common and often misused. A spy could earn a handsome profit by selling it on.

Yet Franton didn't look like an evil conspirator. He seemed

ordinary, slightly pathetic, and Pippa couldn't help a surge of unwilling sympathy for him.

'I never meant it to happen the way it did,' he pleaded.

'Understand me once and for all,' Roscoe replied in a hard voice. 'I care nothing for what you meant. I care only for what you did. And what you did was this. You ignored my specific instructions. You lied. You spread unsubstantiated rumours and caused a false rise in prices that cost a lot of people a lot of money—'

'Including you.' Despite his pathos, Franton couldn't resist a spiteful sneer.

'Yes, including me, but it's not the money that counts. It's my reputation that you've damaged and I don't want to see you on these premises ever again. You're out, and that's final.'

'But I need a job,' Franton screamed, collapsing again. 'I've got a family to support, debts—*look*!'

He ran to the window, pointing out to where the snow could now clearly been seen cascading down.

'Snow,' he cried. 'Christmas is coming. What do I tell my children when they don't get any presents?'

'Don't try playing the pathetic card with me,' Roscoe said coldly. 'You nearly caused a disaster throughout the financial world, and you did it by dishonesty. If you've brought a tragedy on yourself the responsibility is yours.'

'You heartless swine!'

Roscoe's face was as stony as his voice. 'Get out,' he said, softly threatening. 'Get out and stay out. You're finished.'

His last card played, Franton seemed to collapse. Slowly, he backed out, casting one last beseeching look. Roscoe didn't even see it.

'Now, perhaps we can finally get on,' he said, seating himself. 'Miss Jenson, I have some papers here—'

'Wait a minute,' Charlie said. 'You're not just going to let him go like that?'

'He can think himself lucky I'm not doing worse.'

'But this is Bill Franton—he's been here for years and he's a family friend—'

'Not any more.'

'Wait,' Charlie said, dashing out in pursuit.

'I'm afraid Charlie is too soft for his own good,' Roscoe said. 'One day I hope he'll learn a sense of reality.'

'Of course insider trading is dishonest and can't be defended,' Pippa agreed, 'but that poor man—'

'Why do you call him a "poor man"—because you saw his distress? You didn't see the distress he caused other people, and the much worse distress that was narrowly averted.'

'I suppose you're right,' she sighed.

'But you don't really think so, do you? I guess I'll just have to endure the burden of your disapproval.'

'It certainly doesn't bother you.'

'I've met it before and it's based on sentimentality.'

'Is it sentimental to say you can attach too much importance to money?' she demanded indignantly.

There was an ironic humour in his eyes, as though he was enjoying a grim joke at her expense.

'Not money, Miss Jenson,' he said. 'Honesty. That's where I attach importance. Nowhere else.'

And he was right, she thought furiously. He was beyond criticism, totally honest, upright, honourable, incorruptible.

And merciless.

'Ah, Charlie, there you are.' Roscoe sounded coolly collected at the sight of his brother. The last few minutes might never have been.

'Roscoe—'

'Come and sit down.'

'But Franton—'

'The subject is closed.' Roscoe's voice was final and Pippa shivered.

She made a mental note not to get on his wrong side, but reckoned that was probably easier said than done.

Then she pushed all other thoughts aside to concentrate on the case, but now that was hard because something was causing Charlie to become uncommunicative, as though protecting a secret. When his secretary looked in, saying, 'That call has come,' he vanished at once.

'How do you think it's going?' Roscoe asked her.

'I think there are problems. He's holding something back.'

'You amaze me. Last night he didn't seem to be holding anything back. You're doing brilliantly, as I expected.'

'That's why you came along, to keep watch, is it? To make sure I didn't lead Charlie along the wrong path?'

'Are you angry with me?'

'I suppose I might be. I can't think why.'

She spoke ironically, but there was truth as well. Beneath the polite surface, this meeting seethed with undercurrents of mistrust. The visit to Roscoe's home had left her feeling more kindly to him, but last night had reversed that. Now she remembered the awkwardness on which their relationship was based and she couldn't wait to get away from him.

'Maybe I'm not managing this very successfully,' he said, 'but it's a new situation for me too.'

'You mean you don't hire women for romantic relationships every day? You amaze me. I thought you were an old hand.'

'All right, attack me if you wish. You're angry about last night, and perhaps you have reason, but I only wanted to... to study the situation.'

'You wanted to find out if you were getting what you paid for. Or if Charlie was getting what you paid for.'

'Stop it!' Roscoe snapped, suddenly finding his nerves fraying. 'Don't talk like that.'

'I'll talk as I like. It's been "like that" ever since you hired me. Well, I don't sleep with the men I date. None of them. Sorry to disappoint you.'

'How dare you say that?' he raged.

Far from disappointing him, Pippa's words gave him a surge of joy so intense it was almost frightening. Until now, he hadn't known how much it mattered. But the discovery left him more confused, even more angry. He wanted to roar up to the heavens.

'Don't ever say anything like that,' he commanded, breathing hard. 'It wasn't our bargain, and you have no right to imply that it was.'

'Maybe not in words, but it's what you were thinking.'

'Don't *dare* tell me what I'm thinking. You know nothing. *Nothing!*'

'Perhaps I know more than you realise.'

'Pippa, I'm warning you—'

'Then don't. What right do you have to warn me? You're so arrogant, you think you can give orders left, right and centre, but not to me.'

'*I'm* arrogant?' Roscoe snapped. 'What about you? You assume all men are slavering for you and you despise them accordingly. I only hope one day you'll meet a man who's totally indifferent to your charms. It would teach you a lesson.'

'But surely,' she said with poisonous sweetness, 'I've met him already—in you. Haven't I?'

If she'd been easily scared she might have quailed at the look he threw her.

'You *are* indifferent to my charms, aren't you, Roscoe?'

'Totally!' he said in a voice of ice.

'And, since I'm equally indifferent to yours, neither of us has a problem. Just the same, I think it's time this arrangement came to an end. Another lawyer will suit you better.'

She rose and made for the door, but he was there before her.

'Don't be absurd. You can't just go like this.'

'So anyone who disagrees with you is absurd? No, I was absurd the day I let myself get embroiled in this. I should have had more sense of self-preservation. Now, please stand aside.'

'No,' he said stubbornly. 'I'm not letting you leave here.'

'Roscoe, stand aside. I won't be treated like this.'

Pippa thought he would defy her again, but then his shoulders sagged.

'All right, I'll stand aside,' he said. 'But I'm going to say something first.'

'Then get on with it.'

'Don't go. Hate me as much as you like, but don't abandon Charlie, *please*.'

'Roscoe—'

'I'm begging you, do you understand that? Begging.'

His eyes left no doubt that he meant it. They were brilliant, feverish, amazing her so that she couldn't speak.

'Well?' he asked. 'Do you want me to go down on one knee?'

'Oh, don't be ridiculous,' she said, backing away. 'Suppose someone came in.'

'Then they'd see me as never before, and they'd think it was a good laugh. Is that your price? You want me to make a fool of myself, and then you'll do as I ask? Is that it?'

'Suppose I said yes?' she asked. 'Would you pay the price?'

'Yes,' he said simply. 'Shall I? Go on, you've been wanting to take me down a peg since we met. Now's your chance.'

'No!' she exploded. 'That's the last thing I'd want. I'm not that kind of harpy.'

'Then what is your answer? Will you stay?'

'*Yes!* Now get back behind your desk and stop talking nonsense.'

He gave her a wry look, but moved away behind the desk.

Suddenly the door came flying open and Charlie stood there. 'I won!' he carolled.

'You don't mean that three-legged hack came home?' Roscoe asked ironically, and only Pippa noticed the strain in his voice.

'Ten to one!' Charlie yipped joyfully. 'I made a packet. Hey, I'll be able to pay you back the money I owe you—well, some of it, anyway.' He gave Pippa a bear hug. 'And it's all due to you. Since you came into my life, everything has gone well. The sun shines, the world is beautiful. Isn't that so, Roscoe?'

'Miss Jenson is certainly having a beneficial effect,' he replied loftily. 'In fact I was explaining how pleased we are with her efforts when you came in. Now, if you'll kindly sit down, Charlie, we can return to work.'

Pippa had to give him ten out of ten for a sense of wicked irony. She tried to meet his eyes, perhaps even encourage him to share the joke. But he wasn't looking at her. The paperwork seemed to absorb him.

The rest of the meeting was conducted with strict propriety, with as few words as possible. Pippa asked questions, made notes and finally rose briskly, declaring, 'I'll be in touch when I've investigated some more.'

'Tonight,' Charlie said eagerly.

'Tonight I've got some boring reception to go to. Don't be in a rush. I'll see myself out.'

She escaped.

CHAPTER SEVEN

PIPPA had spoken the truth about the coming evening. A client was giving a lavish reception to celebrate acquiring sole rights to a piece of valuable computer software and had offered several invitations to Farley & Son, whose work had been crucial in securing the contract in a bidding war. A little group of them were going, including David and herself.

'Dress up to the nines,' he told her. 'Knock their eyes out. It's good for business.'

She laughed but did as he wished, donning a shimmering white dress that combined beauty with elegance. The reception was held at London's most costly hotel. They arrived in a fleet of expensive cars and were shown upstairs to the Grand Salon where their hosts were waiting to greet them effusively.

One of the younger wives, friendly with Pippa and new to this kind of function, was in transports. 'Everybody who's anybody in finance is here tonight,' she said. 'You probably know most of them.'

Pippa did indeed recognise many faces and began working the room, champagne in hand, charm on display, as was expected of her. As her friend had said, the cream of London's financial establishment was gathered there, so it shouldn't have been a surprise when her eyes fell on Roscoe Havering. Yet it was.

'Good evening, Miss Jenson.'

'Good evening, Mr Havering.'

'I suppose I shouldn't be surprised to see you here,' he said, unconsciously echoing her own thought. 'It's the sort of gathering in which you shine.'

'Strictly business,' she said. 'I can help to attract new clients here, and that's what David expects me to do, so, if you'll excuse me, I must get to work.'

'Wait.' His hand on her arm detained her. 'Are you angry with me?'

'Certainly not.'

'Then why are you so determined to get away from me?'

'Because, as I've tried to explain, for me this is a business meeting.'

'Tell me the real reason. That's not just efficiency I see in your eyes. It's coldness and hostility. How have I offended you now?'

'You haven't.'

'Little liar. Tell me the truth.'

'You haven't offended me, but I can't pretend that you're my favourite person.'

'Because of Charlie?'

'No, because of…lots of things.'

'Name one.'

'Stop interrogating me. I'm not in the dock.'

'No, your victim is usually in the dock with you pressing home the questions. So, you can dish it out but you can't take it?'

'How dare you!'

'Name something I've done to offend you—a new offence, not one you've told me about before.'

She ground her teeth, wondering how she could ever have sympathised with him.

'All right,' she said at last. 'Franton.'

'Who?'

'You've forgotten him already, haven't you? That poor man who burst into your office this morning.'

'That "poor man"—'

'Yes, yes, I know. Insider trading is wrong, but he's not the only one who's sailed a bit close to the wind, is he? I know someone else whose activities threaten your firm's good name, but he doesn't get chucked out. He gets protected. You hire a lawyer to keep him on the straight and narrow.'

'He's my brother—'

'And Franton is a man with a wife and children. Maybe he doesn't deserve a position of trust any more, but you threw him onto the scrap heap without a second thought.'

Pippa waited for Roscoe to speak but he was staring as though he'd just seen her for the first time.

'All right,' she said. 'I'm a soppy, sentimental woman who doesn't understand harsh reality and sticks her nose into what doesn't concern her. There, now, I've saved you the trouble of saying it.'

'Soppy and sentimental is the last thing I'd ever call you,' Roscoe said. He seemed to be talking in a daze.

'Well, anyway...since you're employing me I suppose I had no right to fly at you like that.'

His voice was unexpectedly gentle. 'You can say anything you like to me.'

'No, really—it's none of my business.' Suddenly she was desperate to get away from him.

'I wish I could explain to you what the pressures are—I think I could make you understand, and I'd like to feel that you did.'

'As you say, I don't know what it's like for you.' She gave a brittle laugh. 'I don't suppose I could imagine it.'

'Pippa—'

'Don't let me keep you. We both need to drum up new business.'

She gave him a brilliant smile and moved firmly away. She didn't even look back, but plunged into networking—smiling, laughing, making appointments, promising phone calls. It was an efficient evening and by the end of it she'd made a number of good contacts.

At last she found herself on the edge of a little group surrounding the managing director of the firm celebrating its triumph. He was growing expansive, making jokes.

Roscoe, standing nearby, joined in the polite laughter, while his eyes drifted over the crowd until he saw the person he wanted and watched her unobtrusively.

'It's been a good celebration,' the managing director said. 'Of course, I really wanted to arrange this evening a couple of weeks later, so that we could make it a Christmas party as well, but everyone's calendar was crowded already.'

'Such a shame,' said a woman close by. 'I simply adore Christmas.'

There were polite murmurs of agreement from almost everyone.

But not from Pippa, Roscoe realised. Beneath the perfectly applied make-up, her face had grown suddenly pale, almost drawn. She closed her eyes, keeping them shut just a moment too long, as though retreating into herself.

David spoke in Roscoe's memory. *'The nearer to Christmas it gets, the more of a workaholic she becomes... It's as if she's trying to avoid Christmas altogether.'*

He studied Pippa, willing her to open her eyes so that he might read something in them. At last she did so, but when she saw him she turned quickly, as though she resented his gaze.

As she moved away a strange feeling assailed him. She was young, beautiful, the most alluring, magnetic woman in the room. And she was mysteriously alone. No man claimed her, and she claimed none either. For a blinding moment the sense of her isolation was so strong that it was as though everyone else had vanished, leaving her the sole occupant of the vast, echoing room.

Or a vast, echoing world.

He told himself not to indulge fanciful thoughts. But they wouldn't be banished. He started to go after her but somebody called him, forcing him to smile and go on 'business alert'. When he managed to escape, Pippa had vanished.

Along the front of the hotel were some elaborate balconies, decorative stonework wreathed in evergreen. Pippa wandered out, thankful to escape the air inside, heavily perfumed with money, seduction and intrigue. But it was too chilly to stay out long and after a few minutes she turned back. Then she stopped at the sight of the man standing there.

'Good evening,' he said.

After a moment memory awoke. This was the 'big noise' in the financial world, with whom Roscoe would soon merge his firm, becoming, if possible, more powerful and autocratic than he already was.

'Mr Vanlen. I think we met briefly in Mr Havering's office.'

'You could say we "met". It was more you putting yourself on display. Mind you, there's plenty to display, I'll give you that. You knew you were driving me crazy, and you meant to do it. Fine, I fell for it. Let's talk.'

'No, I—'

'Oh, spare me the modest denials. You came out here knowing I'd follow you.'

'No, I didn't know you were here.'

'I've been watching you all evening. Don't pretend you didn't know. Here's the deal. You and I, together, for as long as it suits me. And you'll find me generous.'

'You're mistaken,' she said coldly. 'I am *not* interested in you in any way, shape or form. Is that clear?'

But, as his self-satisfied smirk revealed, he interpreted this in his own way.

'Evidently I didn't make *myself* clear,' he said. 'Does this say it plainly enough?'

Pulling out a flat black box, he opened it to reveal a diamond pendant of beauty and value.

'And that's just the start,' he added.

She regarded him wearily. 'I'm supposed to be impressed by this, aren't I?' she said. 'But I'm not interested. Can't you understand that?'

'Come, come. You're a woman of the world. You know the score. You're used to rich, powerful men and you like them that way, don't you?'

'Only if they're interesting. Not all rich men *are* interesting. Some of them are plain bores.'

'Money is never boring,' he riposted. 'Nor is power. You see them?' He flung a hand in the direction of the room behind them. 'The richest, most powerful men in London, and there isn't one of them I couldn't crush. Ask Havering. His investigations about me have shown him a few things that surprised him.'

'He's had you investigated? You sound very cool about it.'

Vanlen shrugged. 'It's no more that I expect, ahead of our tie-up. I've done the same to him, and I found things that surprised me too. It's par for the course.'

He was right, she realised. This level of sharp-eyed suspicion was normal in the world of high finance where Roscoe inhabited a peak. But it made her shiver.

'I know a few things about you too,' Vanlen went on. 'You like to play the field. No permanent lover to make things awkward. Fine, then we understand each other.'

His hand slid around her shoulder, making her move away quickly.

'The one thing you don't seem to understand is the word no,' she snapped. 'I'll say it as often as I have to.'

'But you don't mean it,' he protested. 'Come on, just one little kiss to seal our bargain.'

Before she could stop him, he'd pulled her close and brushed her lips with his own. Exerting all her strength, she wrenched free.

'Try that again and I'll slap you so hard you'll bounce into next week,' she said breathlessly.

What he might have done then she never found out, for a cough from the shadows made them both turn. Roscoe was standing there.

'I came to fetch you, Vanlen,' he said. 'There's a big deal going on and they want you to be part of it.'

'On my way,' the man replied and vanished without a backward glance at Pippa. The scene between them might never have happened.

'Thank you,' she said coolly. 'He was becoming a bore.'

He made a wryly humorous face. 'Don't tell me I arrived in time to save a damsel in distress?'

'Certainly not. Another moment and I'd have tossed him off the balcony, so you might say you spoilt my fun.'

'My apologies.'

The feel of Vanlen's mouth was still on hers, filling her with disgust and making her rub her mouth hard with tissues.

'Yuck!' she said.

'It's a pity he affects you like that. You could have been queen of London.'

'Don't you start. Did you hear what he said about you?'

'Investigation? Sure. We each know enough to confront the other. Pippa, are you all right?'

She was still rubbing her mouth, and he caught himself up at once.

'No, of course you're not all right. Stupid of me. Don't go at it so hard, you'll hurt yourself.'

'I can't help it. He's disgusting.'

'Here, let me.' Taking a clean handkerchief from his pocket, he began to rub gently.

'It's no use,' she sighed. 'I can still feel him. Perhaps another glass of champagne would wipe him away.'

'I know something better,' he said softly and laid his mouth against hers.

It was over in a second. His lips touched hers for a brief moment, just long enough to obliterate Vanlen, then they were gone.

Through the dim light, he saw the wild astonishment in her eyes and could just make out her lips shaping his name.

'I'm sorry,' he said stiffly. 'I thought it might help.'

'I—'

'Come on.' Taking her hand firmly, he led her back to where the crowd was beginning to disperse.

David was there, looking around, brightening when he saw her. 'Ready to go?' he asked cheerfully.

'Yes...yes...'

'I think she's tired,' Roscoe said. 'The sooner she goes home, the better. Excuse me.'

He was gone.

In the car home Pippa pretended to be asleep so that she could avoid talking. But later, when she got into bed, she lay awake all night, staring into the darkness, trying to see what could not be seen and understand what could not be understood.

The following evening she went to have a family dinner at her beloved grandparents' house on Crimea Street, and where she herself had lived for the last two years of their lives. These days Frank, his wife and children, lived there, with her other brother, Brian, just down the street. Now they returned her car with an air of triumph at having made it usable again.

Pippa hadn't been back to the old home much recently, and for a while she could enjoy the company of her parents, nephews and nieces, most of whom lived no more than two streets away.

With so many children, it was inevitable that the Christmas decorations should go up early.

'I keep telling them that it's still too soon,' Brian's wife, Ruth, said in laughing despair. 'But you might as well talk to the moon. As far as they're concerned, it's Christmas already. Hold that paper chain, would you?'

Pippa smiled mechanically. It was true, as David had suggested, that she had her own reasons for shying away from Christmas—for her, it had been a time of heartbreak. But this was no time to inflict her feelings on her family, so she spent a conventional evening climbing a stepladder and hanging up tinsel.

There was a moment of excitement when a box was brought down from the attic. Dust rose as it was unpacked, but the contents were disappointing.

'A couple of tatty scarves,' Ruth said disparagingly. 'Gloves. Some old books. Let's throw them out.'

'No, give them to me,' Pippa said quickly. She'd recognised the gloves as a pair Dee had worn, and it would be nice to keep them as a memento.

She wandered through the house, glancing into the bedroom where they had slept together until the end. Pippa's mother Lilian crept in behind her and surveyed the double bed, which was still the same one where the old people had embraced each other as they'd drifted contentedly to the end of the road.

'They were very happy together,' she sighed. 'And yet I can never see this room without feeling sad.'

'I came in one morning to find that Gran had died in the night,' Pippa remembered, 'and Grandma was holding him. It wasn't very long after they took that trip to Brighton, the honeymoon they never had.'

'And they wouldn't have had even that if you hadn't taken them,' Lilian recalled. 'They told me it was the last thing that made everything perfect. Afterwards, they just slipped away.'

'And that was what they both wanted,' Pippa said. 'Even missing them terribly, I couldn't be unhappy for them. All they cared about was being together, and now they always will be.'

'And one day that's what you'll have,' Lilian said, regarding her tenderly. 'Just be patient.'

'Honestly, Mum, I don't think like that any more. You start off telling yourself, "Never mind, there's always next time". But there isn't really. There won't be a next time for me, and it's better if I face that now.'

'Oh, darling, don't say that,' Lilian protested, almost tearful. 'You can't live your life without love.'

'Why not? I have a great time, a successful job, a good social life—'

'Oh, yes, every man falls at your feet in the first ten minutes,' Lilian said with motherly disapproval.

'Not quite every man,' Pippa murmured.

'Good. I'm glad some of them make you think.'

'Mum, please stop. I did my thinking years ago when a certain person did his vanishing act. That's it. The man who can change my mind hasn't been born.'

'You're only talking like this because you're always depressed at Christmas, but I just know that one day someone will make your heart beat faster.'

'You mean like Dad does with you?' Pippa asked mischievously.

'I admit your father's no romantic hero, but he's a decent man with a sweet temper. If he'd only stop breeding ferrets I'd have no complaints.'

'Is someone talking about me?' came a voice from the stairs as Pippa's plump, balding father appeared.

In the laughter that followed, the subject was allowed to die and she was able to escape.

They all think it's so easy, she mused. *Find a man who makes your heart beat faster and that's it. But suppose you don't like him because he's hard and cynical, and he looks down on you even while he's looking you over. Suppose he infuriates you because you can't stop thinking about him when you don't want to, so that you just get angrier and angrier. Suppose he's the wrong man in every possible way but that doesn't seem to help because when he looks at you it makes you think of things you'd rather not think of. And then he does something—the last thing you expected—and it makes you want...it makes you want...oh, to hell with it! And him!*

Charlie called her the next day and they arranged to meet for dinner the following evening.

'And don't worry about Roscoe turning up because he's gone to Los Angeles,' Charlie added.

'Los Angeles?' she murmured, recalling the words she'd overheard in his office. 'But he was so definite about not going, said it was a waste of time.'

'I know, and then suddenly he changed his mind, which is something he never does.'

'Everybody does sometimes,' she said mechanically, trying to ignore certain thoughts that clamoured for entrance to her mind.

They were astounding thoughts. They said he'd gone away to escape her after their two encounters, so confusingly different. He seemed to fight with her and kiss her, just as easily.

No, she corrected herself quickly. It hadn't been a kiss, just a kindly gesture; almost medical in intent. But it had misfired. Meaning only to obliterate the memory of Vanlen's lips, he'd replaced it with his own. Which surely hadn't been his intention.

She remembered how quickly he'd backed off, clearly shocked. By himself, or by her? What had he read in her eyes that had sent him flying to the far side of the world?

The memories and questions raged inside her, warning her that the time was coming when she would have to face the truth. And the truth scared her.

At her insistence, Charlie took her to a sedate, conventional restaurant, where he was on his best behaviour. And, without Roscoe there, Pippa could raise the suspicion that had been nagging at her since the office meeting.

'Now tell me the truth,' she said. 'You never did go into that shop, but Ginevra did, probably dressed in jeans with her hair covered. In the near darkness she looked like a man, so when she escaped and the owner caught up with you—well, it was her, wasn't it?'

Charlie set his chin stubbornly. 'You're just imagining things.'

'You gave the game away when Roscoe said people thought all lads were the same and you had that coughing fit. I suddenly saw what had happened. You were mistaken for her, and she just ran off and left you to suffer.'

'Look—we were good together once and I can't just drop her in it.'

Nothing would budge him from this position. Pippa seethed with frustration and ended the evening early.

Before going to bed, she sent an email to Roscoe. For some

reason it wouldn't come right and she had to reword it three times, eventually settling on:

Mr Havering,
I've just had a worrying talk with your brother. He didn't break into the shop. It was Ginevra and three others. Mr Fletcher caught them but they ran off and by the time he caught up she'd vanished, and he assumed Charlie was the fourth.

Charlie's having an attack of daft chivalry. I've tried to make him see sense, but he's deaf to reason.

I'm afraid the 'charms' for which you hired me are drawing a blank, and it seemed only right to inform you of my failure.

I await your further instructions.
Yours sincerely,
Philippa Jenson

She read it through repeatedly, finally losing patience with herself for shilly-shallying and hitting the 'send' button violently. Then she threw herself into bed and pulled the covers over her head.

Next morning, she checked for a reply. But there was nothing.

Too soon. Think of the time difference. He must be asleep.

At work she accessed her home computer every hour, sure that this time there would be a response. Nothing.

Her email would have gone to his London office, she reasoned, and perhaps he wouldn't see it until he returned. No way! An efficient man like Roscoe would link up from Los Angeles. He was ignoring her.

Her disappointment was severe—and irrational, she knew. This didn't fit with her mental picture of him as a better man inside than he was on the outside. She felt personally let down.

She worked late that night, finally reaching home with relief.

Then she stopped, astounded, at the incredible sight that met her eyes. Roscoe was in the hall, seated on an ornate wooden bench. His head leaned back against the wall, his eyes were closed and his breathing suggested that he was asleep. He looked almost at the point of collapse.

CHAPTER EIGHT

PIPPA touched him gently on the shoulder and his eyes opened slowly.

'Hello,' he said.

'Roscoe, what on earth—? Come upstairs.'

He retrieved the two suitcases near his feet and followed her into the elevator, where he closed his eyes again until they arrived and she led him out, along the corridor and into her apartment.

'Sit down,' she said, pointing to a comfortable sofa.

'You must be thinking—'

'Tea first, explanations later,' she said.

'Thank you.'

She was smiling to herself as she filled the kettle. Her email had brought him home. The world was good again.

He drank the tea thankfully, but didn't seem much more awake.

'When did you last sleep?' she asked.

'I can't remember. I was unlucky in catching a flight. I reached the airport just in time to miss one plane and I had to grab the next one. Only it went to Paris, so I had to get a connecting flight to London.'

'You walked out on your conference?' she breathed.

He shrugged. 'After your email, what did you expect me to do?'

'Email me. Text me. Call me.'

'No, I had to talk to you properly.'

And for that he'd walked out on business.

Of course he'd done it for Charlie and his mother, Pippa reminded herself.

But common sense spoke with a feeble voice, defeated by the surge of awareness of Roscoe as a man. A man who'd tried to escape her and been defeated.

What was happening between them alarmed him because it threatened the life he'd achieved with such a struggle. But he'd seized an excuse to come back to her and now he was here, laying his gesture at her feet, waiting to know what she would do with it.

She was silenced for a moment. She'd misjudged him so badly.

'The flight to Los Angeles is eleven hours,' she said at last, 'and then you came straight back—'

'And I don't even like flying,' he ground out. 'In fact, I hate it.'

'I hate it too,' she admitted. 'It's boring, you're trapped, and I'm always sure we're going to crash at any moment.'

He gave her a faint grin of understanding.

'No wonder you're exhausted,' she said. 'But why did you wait downstairs? There's a sofa in the hall outside my front door where you could have been more comfortable.'

'Yes, but I wasn't sure if you'd be coming home alone, and if your companion had seen me lolling by your door... well...'

'Am I understanding you properly?' she asked, regarding him with her head on one side.

'I just didn't want to embarrass you.'

'You've got a nerve,' she breathed, feeling a return of the annoyance he could inflame so easily in her.

'I'm only suggesting that you might have company tonight. What's wrong with that?'

Pippa drew a deep breath, but instantly checked herself.

'No—no!' She held up her hands with the air of someone backing off. 'Let's leave it for now. I'll say it later, when you're back in the land of the living.'

'Thank you for that mercy,' he said. 'So when "later" comes I can expect to be knocked sideways, beaten to a pulp—'

'Walked over with hobnailed boots,' she agreed. 'But first I'll make you some supper.'

'Just a little, thank you. I'll probably fall asleep over it.'

'Then I shall wake you and make you eat something anyway.'

Roscoe gave her a look of appreciation. Then he followed her into the kitchen and tried to help, but finished up sitting on a stool, watching her out of bleary eyes.

'It's not just tiredness,' he said. 'It's jet lag, which always hits me like a rock. I don't know why I get it worse than most people. Everyone else seems to brush it off, but not me. And it's not just the flight home. I'm still lagged from the flight out there, so I'm—' he made a helpless gesture '—not at my best.'

'That's what comes of dashing off to conferences at the last minute,' she suggested gently.

'Yes, well…things happen. You can't always plan for…' again the gesture '…well, anyway…'

'Did you hear anything useful while you were there?' she asked in a neutral voice.

'I couldn't tell you,' he said with a humorous sigh. 'I can't remember a thing.'

'Is this Roscoe Havering talking?' she asked lightly. 'The man who makes the financial world tremble, whose tough decisions can shake the market—?'

'Oh, shut up!' he begged.

She laughed. 'Sorry.'

'You're not.'

'Hey, you're right. I'm not.'

She made a light meal of scrambled eggs on toast, and he pleased her by eating every last crumb.

'That was delicious. Do you want some help with the washing up?'

'No, thank you,' she said with more haste than politeness. 'But you've made your offer so you can go and sit on the sofa with a clear conscience.'

'That's what I like. A woman who understands.'

He wandered away with the air of a man who had arrived in heaven.

When she joined him a few minutes later he said, 'Do you really think Charlie's protecting Ginevra?'

'Oh, yes. But I can't prove it without his help. I guess I'm just not doing my job properly. I haven't beguiled him very well if he's defending her against me.'

'Charlie's loyal. If he had feelings for her once, he wouldn't drop her in it now.'

'That's nice of him but don't you see what it means?'

'It means my brother's an idiot, but we knew that.'

'It means I've failed. He was supposed to be so much under my spell that he'd do anything I said. Hah! Some spell! I'm useless.'

'That's enough. You're not useless. It's only been a few days.'

'But you thought he'd take one look at me and become my willing slave,' she said wryly. 'Or something like that. This isn't what you expected when you hired me. Perhaps you should get someone else.'

'Someone else?' he echoed. 'Someone else with your eyes, your laughter, your charm? *Is* there anyone else? Pippa, you knocked Charlie sideways in the first moment.'

'You're just being kind.'

'I'm not known for my kindness,' he said drily. 'And once you'd have been the first to say so. I knew from the start that you were exactly what I wanted—for Charlie, I mean. And you're doing well. Look how you found out about this. I had no idea.'

'But I'm failing.'

'Why are you so hard on yourself? It's not like you.'

Now she was all at sea, taken by surprise by his understanding.

'You don't know what's like me,' she muttered.

'Don't I? Well, perhaps I'm learning, and perhaps the things I'm learning are surprising me.'

She tried to be sensible, but it was hard with Roscoe's gentle eyes on her.

'Obviously I don't have the hold on him that you wanted,' she murmured.

'I think you do. The other night, when you were dancing together and he tried to kiss you at the end—'

'That didn't mean anything,' she said quickly. 'He just saw it as part of the dance.'

'But earlier that evening, when you were at the table and you—'

'I didn't kiss him.'

'No, but you did this.' Roscoe leaned forward, putting his hands on either side of her face and looking into her eyes. 'You did this,' he repeated. 'Don't you remember?'

'Yes,' she said breathlessly. 'I remember now.'

She waited for him to release her, but for some reason he didn't. She had the strangest impression that he was imprisoned in himself, wanting to move but unable to. Then she knew that the feeling was there inside her also. His hands were warm and firm against her cheeks, his eyes uncertain and questioning as she'd never seen them before. How dark and mysterious they were, inviting her to explore depths that enticed her. His lips, so often set in a firm line, were slightly parted, the sound of his breathing reaching her softly.

He'd been watching her all the time in the nightclub, she realised; not just dancing but when she was sitting at the table with Charlie, laughing with him, smiling at him. He'd noted every gesture, every moment of warmth.

She felt a tremor go through her and realised that it came from him. He was shaking. She drew in a sharp breath and in the same moment he dropped his hands, as though the touch of her burned him.

And she saw fear in his eyes.

His alarm had an instant effect on her, reminding her of her own caution about getting too close.

'You misunderstood what you saw,' she said quickly. 'It was just friendly. That's all I can ever manage. Just friendly. That's why you didn't have to worry about me bringing anyone home tonight. I know what I look like, but it's not real. People would be amazed to know how virtuously I live.'

'I wouldn't,' he murmured, but she didn't hear him.

'It's all front, all presentation,' she hurried on, gabbling slightly. 'So I suppose that makes me a tease. I meet a man, we go out, have a good time, exchange a few kisses—oh, yes, I don't deny that—and he thinks that sooner or later he's going to have a night of pleasure. I don't intentionally deceive them, but pretty soon I realise that I can't go through with it. He isn't "the one" and the kindest thing to do is tell him.'

'Yes, I saw that the first night,' he reminded her. 'But why, Pippa? You could have any man you wanted.'

'No, I couldn't,' she said. Pippa turned sharply away and walked to the window, filled with shrieking alarm at the way the distance between them was closing by the minute. It was safer to pull apart now.

But perhaps Roscoe's courage was greater than hers

because he followed and stood just behind her, not touching but barely an inch apart.

'What happened?' he asked softly.

'It doesn't matter.'

'Yes, it does. It matters because you've made it your whole life. If it didn't matter, it wouldn't scare you as much as it does.'

'I'm not scared,' she said brightly. 'What is there to be scared of?'

'You tell me—if you can put it into words.'

'You're making something out of nothing. I had a bad experience, but so does everyone.'

'Yes, but yours went deep enough to damn near destroy you,' he said in a voice that was mysteriously fierce and gentle at the same time.

That almost shattered her control. Out of sight, she clenched her hands and forced herself to shrug.

'Look, I lost the man I wanted and it cured me of silly fantasies.'

Hands on her shoulders, he turned her to face him. He was frowning slightly. 'And what do you define as "silly fantasies"?'

'Love lasting for ever. Moon rhyming with June. It's all a con trick. Have fun, but don't start believing in it, that's my motto.'

'Do you really not believe in people truly loving each other, wanting to give to each other, make sacrifices for each other?'

She gave a little laugh. 'I believed in it once. Not any more. Let's leave it.'

'What happened?'

She shrugged. 'It turned out that he didn't believe in it, that's all. Unfortunately, he discovered that rather late in the day. The wedding was planned, everything booked—the church, the honeymoon. So we had to cancel the arrangements. Very boring, but a useful lesson in reality.'

She finished with a tinkling laugh that made him look at her shrewdly.

'I see,' he said, nodding.

'Do you? I wonder. I don't suppose you know much about being jilted.'

He didn't reply for a moment. Then he said simply, 'Don't jump to conclusions.'

Suddenly, as though he too had heard the sounding of an alarm, he stepped back, asking, 'Is there any more tea?' in a voice whose brittleness matched her own.

'Yes, I'll make a fresh cup. Sit down and wait for me.'

He'd revealed more than he'd meant to and was hastily blocking a door he'd half opened. Pippa understood the feeling, having done the same. Now she was glad to escape to the kitchen and have a few moments alone to calm her riotous feelings.

When she felt she'd returned to some sort of normality, she took in the tea and found him studying Dee and Mark's wedding picture.

'They were my grandparents,' she said. 'They married during the war.'

'You're very like her,' he said.

'Really? Nobody's ever said that to me before.'

'Not in features, but she's got a cheeky look in her eyes that I've seen in yours. It says, "Go on, I dare you!"'

'Hey, that was her exactly.'

'Did you know her well?'

'I lived with the two of them near the end of their lives. When she died, she left me some money on condition I used it to train for a career. It's funny, I love both my parents, and my brothers, but I was closer to Gran than anyone else. She didn't stand for any nonsense.'

'You see; I said you were like her.'

'Well, she taught me a lot, especially how to get the better of a man.' She gave a merry chuckle. Now that the dangerous moment had passed, she was slipping back into the persona of Pippa the cheeky urchin. '"Let him think he's winning", that was her motto. "Make sure he doesn't find out the truth until it's too late".' She glanced at the picture on the sideboard. 'And I was a good pupil, wasn't I, Gran? Top of the class.'

'You want to be careful having that kind of conversation with your grandmother,' Roscoe said, grinning. 'Your grandfather might eavesdrop and discover your secrets.'

'If he doesn't know them by now—' She stopped suddenly, aghast as she heard herself talking as though they were living people. She must sound really mad. 'That is…' she resumed hastily '…what I mean is…'

'Pippa—' he interrupted her gently '—you don't have to tell me what you mean. You really don't.'

And she didn't, she realised with a surge of thankfulness. Roscoe understood perfectly.

'How long were they married?' he asked.

'Sixty years. We had a big celebration of their anniversary, and neither of them lived very long after that. He died first, and then Gran was just waiting to join him. She used to say he appeared in her dreams and told her to hurry up because he could never find anything without her. In the end, she only kept him waiting three weeks.

'I remember her saying that she wanted to outlive him, but only by a little. She wanted to be there to look after him as long as he needed her, but then she wanted to follow quickly. And she got her wish.'

Roscoe gave her a strange look. 'So love does sometimes last for ever?'

'For their generation, yes. In those days it was expected.'

'And that's why they stayed together for sixty years? Because of convention?'

'No,' she sighed. 'That's not why. They loved each other totally, but just because they could manage it doesn't mean that everyone... Drink your tea before it gets cold.'

'Then I must call a taxi and go home. Perhaps you'd have lunch with me tomorrow, when I'm more awake. We'll discuss the most sensible way to proceed.'

He took out his cellphone but, instead of making the call, he stared at it, then put it down suddenly as though reeling from a blow.

'If I can just rest for a moment,' he murmured.

'Not just for a moment,' she said. 'All night.'

'What was that?'

'You're not leaving while you're in this state. You'd forget where you were going and end up heaven knows where. Come on.'

She reached for him to help him to his feet. Dazed, he let her support him into the bedroom, where a gentle push sent him tumbling onto the bed. She went to recover his suitcases and when she returned he was sprawled out, dead to the world. Quietly, she drew the curtains and turned out the light.

'Goodnight,' she whispered, closing the door.

She washed up quietly so that no noise should intrude on him even through the door. As she worked, she tried to believe that this was really happening. Her email had brought Roscoe flying home, despite his problems with jet lag, despite his work, despite his intense need to stay ahead of the game. Despite everything, he'd come speeding back to her.

Before retiring for the night, she opened the door of the bedroom just a crack. Roscoe was lying as she'd left him, his breath coming evenly. She backed out and went to curl up on the sofa.

Who would have imagined that he had an unsuspected

frailty? she thought. More—who would have imagined that he would allow her to see it?

Just before she fell asleep, she wondered if Teresa had ever been allowed to know.

She awoke in darkness, feeling slightly chilly. The weather was growing cold as autumn advanced, so she turned the heating up, then recalled that the bedroom radiator was sometimes temperamental.

Quietly, she slipped into the room, realising that she'd been right. The temperature was low and it took some fiddling before the radiator performed properly. In the darkness she could just make out Roscoe, lying still, then turning and muttering.

He must be cold, she thought, taking a blanket from the cupboard and creeping to the bed, hoping to lay it down without waking him. But his eyes opened as she leaned over.

'Hello,' he whispered.

'I just brought you this so that you don't catch cold,' she said.

She wasn't sure if he heard her. His eyes had closed again while his hands found her, drawing her down against him. There was nothing lover-like in the embrace. She wasn't even sure he knew what he was doing. But his arms were about her and her head was on his chest, and he seemed to have fallen asleep again.

It would have been easy to slide free, but she found she had no desire to do so. The feeling of Roscoe's chest rising and falling beneath her head and the soft rhythm of his heart against her ear were pleasant and peaceful. That was missing in her life, she realised. Peace. Tranquillity. This was the last man with whom she would have expected to find those elusive treasures, yet somehow it seemed natural to be held against him, drifting on a pleasant sea in a world where there was nothing to fear.

Which just went to show.

Show what?

Something or other.

She slept.

She was awoken by a sudden movement from Roscoe. His hands tightened on her and he looked into her face, his own eyes filled with shock.

'What...how did you...?'

'You pulled me down while I was putting a blanket over you,' she said sleepily. 'It was like being held in an iron cage, and I was too tired to argue so I just drifted.'

He groaned. 'Sorry if I made you a prisoner. You should have socked me on the jaw.'

'Didn't have the energy.' She yawned, letting him draw her back against his chest. 'Besides, you weren't doing anything to deserve getting socked.'

And what would I have done if you had? The words ran through her mind before she could stop them.

'Are you sure? Pippa, tell me at once—did I...I didn't...?'

'No, you didn't. I promise. You were right out of it. You wouldn't have had the energy to do anything, any more than I'd have had the energy to sock you.'

She was laughing contentedly as she spoke and he relaxed, also laughing.

Suddenly he said, 'What on earth is that?'

He'd noticed the shabby toy on her bedside table. Now he reached out and took it.

'That belonged to my Gran—the one in that photo,' she said. 'She called him her Mad Bruin, and I think he represented Grandpa to her. After he died she cuddled Bruin and talked to him all the time.'

Roscoe surveyed Bruin, not with the scorn she would once have expected from him, but with fascination.

'I'll bet you could tell a secret or two,' he said.

Pippa choked with laughter and he drew her close, laying the little bear aside as carefully as though he had feelings.

'Will you believe me if I say I never meant this to happen?' he murmured against her hair.

'Of course. If you'd had anything else in mind you would have gone to Teresa.'

'Teresa isn't you,' he said, as though that explained everything.

'Ah, yes, you couldn't have talked stern practicalities with her.'

'As a matter of fact, I could. She's my oldest friend.'

'She's a great beauty,' Pippa mused. 'Useful kind of "friend".'

'The best. She's helped me out of several awkward situations. Her husband was also my friend. In fact I introduced them. He died a few years ago but she's never looked at anyone else, and I don't think she ever will. She's still in love with his memory.'

Roscoe wondered why he was telling her all this. Why should he care what she thought? Then he remembered her with Charlie the other night, holding his face tenderly between her hands. And he knew why.

He waited for her to say something, and was disappointed when she didn't. He couldn't see that she was smiling to herself.

CHAPTER NINE

AFTER a moment Pippa summoned up her courage and said, as casually as she could manage, 'So you went on being friends with her husband? He didn't steal her from you?'

'Goodness, no! Teresa and I had just about reached the end of the line by then. She was a lovely person—still is—but that connection wasn't there. I don't know how else to put it. I enjoyed our outings, but I wasn't agog with eagerness for them.'

'Now that's something I can't imagine; you, agog with eagerness—not over a woman. A new client, yes. A leap in the exchange rates, yes. But a mere female? Don't make me laugh.'

He was silent and she feared she'd offended him, but then he said quietly, 'It might really make you laugh if you knew how wrong you were.'

The proper response to this was, *You don't have to tell me. I didn't mean to pry.*

But she couldn't say it. She wanted him to go on. If this lonely, isolated man was about to invite her into his secret world then, with all her heart, she wanted to follow him inside. If he would stretch out his hand and trust her with his privacy it would be like a light dawning in her life.

'Well, I've been wrong in the past,' she mused, going carefully, not to alarm him. 'If you knew the things I was thinking about you that first day, and even worse on the second day.'

'But I do know,' he said, and even from over her head she could hear the grin in his voice. 'You didn't bother to hide your terrible opinion of me—grim, gruff, objectionable. And that was when you were thanking me for helping you over those lost papers. When I landed you the job from hell with Charlie your face had to be seen to be believed.'

'But I soon realised that you were right,' she said. 'I'm the ideal person to do it because I can enjoy the game. A woman with a heart would be in danger.'

'And you don't have a heart?'

'I told you, my fiancé finished all that.'

'I've begun to understand you,' Roscoe said slowly. 'You come on like a seductive siren but it's all a mask. Behind it—'

'Behind it there's nothing,' she said lightly. 'No feeling, no hopes, no regrets. Nothing. Just a heartless piece, me.'

'No!' he said fiercely. 'Don't say that about yourself. It's not true. Once I thought it was but now I know you better.'

'You don't know me at all,' she said, fighting the alarm caused by his insight. 'You know nothing about me.'

'You're wrong; I do know. I know you're kind and sweet, gentle and generous, loving and vulnerable—all the things you've tried to prevent me discovering, prevent *any* man discovering.'

'Nonsense!' she said desperately. 'You're creating a sentimental fantasy but the truth is what's on the surface. I have no heart because I've no use for one. Who needs it?'

'That's your defence, is it?' he asked slowly. 'Who needs a heart? I think you do, Pippa.'

'Mr Havering, I am a lawyer; you are my client. My private life does not concern you.'

Her voice was soft but he heard something in it that was

almost a threat, and he backed off, worried more for her than for himself. There seemed no end to the things he was discovering about her, but he feared to put a foot wrong, lest he harm her.

'All right, I'm sorry,' he said in a soothing voice. 'It's none of my business, after all. Don't cry.' He could feel her shaking against him.

'I'm not crying,' she said. 'I'm laughing. Me, saying I'm a lawyer and you're a client, when we're lying here—'

'Yes, we've got a bit beyond that point, haven't we?' he said. 'We've both experienced things to make us bitter. Like the way when someone has promised to marry you, they become the person above all others you have to beware of.'

'That's true,' she said in a voice of discovery. 'Once you start twining your life with theirs, they have a whole sheaf of weapons in their hands—the house you chose together, the secrets you tell each other—all the things they know about you that you desperately wish they didn't. Ouch!'

She gasped for Roscoe's hands had suddenly tightened.

'Sorry,' he said.

'Did that last one—?'

'Struck right home,' he agreed, drawing her head down against his chest once more. 'You brood about it, which is nonsense because she and her new love have other things to talk about apart from you. But you picture them laughing, and wonder how you could ever have trusted her so much.'

'And then you don't want to trust anyone again,' she whispered. 'So you promise yourself that you won't.'

'But it isn't so easy. If you go through life drawing away from people, at last you turn into a monster. I don't want to turn into a monster, although several people would probably tell you that's what I am.'

'Sometimes it feels safer,' she agreed.

'I won't believe anyone's ever said it of you.'

'Why? Because I've got a pretty face? Haven't you ever heard of a pretty monster? It's all part of the performance, you see. The lad who was here the first night, the one I half crippled, don't you think he sees me as a monster?'

'That doesn't mean you are one,' he said with a touch of anger in his voice. 'Stop this.'

'I led him on, didn't I? You'd think I'd know better by now, but a girl must have some fun in her life. You knew that, even then. That's why you hired me.'

He groaned and raised his hands to cover his eyes. 'And this is what he did to you? Your fiancé?'

'Or maybe I was always like that. It's hard-wired into me and it took him to bring it out.'

'You don't really believe any of that stuff.'

'Don't tell me what I believe.'

'I will because someone's got to show you how to see yourself straight. You're as beautiful inside as you are out.'

She pulled herself up on the bed so that she could see him better in the dim light and pull his hands down.

'We've known each other only a few days,' she reminded him.

'I've known you a lot longer than that. I knew it when I saw you in the graveyard, swapping jokes with a headstone. It was the kind of mad, daft—'

'Mutton-headed,' she supplied.

'Glorious, wonderful—I knew then that you had some secret that was hidden from me, that you could teach it to me and then I'd know something that would make life possible.'

He lay looking up at her, defenceless, all armour gone, nothing left but the painful honesty with which he reached out to her.

Pippa felt dizzy, knowing that she'd come to one of those moments when everything in her life might depend on what she did now. Roscoe's eyes told her that this was her decision, and she was stunned by how quickly it had come to pass. Just a few days.

He was reasonably attractive without being handsome. Yet the experience he'd given her tonight—of peace, joy and safety—had astounded her by outshining all other experiences in her life, and now the desire to kiss him was the strongest she had ever known. The tantalising half kiss he'd once given her had lived with her ever since, taunting and teasing her onwards to discover everything about him.

His eyes asked a silent question. Would she kiss him? The decision was hers.

And yes! Yes! The answer was yes!

As she adjusted her position he saw her intention and opened his arms. A little smile curved her lips, one she hoped he would understand. He did understand. The same smile was there on his own lips as she leaned forward, closer—closer—

The doorbell shrieked.

In an instant the spell died. They froze in dismay.

'At this hour of night?' Pippa whispered, aghast.

Stiffly, she moved off the bed and made her way to the front door, calling, 'Who is it?'

The voice that answered appalled her.

'Pippa? It's Charlie. Let me in.'

She turned to see Roscoe standing in the bedroom doorway. Horrified, they stared at each other. Nothing more terrible could have happened.

'Let me in,' Charlie cried.

'No, I can't,' Pippa called back. 'Charlie, go home; it's late. We'll talk tomorrow.'

'Oh, please, Pippa. I've got something to say that you'll be glad to hear. Open up!' He rapped on the door.

'Stop making so much noise,' she cried. 'You'll wake my neighbours. Just give me a minute.'

She was talking for the sake of it while her gaze frantically went around the apartment, seeking evidence of Roscoe's presence. He was doing the same, seizing his baggage, hurrying with it into the bedroom. When he was safely out of sight, Pippa opened her front door.

Charlie immediately came flying through and seized her in his arms.

'What...what do you think you're doing?' she spluttered.

'Telling you that I've given in. I'll do it your way. I'll tell the police about Ginevra. I've been thinking for hours, and I know I have to do what you think is right.' He searched her face. 'Aren't you pleased?'

'Pleased?' she snapped. 'Of all the selfish schoolboy pranks—waking me at this hour to tell me something you could have sent in a text message. How old are you? Ten?'

She was consumed by rage. At this moment she could almost have hated the silly self-centred boy.

'Oh, sorry!' he said. 'Yes, I suppose it is a bit late.'

'Get out, *now*!'

Reading dire retribution in her eyes, he backed out hastily, gabbling, 'All right, all right. We'll talk tomorrow.'

He was gone.

She listened as the footsteps faded, followed by the sound of the elevator going down. Roscoe emerged from the bedroom, walking slowly, not coming too close to her.

The memory of what had so nearly happened was burning within her. Another moment and she would have been in his arms, kissing him and receiving his kiss in return. She had wanted that so much and come so close—so close—and it had been cruelly snatched away.

What she saw when she looked at him made a cold hand

clutch her heart. His face was calm and untroubled. Whatever had happened to her, no earthquake had shaken him.

'I'd better leave now,' he said.

'No!' she said urgently. 'That's what you can't do. He might linger downstairs, and then he'd see you.'

Going to the window, she drew the curtain an inch and looked into the street below.

'There's his new car,' she murmured. 'But there's no sign of him. I reckon he's still in the hall, planning to come back up here.'

'You're right,' Roscoe groaned. 'I'll have to stay for a while. Sorry.'

A few minutes earlier she'd felt him tremble in her arms and known that he would gladly remain all night. Now he spoke as though staying with her was a duty that he dreaded.

'I'll stay out here,' he said, settling on the sofa. 'You take the bedroom.'

The spell was broken. And that was good, she tried to tell herself. She'd had enough of spells.

She lay awake for the rest of the night, and finally went out to find Roscoe on the phone to Angela.

'Charlie's arrived home,' he said as he hung up.

'Don't mention Charlie to me,' she said crossly. 'Turning up like that in the middle of the night! Does he think nobody has a life apart from him? I feel really sorry for your mother, pinning so many of her hopes on that overgrown infant.'

She was still full of nerves or she would have been careful not to say the next words.

'She's had so much to bear in her life already. Losing your father, knowing he killed himself—'

Too late, she saw the strange look on Roscoe's face.

'How did you know that?' he asked. 'Charlie, I suppose?'

'I already knew. David said something.'

'So you've known from the start. You never mentioned it to me.'

'I knew you wouldn't like it, and it was none of my business.'

'That's right,' he said lightly. 'Well, I'd better be going.'

She could have kicked herself. Roscoe's cool tension told her more than any words that he resented her for what she'd just revealed. In time, he might have told her, but he disliked her knowing without his being aware.

'I'll make you some breakfast,' she offered.

'No, I'd better be off. I'll be in touch.'

She doubted it. He couldn't get away from her fast enough.

There was nothing to do but stand back while he collected his things. Suddenly a chill wind was blowing. He gave her a polite smile, thanked her for everything, just as he should, but something was mysteriously over. Worst of all was the fact that she couldn't be sure what had ended, because she didn't know what had begun. She only knew that the sense of aching loss was unbearable.

Then a strange thing happened. Charlie became elusive. He didn't call, wasn't in his office and his cellphone was switched off. Without him, the trip to the police had to be postponed.

After two days, Roscoe texted: *Is Charlie with you?*

She texted back: *I was about to ask you the same thing.*

The next time Pippa's work phone rang it was the last person in the world she'd expected to hear from.

'Biddy—or should I call you *Ginevra*? Where are you?'

'Abroad; that's all you need to know. Charlie's a real gent, I'll say that for him. I'm not coming back but I've written to the police and told them it was me in the shop, not him. I wasn't going to, but then I got to thinking I owed him something, so I sent the letter from...the country I was in. I'm in a different place now, so the postmark won't help them. But I wanted you to know about something else, so listen.'

Pippa did so, growing wide-eyed as Ginevra's information grew clear.

'Thank you,' she said at last. 'That'll be very useful. Where can I get hold of you?'

'I'm moving around, but you can call this mobile number. I've sent you a copy of the letter so that you'll know exactly what I told the police. 'Bye.'

She hung up.

Pippa sat, deep in thought. Then she made a call.

'Gus Donelly? Good, I need your help, fast. Listen carefully.' After a terse conversation she swept out, announcing, 'I won't be back today.'

David, who'd been shamelessly eavesdropping, exclaimed, 'Donelly? I seem to recall that he's a private detective, and a very shady one. I hope you're careful.'

Pippa was not only careful but successful. Returning, triumphant, she knew she had all she needed to achieve a victory—thanks, ironically, to Ginevra.

Charlie presented himself at her office with a shamefaced smile that was clearly meant to win her over. She dealt with him briskly.

'So much for telling everything to the police! You offered a grand gesture that meant nothing. Now there's no need. I'll see you at the trial tomorrow. Now, go before I lose my temper.'

He fled.

The next day, they were all present in the courtroom—Angela clinging to Charlie's arm, Charlie trying to read Pippa's expression without success, Roscoe, aloof and isolated.

The court assembled, the magistrates seated themselves,

the accused were produced. Mr Fletcher entered the witness box and Pippa confronted him. There was nothing in her manner to suggest tension. On the contrary, she seemed at ease, cheerful and smiling. So that the sarcastic words that poured from her came as a greater shock.

'Tell the truth, Mr Fletcher. You haven't the faintest idea what actually happened that night, have you?'

'I certainly have,' he declared indignantly. 'I gave a full statement to the police.'

'Your statement is an invention. You should take up fiction writing, you do it so well.'

'Here—'

'You don't know what really happened because you'd spent the evening in the pub. I gather you put away quite an impressive amount, far too much for you to be a reliable witness. Isn't that so?'

'No, it ain't so. Nobody said I was drunk. The police never said so.'

'True, but then you're a past master at seeming more sober than you are, aren't you? As the police have found out to their cost before.'

'I dunno what you mean.'

'Then let me refresh your memory. About five years ago, there was a case that had to be dropped because you turned up in court the worse for wear.'

'That's not true,' Fletcher squeaked.

'Perjury is a crime, Mr Fletcher, and you've just committed that crime. I have the papers here.' She waved them. 'The case had seemed to be watertight, but then you ruined everything, as the constable in question will tell us.'

After that, it was over quickly. The policeman from the previous case, still furious at having his hard work undone by an unreliable witness, gave evidence that totally undermined Fletcher. The magistrate declared Charlie not guilty, then asserted that the case against the other three was also unsafe and should be dropped.

The court erupted.

Angela bounced around, throwing her arms about Charlie, then Roscoe, then Charlie again, squeaking and weeping with joy.

Pippa was surrounded by people congratulating her. She smiled but concentrated on gathering up her papers, the very picture of an efficient lawyer who cared only about her case. She resisted the temptation to look around for Roscoe. Secretly, she was afraid he wouldn't be there.

The lawyers for the other three defendants regarded her in astonished admiration.

'How did you *do* that?' one of them demanded.

Another one merely touched her arm, saying, 'I'll call you tomorrow.'

'You can call all you like,' David said, appearing behind her. He'd taken the precaution of coming to watch. 'Just remember she's signed up to my firm for the foreseeable future.'

'I can offer a very good fee,' said yet another.

'Forget it, she belongs to Farley & Son,' David declared firmly.

Angela embraced her wildly, declaring, 'You're a magician. You just waved a magic wand.'

'No, it was really Ginevra who waved the wand,' Pippa said. 'She's still got a soft spot for you, Charlie, especially after you helped her escape. Fancy telling me you were going to shop her to the police! You didn't mean a word of it.'

He had the grace to blush. 'I sort of meant it,' he said awkwardly. 'But then it seemed such a terrible thing to do that I got her away fast.'

'So I gathered. She wrote to the police telling them what had really happened, but that wouldn't have been enough on its own. Anyone can take the blame for anything from a safe distance. That's probably why she gave me all the other information about Fletcher's past.'

'But how did she know all that stuff?' Charlie asked.

'She has friends in the police,' Pippa said cautiously.

'Ah, yes, I see.' He grimaced.

'She told me what I needed, I hired a very good private detective and he did the rest.'

She was talking mechanically. Something was missing. Where was Roscoe? What would he say?

Then he seemed to appear from nowhere, standing before her.

'You were wonderful,' he said. 'Past my wildest hopes. When you wouldn't look at me just now I was afraid you were going to snub me. I guess I deserve it.'

'No, of course not. I'm just glad things worked out for you.'

'For me?' he queried. He added quietly, 'Or for us?'

'I don't know,' she said huskily.

'No, that's what we still have to find out, isn't it?'

He took her hand, holding it between both of his. She met his eyes and saw in them—what? Everything she wanted? No, because she didn't know what that was. But something that pointed the way.

'Yes,' she whispered. 'We still have to find out.'

'Will you come to my home tonight? I don't want to come to your place in case Charlie turns up.'

'I'll be there,' she promised.

Neither of them noticed Charlie standing a few feet away, his head on one side, a little smile of cheeky understanding on his lips.

Back at the office that afternoon, she had a long talk with David, who made it clear that her value had dramatically increased. The word 'partnership' was mentioned.

'Not right now, because it's a bit soon,' he said, 'but we've got our eyes on you and will take drastic steps to stop you being poached by any other firm. In the meantime, you'll have to make do with a raise.'

Her career was heading for the heights. She wondered when Roscoe would call her.

The phone rang. She snatched it up. But it wasn't Roscoe. It was Lee Renton, the impresario she'd last seen in The Diamond.

'You were right,' he boomed. 'I do need a pre-nuptial agreement.'

'I'll get to work—' Suddenly Pippa sat up straight in her chair as inspiration came to her. 'Lee, could you do me a big favour?'

'Name it.'

She explained what she wanted.

He listened with the occasional grunt, ending with, 'Consider it done. I'll be in touch.' He hung up.

The next call was the one she longed for.

'I'm going home now,' came Roscoe's voice.

'I'm on my way.'

CHAPTER TEN

ROSCOE's apartment was high up in a tall, plain block, which once she would have said was typical of the man. But that was before she'd discovered the hidden, complex depths that meant there was no such thing as 'typical' of him.

Who would ever have thought that this man would be waiting at his open door, would pull her inside and crush her in his arms as though he'd waited all his life for this moment? Or hear him say in a shaking voice, 'I was so afraid you wouldn't come.'

'Never fear that. I'll always come if you want me.'

'And I'll always want you.'

He had even started to cook a meal for her. He wasn't a great cook, but he could manage a microwave and between the two of them they managed to get something onto the table. There was much more to deal with this evening, but, as if by a silent signal, they were each taking it slowly.

'So where do we go from here?' he asked, filling her wine glass. 'I leave the decision to you because it's clear you're several steps ahead of me. All those rabbits you produced out of the hat at the trial. You don't need me or anyone. You're queen of all you survey.'

'Hey, stop buttering me up.'

'Just trying to find the way forward, or hoping you can find it for us. There are so many things yet to be decided.'

'Like what?'

'Charlie. His feelings for you. I contrived the situation and, now that he's fallen for you, how can I just tell him everything has changed and he must forget you?'

She stroked his face, taking care that he should feel her warmth and tenderness towards him because her words would be a shock.

'You know something?' she said. 'Anyone hearing you say that would think you came straight out of the nineteenth century. You're a real male chauvinist pig.'

'Am I?' he asked, startled. 'How?'

'You talk about what *you* can do, but what about me? Don't I get a say? *You* fixed it so that Charlie should come under my influence, like I didn't have anything to do with it. But maybe *I* fixed it, oh, powerful one!'

'I guess I deserved that,' he said gruffly.

'Don't get me started on what you deserve. And there's one thing you have to understand. Charlie isn't in love with me. When we met, he took one look at me and thought *Wow!*, just as we both meant him to. But it was purely physical. He's up for new experiences and he pursued me when he thought he might get one. But there was no emotion in it. He's closer to Ginevra than he is to me. About an hour after the trial she texted me saying, *We did it!*'

'How did she know?'

'Exactly. Charlie must have called her.'

'Oh, no,' Roscoe said at once. 'I won't have this.'

'But it's not up to you. You've got to let Charlie be himself, not some creature you've created.'

'I only want to keep him out of danger. Is that wrong?'

She thought it might be impossible if, as she was beginning to suspect, danger was Charlie's natural medium. But this wasn't the time to say so. They had more urgent matters to attend to.

'The point is that Charlie's not in love with me,' she repeated, 'and his heart can't be broken by us. So we're free.'

'Free,' he echoed slowly. 'Free to—?'

'Free to do anything we want. Be anything we want.'

'Do you have any ideas about that?'

'Plenty. Don't ask me to list them because that would take all night.'

He became hesitant, almost as though nervous of saying the words.

'About...all night. Does it seem to you...?'

'Yes,' she whispered. 'It does.'

Like everything else in this new relationship, their lovemaking was tentative, cautious, watching and learning from each other. He was a patient lover, fervent, but with the control to take everything slowly. How softly his fingers caressed her breasts, and how mysterious was his smile as he did so.

She smiled back, feeling more and deeper mysteries unfold within her. The sweetness at being one with him was greater than anything she had ever known. She wanted to be with him. She wanted to *be* him. And she wanted it for ever.

Afterwards, he murmured, 'Are you really mine?'

'Can you doubt it?' she whispered.

'Yes. Nobody has ever been mine before.'

Before she could reply, he enfolded her in his arms again and in the passion that followed she forgot all else. But after passion came safety and contentment, both as precious as desire.

'Nobody was ever yours before?' she murmured. 'Surely that can't be true?'

'You'd think not, wouldn't you?' he agreed. 'I don't usually go around telling people that I need them. It's too dangerous, for one thing.'

'Oh, yes, I know. They have to discover it for themselves.'

'Yes. And they don't. Except you. But before you...' His voice died away into silence.

'What about your fiancée?' she asked. 'You must have been in love with her.'

'Yes, desperately. I thought I'd found the answer—a woman I could love and who'd love me—but it wasn't right between us. I couldn't be the man she wanted, giving her all my attention. She resented my other responsibilities.'

'Did she force you to choose between her and them?'

'In a way, yes. I can't blame her. I put them first, but how could I not? Charlie was still basically a kid and Mother was still stuck in a state of bewilderment. They needed me. In the end, Verity and I agreed to call it a day.'

But to outsiders it had looked like a cold-hearted parting, she thought. Perhaps Roscoe bore some of the blame for that, hiding his feelings and turning a blank face to the world, but it had left him in terrifying isolation. He'd said that nobody had ever been his before, and it was true. Pippa clasped him more closely, seeking to offer him a warmth and love that would make up for the aching loneliness in which he'd lived, a loneliness that left him always prepared for betrayal, ready to expect it as natural and inevitable.

Now she recalled the words with which he'd greeted her, a few hours and a lifetime ago.

'Why did you think I wouldn't come? Surely we'd agreed?'

'Yes, but I thought you'd remember that you were angry with me, and with reason. I behaved badly.'

'When? I don't remember.'

'When I discovered that you knew something I hadn't told you, about my father. You'll despise me, but I couldn't bear that. It made me feel spied on.'

'You like to control how much people know about you,' she mused. 'It's safer, isn't it?'

'Much safer. No—' he checked himself instantly '—it *feels* safer but, if you give into it, it's actually the way to go mad. Once I knew what you'd discovered, I had to head in the other direction, even though leaving you was the last thing I really wanted. But it was like being driven by demons.'

'Mmm, I know about those demons,' she murmured. 'They scream, *This way lies safety*. So you take that path, but you find that it leads to a howling wilderness, then to a cage. And you know you must escape it soon or there'll never be a way out.'

'You have to decide whether you want to live in that cage for ever, or venture out and take the risks of being human,' he agreed. 'But if you don't take those risks—' his arms tightened about her '—then you stop being human. And perhaps you need to find the one person who can make you want to take them.'

'Then maybe it's time I took a risk,' she said.

'How do you mean?'

'Asking you about your father. You've already told me to back off—'

'I didn't mean—'

'But I'm not going to do that. I'm going ahead, even if it makes you angry. Perhaps you *need* to be angry, so tell me what happened when he died. Were you very close to him?'

'Close?' He seemed to consider the word. 'I hero-worshipped him. I thought he was a great man, starting from nothing and building up a huge business. He had power and that was wonderful. Which just goes to show how naive I was. I was as immature in those days as Charlie is now.

'I was so proud when he took me into the business, told me I had the brains for it. We were a team, working together to conquer the world, so I thought. It was only after he died that I discovered the mountain of debt, the rip-offs, the deceit.

He'd lied to everyone; my mother, who never knew he had a succession of mistresses bleeding him dry; virtually everyone he ever worked with, and me, who trusted him totally, was so proud at being close to him, and then discovered that we weren't close at all.

'I'd been so smug, so self-satisfied, sure of my place inside the loop, and all the time I'd been kept on the outside, like the fool I was.'

Pippa pulled herself up, turning so that she could look down at his head on the pillow. 'Don't put yourself down,' she said.

'Why not? A fool is the kindest thing I can call myself. If you knew how ashamed and humiliated I felt at how easily he took me for a ride. He knew he could deceive me more than anyone else.'

'Because you were his son and you loved him,' she urged. 'He made use of that. Shame on him, not you.'

In the dim light she could just make out his wry smile.

'That's the sensible point of view. Back in those days it didn't help a distraught boy who'd been conned by a father he damn near worshipped and only found out when it was too late to ask any questions. He was dead. I went to see him lying on a slab—cold, indifferent, safely gone beyond the world, beyond me. I wanted to scream at him—why hadn't he trusted me? We could have fought for the business together. But he'd chosen to walk away, leaving me behind.'

'He rejected you,' she said softly, 'left you stranded without warning. No wonder you're sensitive about what other people know about you.'

'Stranded without warning,' he murmured. 'Yes, that was it. Suddenly I was standing on the edge of a cliff that I hadn't even known was there. No way forward, no way back, nobody I could talk to.'

Nobody I could talk to. The words were like an epitaph

for his entire life. His bond with his father had been an illusion, his mother took everything and gave little, Charlie took everything and gave nothing. He was like a castaway stranded on a desert island.

'Was anyone with you when you went to see him on the slab? Your mother?'

'No, she couldn't bear very much. There were so many things she mustn't be allowed to know.'

'The other women?'

'Yes. She'd heard rumours, I denied them, swore that I'd never heard of his being untrue to her. I was afraid she'd kill herself as well if she knew. It's ironic. I blame Charlie for telling stupid lies, but I've lost count of the really black lies I've told, the deceptions I've arranged, the people I've bribed to stay out of my mother's way in case they let something slip.'

'That's different. Sometimes you have to lie to protect people you love. That's not the same as self-serving lies. I don't suppose you told her the state the firm was in either.'

'Not completely. I hinted that we weren't as prosperous as we might be, but I spared her the worst. Sometimes I think stocks and shares are the only part of my life where I'm actually honest.'

'Deception doesn't make you dishonest,' she said seriously. 'It's the kind of deception that counts. You're the most honest man I've ever met. I *know* that Roscoe, because I know you.'

After what he'd told her about how he resisted anyone's eyes, it was a daring thing to say. Perhaps it was too soon for him to relax under a knowing gaze, even hers. But then she saw his face transfigured by joy and relief.

'You know me,' he echoed softly. 'That's the most beautiful thing I've ever heard. Now I'll never let you go.'

Heaven must be like this, she thought, nestling against him. If only they could be undisturbed for ever.

Pippa was to remember that feeling because, looking back, she could see that it was the moment everything began to fall apart. She wondered if it was the Christmas carol that triggered the catastrophe or if it would have happened anyway, for she awoke next morning to find herself in a dark wilderness.

She tried to shake it off, wondering how she could feel this way after the wonderful events of the night before. But the darkness seemed to be rooted in those very events and her confusion grew.

Roscoe was still clasping her with loving possessiveness, which should have touched her heart but suddenly seemed like a threat. She began to ease away.

'Don't go,' he said. 'Stay here a little longer.'

'I can't,' she said. 'I've got work to go to. So have you.'

He grinned. 'To hell with work. To hell with the markets.'

Another time she would have teased him fondly for such an attitude, but now she needed to get away from his warmth and gentleness, far, far away from everything that made him lovable. She must think, calm her howling demons, refuse to let them ruin her life.

She slipped out of bed and went to the window, pushing it open a little way. It was a bright, fresh morning with a little snow in the air and she stood taking deep breaths, trying to make the darkness lift.

She could do it—just a few minutes more.

But then Roscoe did the thing that made her efforts collapse. He turned on the radio and the sound of a Christmas carol floated out. As Pippa heard the words she stiffened.

'On this happy morning,
All is well with all the world.'

All is well. Once before she'd heard those words, just before the betrayal that had devastated her.

'Don't catch cold,' he said, coming up behind her and putting his arms about her. 'Hey, what's the matter?'

'Nothing,' she said hastily. 'Nothing.'

'You're shaking.' He shut the window and drew her back. 'Come back into the warm.'

But she tensed against his embrace, resisting him silently, unable to meet his eyes.

'Now the sun will always shine,
Joy is here for ever.'

But joy hadn't been there for ever. Joy had ended in the next few moments, leaving her unable to hear that carol again without reliving terrible memories.

Roscoe tightened his embrace, tried to draw her closer, felt her fight against it.

'Pippa, for pity's sake, what's the matter? It's not the cold, is it? There's something else.'

'No, I...I just have to be getting to work. And so do you.' She gave a brittle laugh. 'We still have to be sensible.'

'Sensible? You dare say that to me after the way we were together last night? Was the woman who lay in my arms and cried out to me to love her being sensible? Was I being sensible when I gave her everything I was and received back everything she had in her soul?'

Pippa didn't reply. She couldn't. There were no words for the terror she was feeling. Roscoe's face darkened.

'Or didn't I?' he said. 'Was I fooling myself about that, because the woman in my bed would never have wanted to be sensible?'

'Well,' she said brightly, 'perhaps that wasn't me, just someone who looked like me.'

'What's got into you? If this is a joke, it isn't funny.'

The music swelled. Now the carol was being played louder, sung by joyful voices, and her nerves were being torn. She had to get out of this or go mad.

'It's not a joke,' she said breathlessly. 'It's just that things look different in the morning.'

'Yes, they can look different,' he said slowly. 'Better or worse, depending on what you want to believe.'

'But that's the problem,' she said quickly. 'Wanting to believe is dangerous—talking yourself into things because it would be so nice if…if…'

Roscoe was still holding her, trying to understand the violent shaking he could feel throughout her body.

'What is it?' he asked urgently. 'Tell me. Don't bear it alone.'

She slumped against him in despair. How could she make him understand what she didn't understand herself? She only knew that she'd been brought to the edge of a deep pit, a place that many people found joyous but where she'd vowed not to venture. Now she stared down into the depths, appalled at herself for backing away but unable to do anything else.

Last night they'd talked happily about the risks they would take for their love. Now she knew she hadn't the courage and nothing mattered but to get away.

The words of the carol were still pouring from the radio.

'New day, new hope, new life.'

That was how it should have been and how it never would be again. It was all folly, all illusion, and she must put right the damage now.

'Pippa, my darling—'

'Don't—it's better not to call me that. We had a wonderful time last night, didn't we?'

'I thought so,' he said quietly.

'But now it's time to wake up and return to reality.'

'And what do you call reality?'

'We both know what we mean by it.' She gave another brittle laugh. 'I'm sure we'll see each other again, but nobody can live too long in that fantasy world.'

At last Roscoe released her. It was what she'd wanted but the feeling of his hands leaving her was achingly wretched because, deep inside, she knew he would never hold her again.

'I see,' he said. And now his voice was ominous. 'So that's how it is. We had a good time, now it's over and it had nothing to do with the real world. Is that what you're trying to tell me?'

Pippa summoned a carefree smile. 'Why, that's just it. A good time. And it was great fun, wasn't it? But now...well, you knew from the start that I was a good time girl. I think you even called me a few worse things in your head.'

'Before I *thought* I knew you,' he corrected harshly.

'Well, maybe first impressions are the most reliable. Floozie, tart, heartless piece—'

'Stop it!' he shouted, seizing her again. 'I won't listen to this. I never thought that of you—or if I ever wondered for a moment you showed me how wrong I was—'

'Did I? Or did I show you what you wanted to see? You were a real challenge, you know. Anyone can lure a man into her bed, but luring his heart—that's another matter.'

Pippa felt dizzy as she said these terrible words. In her desperation to escape she had gone much further than she'd meant to and for a moment she hesitated on the edge of recalling them, hurling herself into Roscoe's arms and swearing she meant none of it.

'Do you mean that?' he whispered.

She had one last chance to deny her words, reclaim all the joy life could offer her.

'Do you mean it?' he repeated. 'Is that all there's been between us? You trying to bring me down, to punish me for my attitude in the first few days? *Is that the truth?*'

One last chance.

'Now the sun will always shine,
Joy is here for ever.'

Frantically, she switched the radio off.

'You know the saying,' she said with a shrug. 'You win some, you lose some. I like to win them all.'

Now it was too late. The last trace of feeling had gone from him. His eyes were those of a dead man.

'I suppose I should be glad you came clean so soon,' he said. 'You might have taken it much further before you...but it's always wise to face the truth.'

A sneering look came into his eyes.

'So all the worst I thought of you was right after all. I should have more faith in my own judgement. Are you pleased? Does it give you a nasty little thrill to have brought me down?'

She managed a cynical laugh. 'I came to your bed and gave you a good time. That's hardly bringing you down.'

His eyes as they raked her were brutal.

'Oh, but you did much more than that,' he breathed. 'You put on the sweet, generous mask and it fooled me so thoroughly that I told you things that never before...' He drew a shuddering breath. 'Well, I hope it gave you a good laugh.'

She was about to protest wildly that he was terribly wrong, but she controlled the impulse in time and offered him a smile precisely calculated to infuriate him. It would break his heart, but if it drove him away from her it would be better for him in the long run. And for his sake she would hide her own broken heart and endure.

'I see that it did,' he grated. 'Well, don't let me keep you.'

'You're right,' she said brightly. 'We've said all we have to say, haven't we?'

He made no attempt to follow her into the bedroom as she gathered her things and when she came out he was waiting by the front door, as though determined to make sure that she left.

'Good day to you,' he said politely.

'Goodbye,' she told him, and fled.

A robot might have functioned as Pippa did for the rest of the day. Her efficiency was beyond reproach, her smile fixed, her work done to the highest standard.

'What the devil is the matter with her?' muttered David, her employer and friend.

'Why not ask her?' his secretary suggested.

'I daren't. She terrifies the life out of me.'

At last it was time to escape back to the apartment that would now be her cage. As if by a signal, Pippa began to tidy the place, although it was already tidy. From now on order and good management would be her watch words. She would concentrate on her career, be the best lawyer in the business and never again try to break out of the prison created by her nightmares. Life would be safe.

At last, when she'd put everything else away, she came to the box rescued from the attic in Crimea Street. Taking out the gloves and scarves, she discovered some handwritten books at the bottom.

'That's Gran's handwriting,' she breathed. 'But surely she didn't keep a diary? She wouldn't have had time.'

Yet the diaries went back to Dee's early life, when she had

been a nurse, and had still sometimes found the time to jot down her thoughts about the life around her. Sometimes amusing, sometimes caustic, sometimes full of emotion, always revealing an ebullient personality that Pippa recognised.

There were the long, anguished months when she'd loved Mark Sellon hopelessly, becoming engaged to him, then breaking it off because she couldn't believe he loved her. But he'd been returned to her in the hospital, shot down by enemy planes, and she'd sat by his unconscious form, speaking more freely than she could have done if he'd been awake. Dee had written:

> I told him that I must believe that somewhere, deep in his heart, he could hear me. Wherever he was, he must surely feel my love reaching out to him, and know that it was always his.

Pippa read far into the night, until she came to the passage that, in her heart, she had always known she'd find, written just after her grandfather's death.

> I saw you laid in the ground today and had to come away, leaving you there. And yet I haven't really left you behind because you're still with me, and you always will be; just as I'll always be with you in your heart, until we really are together again. It doesn't matter how long that is. Time doesn't really exist. It's just an illusion

Pippa dropped her head into her hands. That was how love should be, how it never would be for her. She knew that now.

She laid everything away tidily, turned out all the lights and went to bed. A faint gleam from the window showed her the toy bear on her dressing table. In this poor light his shabbiness was concealed and his glass eyes seemed to glimmer softly.

'No,' she told him. 'I'm not listening to you. You want me to believe one thing, and I know it's different. I believed you once. I believed Gran. She used to talk to me about her and Grandpa, saying that one day it would happen to me. And I thought it had when I met Jack. He made me feel so safe and loved, and sure of the future. And now I don't *want* to feel safe and loved. *Ever.* Do you understand?'

But he had no reply for her.

CHAPTER ELEVEN

CHARLIE called the next day, his voice full of excitement over the line.

'Bless you for what you've done for me,' he said. 'And I'm not talking about the trial.'

'You've seen Lee?'

'Yes, I've just had a long talk and it's looking good for a couple of weeks' time. Oh, boy, wait until Roscoe hears about this!'

'Don't be in a rush to tell him, Charlie, and don't do anything rash. Wait until you're a little more certain.'

'All right, Miss Wise and Wonderful. I'll do it your way. And thank you again.'

She wondered if she would hear from Roscoe but days passed in silence. Just as well, she told herself. If she saw him she might weaken, and that must not happen. Much better this way.

But the ache persisted.

Days passed, nights passed. She told herself that it was getting easier, except that every knock at the door was him. Until it wasn't.

But then, one evening, it was.

One look was enough to tell her that if anything had changed it wasn't for the better. Now his face wasn't just cold but furious.

'We need to talk,' he said.

She stood back and he walked in, turning on her as soon as the door closed.

'My God, I never thought you'd stoop to this,' he raged.

'I don't know what you mean.'

'Oh, please, you wreck his life and then you don't know what I mean?'

'If you're talking about what I think you are—'

'I'm talking about Charlie walking out of the firm, blowing his life chances to chase a chimera. I'm talking about you persuading him to do it. How could you sink so low? Were you really that desperate for revenge?'

'Revenge?' she echoed, astounded. 'I didn't want revenge. Why should I? You did me no harm. If anything, it was me who... What did you mean about Charlie leaving the firm? That wasn't in the plan.'

'But there was a plan? You admit that?'

'Yes,' she said, her temper flaring, 'there was a plan—an innocent plan to help Charlie follow his own path in life. He's a natural entertainer and I have a friend, Lee Renton, who's in the business. He sets up those television programmes where amateurs perform and viewers vote. I recommended Charlie to him after that evening we spent at The Diamond. He did an impromptu performance for me at the table and he was so good that I thought he should take it further.

'Lee has auditioned him and because he's the big boss he's been able to pull strings and include Charlie in a show in two weeks' time. If he's no good, OK, but the top two performers go through to the next round, and I'd back Charlie to be one of them.'

'And then what?' Roscoe demanded scathingly. 'An existence spent on the grubby fringes of show business?'

'Or as a star, however it turns out.'

'However—? That's how you see life, is it? Leave it to chance?'

'What do you suggest instead? Opt for safety every time? Choosing safety doesn't always *lead* to safety. We know that, don't we? But it can, if it's your own free choice. But being a stockbroker isn't Charlie's choice. It was your choice for him, and it won't work.'

He turned away from her, walking about the room like a man who no longer knew where he was going.

'You said Charlie walked out,' Pippa reminded him. 'Did he? Or did you force him out because you were so determined to make him do it your way?'

He turned a haggard gaze on her. 'I wanted him to go on a course to learn some more about the business,' he said. 'He'd have acquired an extra qualification, boosted his prospects. He refused to go because it would have meant missing the television show. I told him he had to make a choice.'

Pippa groaned and clutched her forehead. 'Tell me I'm not hearing this,' she muttered. 'You forced him to choose and you're surprised that he chose his freedom?'

'Freedom? You call that kind of life freedom?'

'To him, yes. Freedom isn't just not being in prison. You could keep Charlie out of trouble with the law but you'd do it by trapping him behind the bolts and bars of finance. For him, that would be a life sentence. He's made his choice.'

'Or you made it for him.'

'No, I helped him do what he wants to do.'

'Behind my back. You did encourage him to deceive me, didn't you?'

'I advised him not to tell you too much too soon, in case you tried to interfere.'

'Interfere? I'm his brother.'

'Yes, his brother, not his keeper. And you did interfere with that damn fool choice you forced on him. "Do it my way or get out." The clever thing to do would be to leave the door open for him to come back if his new career failed. But you slammed that door shut so you're not really a clever man at all, are you?'

The next moment she was sorry she'd said it because his face changed. The anger died out of it, replaced by a weary sadness that broke her heart.

'No,' he said slowly. 'I guess the truth is that I'm a fool. I've always been a fool. I've trusted people who couldn't be trusted, and I never learned from my mistakes.' He gave a soft, mirthless laugh. 'How big a fool is that? The biggest in the world.'

They weren't talking about Charlie any more. He was saying that he'd trusted her, and he felt betrayed by her. Nor could she blame him when she remembered how he'd confided in her that night, talking about his father, his fiancée, his desolation at the way he'd been abandoned. He'd confided in her as to nobody else in his life, and just a few hours later she'd rejected him, her rejection coming out of the blue, with no real explanation.

And it had to stay that way. She didn't dare tell him the whole story of her inner destruction in case he opened his arms to her in sympathy and understanding. Then she would weaken, seeking his love where once she'd found the strength to reject it. And she would destroy him.

Whatever happened, she would protect him from that. Protect him from herself.

'I see you don't deny that you made a fool of me,' he said. 'And that's all I was—just one more fool among many. I fell for you totally, nothing held back. Boy, that must really have given you a laugh.'

'No, I'm not laughing,' she said quietly. 'But I do know that I'm no good for you. I'm poison, and you're better off without me.'

'Oh, please!' He warded her off again, this time actually backing away. 'Spare me the pathos. You've done so well up to now. I was a scalp you had to add to your collection. You as good as admitted it.'

'I didn't—'

'As close as, damn it. You had your victory and then I was no more use. I congratulate you. Cutting out the dead wood is good business practice, although even a heartless robot like myself hesitates before using it on people.'

'Don't call yourself a heartless robot,' she cried. 'I've never said that—'

'Can you swear you've never thought it?'

'No...never...' she said jerkily.

'You're lying. The truth is there in your face. You've thought that and worse. Charlie told you I'm a control freak, didn't he? And perhaps I am. But I'm not the only one, Pippa. Maybe I have pulled the strings of Charlie's life, but so have you. The difference is that I pull strings in the open, not behind anyone's back.'

Seeing that she was too stunned to speak, he turned with an air of finality and went to the door.

'Be sure to send me your bill,' he said, and walked out.

She could hear his retreating footsteps, followed by the sound of the elevator going down. She felt cold—deeply cold, too cold to move—with a coldness that would last for the rest of her life, freezing her heart, turning her to something inhuman.

But Roscoe already saw her as inhuman. His contempt left no doubt about that.

And that was good, she told herself resolutely. He was safer that way. As long as he was safe, she could bear anything.

Charlie called her, full of excitement about his approaching big night.

'Mum's giving a big party that night,' he bubbled, 'and

she wants you as the guest of honour because you made it all happen. She's thrilled about my new career. Roscoe can't understand it.'

'Obviously he isn't thrilled.'

'He wouldn't be, would he? I don't see him any more now I'm out of the firm, and he won't be at home on the night. OK, so I'll tell Mum you're coming.'

'Charlie—'

But he'd hung up, leaving her reflecting that Roscoe wasn't the only member of his family who liked to call the shots.

The day of Charlie's show started badly, with another car breakdown. This time Pippa faced the inevitable and dumped the vehicle. She took a taxi to the Havering house, arriving to find all the lights on and Angela waiting for her on the front step, flanked by neighbours who clapped and cheered as her taxi drew up.

'Roscoe's not here,' Angela confided. 'He's so annoyed about the programme that he's not coming.'

'How do you feel about it?' Pippa asked.

'It's what Charlie wants. And besides,' Angela added in a low, confiding voice, 'he can be a bit of a naughty boy, and if he gets into a little trouble now and then, well—it won't matter so much, will it?'

So, despite appearances, there was a realistic brain beneath that fluffy head of hair, Pippa thought. More realistic than Roscoe about some things.

Dinner was a banquet, and then everyone crowded around the huge television screen on the wall. There was the opening music and the announcer came on.

'Hello, folks! It's time for *Pick a Star*, the programme where you, the viewer, vote the star in and the dunces off. And tonight's contestants are—'

As soon as Charlie began his comedy act, everyone knew

this was the winner. None of the other seven contestants could hold a candle to him. Even Pippa, who knew how rigorously Lee had had him trained as a favour to her, was impressed by his quality.

'Now it's voting time, folks—the moment when you choose the winner. Here are the phone numbers.'

When he got to Charlie's number everyone scribbled frantically and hauled out their cellphones to ring and cast their votes. Angela dived for the house phone and put her call through.

'How long do we wait?' Angela asked.

'Half an hour,' Pippa told her, 'but Lee said there wouldn't be any question. He's sure Charlie will win and go on into the next round but, even if he doesn't, Lee's got an agent already interested in him.'

The minutes crawled past and at last it was time to gather around the set to learn the winner. When Charlie's name was announced, the room erupted.

There he was on screen, triumphantly repeating his act, his face full of delight, and more than delight: fulfilment. The applause grew, the credits rolled. It was over.

One by one, the guests departed. A beseeching look from Angela made Pippa stay behind the others and she understood that Angela didn't want to be alone. Her house was going to be very empty now.

She led the way into the conservatory and poured Pippa a glass of champagne.

'It's so kind of you to stay a while, my dear. I know everything's going to change now, and I'm ready for it as long as Charlie is doing what will make him happy.' She added in a confiding tone, 'I must admit that I hoped you and Charlie... but there, he says you're like a friendly big sister.'

'I hope I am.'

'Oh, dear, how sad.'

'Sad?'

'I would have loved to welcome you into the family as Charlie's wife.' An idea seemed to strike her. 'You don't think you could make do with Roscoe, do you?'

'What?'

'I know it's a lot to ask, but you never know, you might make him human.'

'Angela, please don't go thinking like that. There's no way Roscoe and I could ever...please don't.'

'No, I suppose you're right. I'm being selfish, I suppose. I've always wanted a daughter because you can't talk to a man as you can to a woman, and I've had nobody to talk to since my husband died. Charlie was just a child and Roscoe...well, he's only interested in making money. To be fair, he gives it too, but he seems to think that's all that's needed.'

'Gives it?' Pippa echoed cautiously.

'He's got charities he gives to, hospitals in the Third World, that sort of thing, but signing cheques is easy. It's affection he finds difficult.'

'But maybe it's just a different way of showing affection,' Pippa said urgently. 'Putting your arms around a sick child is fine and beautiful, but if that child is dying for lack of the right medicine, then surely it's the man who signs the cheque that buys the medicine who's shown the real feeling? At any rate, I'll bet that's what the child's mother would say.'

Angela stared at her. 'You sound like Roscoe.'

'And he's right,' Pippa said robustly. There was a curious kind of satisfaction in defending Roscoe when he wasn't there. It was when he was there that the trouble started.

'Have you ever tried to talk to him?' she asked gently. 'You might find more sympathy in Roscoe than you thought.'

'Do you think so? Have those wonderful all-seeing eyes of yours bored into him and found something the rest of the world missed?'

This was so close to the truth that Pippa was momentarily lost for words. She recovered enough to say, 'Who knows? He works so hard at not letting people see what he's really like, almost as though part of him was afraid.'

'Afraid? Him?'

'Sometimes the man with the strongest armour is the one who needs it most for...whatever reason.'

'You may be right,' Angela sighed. 'It's just that I've always found it hard to forgive Roscoe for William's death. If he'd taken on a bigger share of the work—'

'But he was just a boy,' Pippa protested. 'About the same age Charlie is now. Would you blame Charlie in the same way?'

'No, of course not, but—' Angela checked herself as though the realisation had startled her. 'Roscoe has always seemed different.'

'*Seemed* is the word,' Pippa said. 'He was young, learning the business and probably completely confused. Then his father died. Maybe he blamed himself, then he discovered that you blamed him—'

'I never said so,' Angela hurried to say. 'Oh, but I wouldn't need to say so, would I?'

'No. But he wouldn't say anything either, and so you lost each other all these years ago.'

Angela was silent, looking sad, and after a moment Pippa ventured to ask, 'Was your husband at all like that?'

'Oh, no. William was talkative and open-hearted. He told me everything—absolutely everything. Our marriage was blissfully happy.'

She held up the hand with the glittering diamond ring. 'At least I've always had this as a symbol of his love. I kiss it goodnight every evening when I go to bed, and for a moment I can imagine he's still there. We loved each other so much until he...until he...' She was suddenly shivering. 'He died in a car crash. Taken from me suddenly, with no goodbye. Oh, if he'd had the chance to say goodbye he would have been so kind—'

With a feeling of sick dread, Pippa realised that Angela knew the truth, despite her frantic denials. Beneath her smiling facade, she was hiding another self, permanently tormented. It was a self that the outside world must never be allowed to see, and in that she was just like her elder son.

Now Pippa knew what she must do. Going to sit beside Angela, she put her arms gently about her and held her close.

'You remember him as a kind man who loved you,' she said. 'And that's what really matters—all the good years you shared—loving each other—'

'Yes, yes—*no*!' Angela's voice suddenly rose to a shriek and sobs shook her. 'No, he left me,' she wept. 'He took his own life, although he knew I loved him. He went away from me because he wanted to, and it destroyed me and he didn't care. *He didn't care.*'

'That's not true,' Pippa said, tightening her arms. 'He didn't stop loving you. He was just full of despair. His mind was so dark that he wasn't his real self. It was another man who took his own life, not the one you knew. He didn't reject you. That was someone else who only looked like him.'

She wondered if she had any right to say this when she didn't really believe it. William Havering's suicide had indeed been a betrayal of those who loved and needed him, and she'd said as much to Roscoe. But this desperate woman could not have endured it.

She knew she'd made the right decision when Angela raised her head, her eyes frantically searching Pippa's face.

'Do you mean that?' she whispered.

'Yes, I do. He must have been terribly ill, and it was the illness that made him act, not his own heart. He never rejected you, and I know that wherever he is now he wants you to understand that. He can't have peace until you have it first. You still love him, don't you?'

'Oh, yes—yes—'

'Then do this for him. Speak to him in your heart and tell him you forgive him because you know he didn't mean it. Tell him—'

She stopped for the air was singing. Suddenly, Dee was there with her, pointing to the words in her diary—words she'd spoken to the man she loved, not knowing if he could hear them, if he would ever hear them.

'Tell him…tell him…'

'What is it?' Angela asked in wonder. 'You look as if you'd seen a ghost.'

'No,' Pippa whispered. 'You don't need to see a ghost to feel it.'

'What should I tell him?'

'That he's still with you,' Pippa said slowly, 'and he always will be, just as you'll always be with him in your heart, until one day you really will be together again.'

'And he won't reject me?' Angela whispered longingly. 'After so long?'

'It isn't long. Time doesn't really exist. It's just an illusion.'

'Yes, yes,' Angela said eagerly. 'I didn't understand before, but I do now. You're so kind and understanding.'

She buried her face against Pippa, still trembling, but no longer in agony

A sound from the door made Pippa look up, and what she saw made her stiffen with shock.

Roscoe stood there. He was staring, seemingly dazed by the sight that met his eyes—his mother, in transports of joy and relief, in Pippa's arms.

This was what he was trying to do for her, but never managed it, she thought. Perhaps he'll hate me.

She recalled his chilly hostility when he'd discovered she knew about his father's suicide. To him, this would seem even more of an intrusion.

She patted Angela's shoulder. 'Roscoe's here.'

Angela raised her head. To Pippa's pleasure, she smiled at the sight of Roscoe and reached out a hand.

'Mother, what is it?'

'It's all right. Dear, dear Pippa has made me understand so much—she said such wonderful things—'

'I heard what she said,' Roscoe told her quietly. He took out a handkerchief and dabbed Angela's face. 'Don't cry, Mother. There's nothing to be sad about.'

'I know. It was wonderful. Charlie won and he'll be in the next round and, before we know it, he'll be rich and famous.'

The phone rang and she snatched it up. 'Charlie, darling, we were just talking about you—'

Pippa took a step away from Roscoe. Everything—her mind, her heart, her flesh—all were in turmoil at his appearance and the uncertainty over what he'd heard. Only one thing was sure. She must get away from him.

But she felt her hand taken between his in a grip she couldn't resist, and he drew her away, out of Angela's sight.

'How can I ever thank you?' he asked in a low, passionate voice. 'I never dreamed I could see her so at peace again, and you did it.'

He raised her hands to his lips, kissing them, while she felt a happiness she'd feared never to know again. She tried to fight it, but it wouldn't be fought.

'You don't mind that it was me?' she asked.

'If you mean would I rather have been the one who brought my mother peace again, then yes, I would. But as long as somebody can make her such a priceless gift, that's the only thing that matters.'

'Thank you,' she said softly. 'It hurt so much when we quarrelled, but at least we can part friends.'

'Part? Are we going to part?'

'We've already parted, Roscoe. You know that.'

'But I don't. Just because we said some terrible things—you pretended to be a floozie and I pretended to believe you. We can get past that if we want to.'

The turmoil of feeling that went through her was part joy at his love, part misery at the parting that she knew was inevitable, although he could not see it, and part terror that her own nerve might fail. She must leave him, but the knowledge filled her with anguish.

'Surely you're ready to try again,' he said in a pleading voice. 'The fact that you're here—'

'Charlie told me you wouldn't be here tonight.'

'He said that? Surely not? He knew I was coming.'

'Maybe I misunderstood,' she said huskily. 'But it's too late for us.'

'It'll never be too late while we love each other.'

She didn't answer that. She didn't dare.

Hearing Angela hanging up, Pippa said quickly, 'I've got to go.'

'I didn't see your car outside.'

'It's finally had it.'

'Then I'll drive you. Don't argue.'

Angela kissed her goodbye and watched them depart with a smile that said she was crossing her fingers for her hopes to come true.

'Wrap up warmly; it's snowing again,' Roscoe said as he helped her on with her coat, drawing the edges together. 'Your trouble is that you haven't got anyone to look after you. Never mind, you'll have me in future.'

She didn't protest. It wasn't true but she didn't have the strength to dispel the beautiful dream right now. There would be time enough for heartbreak later.

CHAPTER TWELVE

As they headed for Roscoe's car they realised that there was a ghostly figure standing beside it, half obscured by the driving snow. Pippa gasped with horror when she realised who it was.

'That's Franton,' she said urgently. 'The man you fired for insider trading. He's probably damaged your car.'

But there was nothing threatening about Franton's appearance as he stood waiting for them by the road.

'What are you doing out here in this weather?' Roscoe asked him, sounding irritated. 'Do you want to catch your death?'

Franton loomed at them through the flakes.

'I'm not staying long. I only came to thank you. I found out who got me the job.'

'I told them you'd do it well and I know you will,' Roscoe said gruffly.

'And the paper you signed about my debts...'

'It's only a guarantee. You still have to pay them.'

'But, thanks to you, I have time now. I had to come and thank you.'

'Fine, but clear off now before you get pneumonia,' Roscoe snapped, sounding annoyed. 'Where's your car?'

'I sold it.'

'Get in; I'll drive you home.'

Franton tumbled thankfully into the back seat. Pippa, sitting in the front, tried to sort out her tangled thoughts but without success.

Why, she thought fretfully, couldn't Roscoe stay the same person for five minutes at a time?

Franton's wife and three children were waiting at the window, looking anxious. They streamed out to embrace him and Roscoe sat watching the family scene, before firing the engine and driving off.

'I don't believe what I'm seeing,' she breathed. 'You got him another job? After what happened?'

'What else could I do?' he demanded. 'You saw his family. It's not much of a job, handling the finances of a little group of shops.'

'But didn't you have to tell the owners why you fired him?'

'I'm a partner in the business.'

'So you pulled strings for him?'

He grunted.

'And you've guaranteed his debts?'

'Guaranteed them. Not paid them. Now, can we drop this?'

'I just can't get my head around it. Nobody would guess the truth about you.'

'But you think you know the truth?' he asked savagely. 'After the way you attacked me about him, what did you expect me to do?'

'I didn't expect you to take any notice of anything I said. And I'm not even sure you did. I have a suspicion that you'd have done it anyway. Scrooge outside and Santa inside.'

'How dare you?'

'I don't know,' she mused. 'But I dare.'

After a while she said, 'This isn't the way to my home.'

'I'm taking a detour. The traffic's heavy because we're close to Trafalgar Square.'

'Ah, yes. That's where they set up the huge tree that the Norwegians give us every year.'

'Let's go and see it,' he said, turning into a side road and stopping.

Taking her hand, he drew her forward to where the crowds were gathered. There was the great tree rearing up into the night, covered in lights. More lights set the fountains aglow and the huge buildings around the edge of the square. All around, carol singers gathered, their voices rising into the chilly air.

'Beautiful,' Roscoe murmured.

Receiving no reply, he turned to see Pippa standing with her eyes closed, her face wet from snow, or maybe tears. Her head was uncovered and now her glorious hair was drenched and hanging drably.

'Pippa,' he said urgently. 'Pippa, what is it? Tell me, for pity's sake.'

He shook her shoulders gently and, when she didn't react, he drew her close, kissing her with the fierceness of a man trying to reawaken life.

'Pippa,' he whispered. 'Where are you?'

'I don't know,' she said helplessly. 'But I can't escape. I'm trapped there and I always will be.'

'You can. Let me help you.'

He kissed her again and again and she gave herself up to the feeling, trying to find in it a way out of the fears that tormented her. But she knew there was no way out and she must try to make him understand.

'Let me go,' she said desperately. 'I have to get out of here.'

She wrenched herself free and darted away, vanishing into the crowd so that for a moment Roscoe lost her and looked around desperately. She had vanished into thin air, gone for ever, and for a moment the demons that pursued him seemed to be mocking him.

Then he saw her at the end of the street, fleeing him without looking back. He gave chase and managed to catch up before she vanished again.

'No,' he said fiercely. 'We can't leave it like this. It's too important. Let's go back.'

'Not to that place,' she said, pointing to Trafalgar Square, whose lights could just be seen in the distance. 'I couldn't bear it.'

'But why?'

'Christmas,' she said simply. 'I just can't cope.'

'Let's go home.'

He led her back to the car, saw her tucked in and headed back to her home. She sat in silence, her arms crossed over her chest for the whole of the journey, then let him shepherd her upstairs. She knew this moment had to come. They must have a long talk, and she must make him understand why this path was closed off to her. Then, and only then, would she be ready to face the bleakness of life without him.

When they reached her apartment he fetched a towel and began to dry her hair, which was sodden from the snow, pulling it down so that he could work on it properly. The movement reminded him of that first day, when he'd seen her hair and her young, voluptuous body in their full glory.

Now there was nothing young or glorious about her. With her hair bedraggled, her face pale and strained, he had a sudden blinding glimpse of how she would look as a weary old woman.

He had never loved her so much.

At last he tossed the towel away, but still kept hold of her.

'I can't believe the way things went wrong with us without warning,' he said.

'There may have been no warning to you,' she said. 'For me, there was.'

'But everything was beautiful between us. We made love and found that our hearts and minds were open. We could talk and trust each other. I thought it was wonderful. Was I wrong?'

'No,' she cried passionately. 'It was wonderful. But that was what scared me. It was wonderful once before. All that trust and hope for the future. I know how little it means because I had those feelings with Jack, and they ended in a smash-up. I loved him so much. I was ready to give him everything I had, everything I was, everything I might be, and I thought it was the same with him.'

She began to pace the room.

'After that night you and I spent together, I woke up full of fear. It made no sense when things were so good between us, but I had this terrible sense of darkness. I tried to force it away, and I might have managed it, but then that Christmas carol came on the radio. And suddenly I was back there with Jack.

'Christmas was coming and our wedding was set for the New Year. The church was booked, the reception, the presents had started to arrive. I went to see him at his flat, and I was so stupid that I never realised anything was wrong. I could see he had something on his mind but I thought he was planning a special surprise for me.

'There were carol singers in the street below. They were singing *that* carol; how joy was here for ever and there would be "*New day, new hope, new life*". And it seemed to fit us so exactly that I began to sing the words. Jack looked a bit embarrassed. I'll never forget that look on his face, but of course it was because he was about to tell me that it was all over.

'I had some mistletoe that I'd been keeping hidden, waiting

for the right moment to produce it. I thought it was the perfect moment. I brought out the mistletoe and held it up, saying "This is where you're supposed to kiss me."

'But he just looked more embarrassed, and suddenly blurted out that he would never kiss me again. It was over. He was marrying someone else. I just stood there, trying to take it in, and all the time those words were floating up from the street. Since then, I've never been able to hear them without a shudder, but until that day I didn't know how deep it went.'

'But one song—'

'That's what I've tried to tell myself, but it's more. That one carol seems to sum it all up. The very fact that we were so happy seems like a threat. I'm afraid of happiness. I daren't let myself feel it because I can't face what happens when it ends.'

'And you think it will end with us? You don't trust me to be true to you? How can I prove it?'

'You can't. It's my fault, not yours. After Jack, I shut out love, hid myself away from it. That's why I live as I do, because it keeps love away. Let people think of me as a floozie who doesn't need real feeling! It makes me angry sometimes, but it also keeps me safe, and safe is what I want to be more than anything in the world.'

'More than anything in the world?' Roscoe echoed slowly. 'More than everything we could have together? More than the love we would share over the years, more than our children, our grandchildren?'

'Stop it,' Pippa whispered. 'Please, please stop it.'

He moved closer, not holding her, but letting her feel the warmth of his breath on her face.

'No, I won't stop it,' he whispered. 'I won't stop because I'm going to make sure that you remember me. I won't let you just shut me out as though our love didn't count. Do you think I'm going to let you off so easily? I'm not. I'm going to make sure you remember me every moment.'

Now he touched her, laying his mouth against hers, caressing her with his lips, then whispering, 'Feel me, and remember me. I'll always be here. You'll never be rid of me, do you understand?'

'Yes,' she murmured. 'I don't want to be rid of you, but I can't be with you. I'd make you wretched and destroy you, and I won't do that.'

'Tell me that you love me.'

'I love you—I love you—'

'And you belong to me.'

'Yes, I belong to you, and I always will. But please go away, Roscoe—please forget me—'

'Never in life. When I leave this room I'll be with you. When you wake up tomorrow morning I'll be with you. When you go to bed I'll be with you. When you dream of love and feel hands touching and caressing you, they'll be my hands, although I may be far away. As the years pass I'll be with you. I won't set you free—ever.'

His kiss intensified. She felt his mouth crushing hers for one fierce moment, before it softened again, leaving only tenderness behind. Then she was alone and he was backing away to the door, not taking his eyes from her.

'Forgive me,' she cried. *'Forgive me!'*

'Perhaps,' he said quietly. 'One day.'

He walked out.

An unexpected knock on her door turned out to be Charlie, dressed in a heavy overcoat, swathed in a scarf.

'It's freezing out there,' he said, coming in. 'I came because I wanted to tell you myself. Even if I don't win the show, my agent has fixed me up with a load of dates and *I'm on my way.*'

He finished with a yell of triumph and they embraced eagerly.

'Is Ginevra pleased for you?' she asked.

'Probably. We're not in touch. Last I heard from her was a text wishing me luck and saying not to contact her any more.'

'Do you mind?'

'Nope. There's a girl...well, anyway...'

'Have fun,' Pippa chuckled. 'You've been taking things too seriously for too long.'

'Well, that's over and I'm glad. I swear I'll never take anything seriously again.'

'How's Roscoe coping with the change in you?'

'Resigned, I think. I hardly see him now. Since the tie-up with Vanlen came to nothing, he's in the office all the time.'

'There's not going to be a merger?'

'No. I'm not sure what happened but I've heard there was a big row. Vanlen wanted to go ahead and merge; Roscoe didn't. Vanlen made threats; Roscoe told him to do his worst. Vanlen stormed off.' Charlie suddenly became awkward. 'Actually, I thought you might have seen Roscoe more recently.'

'The last time I saw him was at your mother's house on the night of the show, and I only went because you assured me he wouldn't be there.'

He was wide-eyed. 'Did I say that? I don't remember.'

'Stop telling porkies. You promised I wouldn't bump into him. But he said you knew he'd be there. How did you get that so wrong, Charlie?'

'Ah—well—'

She surveyed him suspiciously. 'You set us up to meet, didn't you?'

'Who, *me*?' His air of innocence was perfectly contrived,

and she would have believed it if she hadn't known him so well by now.

'Yes, you.'

'How can you think that I—? Oh hell, yes of course I did. I was hoping the two of you would see sense if I helped things along.'

'You've got an almighty nerve, playing Cupid.'

'Why shouldn't I? I need a big sister, and I've chosen you. Besides which, it's always handy having a lawyer in the family. There are bound to be times in the future when—well, you know.'

Her lips twitched. 'Yes, I do know.'

Charlie became briefly serious. 'But that's not really the reason, Pippa. Both Mother and I want you in the family because you make Roscoe human. Without you he'll go to the dogs.' He resumed his clowning manner. 'So get on with it, OK? Right, now I've got to go. I just wanted to see you again and say thanks for everything.'

He gave her a brotherly kiss and was gone, taking with him her last connection with Roscoe.

At their parting she'd said a final goodbye, but still she clung to the hope that he would refuse to accept her rejection. But he neither called her nor turned up on her doorstep. In the next few days their only contact was a letter:

I had a long talk with Mother last night. I think we were both equally surprised that it was possible, but once we started it grew easier. She told me how she'd felt, things that I hadn't known, and actually asked my forgiveness if she'd failed me. I told her there was nothing to forgive. Without you, it would never have happened. For the rest of my life you can ask anything of me that you wish and it will be yours. As I am yours.

It was signed simply, *Roscoe*.

He had said that she would never be alone and she found that, mysteriously, it was true. The apartment echoed with emptiness, yet he was always present, along with her other silent companions. There was Dee, accusing her of cowardice, and Mad Bruin, echoing Dee's thoughts, as he always had.

Cowardice? Am I really a coward?

If you had any real nerve, Dee told her, *you'd go back to Trafalgar Square and face that Christmas tree and those carols.*

That's what you'd have done, isn't it? But I'm not brave enough. I'd always be watching Roscoe, wondering if his love was failing, and I won't do that to him.

It's nearly Christmas. Soon the lights will go out and it'll be too late for another year. It's now or never.

Then let it be never. Better for him. I'd only break his heart.

Yet she began wandering past Trafalgar Square every night on her way home, standing there, apart from the crowd, trying to listen to the carols without hearing them. But it was no use. The darkness did not lift and after standing in the cold for an hour she would turn and make her way drearily to the nearest underground station, trying to find relief in the thought that this self-inflicted punishment would soon be over, and she could be strong for another year.

'I won't go back in the future,' she murmured. 'I can't.' Just one last visit, she thought. Then never again.

'And you'll come with me,' she said, taking up Mad Bruin from his place by her bed. 'We'll say goodbye together, then maybe you'll understand and stop nagging me. And tell *her* to stop nagging me. Not that she ever does stop. Look at that.'

The exclamation was drawn from her by one of Dee's diaries, on which Bruin had been sitting, and which fell to the floor when he was moved. Picking it up, Pippa found it falling open at a page in the centre. Dee had written:

> I suppose I'm a bit mad. I swore I'd never marry him. I even ended our engagement. That broke my heart. I thought I was doing the best thing, but who gave me the right to decide for both of us? When he came back to me, injured, vulnerable, I knew that my place was by his side, no matter what.
>
> We're marrying now because I'm pregnant, so I don't know if he really loves me. But IT DOESN'T MATTER. I love him, and that's what matters. Nobody knows the future. You can only love and do your best. Perhaps it won't work. Perhaps he'll leave me.

Here some words were scribbled in the margin. Pippa just managed to make out her grandfather's writing: *Daft woman! As though I could.*

Dee went on:

> I'll take that risk and, at the end, whenever and whatever the end will be, I'll be able to say that I was true to my love.

'You were so strong,' Pippa murmured. 'If only I could be like you. But I can't.'

She put the diary carefully into a drawer, then tucked Bruin into her bag and hurried out.

She could hear the carol singers from a distance and ran the last few yards, suddenly eager to see the beautiful tree, its lights streaming up into the darkness, promising hope. That hope would never be hers, but she would carry the memory of this night all her life.

A vendor was wandering through the Square, holding

up sprigs of mistletoe and doing a roaring trade as couples converged on him, paying exorbitantly for tiny sprigs, then immediately putting them to good use. Tears sprang into Pippa's eyes as she watched them.

All around her people were singing. Someone was yelling, 'Come on, everyone. Join in.'

But she couldn't join in. That was the one final step that was still beyond her courage. Sadly, she pressed Bruin against her cheek before turning away.

But then someone crashed into her from behind and made her fall to the ground, sending him flying.

'No,' she cried. 'Where are you—where—?'

'It's all right; I've got him,' said a familiar voice, and she found herself looking into Roscoe's eyes.

He helped her to her feet and pressed Bruin back into her hands. 'Take care of him.'

'How long have you been there?' she stammered.

'Since you arrived. And last night, and the time before. I know why you've come here and I've followed, hoping that what you found here would make you believe in me again.'

'But I do believe in you. It's myself I don't believe in. I'm afraid.'

'You? Never. You're not afraid of anything.' He made a wry, gentle face. 'Many people are afraid of me. Not you. That was the first thing I liked about you.' He went on, almost casually, 'I could do with you around just now. Vanlen's turning nasty and your moral support would mean a lot to me.' He gave a small grin. 'Plus, of course, your legal expertise.'

'I heard the merger was abandoned and he didn't like it.'

'Since a certain night, I want nothing further to do with him. He blames me for you knocking him back.' He gave a grunt of laughter. 'If only I could believe that. I could hardly tell him that you have no more use for me than for him.'

'That's not true; you know it's not,' she whispered. 'It's because you matter so much that I—'

'If I could have spoken freely I'd have told him that you're a woman so special that I'd take every threat he could throw at me, make any sacrifice asked and call it cheap at the price. Except that there is no price. There never was and there never could be. What isn't given freely has no value.'

Pippa clutched her head, almost weeping. 'You make it sound so wonderful, but I have nothing to give.'

'That's not true. You've already given me things that matter a million times more than anything else in my life. If you choose to be more generous it will be the most precious gift of all. If not, I'll always live in the knowledge that I knew the most glorious woman in the world, and my life was better for knowing her.

'If you won't marry me, Pippa, I'll never marry anyone else. I'll live alone, dreaming of you. It'll be a sad life when I think of what could have been mine instead. Will you abandon me to that loneliness? Do you love me so little that you'll do that to me?'

'No,' she cried. 'I love you with all my heart; it's just that… the fearful part of me is still fighting it. If only I could…if only…'

Everything in her yearned towards him. If only she could find the inspiration that would take her that last step into the unknown.

But it wasn't unknown. It was filled with problems, fears, difficulties, but also with love. That much she knew. As for whether the love would be enough, that was up to her, wasn't it?

Nobody knows the future. You can only love and do your best.

Dee's words seemed to echo so resoundingly that she

gasped and looked up, almost expecting to see the mysterious presence.

'Where are you?' she whispered.

Here, the presence replied. *Here, there and everywhere. In your heart.*

'What is it?' Roscoe asked.

'Nobody knows the future,' Pippa repeated slowly. 'You can only love and do your best. She knew that. She tried to tell me.'

Roscoe had laid all that he was, all he had and all he ever could be at her feet. He could do no more. Now the future lay in her hands.

'Roscoe,' she said, reaching out to him, 'if only I could—'

'But you can,' he said. 'You can if you believe. We can do it together because now I know the way.'

The choirmaster was just waiting to start the next carol. Roscoe tugged at his arm, spoke a few words and the man nodded. The next moment the first notes of '*A New Day Dawns*' floated out on the air.

'Not that one,' she said quickly.

'Yes, that one,' he said. 'That's the one that haunts you, and once we've defeated it together, the way is clear for us. Don't you see?'

'Yes, I do, but—' Still the fear lurked.

He took her face between his hands.

'No buts. From now on we face everything together, including this. Especially this. So now you're going to sing this with me. Understand?'

'Yes,' she whispered.

'Then do it. Do it now, I order you. Yes, I'm a control freak and a manipulator, *but so are you*. When we're married I'll give my orders and expect you to do as I say. But be honest, my darling. *You'll* give *your* orders and expect me to do as you say. And I will. In the end we'll know each other so well that nobody will have to give orders. We'll each know how to please the other.

'And, since you're a bigger control freak than I am, it'll be me doing most of the obeying. But this time it's me giving the orders. Sing with me, for this hope is ours and it's time to claim it.'

Around them the voices rose, seeming to shimmer with the lights that glowed up high, to the star at the top of the tree, blazing against the darkness.

'A new day dawns, a child is born.
Behold the shining star,'

'Sing,' he said. 'Sing with me. *Sing*.'
And suddenly she could do so, clinging to him for the strength only he could give her. Now and only now the words would come.

'It leads us on to hope revived,
New day, new hope, new life'

It was there, the miracle she'd thought could never happen, rolling back the fear, setting her free, but only free as long as he was there.

She saw the question in his eyes and nodded as their voices rang out together.

'For darkness flees the coming light,
And we are all reborn.'

'Reborn,' she whispered.
'Does that mean you'll marry me?'
'Yes, I'll marry you.'

From his pocket he took a small box containing a diamond ring, which he slipped onto her finger. She gasped. 'That's your mother's.'

'She gave it to me. She said her time for wearing it was over, but yours had just begun. It's her way of welcoming you into the family, but also—I don't know how to put it—'

'She gave it to you, not Charlie. That's her way of opening her heart to you again, saying you're her son?'

'Yes. It's taken so long. I thought I was resigned, but I wasn't. After all these years it has brought me more joy than I can say, and that's another thing I owe to you. You brought us together and helped us understand each other. I could never give this ring to anyone but you, and you must promise me to wear it all your life.'

'I'll wear it as long as you want me to wear it.'

'All your life,' he repeated.

A vendor glided past them, waving a sprig of mistletoe. 'Go on, buy it,' he begged. 'Then I can go home.'

Roscoe grabbed the first note he came to and proffered it without looking to see how large it was. The vendor's eyes opened wide and he vanished quickly.

Slowly, Roscoe raised the mistletoe over her head.

'Do you remember what you said to that fool who let you slip through his fingers?' he asked.

'"This is where you're supposed to kiss me",' she recalled.

'Very willingly,' he said, lowering his mouth to hers for the first kiss of their engagement.

She kissed him back fervently, trying to tell him that she was entirely his, despite her fears. With his help she would conquer them and be everything he wanted. Nothing else mattered in her life.

Afterwards they hugged each other. Later there would be passion, but just now what mattered was the warmth and comfort they could bring each other. As her spirit soared she even managed a tiny laugh.

'What is it?' he asked, lifting her chin and gazing searchingly into her face.

'That was a twenty pound note you gave him.'

'If it had been a million pounds it wouldn't have begun to be enough for what I've won tonight.'

As they finally walked away, arms entwined, she murmured, *New day, new hope, new life.* All the best things to wish for.'

'I don't have to wish for them,' Roscoe said. 'You have given them to me already, and they will last for ever.'

They set the wedding date for soon after Christmas. It would take place in the church belonging to the graveyard where they had first met, where Pippa's family lay in the grounds. The day before, they paid a visit together and went to look at the graves of Mark and Dee. Roscoe brushed the snow away, revealing the faces beneath, not just happy, but with a contentment that spoke of many years of successful marriage.

'I'm glad they'll be at our wedding,' she said.

'They'll always be part of our lives,' he agreed. 'Because without them we'd never have met. Do you think your grandmother likes me?'

'Oh, yes, I can tell from the way she's looking at you.'

'So can I.'

When she went to visit the other family graves he stayed behind to talk to Dee.

'You've been such an influence in her life—and mine—that I want to know you better. Without you, she wouldn't be who she is, and I wouldn't be the happy man that I am. Thank you with all my heart.'

He stepped back.

'I'll see you both at the wedding tomorrow. I hope you enjoy it.'

He walked away to find the woman he adored more than life, and even now he had the sense that two pairs of eyes were following him. He smiled, happy in the knowledge, and resolved to tell Pippa all about it.

HIS DIAMOND BRIDE

BY
LUCY GORDON

DID YOU PURCHASE THIS BOOK WITHOUT A COVER?

If you did, you should be aware it is **stolen property** as it was reported *unsold and destroyed* by a retailer. Neither the author nor the publisher has received any payment for this book.

All the characters in this book have no existence outside the imagination of the author, and have no relation whatsoever to anyone bearing the same name or names. They are not even distantly inspired by any individual known or unknown to the author, and all the incidents are pure invention.

All Rights Reserved including the right of reproduction in whole or in part in any form. This edition is published by arrangement with Harlequin Enterprises II B.V./S.à.r.l. The text of this publication or any part thereof may not be reproduced or transmitted in any form or by any means, electronic or mechanical, including photocopying, recording, storage in an information retrieval system, or otherwise, without the written permission of the publisher.

This book is sold subject to the condition that it shall not, by way of trade or otherwise, be lent, resold, hired out or otherwise circulated without the prior consent of the publisher in any form of binding or cover other than that in which it is published and without a similar condition including this condition being imposed on the subsequent purchaser.

® and ™ are trademarks owned and used by the trademark owner and/or its licensee. Trademarks marked with ® are registered with the United Kingdom Patent Office and/or the Office for Harmonisation in the Internal Market and in other countries.

First published in Great Britain 2011
Harlequin Mills & Boon Limited,
Eton House, 18-24 Paradise Road, Richmond, Surrey TW9 1SR

© Lucy Gordon 2011

ISBN: 978 0 263 88852 2

23-0111

Harlequin Mills & Boon policy is to use papers that are natural, renewable and recyclable products and made from wood grown in sustainable forests. The logging and manufacturing processes conform to the legal environmental regulations of the country of origin.

Printed and bound in Spain
by Litografia Rosés S.A., Barcelona

Dear Reader,

Given the way my last heroine, Pippa, was influenced by Dee, her grandmother, there was no way I could write Pippa's story without also writing Dee's. She came from another age, when men and women saw each other in more traditional roles and the obstacles to love were different—one of which was the turmoil caused by war.

Unlike Pippa, Dee was not spectacularly beautiful. Pleasant, but unremarkable, she chose a useful life as a nurse. The beauty of the family was her sister Sylvia and, when she brought home the handsome Mark Sellon, Dee was content to admire him from a distance.

Then the Second World War broke out and he became a pilot, flying daring missions and being hailed as a hero. To Dee, this glamorous man seemed more out of her reach than ever. How could he ever love her? And how could she ever believe in his love?

Mark, struggling to recover from terrible experiences, lost in confusion, could make his way only slowly towards the love of his life. But when he saw his destiny, lit up and beckoning, he pursued it with determined purpose.

Their road to each other was complicated and troublesome, with pain and despair as well as joy. At the end of it lay their sixtieth wedding anniversary, celebrated publicly with diamonds, but privately with a contentment of heart that they would once have thought impossible.

It was the triumphant achievement of that joy that gave Dee a new mission in life: to reach out to her beloved granddaughter, helping Pippa find the way to her own happiness.

Warmest wishes,

Lucy Gordon

CHAPTER ONE

5th August 2003

'HE MUST have been the most handsome man who ever lived,' Pippa sighed, her eyes fixed on the framed photograph in her hands. 'Look at those film star features and the way he's half smiling, as though at a private joke.'

'That's what used to drive the other girls wild,' Lilian said. 'Mum said he could charm the birds off the trees, and always keep them wondering.'

She was fifty-eight, with grey hair and a vivid face. She smiled when she spoke of her parents.

The photograph had been taken sixty-three years earlier. It showed a fine-looking young man, splendid in airman's uniform, his head slightly cocked, his features alive with sardonic humour. It bore only a faint resemblance to the old man that he was now, but the glint in his eyes had survived.

He was crouching on the wing of an aeroplane, one arm resting on a raised knee, his face turned to the camera, yet with a mysterious air of gazing into the future, as though he could see what was coming and was eager to meet it. Everything in the picture was redolent of life and masculine attraction.

'He may have been a hero back then, but I'll bet he was a devil, too,' Pippa said gleefully.

She was just twenty-one and beautiful. Her mother was immensely proud of her but she didn't let that show too often.

'Too attractive for her own good,' was her favourite expression to conceal her pride.

'Yes, I've heard he was a devil, among many other things,' she agreed, looking back at the picture of Flight Lieutenant Mark Sellon. 'By the way, the local TV station has been in touch. They want to do a piece—hero and wife celebrate sixty years of marriage. And the local paper. They're both sending someone to the party this afternoon to get some pictures and a few words about all the fantastic things he did in the war.'

'Grandpa won't like that,' Pippa observed. 'He hates going back over that time. Have you ever realised how little we actually know about it? He always avoids the subject. "Ask Gran", he says. But she doesn't tell much either.'

'I wish they'd let me throw the party in my house,' Lilian said. 'It's bigger and we could have got more people in.' She looked around disparagingly at the modest little property that stood at the far end of Crimea Street on the outskirts of London.

'It's where it all began,' Pippa reminded her. 'They met when he came to stay here with the family the last Christmas before the war, and all over the house there are places that remind her of him as he was then.'

'I suppose now you know them better than any of us,' Lilian said.

Pippa was her youngest child, several years younger than her siblings, arriving when the others were all at school and Lilian had resumed her career as a midwife. Lilian's mother had come to the rescue, announcing that, as they lived only three streets apart, she could take on most of the baby's care. The result was that Pippa had always been close to her grandparents, regarding them almost as extra parents.

She was spirited, even rebellious and in her teens this had led to difficulties with Lilian, resulting in her taking shelter in Crimea Street. The trouble had been smoothed out. Mother and daughter were friends again, but Pippa now lived with her grandparents, keeping a protective eye on them as they grew old and frail.

On the surface it was a perfect arrangement, yet Pippa was a worry to all who loved her. With her brains and beauty she should have been doing something more demanding than a dead-end job, and her social life should have consisted of more than staying at home almost every evening.

All the fault of Jack Sothern, Lilian thought bitterly. He'd seemed like a decent fellow, and everyone had been happy when he became engaged to Pippa. But he'd broken it off ruthlessly just a few weeks before the planned Christmas wedding, leaving Pippa devastated.

That had been nine months ago. Pippa had seemed to recover, but the life had gone out of her, as though she was emotionally flattened. She still smiled and laughed with a charm that won everyone over, but behind her eyes there was a blankness that never changed.

The doorbell rang and Lilian went to answer it. After that she was kept busy letting in guests until the house was overflowing. Pippa welcomed everyone with a finger over her lips.

'They're upstairs lying down,' she whispered. 'I want them to rest until the last minute. Tonight's going to be very tiring for them.'

Lilian's brother Terry appeared. He was in his fifties, heavily built with greying hair and bullish features that radiated good nature. With him was his wife Celia, two children and three grandchildren. Hard on his heels came Irene, his first wife, now remarried, also with a herd of youngsters.

'I can't even keep track of them,' Pippa confided to her Uncle Terry. 'Are we related to them all?'

'We're definitely related to that one,' Terry observed, indicating a boy of fourteen who seemed possessed by an imp of mischief. 'Mum says he's exactly like Dad was years ago: into everything, driving everyone mad, then winning them over with that smile. But he's bright; always top of the class, apparently.'

'He didn't get that from Grandpa,' Pippa remarked. 'He was bottom of the class, according to him. He says there was always something more interesting to do than read dreary books, and there still is.'

Terry laughed appreciatively. 'That sounds like Dad. His idea of serious reading is a magazine with pretty girls. I hope he doesn't let Mum see them.'

Pippa chuckled. 'She's not bothered. She buys them for him.'

Terry nodded. 'That sounds just like her.'

'Have you got all the pictures out?' Terry asked.

'Yes, they're in here.' She led the way to a room at the back, decorated for the party, hung with paper chains and flowers and full of photographs. Some were family groups, but most were individual shots.

There was Lilian on her twenty-first birthday. There was Terry dressed for mountain climbing, which was his passion.

'What about Gran's parents?' Pippa asked, pointing to a picture of a middle-aged couple dressed in the clothes of the thirties. 'Should I have put them a bit further forward?'

'Yes, I think so. It would please her.' He reached for another picture, showing a beautiful young woman with a ripe, curvy figure. 'And this one, of her sister Sylvia.'

'Ah, Great Aunt Sylvia,' Pippa said. 'I often wish I'd known her, she sounds so interesting. Wasn't she the one who—?'

'Yes, she was. It was an earth-shattering scandal at the time, but these days nobody would think anything of it. Times have changed. Put her where she can be seen. Mum was very fond of her.' He looked around for a moment before adding, 'There's one missing. Polly should be there, too.'

'Should she? I did wonder, and I've got some pictures of

her, just in case. But she was only a year old when she died. She barely existed.'

'Don't let them hear you say that,' Terry said in alarm. 'Dad absolutely adored my baby sister. It's nearly fifty years since she died, but she's still part of the family, and if you leave her out he'll be upset.'

'Yes, of course. Here she is,' Pippa agreed.

She produced two photographs, one a portrait of a baby girl, beaming at the camera, the other showing the same child in her father's arms. Their eyes were locked, each totally entranced by the other.

'He was a terrific dad,' Terry said, studying the picture. 'But I don't think he ever looked at any of the rest of us quite like that. It was just something Polly had, maybe because she was the image of Mum...I don't know...'

'You think it had something to do with the way he felt about Gran?'

'I'm not sure, but when Polly died, I think he'd have gone crazy if it hadn't been for her.'

'When he walks into a room he always looks to see if she's there,' Pippa reflected. 'If she isn't, he keeps looking at the door, waiting for her to arrive. And when she does arrive, he seems to settle down.'

The bell rang and she went to let in the reporter from the local TV station, a young woman called Stacey, and the photographer, who prowled around looking for angles.

'I just can't get over anyone being married sixty years,' Stacey said, awed.

'It was different in their day,' Pippa said. 'People married for life. And I think Grandpa was courting her for a long time so he wasn't going to let her go easily.'

'Long courtship,' Stacey muttered, making notes. 'Good, that gives me something to go on.'

At last everyone was there: Mark and Dee's children and

grandchildren, cousins, in-laws, a representative from the local hospital where Dee had once worked.

'Quiet everybody! They're coming.'

The photographer got into position at the bottom of the stairs, ready to capture the stars of the evening as they appeared above: Mr and Mrs Sellon, Mark and Deirdre, known to everyone as Dee. They were in their eighties, white-haired, thin and frail-looking, but holding themselves erect, with smiling eyes.

They descended the stairs arm in arm, seeming to support each other equally, until the moment Dee stumbled and clung to her husband for safety.

'Careful, my love,' he said, guiding her to a chair. 'What happened?'

'Nothing; I tripped on the carpet.'

'Are you sure you're all right? You'd better have a cup of tea.'

'Tea?' she said in mock outrage. 'Today? I want a good strong sherry.'

He hurried to get her a glass and Lilian regarded them with delight.

'Look how he dances attendance on her,' she sighed. 'After all these years. So many husbands become indifferent.'

'I've never known Grandpa indifferent,' Pippa said. 'In fact, he sometimes smothers Gran with his concern. He's so scared that she'll go first.'

'You know the saying. There's always one who loves and one who lets themselves be loved,' Lilian reminded her. 'No prizes for guessing which is which with those two.'

Even as she spoke, Dee's voice rose, full of affectionate laughter. 'Darling, I'm all right. Will you stop fussing?'

Everyone heard that, but only she heard his murmured response. 'No, I won't, and you know that I won't. You've been telling me for years to stop fussing over you and I've never listened yet, so why don't you just give up?'

'I never give up where you're concerned,' she whispered back. 'You should know that by now.'

'I do know it. I rely on it.'

He touched her face gently. It had never been a beautiful face, but it had always been rich in warmth and generosity, qualities that the years had left untouched. Watching them, the family knew that what he'd first seen in her years ago, he saw there still.

The elderly couple were shown into the main party room and went around the collection of family photographs, pausing occasionally to murmur to each other, words that nobody else could hear. When it came to baby Polly, Gran lifted the picture and they looked at it together before they met each other's gaze and nodded.

'I swear there were tears in Grandpa's eyes,' Pippa murmured afterwards.

At last they were seated together on the sofa while family members approached them, hugging and murmuring words of congratulation. Champagne was poured and glasses were raised in toasts. Speeches were made. Everyone wanted to have their say.

Then Stacey got to work, talking to the camera.

'…one of the last of a dying breed…heroes of World War Two, who gave their all for their country…night after night, climbing into their Spitfires, taking off into the darkness, not knowing if they would return to their loved ones…how proud we are that one of them is still among us…'

'Is she going to witter on like that for ever?' Mark growled under his breath.

'Hush,' Dee murmured. 'Let your family take pride in you.'

'My family know nothing about it,' he insisted.

'How can they? They weren't born then. Don't blame them for that.'

Out of sight, they squeezed each other's hands.

Now Stacey turned her attention on them. To her questions about the war Mark gave polite but uninformative replies, claiming to have forgotten the details. Finally she said, 'But I understand that yours is also a great romance. Mr Sellon, is it true that you courted your wife for years before you persuaded her to marry you?'

'Oh, yes,' Mark said. 'She wasn't won easily. I really had to work hard to impress her.'

Everyone smiled at this. Only the most perceptive noticed the look of surprise on Dee's face.

'But how romantic!' Stacey exclaimed. 'The lover who yearns hopelessly from afar. Mrs Sellon, why did you make him wait so long?'

'I'm not sure now. We weren't the same people back then.'

'Would you do it any differently now?'

Dee's lips twitched. 'Oh, yes,' she said. 'I'd make him wait *much* longer.'

The newspaper journalist followed, with similar questions, but he had his eye on the photograph of Flight Lieutenant Sellon that the family had studied earlier.

'This is a fantastic picture,' he said. 'I'd like to use it in the paper. I'll need to borrow it—'

'No,' Dee said at once. 'I'm sorry; you can't take it away.'

'Just for a few hours. I'll take care—'

'I'm sure you will, but I can't take the risk. I'm sorry.' Her manner was polite but very firm as she removed the picture from his hand. 'This is mine.'

The young man looked round for help, but none of the family would yield. They knew Gran when she spoke like that.

The evening moved gently on to its conclusion, everyone feeling that it had been a triumphant success. In the spotlight, Mark and Dee seemed to be enjoying themselves but, as he slipped his arm about her waist, he murmured, 'When will they go?'

'Soon,' she promised.

They smiled at one another and the camera clicked. The picture appeared in the local paper the next day. Neither of them noticed it being taken.

At last it was all over. The guests departed, and Lilian accompanied her parents up to their room.

'How is Pippa coping?' Dee wanted to know. 'I worried about her this evening. A wedding anniversary. How that must have hurt her! If her wedding had gone ahead, it would have been her own first anniversary soon.'

'I know, but you'd never guess it, she seems so bright,' Lilian sighed. 'Oh, I could kill that man for what he did to her.'

Pippa's entry silenced the topic. Together, they helped the old people to bed, kissed them goodnight and retreated to the door.

'You're not too tired after all the goings-on?' Pippa asked.

'Tired?' Mark echoed. 'We're only just starting. We're going to get revved up, then swing from the chandeliers and indulge in some mad lust. You youngsters! You don't know how to enjoy life. Ow! No need to beat me up.'

Dee, who'd delivered the lightest tap on his shoulder, chuckled. 'Behave yourself!' she commanded.

'You see how she treats me,' Mark sighed. 'I expect you bully your menfolk too, and they wonder where you get it from. They should see what I put up with. Ow!'

As the two old people collapsed with laughter, Lilian drew her daughter away.

'Let's leave them to it. Honestly, they're like a couple of kids.'

'Perhaps that's their secret,' Pippa said.

'Yes,' Lilian said thoughtfully. 'They do seem to have a secret, don't they?'

They went downstairs to get on with the clearing up.

In the darkness, Mark and Dee listened to the fading footsteps.

'We're very lucky,' she mused, 'that our family takes such care of us.'

'True, but I hope they don't come back,' he admitted. 'Right now, I want to be alone with you. What are you giggling for?'

'I was remembering the first time you ever said that to me. I was so thrilled. Suddenly every dream I'd ever had was coming true.'

'But it wasn't, was it?' he reminded her. 'I was a dreadful character in those days. I can't think what you saw in me.'

'Well, if you don't know, I'm not going to tell you,' she teased. 'We had our troubles, but we reached home in the end. That's all that matters.'

'Yes, we reached home and shut the door against the world,' he mused. 'And, ever since then, we've kept each other safe. Sixty years you've put up with me! I can't imagine how!'

'Neither can I, so stop fishing for compliments. And, by the way, what game were you playing tonight?'

'Game? I don't know what you mean.'

'Don't play the innocent with me. All that talk about how you had to court me for years and work to impress me. You know that's not what happened.'

'Yes, it is.'

'It most certainly is not. Don't you remember—?'

He stopped her with a gentle finger over her mouth. 'Hush! I remember what I remember, and you remember what you remember, and maybe it's not the same thing, but does that matter?'

'No, I suppose not,' she said thoughtfully. 'I dare say we'll never know now which of us has remembered it right.'

'Both of us and neither of us,' he said.

She smiled. 'You're very wise tonight.'

'I'll swear that's the first time you've ever called me wise. Now, tell me, did you like your present?'

'I loved it, but you shouldn't have splashed out on diamonds.'

'*One* measly little diamond,' he corrected. 'I was determined you were going to have that on our diamond anniversary.' Then his voice rose in horror. '*Good grief; I almost forgot!* Your other present.'

'I've been wondering about that, ever since you told me this morning that the diamond was only the "official" present, and that you had something else for me that meant much more. You said you'd give it to me later, when the crowd had gone.'

'I forgot until now,' he groaned.

'Never mind, darling,' she said tenderly. 'People of our age become forgetful.'

'Our age?' he echoed, affronted. 'Are you suggesting that I'm old?'

'Of course not. You could be a hundred and you still wouldn't be old.'

'Thank you, my dear.'

She couldn't resist adding cheekily, 'But give me my present before you forget again.'

He gave her a look, then switched on the little light by the bed and fumbled in a drawer, producing a small object that he hid behind his back. 'Close your eyes and hold out your hands,' he ordered.

Smiling, she did so, until she felt the soft touch of fur in her palm, and opened her eyes to find a small teddy bear. She gave an excited squeal and rubbed him against her cheek. 'Now, that's a real present,' she said. '*Much* better than diamonds.'

There seemed little in the toy to explain her delight. Six inches tall, with beady eyes and nylon fur, he was like a thousand other cheap trinkets, but Dee was overwhelmed with joy.

'Do you remember the first one I gave you?' Mark asked fondly.

For answer, she reached under her pillow and produced another toy bear. Once, long ago, he might have been like the new one, but now all his fur had worn away, he was shabby and mended at the seams.

'He's still here,' Dee said, holding him up. 'I never let him get far away.'

'You talk as though he was alive and trying to escape.'

'He is alive, and he knows he can never escape me,' she said, looking at her husband with meaning. 'That night you said you'd given him to me so that I didn't forget you. I loved you so much that nothing in the world could have made me forget you, but you didn't know that.'

'I took too long to understand,' he agreed. 'So many things I didn't see until it was nearly too late.'

'But I always had my Mad Bruin,' she said, indicating the threadbare toy.

'Mad Bruin,' he said, taking the bear from her and holding him up to consider him. 'I remember when you called me that. You were so angry. You were an impressive woman when you got really mad. Still are.'

'You scared me, doing something so stupid,' she recalled. 'You were the real Mad Bruin. Mad as a hatter, always doing something no sensible man would have done.'

'And we both got told off,' he remembered, addressing the toy.

She held both of the tiny bears together. 'He'll enjoy having a companion. I'm glad you gave me this. It was a lovely thing to think of. I thought you'd forgotten all about Bruin.'

'No, I didn't forget, but I noticed that you keep him hidden away.'

'Nobody else would understand.'

'Nobody but us,' he agreed.

She slipped both toys under her pillow. Mark turned out the lamp and they settled down together in the darkness. She felt his arms go around her, while her head found its natural place on his shoulder.

'Bliss,' he mused. 'This is what I've been waiting for all evening. Everyone is kind to us, but they don't understand. They just never know.'

'No,' she murmured. 'Only we know, but only we *need* to know.'

'Goodnight, my darling.'

'Goodnight.'

After a moment she heard the change in his breathing that meant he was asleep. But she wasn't ready to sleep. The evening had revived sixty years of memories and now they seemed to be there, dancing in the darkness.

The old man beside her disappeared, leaving only the dazzling young hero of long ago. How stunned she'd been by her first experience of love, blissful if he smiled at her, despairing because she knew he could never he hers.

Slowly she raised herself on one elbow to look down on him in gentle adoration. He awoke at once.

'What is it?' he asked quickly. 'Is something wrong?'

'Nothing,' she reassured him, settling back into his arms. 'Go to sleep.'

Content, he closed his eyes again. But she did not sleep. She lay looking into the distance, remembering

CHAPTER TWO

December 1938

'ANY sign of them yet?' Helen Parsons' voice sang out from the kitchen.

Dee, her seventeen-year-old daughter, paused from studying a box of Christmas decorations and went to the window. The narrow London street outside seemed empty, but the darkness made it hard to see far so she slipped out of the front door and down the small garden to the gate.

'Not a sign,' she said, returning to the house and hurriedly closing the door.

Her mother appeared, frowning. 'Have you been out without a coat, in this weather?'

'Just for a moment.'

'You'll catch your death of cold. You're a nurse; you should have more sense.'

Dee chuckled good-humouredly. 'It's a bit soon to call me a nurse. I've barely started my training.'

'Don't tell your father that. He's dead proud of you. He tells everyone that his daughter became a nurse because she's the bright one of the family.'

The bright one, Dee thought wryly. Her older sister, Sylvia, was the beautiful one, and she was the bright one.

'Now, don't start that again,' her mother said, reading her face without trouble.

'It's just that sometimes I'd like to be gorgeous, like Sylvia,' Dee said wistfully.

'Nonsense, you're pretty enough.' She bustled back to the kitchen, leaving Dee to gaze into the mirror.

She had pleasant, regular features under short brown hair, with dark brown expressive eyes. Pretty enough. That was about the best anyone could say and, if it hadn't been for Sylvia, Dee might have been content with it. But when she compared Sylvia's luscious features with her own, which were pleasant but not spectacular, she knew she could never be content.

Her figure was slender, almost too much so, which would have pleased many girls. But they didn't have the constant comparison with Sylvia's ripe curves. Dee didn't appreciate her own shape—with all the yearning of seventeen, she wanted Sylvia's.

She wanted to be beautiful, she wanted boyfriends trailing after her, and a throaty, seductive voice. Instead, she was 'the bright one' and 'pretty enough'. As though that was any comfort. Honestly! Older people just didn't understand.

'I wonder what this one's like,' her mother said, returning with a duster that she put into Dee's hand.

No need to ask who 'this one' was. Yet another of Sylvia's conquests. There were so many.

'She'll get a bad name, having a new young man every week,' Helen observed.

'But at least she's got some choice,' Dee observed wistfully. 'Not like being stuck with Charlie Whatsit down the road, or the man who comes round with the pies every week.'

'I don't want this family being talked about,' Helen said firmly. 'It isn't nice. Anyway, what about all those doctors you meet at the hospital?'

'They don't look at student nurses. We're the lowest of the low.'

'The patients, then. You wait, you'll meet a millionaire. He'll take one look at you and fall madly in love.'

They laughed together and Dee said, 'Mum, you've been reading those romantic novels again. That's just dreaming. Real life isn't like that—unless you're Sylvia, of course. I wish she'd hurry up and get here. I'm longing to see her latest.'

Sylvia worked in an elegant dress shop on the far side of London. As Christmas neared, business was booming and her hours were longer. Today she was arriving home late, along with her new young man.

Mark Sellon was a mechanic, newly out of work because his employer had lost all his money. Sylvia was bringing him home for Christmas in the hope that her father could offer him a job in the tiny garage he owned beside the house in Crimea Street. In that shabby corner of London, Joe Parsons counted as a prosperous man.

'Of course, he might simply be a good mechanic, and she's bringing him for Dad's sake,' Dee mused.

'Then why would she want us to invite him to stay the night? By the way, have you finished putting the spare bed into her room?'

'Yes, but—'

'You'll sleep there with Sylvia. And make sure you stay with her as much as possible. I don't want any hanky-panky in this house.'

'You mean—?'

'Yes, that's exactly what I mean, so you see that Sylvia behaves herself. Thank goodness I don't have to worry about you!'

Dee knew better than to answer this. To say that she yearned to be a 'bad girl', in theory if not in practice, would bring motherly wrath down about her head and she had some urgent dusting to do.

In this she was helped by Billy, the family dog, an enormous mongrel who tackled everything with gusto. His contribution to the cleaning was to follow Dee everywhere, pouncing on the dusters and shaking them.

'Let go,' she told him, trying to sound stern and not succeeding. 'Billy, I shall get cross with you.'

His glance said he'd heard that before and knew better than to believe it.

'Stop it, you idiot!' she said through laughter, managing to rescue a duster. His response was to seize another and run off.

'You haven't got time for play,' Helen said, appearing. 'They'll be here soon.'

'Yes, Mum.'

She applied herself to the work, finished it as soon as possible, then said, 'I'm taking Billy for a walk. He needs exercise or he won't behave himself.'

'All right, but don't be too long.'

She pulled on a thick coat and slipped out of the door, with Billy on a lead. It was a beautiful clear night, stars and moon shining down with a dazzling intensity that revealed her surroundings sharply.

'Shame there's no snow,' she mused. 'Never mind. Still, a little time before Christmas Day... All right Billy, *I'm coming.*'

Down the street he hauled her, across the road into another long street and down a narrow path that went along a string of back gardens. Voices greeted her as she went, for she had lived here all her life and knew the neighbours.

Now Billy was on his way back, taking her for a walk rather than the other way round. As they reached Crimea Street, she heard a sound in the distance, quickly growing louder and louder until it was deafening.

Then she saw a motorbike turning the corner, coming towards her, driven by someone in a helmet and goggles that obscured his head. In the sidecar was another person, also mysterious until it raised an arm to wave at her and Dee realised that it was Sylvia.

So the driver must be her young man. Dee stared in wonder. She'd sometimes seen motorbikes being repaired in her father's garage, but she knew nobody who actually owned one.

The bike stopped and the driver got off to help Sylvia out, then remove her helmet. She clung to him, wide-eyed.

'Oh, goodness!' she gasped. 'That was—that was—'

'Are you all right?' Dee asked.

Sylvia's response was to release her companion and throw her arms around Dee as if her legs were giving way beneath her, so that Dee had to support her.

She glanced at the young man. He was removing his goggles and the first part of him she saw was a smiling mouth—something she afterwards remembered all her life.

Then his whole face was revealed—handsome, lively, full of pleasure.

'Sorry if I was a bit noisy,' he said ruefully. 'When I'm going really fast the excitement tends to carry me away. I'm afraid I've offended your neighbours.'

The words sounded contrite but there was nothing contrite about him. He'd enjoyed himself to the full and was fizzing with delight. All around them curtains were being pulled back, shocked faces appearing at windows. He greeted them with a cheeky wave before turning back to Sylvia.

'I'm sorry,' he repeated. 'I didn't mean to scare you.'

'I never dreamed you'd go so fast,' Sylvia gasped. 'It was—oh, goodness!'

She took a deep breath and remembered her manners. 'Mark, this is my sister, Dee. Dee, this is Mark.'

Now Dee could look at him properly and her head swam. He was too good-looking to be true. It didn't happen outside the cinema. She held out her hand and from a distance heard him saying that Sylvia had told him all about her.

'Nothing bad, I hope,' she said mechanically and immediately cursed herself for talking nonsense. But it was as much as she could do to talk at all.

A moment ago she'd been content with life trundling along in the same old way. Now it was as though a thunderbolt had struck her.

'Let's get inside,' Sylvia said. 'It's freezing out here.'

Joe and Helen had come to the door to see what all the commotion was about. The sight of Mark wheeling his motorbike brought Joe hurrying down the path of the tiny front garden.

'That's yours?' he asked with a hint of awe.

'Yes. Is there somewhere I can put it?'

'In my garage next door. I'll show you the way.'

When the two men had vanished, Helen said, 'Well! So that's him! Noisy young fellow, isn't he?'

'He likes people to know he's there,' Sylvia said.

'Hmm! Not the retiring type, obviously.'

'Nobody could call Mark the retiring type,' Sylvia agreed, following her mother into the house.

In the better light Helen could see her daughter properly and was horrified.

'What are you wearing?' she demanded. 'What's that—thing in your hands?'

'I wear it on my head, and these are goggles to protect my eyes.'

'What do you want to go gadding around on that contraption, dressed like that for? To suit him?'

It was clear that Mark had got off on the wrong foot with Helen. With Joe, however, he had better luck. The motorbike had made an excellent impression and, as Dee watched them returning to the house, she could see that they were already in perfect accord.

'So now your dad's found someone to talk nuts and bolts with, he's happy,' Helen observed. 'I reckon that lad's got the job already.'

Then it happened. Mark threw back his head and roared with laughter, a rich, vibrant sound that streamed up to the heavens. It seemed to invade Dee through and through, filling her with helpless delight. All of life was in that sound; everything good and hopeful, all that was promising for the future. How could anything possibly go wrong with the world when a young man could laugh like that?

But then, mysteriously, she knew a flicker of alarm, as though a hidden danger was approaching her behind a smiling front. But it passed and she chided herself for being fanciful. Sylvia had found herself a pleasant young man. Surely all was well?

'Are you two coming in for your tea?' Helen called, and the two men obediently returned to the house.

Some instinct seemed to warn Mark that he was doing badly with Helen. He behaved charmingly, thanking her for allowing him to stay for Christmas.

'Any friend of Sylvia's is a friend of ours,' Helen said politely, and Dee might have imagined that she slightly emphasised 'friend'. 'Joe needs a good mechanic, so I hope things work out.'

'He *is* a good mechanic, Mum,' Sylvia said eagerly. 'The best.'

'Well, we'll see. It's almost teatime and I expect you're starving, Mr Sellon.'

'Please, call me Mark. And yes, I'm starving.'

'Come upstairs and unpack first,' Sylvia suggested. 'Where's he sleeping, Mum?'

'In Dee's room,' Helen said. 'She'll be in with you.'

'I thought Dee was going to sleep on the sofa down here,' Sylvia protested. 'That's what you said this morning.'

Helen dropped her voice to say, 'I've changed my mind. Now, get going and tea will be ready in a few minutes.'

At that moment Joe Parsons signalled for Mark to join

him in the sitting room. Sylvia went too and, when they were safely out of earshot, Helen said, 'If she thinks I'm letting her be alone in that room while he's here—well! That's all I can say.'

There was no need for her to say more. Her suspicions stood out brilliantly.

'You think he'd—you know—?'

'Not now, he won't,' Helen said with grim satisfaction.

'He's very good-looking, isn't he?' Dee ventured.

'Hmm. Handsome is as handsome does.'

'*Mum!* It's not his fault he's handsome.'

'Did I say it was? But they're the ones you have to watch, that's all. Now, go and lay the table.'

Over tea, Mark told them about himself. He was twenty-three and lived on the other side of London in a hostel for respectable young men. His father had died when he was six and he'd been reared by his mother alone.

'She had no family, and my father's family had disapproved of their marriage, so I don't think they helped her much. She died a couple of years ago.'

'So you've got nobody?' Helen asked with a touch of sympathy.

'Not really. I trained as a mechanic because my father was one. Luckily, I took to it and now I'm only happy with a spanner in my hand. I had a good job in a garage. At least I thought it was a good job, but the owner lost all his money, the garage was sold to someone who brought his own workforce in, and I was fired.'

'How did you get that motorbike?' Joe asked in a voice full of envy. 'Don't they cost a fortune?'

'Yes, they do,' Mark agreed, 'so I had to use rather unusual methods. It belonged to the son of the man buying the garage. He wanted to sell it because he was getting a new one. I couldn't afford even the second-hand price, so I bet him he couldn't beat me at cards.' The gleam in his eyes had a touch of charming wickedness. 'And he couldn't.'

'No,' Joe breathed in awe. 'You're a bit of a devil, aren't you?'

'I hope so,' Mark said, sounding comically shocked. 'What's the point otherwise?'

'Hmm!' Helen said disapprovingly.

'I didn't cheat, Mrs Parsons,' Mark assured her. 'I just—tempted him a bit further than he'd meant to go.'

'That's what the devil does,' Dee said triumphantly, and was rewarded with his blazing grin that seemed to fill the room.

Helen frowned, disapproving. Sylvia looked as though she was struggling to keep up.

Afterwards, the men retired to the garage while the girls helped their mother in the kitchen.

'If you ask me, he's a bad lad,' Helen said.

'Why, Mum, whatever do you mean?' Sylvia asked.

'I mean he's the sort who goes around telling the world he's there all the time, like he did tonight. You watch out, my girl. Don't you go getting yourself into trouble.'

'Mum,' Dee protested, 'that's not fair. Sylvia's a good girl.'

Sylvia said nothing.

'Maybe she is, maybe she isn't,' Helen said. 'I'm taking no chances, not with him looking like he came off a cinema screen.'

'He is handsome, isn't he?' Sylvia said eagerly.

'Yes, he is—too handsome for his good or yours. That's why Dee's going to be with you in your room tonight. I don't want any of your nonsense.'

'Why, Mum, I don't know what you mean,' Sylvia said, earnestly enough to fool anyone who didn't know her.

'You know exactly what I mean, young lady. You behave yourself.'

Behind her mother's back, Sylvia made a face, but gave up arguing. Nobody won against Helen and they all knew it. When it was time to go to bed, she drew Mark aside in the hall, signalling for Deirdre to go on ahead.

Dee hesitated, mindful of her mother's orders to keep a strict eye on them. But Helen herself was only a few feet away in the kitchen and surely one little goodnight kiss couldn't do any harm?

'Go on,' Sylvia said urgently, jerking her head to the stairs and at last Dee obeyed, trying to sort out her thoughts.

There was another reason for her reluctance to leave them alone; one she couldn't admit to herself because she didn't fully understand it. It made no sense. After all, Mark was Sylvia's property.

Wasn't he?

Upstairs, she undressed slowly, trying not to let her mind dwell on the two lovers enjoying a tender embrace. In bed, she read for a little while, waiting for Sylvia to appear, but nothing happened.

When she could stand it no longer, she crept out into the hall and listened to the soft sounds coming from the bottom of the stairs, trying to picture what they would be doing.

Dee was a child of her time. At seventeen, she'd never known a passionate kiss, or even a non-passionate one. Nor had she seen one, unless you included Robert Taylor kissing Greta Garbo in the film of *Camille*. Apart from that, her knowledge of men and women was gleaned from her studies as a nurse, technical information that told her nothing of the passionate reality. About that she was as ignorant and innocent as any other respectable girl.

But tonight something had changed, making her aware of feelings and sensations that had existed beyond her consciousness. Mark had smiled at her, and he'd sat opposite her at the table, where she could see his face all the time. And nothing was the same. Now she was all avid curiosity to explore, but how could she? Mark was off-limits, and no other man existed.

From downstairs came a soft gasp followed by smothered laughter and a murmuring sound, telling of pleasure enjoyed to the full. Dee closed her eyes, her heart pounding, her breath coming in long gasps. She wanted—what? She couldn't tell. She only knew that she yearned for something above and beyond anything she'd known before.

From the kitchen came the sound of Helen banging pots and pans about, letting them know she was still there and they'd better stop what they were doing. Next moment Dee heard footsteps approaching and hurriedly retreated into the bedroom. By the time Sylvia came in, she was huddled down under the covers.

'Hello,' she murmured in a carefully sleepy voice. 'Have you said your goodnights?'

'Yes, thank you.' Sylvia sounded pleased with herself. 'What do you think of him?'

'He's all right. That motorbike is amazing, though.'

'Oh, the bike!' Sylvia said dismissively.

'I thought you liked it. It must be wonderful to ride with him.'

'Well, it isn't. I thought I was going to die. Of course I didn't tell him, he's so proud of it. You should hear him talk! He's just as bad about cars.'

'You don't sound as though you have much in common,' Dee observed casually.

'You wait until I get to work on him. He'll do anything for me. I'll have him just the way I want in no time.'

Dee didn't answer this, but something told her Sylvia was wrong. Beneath Mark's easy-going charm, she suspected a stubborn will to have his own way.

And yet, how could she tell? she wondered. What did she know of him, except that he was more good-looking than any man had the right to be, that he could make her laugh, and that his mind had a link with her own. At the table they had shared the 'devil' joke, which Sylvia hadn't understood, and that had been the sweetest moment.

More than sixty years later, it still lived in her mind.

I didn't know what had happened to me that night. I thought you were wonderful, but I had no idea of falling in love with you because I didn't know what love was. I only knew I was happy because you were going to stay with us for a few days. You dazzled me, and I didn't think there could be anything better in the world. That's how naive I was.

What is it, darling—are you restless? That's it, curl up against me and go back to sleep. That noise downstairs is them clearing up after the party. I suppose I ought to have offered to help, but I just wanted to be with you and think of all the things that have happened to us.

So many things—so many tears, so much laughter. So long ago, and yet not really a long time at all. I woke up next morning feeling so happy...

She had to be up very early to start work at the hospital and the day was still dark as she left the house, yet the world was mysteriously flooded with light.

At the bottom of the street was a bus stop, from which she could just see the front of the house, and the room that was normally hers. While waiting for the bus, she watched the window and saw it raised and Mark's head come out. He noticed her and waved. She waved back, feeling that the day had had a perfect start.

When she returned in the late afternoon, she saw Sylvia walking Billy in the street.

'I had to get out of the house,' she said crossly. 'Mark's spent the day in the garage with Dad and now neither of them can talk about anything but engines. Honestly! You'd think I didn't exist!'

'I suppose he has to think about engines some of the time,' Dee said mildly.

'Yes, but not when I'm there.'

'He's probably trying to impress Dad so that he can take this job and be near you.'

'Yes, that must be it,' Sylvia said, slightly mollified. 'But I'm going to find a way to get him out of the house tonight and have him all to myself.'

They had reached home by now. There was no sign of Mark, and Sylvia went looking for him. When she'd gone, he appeared so promptly that Dee was sure he'd been avoiding her.

'Is she still annoyed with me?' he whispered.

Mischievously, Dee nodded. 'You've been talking about engines all day, and that's a terrible crime.'

'Do all women find it boring?' he asked.

'Mostly, I suppose.'

'What about you? Doesn't a hospital need machines of some sort?'

'Yes, we do, and I'm learning how to work them, but I suppose it's more interesting if you're doing things yourself rather than just hearing about them.'

He pulled a face full of good-natured resignation, spreading his hands as if to say—what was he supposed to do?

'I keep getting it wrong,' he sighed. 'Sooner or later I always annoy women.'

She was about to tell him not to talk nonsense when she connected with the teasing look in his eye and in the same moment she was invaded by a sweet warmth that shook her to the soul.

'I can believe that,' she said in a voice that trembled slightly. 'In fact, I can't imagine how any woman puts up with you.'

'Neither can I,' he chuckled.

'Mark, are you there?'

Sylvia's voice brought them both back to reality. Dee

thought she spotted a brief look of exasperation on his face, but it vanished at the sight of her, smiling again and so lovely that Dee knew she herself was forgotten.

Supper was a cheerful meal. Joe was warm in his praise of Mark's abilities. The job offer was confirmed, and it was understood that he would stay with them until after Christmas, when he could start looking for a place of his own.

Afterwards, Sylvia announced that she and Mark were going to the cinema. 'There's that new film at the Odeon, *A Christmas Carol*. Mark's longing to see it.'

'Why, what a coincidence!' Helen exclaimed. 'Dee's been saying how much she wants to see it. You can all go together.'

'Mum, I can go another time,' Dee muttered, appalled by this blatant manipulation.

'Nonsense, you go now. You've been working hard. Clear off, the three of you. Have a good time.'

Sylvia seethed at having a chaperone forced on her. Dee was ready to sink into the ground at the suspicion of what Mark must be thinking. But when she dared to meet his eyes, she found them alive with fun.

Of course, she thought. He must have been in this situation a thousand times. The world was full of mothers trying to shield their daughters from his looks and charm.

She felt better. And the thought of an evening in his company was blissful. It was Sylvia who sulked.

CHAPTER THREE

IF MARK was annoyed at Dee playing gooseberry, he didn't show it. At the cinema he paid for her seat, placed her so that he was sitting between them and bought her an ice cream. When the lights went down, she sensed that he slipped his arm round the back of Sylvia's seat and turned his head in her direction.

After a while a woman in the row behind tapped him on the shoulder.

'Do you mind not leaning so close to your girlfriend?' she hissed indignantly. 'You're blocking my view.'

He apologised, and after that he behaved like a perfect gentleman.

When they left the cinema the lovers were in dreamily happy moods, but Dee was disgruntled.

'It was awful,' she complained. 'Not a bit like the book.'

'It's a film,' he objected mildly.

'But the book is by Charles Dickens,' she said, as though that settled the matter. 'And they changed things. The Ghost of Christmas Past was played by a girl, they cut out Scrooge's fiancée and—oh, lots of things.'

'Did they?' he asked blankly. 'I didn't notice. Does it matter?'

'Of course it matters,' she said urgently. 'Things should be done right.'

'Never mind her,' Sylvia said, peevish at having the romantic atmosphere dispelled. 'She's always finding fault.'

Mark grinned, his good temper unruffled. 'Hey, you're a real stickler, aren't you?' he challenged Dee.

'What's wrong with that?' she demanded.

'Nothing, nothing,' he said with comic haste. 'Just remind me not to get on your wrong side.'

Still clowning, he edged away from her, but added, 'I'm only joking.'

'Well, you shouldn't be,' Sylvia put in. 'People do get scared of Dee because she's always so grim and practical.'

'I'm not grim,' Dee said, trying to keep the hurt out of her voice, but failing.

Perhaps Mark heard it because he said quickly, 'Of course you're not. You just like to be precise and correct. Good for you. A nurse needs to be like that. Who'd want to be nursed by someone who was all waffly and emotional? I'll bet when you were at school, your best subjects were maths and science.'

'They were,' she said, warmed by his understanding.

'There you are, then. You've got what my father used to call a masculine mind.'

The warmth faded. He considered her precise, correct and unemotional, practically a man. And she was supposed to be flattered. But then, she thought sadly, he had no idea that his words hurt her. Nor did he care. He'd merely been spreading his charm around to avoid an argument. She pulled herself together and answered him lightly.

'You don't have to be a man to appreciate scientific advances. That film we saw tonight was in black and white, but one day they'll all be in colour.'

'Oh, come on!' Sylvia exclaimed cynically.

'No, she's right,' Mark said. 'They're making a film of *Gone with the Wind* right now, and I've heard that's in colour.'

'Yes, important films, with big stars,' Sylvia agreed. 'But

they'll never make ordinary films like that. It's too difficult and expensive. There are limits.'

'No, there aren't!' Dee said at once. 'There are no limits. Not just in films but in anything. In life. No limits.'

'You're just a little girl,' Sylvia said dismissively. 'You don't know what you're talking about.'

'Yes, she does,' Mark said. 'She's right about that. You can't live life to the full if you set limits on everything.'

From Sylvia's expression, it was clear that she didn't know what he was talking about and was simply exasperated with the pair of them. Mark slipped his arm comfortably about her, but at the same time he gave Dee a wink that was…that was…she struggled for the right word.

Conspiratorial, that was it; a look that said they shared a secret knowledge that Sylvia couldn't understand.

Her heart soared again and she began to make plans for when they got home. She would lure him into a discussion about great matters—knowledge, life, no limits, and the mental bond they shared would grow firmer.

But, once inside, he yawned and said he was tired, which Dee didn't believe for a moment. There was no high-flown discussion, only a time of lying in the darkness knowing that Mark and Sylvia were downstairs, sharing a passionate goodnight. Mental bonds were all very well, but they couldn't compete with Sylvia's curves or the come-hither look in her eye. It was a painful lesson in reality.

Christmas was getting closer. Mark started work in the garage, Sylvia was deluged with customers in the dress shop, but the one with the longest hours was Dee. Coming home late from the hospital one night, she fell asleep on the bus and woke to find Mark shaking her.

'When the bus came I could see you inside, fast asleep. You'd have been carried on, so we had to jump on and rouse you.'

'We?' she asked sleepily, looking around.

Then she realised that Billy was there, too.

'We went for a walk,' Mark explained. 'I saw the bus in the distance and I knew you were due home soon, so we waited at the stop.'

'What's that creature doing 'ere?' the conductor growled. 'He's dangerous.'

'He's not dangerous and we're just getting off,' Mark said, rising and pulling the cord.

'Not until you've paid your fare.'

Then things became comical because Mark had come out without money, and Dee had to pay for him. They descended onto the pavement, hysterical with mirth.

'I guess I'm not cut out to be a knight in shining armour, rescuing a damsel in distress,' he said. 'I'd leave the sword behind and have to borrow hers.'

'It's not your fault,' she protested. 'You didn't know you were going to need money when you came out. I expect even Sir Lancelot was short of four pence sometimes.'

'Which one was he?'

'The most famous one who sat at the Round Table. He flirted with King Arthur's wife Guinevere, and was banished in disgrace.'

'That sounds like me. Did he ever borrow money from Guinevere?'

'The legend doesn't say.'

'I expect he did. He probably took her to a café one evening and she had to pay for it.' He indicated a little café just up ahead. 'That would really annoy her, even if he promised to pay her back afterwards.'

'Very bad.' She nodded solemnly. 'She probably slammed his helmet down on his head. But she bought him a cup of tea afterwards.'

'But how could he drink it if his helmet was slammed down?' Mark wanted to know. 'She slipped up there.'

'I suppose he could raise it,' she mused. 'Unless, of course, it jammed.'

'Bound to, I should think.'

Exchanging ridiculous gobbledegook, they wandered on to the café. At the entrance he said, 'Maybe they won't let Billy in. I should have thought of that.'

'Don't worry. The owner is a friend of Dad's and he likes Billy.'

By lucky chance, Frank, the owner, was standing near the door. He ushered them in and fetched Billy a bowl of water before bringing them tea and buns.

'You won't tell anyone, will you?' Mark begged. 'My reputation would never recover.'

'What, that you drink something as unmanly as tea with two sugars? Of course not. Nothing less than a pint of beer for you.'

'That's not what I meant and you know it. If people found out that I had to let you pay for this, my reputation would never recover.'

'True,' she said in a considering voice. 'Perhaps I won't tell anyone just yet. I'll keep it in reserve to blackmail you with. I'll enjoy that.'

He grinned. 'That's all right, then.'

'Meaning that you think I wouldn't?'

'No, I'm sure you would. I've sized you up as a very tough character and I'm treading carefully. You scare me.'

'Oh, stop talking nonsense!' she chuckled, but in truth she didn't want him to stop. She wanted to sit here talking nonsense with him for ever.

'Yes, ma'am, no, ma'am, anything you say, ma'am. Shall I go down on one knee?'

'I'll chuck this tea over you in a minute.'

'That would be a waste after what you paid for it.'

That sent them both off in more gales of mirth, while Billy

glanced from one to the other with a look that said there was no understanding humans.

'Sylvia tells me you're on duty over Christmas,' he observed.

'Someone has to be. People still get sick.'

'But surely you're still a student?'

'Yes, but there are some things I can do. A dogsbody is always needed.'

He regarded her with admiration. 'Giving up Christmas to fetch and carry. Good for you. I couldn't do it. I like to enjoy myself, but I suppose you get your kicks out of doing good works.'

She made a face. 'Don't make me sound like some dreary embodiment of virtue. I don't want to work over Christmas either, but it's the job I've chosen. The dull bits are worth it for the wonderful bits. Good works, my foot!'

'I didn't mean to offend you.'

'Don't you put up with the dull bits of engines for the sake of the others?'

'There aren't any dull bits in my job. If there were, I wouldn't do it.'

'But life has dull bits. You can't opt out of them.'

'I can try. Live for the moment. Tomorrow may never come.'

'Do you know,' she said, suddenly struck, 'I hear a lot of people talking like that in the hospital. They're convinced there's going to be a war and they must make the most of what time they have now.'

'Very wise of them.'

'Does that mean you think there's going to be a war?' she asked seriously. 'People talk about it but—I just can't believe it.'

'Of course. Hasn't our Prime Minister assured us that Hitler is a man he can trust?'

He was referring to Neville Chamberlain who, following

Hitler's aggressive behaviour in Europe, had gone to meet him in September and returned, apparently reassured. Two weeks later he'd attended a conference with Hitler and signed an agreement accepting the annexation of the Sudetenland. On his return to England, he'd given a speech at the airport promising 'peace for our time'.

'It sounds all right,' Dee said, 'and yet—'

'And yet the government is already issuing gas masks and sending children away to the country for their own safety,' Mark continued. 'Does that look like peace in our time? Of course not. Winston Churchill was right.'

'Who's he?'

'An MP. He's always been a rebel voice and just now he's a bit of an outsider, but he talks a lot of sense. He said you can't make yourself safe by throwing a small country to the wolves. And he's right. We'll know in a few months.'

Until now, Dee had seen mainly Mark's flippant side. Hearing him talk in this serious way was almost like listening to a different man, but the very strangeness made her alert. She shivered. In a little while the skies might darken.

'Will you be drafted into the army?' she asked.

'I won't wait for that. I'll join the Air Force. I've always wanted to fly a plane and this could be my chance.' His eyes gleamed as though for a moment he'd forgotten everything but the hope of adventure.

'Yes, this could be your chance to get killed or horribly injured,' she said crossly.

He shrugged. 'That's the risk you take. The best fun always involves a risk.'

'Fun?' she said, aghast. 'The most terrible danger and you call it fun?'

'The more danger, the more fun,' he said irrepressibly.

'Surely there's more to life than fun?'

'Is there?' he asked innocently. 'What?'

She didn't try to answer. After all, he was right. There was no point in being gloomy. Enjoy the moment, especially if the moment could be spent like this, alone with him, enjoying all his attention, feeling their minds meet.

She guessed that he didn't share such understanding with Sylvia. Her attraction for him was something very different, nothing to do with minds or understanding. Tonight was special because it was hers, all hers.

'I don't suppose it will happen at all,' he said in a reassuring tone.

'That's not what you really think, is it?' she said. 'You're just trying to make the silly little girl stop worrying.'

'I don't think of you as a silly little girl,' he said seriously. 'How can you be? You're a nurse. People depend on you for their lives.'

'Then heaven help them!' she said wryly. 'Mr Royce says it'll be a long time before he'll put anyone's life in my hands because I'd only drop it.'

'Who's Mr Royce?'

'He's a surgeon at the hospital. He's given the students a couple of lectures. I asked him a question once. I thought it was quite clever, but as soon as the words were out I knew it was idiotic. He just looked at me wryly and shook his head. Afterwards, he told me to go and have a cup of tea. He said I looked as if I needed it. And I really did need it.'

'He didn't offer to buy it for you?'

'Goodness, no!' she said, shocked. 'He's the Great Man of the hospital. Students are beneath his notice, unless he's telling them how they did something wrong.'

'Does he tell you that often?'

'All the time. So does Matron, and the ward sisters. In fact, I'm just useless. I'll fail all my exams and probably have to go into the forces.' An imp of mischief made her add, 'Perhaps they'll let me join the Air Force. They say women will be allowed in very soon. I'll fly about the heavens and you can be my mechanic on the ground.' She giggled at the thought.

Mark listened with a sardonic expression. 'Be very careful what you say,' he warned. 'They may let women in the Air Force, but they will *not* let them fly, not if they have any sense. *You* will be *my* mechanic.'

'Aren't you afraid that I'll sabotage your engine?' she teased.

He assumed a lofty tone. 'On second thoughts, I think you should stay quietly in the kitchen, which is where a woman belongs. I don't know why we ever gave you the vote. All right, all right, don't eat me!'

He edged away, holding up his arms in a theatrical parody of self-defence.

'I've a good mind to set Billy on you,' she laughed.

'He wouldn't do it,' Mark observed. 'We're the best of friends.'

As if to confirm it, Billy put his nose on Mark's knee, gazing up at him worshipfully. Mark scratched his ears, returning a look that was almost as loving.

Dee was fascinated by this new side of him. His normal persona—cool, collected and humorous—had relaxed into the kind of daft adoration that dogs seemed able to inspire. She watched them for a while, smiling, until he looked up and coloured self-consciously.

'I always wanted a dog,' he said, 'but my mother wouldn't allow it. I tend to get rather stupid about other people's.'

'I don't think you're stupid because you like Billy,' she said. 'I'd think you were stupid if you didn't. When I set my heart on a dog my parents weren't keen either, but I pestered and pestered until they gave me Billy for my seventh birthday.'

'Pestering my mother would only have brought me a clip round the ear,' he said wryly. 'She didn't like what she called "insolence".'

'She sounds terrible.'

'No, she just had a very hard life. She was devastated after my father left.'

'I thought you said he died.'

'He did, eventually, but he deserted her first. Keep that to yourself, I don't tell everyone.'

She nodded, understanding the message that he hadn't told Sylvia.

'Unfortunately for us both,' he went on, 'I look very much like my father, and it didn't help.'

'She blamed you for that?' Dee demanded, aghast.

'It wasn't her fault,' Mark said quickly. 'She couldn't cope with her feelings, she didn't know what to do with me.'

'How old were you when your father left?'

'Six, and ten when he died.'

'No brothers or sisters?'

'No, I wish I had. It would have helped if there had been more of us. Or one of you,' he added, looking down at Billy. 'You'd have been a good friend.'

'She should have let you have a dog,' Dee said. 'You'd have been easier for her to cope with.'

'I got one once,' he said with a wry smile of recollection. 'It was a stray and quite small, so I took him home and hid him. I managed to keep him a secret for two days before my mother found out.'

'What did she do?' Dee asked, although she was afraid to hear.

'I came home from school one day and he'd vanished. I went through every room looking for him, but he wasn't there. She said he must have run away, but I found out afterwards that she'd thrown him out in the rain.'

'Did she give you a clip round the ear?'

'Mmm! But I was defiant. I went looking for him.'

'Did you ever find him?'

'Yes, I found his body in a pile of rubbish on the street. From the look of him, he'd starved to death.'

'Did you tell your mother?'

Mark shook his head.

She hesitated a moment before asking, 'Did she hit you often?'

'Now and then. When things got on top of her, she'd lash out. I learned to keep out of her way and stay quiet.'

Suddenly he raised his head. 'Hey, what is this? Why are we being so gloomy? It's way in the past, all over.'

She'd liked him before, but now she liked him even more for this brief glimpse into the unhappy childhood that must have made him as he was today. She guessed that it wasn't over, whatever he said.

'Nobody realised Billy was going to grow so enormous,' she said. 'He's really too big for that little house so I take him for walks whenever I can. Thank you for bringing him out.'

'He's marvellous company.' Frowning, he added, 'He must be about eleven, quite old.'

'Yes, I know I won't have him much longer so I make the most of every day. I can't bear to think of life without him.'

'I can imagine. He's exactly the dog I'd have liked.' Mark turned his attention back to Billy. 'D'you hear that? You've got a fan club right here.'

'I'm jealous,' Dee said, regarding Billy, who was receiving Mark's caresses with every sign of bliss. 'Normally he's only like that with me.'

'I guess he knows a willing slave when he sees one. Hey, the owner's trying to attract our attention. I think he wants to close.'

They took the journey home at a gentle stroll, enjoying the pleasant evening, which was mild for winter, with a bright sky. Once Mark stopped and gazed upwards, prompting her to say, 'Are you thinking of how soon you can be up there?'

'If there's a war. There might not be.'

'Then you'd have to forget planes and enjoy motorbikes. It must be thrilling to go at that speed.'

'I'll take you some time. Sylvia didn't like it, but I think you would.'

'Mmm, yes, *please!*'

He laughed and put a casual arm about her shoulders. 'You know, it's funny,' he mused. 'I've only known you a short time—but that's really all you need, isn't it?'

'Is it?' she asked breathlessly.

'Yes. I already feel that you're my best friend. I think I knew from the start, when we understood each other at once. Normally, a man wouldn't want a woman to understand him too well, but in you I like it. It's almost as though you're my sister. You don't mind my saying that, do you?'

'Not at all,' she said brightly. 'I've always wanted a brother.'

'Really? What a coincidence. I've often thought it would be nice to have a sister, preferably a younger one.'

'Yes, so that she could help you out of trouble without complaining, and let you get away with murder,' Dee said tartly.

He laughed. 'You see? You understand my requirements instinctively. What a fantastic sister to have!'

And she really *would* be his sister when he married Sylvia. With a sinking heart, she realised that he was preparing her for the announcement of the marriage.

Sylvia was waiting for them on the front step. 'Where have you been?' she demanded. 'You said you were taking Billy for a walk and you just vanished.'

He explained about rescuing Dee from the bus. 'So naturally I had to take her for a cup of tea.'

'That's right, I was dying for one,' Dee said. 'But Sir Lancelot rescued me.'

'Who?' Sylvia asked.

'Never mind,' Mark said, hastily drawing her aside.

Dee took Billy into the kitchen and released him from his lead while she explained to Helen.

'I hope that doesn't mean you don't want your tea,' her mother said practically. 'It'll be on the table in a minute.'

'I'm starving.'

On her way through the hall she was waylaid by Mark, hastily thrusting some money into her hand.

'That's too much,' she said, examining it.

'Give me the change later,' he muttered. 'Just don't tell—*Sylvia!*'

'What's going on?' Sylvia demanded, seeming to appear out of nowhere. 'Why are you giving Dee money?'

Quick as a flash, Dee replied, 'He's not giving it to me, he's lending it to me. I really try to manage on what I earn but I'm a bit short this week, so Mark's helping me out. Don't tell Mum, will you?'

'Of course not, but why didn't you ask me? I've helped you out before.'

'I know, and I didn't feel I could ask you again, and Mark's been *so* chivalrous.'

Somewhere in the atmosphere she was aware of Mark, torn in two directions; half of him grateful for her quick-witted rescue, the other half fighting to keep a straight face.

Sylvia remained oblivious to the undercurrents. 'You mustn't borrow money from Mark,' she said. 'It isn't proper. I'll lend you what you need. Now, give him that money back.'

'Yes, Sylvia,' she said meekly, handing the cash over but unable to meet Mark's eyes.

Nor could he meet hers. And somehow that made the secret all the sweeter.

It seems so trivial, looking back, but your masculine pride was involved, which made it important. I still laugh when I remember how horrified you were, and how we had to sneak a meeting later so that you could give me the money again. How grateful you were to me for putting Sylvia off the scent, and how happy I was!

Christmas was wonderful, just because you were there.

You gave us all presents, even Billy. He was overjoyed with that noisy toy you bought him and drove us all crazy with it, bless him! You gave Sylvia a pretty necklace, and me a purse saying it was 'to keep my money safe', putting your fingers over your lips. It meant the world to me that we shared a secret, even if you did spoil it a bit by saying, 'What a sister I have!'

That wasn't what I wanted to hear, but she could always take you away from me. She was the one you kissed under the mistletoe, while I looked away, then looked back. Seeing you like that hurt terribly, but I couldn't turn away again.

And then it was New Year's Eve, and that was when I discovered things I hadn't suspected before, things I didn't understand...

CHAPTER FOUR

AS THE hands of the clock crept towards twelve on New Year's Eve, doors were flung open and the inhabitants of Crimea Street poured out into the open, carolling their pleasure up into the night sky.

'Goodbye, 'thirty-eight. Goodbye and good riddance!'
'Hello, 'thirty-nine. This is the year I'll get rich.'

'Listen to them,' Joe murmured. 'So sure it's all going to get better, when in fact—'

'Don't be so gloomy,' his wife advised him. 'There probably isn't going to be a war.'

'They said that just before the last one,' Joe said. 'Some of them were still saying it the day before I was drafted into the army.' He gazed sadly at the rapidly growing crowd, singing and dancing. 'They never think to wonder what the next New Year will be like,' he murmured.

'But we know what the next one will be like,' Dee said wryly. 'Mark and Sylvia will be married, and she'll probably be pregnant.'

'The way they're carrying on, it'll happen the other way round,' Helen observed grimly. 'Look at them. I didn't bring my girls up to act like that.'

Dee smothered a grin. Between her parents' wedding anniversary and Sylvia's birthday was a mere three months, but all the family pretended not to notice.

'*You* wouldn't do a thing like that, would you, Mum?' she asked demurely.

'That's enough from you, my girl. Any more of your cheek and I'll—'

'What, Mum?'

'And don't you think you can snigger and get away with it. Just you be careful.'

'Leave it,' Joe said easily. 'They're young, like we were once.'

He slipped his arm around his wife's shoulders. As she turned her head they exchanged smiles, and suddenly the staid middle-aged couple blurred and there was a faint echo of the young lovers whose passion had overcome them. Dee slipped quickly away.

She tried not to go in the direction of Mark and Sylvia, but she couldn't resist a quick look. As she'd feared, they were locked in each other's arms, oblivious to everyone around them, trusting the night and the excitement to conceal them.

How tightly he was holding her. How passionate his caresses, how tender his kiss. How Dee's heart yearned at the sight of her sister enjoying so much happiness in the arms of this wonderful young man.

She turned away, giving herself a firm lecture. She had no right to be jealous. He belonged to Sylvia. She would get over him and find someone who was right for herself.

But deep inside was the fear that this might never happen, that he was the one and only and she'd met him too late. He would be her brother-in-law, lost to her for ever, and she would become a mean, miserable old maid.

This prospect was so terrible that she forced a smile to her face and began to jump up and down, as if dancing.

'Come on, Dee,' yelled a voice in her ear. Arms went about her, sweeping her round and round.

It was Tom, who lived three doors down. He was gormless but well-meaning and she'd known him all her life, so she willingly danced with him and managed not to look at Mark and Sylvia for a while.

They danced and danced while someone played the accordion and fireworks flared. Then the cry went up, *'It's nearly midnight!'*

The cheers were deafening. *It's almost nineteen thirty-nine. Yippee!*

Laughing, Dee made the rounds of her friends and neighbours, hugging them, wishing them joy. Now she was looking out for Mark and Sylvia again, because surely she could sneak a New Year hug with him. Just sisterly, she promised herself.

In the distance she saw Sylvia and hurried towards her, but then she checked herself, unable to believe what she'd seen.

Her sister was in a man's arms, but the man wasn't Mark.

Nonsense, it *must* be Mark! Who else could it be?

But it wasn't Mark. It was the new milkman.

Never mind, she tried to reassure herself. Just a neighbourly embrace; nothing more.

But it was far more. Sylvia's mouth was locked on the young man's as firmly as it had been locked on Mark's just a few minutes ago.

Firecrackers exploded all around her. The sky was brilliant, but inside her there was darkness. Sylvia had betrayed Mark, had turned from his arms to another man. *How could she?*

Turning, she could see Mark, looking around him as though trying to find Sylvia. She hastened over to him, calling his name and forcing him to turn so that he couldn't see into the shadows, and the heartbreak that awaited him there.

'Dee!' he called cheerfully. 'Come here!'

Before she knew it, he seized her by the waist, raised her high above his head, holding her as easily as if she weighed nothing, then lowered her to deliver a smacking kiss. It was the act of a friend, not a lover. Yet her heart leapt at the feel of his mouth against hers. If only it would last! If only it could be for real!

But it was over. She knew a sad feeling of irony as her feet touched the ground. This was where she belonged. Not up in the air.

'Have you seen Sylvia?' he asked.

'I...no, I...thought she'd be with you.'

'She was, but someone grabbed her and danced her away.'

'And you're not jealous?'

'Because she dances with another fellow? I'm not that pathetic.'

His grin was full of cheeky self-confidence, saying that he had nothing to fear. It plainly never occurred to him that Sylvia might have crossed the line.

Only later did Dee realise that she could have seized the chance to reveal Sylvia's treachery to Mark and break them up, perhaps claim him for herself. At the time, all she could think was that he must be protected from hurt.

'Come on, let's dance,' he said, opening his arms.

It was bliss to dance with him, feeling his arms about her, knowing that the other girls envied her. News of his attractions had gone around the neighbourhood like lightning and everyone wanted to see him. Having seen him, they wanted to stay and see some more, and then to dance with him.

One or two of them tried to break in, claiming to believe that this was an 'excuse me' dance. Dee suppressed the inclination to do murder, swung away to another partner, but then reclaimed Mark as soon as possible.

'You're putting me in danger,' he joked breathlessly as they bounded around together. 'There are at least three men who thought you should turn to them, but you came to me. I'm flattered.'

'Don't be. I'm just keeping Sylvia's property safe for her. I'm a very good sister.'

'Her sister or mine?'

A mysterious instinct to confront the thing she dreaded made her say, 'It's going to be the same thing soon, isn't it?'

His face darkened. 'Who can tell? Where is she?'

'Why don't you go and find her?'

His lips twisted wryly, and she understood the message. Mark Sellon did not search yearningly for a woman, or beg for her attention. He let them beg him.

'You're the only one she cares about,' Dee urged. 'She's probably just trying to make you jealous.'

'Then she's failing,' he said lightly. 'Let's go.'

He swung her higher in the air but, before he could do more, they both saw Sylvia on the edge of the crowd. She was with a different young man, struggling with him, although not seriously, and laughing all the while. She laughed even louder when he managed to plant a kiss on her mouth.

Suddenly Dee found herself alone. There was a yell from the young man as he was hauled away and dumped on the pavement, and a shriek of excitement from Sylvia as Mark hurried her unceremoniously down a side street and into the darkness. The fascinated onlookers could just make out raised voices, which stopped very suddenly.

'No prizes for guessing what's happening now,' someone said to a general laugh.

But then they all fell silent as the church clock began to strike midnight, looking up into the sky as though they could read there the tale of the coming year.

He'll marry her, Dee thought forlornly, *and I'll have to move away so that I don't see him so much. Perhaps I could move into the Nurses' Home.*

'Hey, Dee!' Helen and Joe were waving, beckoning for her to join them as the clock neared twelve.

'Where's Sylvia?' Helen demanded. 'Ah, yes, I can see her.'

There she was, drifting slowly back along the street, arms

around Mark, her head resting on his shoulder, gazing up at him with a look of adoration; a look he returned in full. As the clock reached the final 'bong' he pulled her into a tight embrace, crushing her mouth with his own as the crowd erupted around them.

'It's nineteen thirty-nine!'

'Happy New Year!'

'Happy New Year, everybody! Happy—happy—happy—'

Mark and Sylvia heard none of it. At one with each other, they had banished the world. Nothing and nobody else existed.

'Including me,' Dee whispered softly. 'Happy New Year.'

Two days later, Mark moved out to a local bed and breakfast, and after that Dee saw less of him. They would sometimes pass as she was leaving for work and he was just arriving at the garage, but she was usually home too late to catch him. Once a week Sylvia would bring him to supper. Other nights she would go out and return late. Watching jealously, Dee saw that sometimes she came home smiling, and sometimes she seemed grumpy, but she always denied that there had been any quarrel.

Dee constantly braced herself for news of the engagement, but it never came. As the weeks passed, her nerves became more strained until it would almost have been a relief to know that he'd finally proposed to Sylvia, even set the date. If only it would happen soon, before she fell totally in love with him and it was too late.

And all the time she knew she was fooling herself. The spark of love had ignited in her the night they'd met, but she'd been too inexperienced to know it. Over the next few days it had flared and grown stronger. Now it was already too late. It had always been too late. It had been too late from the first moment.

Day after day, she waited for the axe to fall but, mysteriously, it never did.

There wasn't always time to worry about her own life. As the early months of 1939 passed, the news from Europe grew more ominous and war more likely. Hitler continued to invade weaker countries, annexing them in defiance of the Munich Agreement that he'd signed with Neville Chamberlain the previous September, until even Chamberlain announced that negotiations with him were impossible.

'Mark can't talk about anything else,' Sylvia said sulkily. 'He's set his heart on the Air Force, and he just takes it for granted that I'll stick around.'

'But of course,' Dee said, shocked. 'You couldn't leave him when he was doing his duty to his country.'

'To him it's fun, not duty. I can't even get his attention long enough to make him jealous.'

'Is that what you've been trying to do?' Dee asked curiously.

'Just a little. It worked at New Year but—oh, I don't know. I have to make him realise that I'm here and he's got to notice me.'

'Don't do anything stupid,' Dee warned.

Sylvia's response was a wry look that she didn't understand until later.

Tom, the young man from three doors down who'd danced with Dee on New Year's Eve, began to invite her out. Without encouraging him too much, she agreed to the odd trip to the cinema because she was blowed if she was going to spend her time pining for Mark Sellon, thank you very much!

Tom wasn't brainy, but he had a cheeky humour that appealed to her. Laughing with him wasn't the same as laughing with Mark. There was none of the edgy excitement that made it so much more than humour. But Tom could tell a joke well, and they were chuckling together the night they arrived at her home to find Mark there, looking troubled.

'Is something the matter?' Dee asked quickly.

'No, I'm just waiting for Sylvia. She's a bit late tonight.'

'I thought she was meeting you in town,' Dee said, frowning.

'Did she say that?' Mark said easily. 'I must have got it wrong. Sorry to trouble you.' He was out of the door before they could reply.

'Your sister's got them all running around after her,' Tom said admiringly.

'Funny,' Dee mused. 'I'm sure she said she wasn't coming home early. Oh, well.'

Looking back, it was easy to see this as the first ominous sign. The second came later that night when Sylvia returned, beaming and cheerful, and seemed delighted to know Mark had been looking for her.

'Was he very upset?'

'He certainly wasn't happy. Do you *want* him to be upset?'

Sylvia shrugged. 'It won't do him any harm to worry about me for a change. He winks at every girl who passes.'

'But that's just his way.'

There was a brief pause before Sylvia said, 'That's what I used to believe, but now I think it's more than just a bit of harmless fun. There's something in him—something I can't reach because he won't let me. He seems so outgoing and friendly but it's an illusion. He keeps the important part of himself hidden. He'll flirt and play the passionate lover, but that's not love. Not really. He doesn't like getting close in other ways.'

'Perhaps he doesn't trust the idea of love,' Dee said thoughtfully.

'Why should you say that?'

'I mean after what happened in his childhood—his father leaving and his mother being so withdrawn, you know.'

'No, I don't know. What are you talking about?'

So Mark hadn't told Sylvia what he'd told her, Dee realised. He'd hinted as much but she'd thought that resolution would change as he grew closer to her sister. But it seemed they hadn't grown closer at all.

'Maybe I'd better ask Mark,' Sylvia said shrewdly.

'No,' Dee said quickly. 'I wasn't supposed to repeat it. I forgot. It's just that—'

Briefly, she outlined what he'd told her about his lonely childhood, and the dog his selfish mother had got rid of without even telling him.

'That woman sounds hateful,' she finished. 'However unhappy she was, she had no right to take it out on a child. No wonder he grew up cautious about getting close to people.'

'So that's why he doesn't open up to anyone,' Sylvia mused. 'Including me. But it seems he talks to you.'

'Because he sees me as a sister. A sister can't hurt him like you can, so he feels safe talking to me. But don't tell him I told you.'

'All right, I promise. I'll keep hoping that he'll tell me himself, but he won't, I know that in my heart. You see, I don't matter to him, or not very much. The other night we were going to meet for a date, and he was nearly an hour late. He made some excuse but I think he was with another girl. I'm sure I could smell her perfume.'

'You're imagining things,' Dee said, unwilling to believe the worst of Mark.

'Am I? Maybe. But I resent the time I spend worrying about him. I once thought that he and I would walk off into the sunset and live happily ever after. But now—' She gave an awkward laugh. 'If I don't matter to him, there are plenty of other men who think I matter. I'm going to bed. Goodnight.'

When Dee finally went to her own room she was puzzled. Whatever Sylvia said, Mark was surely under her spell, even if it was only her physical beauty that had drawn him there. She recalled her mother's teaching on the subject.

'They all start off wanting just one thing,' Helen had said. 'A clever woman uses that to get a ring on her finger.'

It was the wisdom of the time. Any woman of Helen's generation, or even Dee's generation, would have said the same. The idea of risking the wedding ring by playing fast and loose with his affections was sheer madness. Dee knew that she could never have done so if she'd been lucky enough to entrance Mark.

'But that's not going to happen,' she told her reflection. 'He's never going to gaze at you as if the sun rose and set on you, so shut up, go to bed, forget him and get on with your life.'

Sometimes lecturing herself helped. Mostly, it didn't.

What did help was walking in the evening with Billy, now their mutual friend. 'You're crazy about him too, aren't you?' she asked the dog as they strolled along.

Billy gave a soft grunt of agreement. The next moment it had turned into a yelp of delight as a motorbike turned the corner of the road. Even in goggles, it was clearly Mark, and Billy shot ahead so fast that the lead slipped out of Dee's hand.

'Billy, no!' she shrieked as the dog went bounding into the road, straight into the path of the speeding motorbike, and to inevitable disaster.

It was all over in a flash. One moment the bike was bearing down on the dog; the next moment there was a crash and a yell as the vehicle swerved violently and smashed into a fence. Mark was flung to the ground and lay still.

'Oh, no!' Dee whispered, running towards him and dropping to her knees beside his frighteningly still form. 'Mark! *Mark!*'

'I'm all right,' he murmured. 'Go and catch that daft animal before he gets killed.'

Catching Billy was easy as he'd come to a halt, staring at

the mayhem he'd caused and whining. As she secured his lead, Mark was already rising painfully from the ground.

'Are you hurt?' Dee begged.

'No, just a few bruises,' he gasped, rubbing himself.

Doors opened. People came running out. Sylvia had seen everything through a window and was weeping as she threw her arms around him.

'I'm all right,' he said, staggering slightly.

Sylvia turned on Dee in fury. 'Why don't you keep that animal under control? Mark could have been killed.'

'But I wasn't,' he said. 'It's not Billy's fault.'

'No, it was mine,' Dee said quickly. 'I'm sorry. Don't stay out here. Let's get inside quickly.'

Leaning on Sylvia, he walked slowly into the house and sat thankfully on the sofa, throwing his head right back, eyes closed.

'Let me have a look at you,' Dee said.

'I've told you, I'm fine.'

For once she lost her temper. '*I'm* the nurse,' she snapped. '*I'll* say if you're fine.'

That made him open his eyes. 'All right, nurse. All right, all right. Whatever you say.'

She gave him a sulphurous look and started undoing the contraption he wore on his head. It was made of some light metal, barely covering his hair, and if he'd landed on his head it wouldn't have protected him, but luckily he hadn't. His shoulder had taken the full impact.

'Fine, let me see your shoulder,' she said, becoming businesslike.

Between them, she and Sylvia eased off his jacket, then his shirt, revealing bruises that were already turning a nasty colour.

'Now your vest,' she said. 'I want to see your ribs. That's it, now lean forward so that I can see the back.'

There were more bruises, but nothing was broken.

'You don't know how lucky you are,' Dee said. 'But I'd like you to come into Accident and Emergency at the hospital tomorrow and they'll take some X-rays.'

'What for?' he demanded with cheerful belligerence. 'I've had the best nurse in the business. If you say I'm all right, then I am.'

'Yes, but—'

'Stop making a fuss, Nurse.'

'Put your clothes on,' Sylvia said.

Something in her voice, perhaps a tense note, made Dee suddenly realise that Sylvia was jealous. She didn't like anyone else to see Mark's bare chest. Nor did she like Dee being free to touch it.

The knowledge was like a light coming on, revealing what she hadn't seen before, that Mark's lean muscularity was as eye-catching as the rest of him. Functioning solely as a nurse, she'd run her hands professionally over that smooth torso, sensing only its medical condition. Now she wondered how she could have failed to notice the rich sheen of his skin, the faint swell of muscles that were strong but not over-developed.

But that was forbidden thinking, so she turned away, saying gruffly, 'Sylvia will help you get dressed.'

Joe came in from the garage where he'd been examining the bike.

'How is it?' Mark asked quickly.

Joe sighed and shook his head. 'Not good. The wheel's bent and there's plenty of other damage.'

Mark groaned.

'It's my fault,' Dee said. 'If I'd kept better hold of Billy's lead, it wouldn't have happened. I'll pay for any repairs.'

'I don't think it can be put right,' Joe told her.

'Then I'll replace it,' she said stubbornly.

'Dee,' Mark said, 'sweet, innocent Dee, it would take you a year's salary to buy another. Forget it.'

'But that bike was your pride and joy and I've ruined it,' she protested.

'So, it's ruined. That's life. Easy come, easy go. I only acquired it in the first place through being thoroughly devious. Something else will come along and I'll be devious again. Don't worry. It comes naturally to me.'

There was a growl of rage and a middle-aged man thrust his way into the room. With a groan Dee recognised Jack Hammond, the neighbour whose fence Mark had smashed, and who was bad-tempered even at the best of times.

'Do you know what you've done to my fence?' he shouted.

'Sorry about that,' Mark said. 'I'll mend it.'

'I should think you will. Why the devil did you have to swerve?'

Mark sighed. 'Because otherwise I'd have killed the dog,' he said, like a man explaining to an idiot.

'So what? It would have been his own fault.'

'Sure. I wonder why I didn't think of that,' Mark said ironically. 'It would have made everything all right, wouldn't it? I've told you I'll mend the fence.'

'You'd better.'

From the corner came a whimper. Billy was sitting there, looking apprehensive, as though he understood.

'You should put that creature down,' Hammond snapped. 'I've a good mind to—'

He didn't finish the sentence. Mark had struggled to his feet, wincing but determined, and confronted Hammond fiercely.

'Leave Billy alone,' he grated. 'I don't even want to see you looking at him. Now get out of here before I make you sorry.'

'Oh, so now you're—'

'Get out!'

Hammond didn't argue further. He knew murder in a man's eyes when he saw it. He fled.

Mark collapsed back onto the sofa and held out his hand to Billy. 'Come here.'

Apprehensively, the dog came to him. Dee held her breath.

'You daft mutt,' Mark said in a mixture of exasperation and affection. 'You crazy, stupid animal; have you got a death wish? You could have been killed back there, do you realise that? Of all the—' Words seemed to fail him. 'Will you be sensible next time? Do you know how?'

Billy whined softly.

'No, you don't,' Mark said. 'Nor do I, according to some people.' He put an arm around the dog. 'Don't worry; it's all over now. But don't take any more silly risks because *she*—' indicating Dee '—can't do without you.'

'Considering he nearly killed *you*—' Helen said, amazed.

'That's all right. I can take care of myself. He can't. He's an idiot.' But, as he said it, he enveloped Billy in a bear hug. Dee barely saw it through her tears.

It was settled that he would stay the night. Dee's room was cleared for him and she moved in with Sylvia, as she'd done last time. She produced some liniment to rub into the bruises, but Sylvia snatched it out of her hand and insisted on doing it herself.

She spent some time comforting Billy, reflecting on Mark's comment that she couldn't do without him. He was right, of course. She wondered how many men would have swerved and accepted injury to themselves rather than hurt an elderly mongrel. He might play the giddy charmer, but this was the real man, she was sure of it.

In her mind she saw him again, bare-chested, lean, strong, powerful. Her hands seemed to tingle with the memory of touching him and an equation began to hammer on her brain, demanding entrance.

Medical condition: satisfactory.

Personal condition: a million times more than satisfactory.

Go to bed, she told herself crossly. And pull yourself together. Remember you're a nurse.

She slept for a few hours and awoke to hear Sylvia getting out of bed and creeping out of the room. She slipped out after her and reached the corridor in time to see her sister go into Mark's room. The whispers just reached her.

'I came to see if the patient's all right.'

'All the better for seeing you,' he said.

'Let's see if I can make you feel better.'

Standing in the bleak corridor, Dee heard muffled laughter ending in his exclamation of, 'Ow! Be careful. I'm delicate.' More laughter.

She crept back to her room and closed the door.

Next morning, she rose early. Even so, he was down before her, in the garden with Billy. She found them sitting quietly together, his hand on the dog's head.

'Have you managed to reassure him yet?' she asked.

'Just about.'

'Mark, I don't know how to thank you for being so nice about this, not just about the bike, but about Billy.'

'Let it go. It wasn't his fault. But listen, keep him indoors for a while. In fact, I'll take him into the garage with me.'

'You think Hammond—?'

'I don't know, but I didn't like the look on his face last night.'

'I do wish you'd come to the hospital—'

But his serious mood had passed and he waved her to silence. 'Who needs a hospital when they've had you looking after them? I didn't hit my head. Look—' he leaned forward for her inspection '—nothing there.'

'That's certainly true,' she said wryly. 'Nothing there at all. Outside or in.'

He grinned. 'I see you understand me. Are you cross with me?'

'How can I be when you were so generous about it? Especially to Billy. But I will help out with the money and—'

'No need. I'll probably get something from the insurance.'

'But if it's not enough, I'll—'

'That's it. This conversation is over. Isn't it time for breakfast? Come along, Billy.'

Man and dog strode into the house, leaving her gazing after them, exasperated and happy.

You barely got anything from the insurance company, did you? Not enough to buy another motorbike, but you didn't tell me. You simply said you'd changed your mind about having one. I might have believed you, but Dad was there when the inspector came and he told me afterwards. I tried to speak of it but you got really cross. It's funny how there were some things you just couldn't cope with. Sometimes you seemed happier with Billy than anyone else. You didn't have to put on a performance with him.

Or with me. That was the nicest thing.

CHAPTER FIVE

DEE's eighteenth birthday was approaching. There would be a party with all the neighbours and for a few hours everyone would forget the approaching war.

On the night, Mark came to meet her at the bus stop.

'I'm the delegation sent to escort you home,' he said cheerfully. 'Your dad let me leave work a little early so that I could shift the furniture for your mum and help her put up the decorations. She's baking a cake for you—the best cake ever, with eighteen candles.'

'Mum always does the best cake ever,' Dee chuckled. 'For Sylvia's twentieth she produced a real masterpiece. Is Sylvia home yet, by the way?'

'Not yet. She'll be along soon.'

As they neared the front door they could see the first guests arriving, everyone waving as they saw each other. Laughing, they all hurried in. After that, the bell rang every few minutes and soon the place was full. Except for Sylvia.

'We're not waiting for anyone,' Helen declared. 'This is your evening. Let's get on with it.'

There were cards and presents to be opened, laughter to be shared. Afterwards, Dee vaguely recalled these things, but the details blurred in the shock of what came afterwards. Neither she, her parents, nor Mark, would ever quite recover from that shock.

She had slipped into the hall, meaning to fetch something

from upstairs, when she noticed an envelope lying on the mat. With a sense of foreboding, she saw that the handwriting was Sylvia's.

She tore it open, telling herself that her worst fears were realised, but even her worst fears hadn't prepared her for what she found.

> I'm sorry to do this now, but I shan't be there this evening. I've gone away for a long time, maybe for good. I'm in love and I have to be with Phil, no matter what else it means.
>
> A friend has delivered this, so don't look for me outside the door. I'm already far away.
>
> Say sorry to Mark for me. I didn't mean to do it this way. Try to make him understand and forgive me. He doesn't love me really, and he'll get over it.
> Love, Sylvia

She read it again and again, trying to understand that it was real and not some wicked joke. Then life returned to her limbs and she tore open the front door, running out in a frantic search for whoever might have thrust this through the letterbox. But the street was empty in both directions.

Her head spinning, she stumbled back to the house and leaned against the wall, shaking. Mark came out and found her like that.

'You're being a long time. Everyone's asking what—Dee, what is it?'

'Sylvia,' she said hoarsely.

He took the note from her hand and read it.

'Well,' he said heartily, 'so that's that.'

But she wasn't fooled. She'd glanced up just in time to see his expression in the split second before the mask came down, and she'd never seen such devastation in any man's face. He actually seemed to wither, mouth growing pinched, eyes closing as if to shut out intolerable pain. The next moment he opened them again and smiled. But the smile only touched his mouth. His eyes were blank.

'She just vanished without a goodbye,' he whispered.

'Mark, I'm so sorry,' she whispered.

He raised his head. His face was set. 'Sorry? What for? Sylvia has the right to do as she pleases. We weren't engaged or anything like that.'

'But to do it like this—'

'Not very polite, but if she wants to be with him—' His voice shook and for a moment he shuddered uncontrollably.

'Dee, are you coming back in?' It was her mother's voice, approaching.

Swiftly, Mark put the letter into his pocket.

'Say nothing until the party's over,' he said.

He was right. She wilted at the thought of telling her parents about this. Their eyes met and they each took a deep breath before heading back into the house.

Someone had brought a gramophone and a collection of dance records, which mercifully made talk impossible for some time. But there was no hiding the way people looked at Mark, or the almost tangible curiosity about Sylvia's absence.

And how they would laugh, she thought angrily. Mark's popularity had always contained a touch of jealousy, even spite. Every girl who'd yearned for him, every young man who'd envied him, would relish seeing him undermined now.

A fierce desire to protect him made her grasp his hand, saying, 'Dance with me, Mark. It's my birthday, and I get to choose.'

He seized her with what might have been eagerness, but she sensed mainly relief that with her he could briefly drop the bright mask.

I wonder where Sylvia's got to. Do you think Mark knows?

The words floated indistinctly through the crowd. Impossible to say who'd uttered them, and nor did it matter.

'Ignore that,' she told him. 'The fact is, you knew Sylvia wasn't going to be here, and you're completely relaxed about it.'

'Am I?'

'All you can think about now is enjoying yourself with me,' she persisted, meeting his eyes urgently and trying to convey her message. 'Hold me close and look deep into my eyes, as though I was all you cared about in the world.'

If only...

He nodded, understanding and following her lead with a good deal of skill. The house was tiny and 'dancing' consisted mainly of taking small steps from side to side, but that, too, was useful, because their 'audience' had a close-up view of the performance.

'Smile,' she whispered, favouring him with a dazzling smile of her own. 'Pretend I'm Sylvia.'

He managed to stretch his lips, although his eyes were still blank. Dee raised her head so that her mouth was closer to his, not kissing, but conveying the impression that she would kiss him if they were alone.

Suddenly she clutched her head and said, 'Oh, I've got such a headache.'

'It's getting late,' Helen said. 'It's been a nice evening, but—'

Obediently, everyone began to drift off. It wasn't really late at all, but everyone knew 'something was up'.

'Shame Sylvia couldn't make it,' someone murmured. 'I wonder what kept her.'

There were several curious looks at Mark, then everyone was gone.

'Right, what is it?' Helen demanded, looking from one to the other. 'What are you two keeping a secret?'

'Sylvia's gone away, Mum,' Dee said. 'She left a letter.'

Mark handed it over and Helen read it, her face becoming like stone.

'She's with a man,' she said harshly. 'My daughter's a bad girl?' She glared at Mark. 'What do you know about this? Why didn't you stop her?'

'Because I didn't know.'

'You're supposed to have been courting her all this time. Why didn't you protect her?'

Dee forced herself to be silent. She longed to cry out that someone should have protected Mark from Sylvia's treachery, but he would have hated that. She contented herself with saying, 'Why don't you save your anger for Phil?'

'Just who is he?' Helen demanded.

'I think I saw him once, when I went to collect her from the shop,' Mark said. 'They were giggling together. We had a row about it.'

Suddenly Helen burst into sobs. Dee moved towards her, but her father appeared from the doorway where he'd been hovering and signalled for them to go. She left them in each other's arms, while she and Mark went out into the garden.

Once outside, Mark leaned against the wall, dazed like a man in a nightmare.

'We can't just leave it there,' he said. 'I have to find her, but I don't know how.'

'She said she was already far away,' Dee recalled. 'They'll probably know more at the shop. It's my half-day tomorrow. I'll go over and see what I can find out.'

'Shall I come with you?' he asked quietly.

She knew what it cost him to make the suggestion, for she felt everything with him: the pain of revealing himself as the rejected one, the shame of admitting how he'd been deceived, the awareness of smothered grins. Her heart ached for him.

'It's best if I go alone,' she assured him. 'They'll talk more freely to me.'

'Thank you.' That was all he said, but she knew he'd divined her understanding and was grateful.

She went to the shop the next day and returned home that evening with a heavy heart.

'They all know Phil,' she said. 'He's the rep for a clothing firm so he was in and out quite a lot, and they got to know each other.'

'But why did they run away?' Helen asked wretchedly. 'Why not just get married?'

'They can't,' Dee said reluctantly. 'It seems that Phil is already married.'

Helen gave a little scream and covered her face. Joe grew pale and said, 'I don't believe it. A married man, and she's living with him. She wouldn't do anything so wicked.'

'I'm afraid it's true,' Dee said. 'His wife was in the shop when I arrived. She'd come looking for him. They have two children and he seems to have just left them all.'

She was giving them only half the story, but there was no way she could tell them about the other things she'd learned—about Sylvia's reputation as a minx who routinely flirted with any man, and perhaps more. His abandoned wife had gone further, calling Sylvia a prostitute, but this, too, she would always keep to herself.

At last Helen dropped her hands and lifted her head. Her face was hard. 'She's no daughter of mine,' she said. 'As far as I'm concerned, she's dead.'

'Mum!' Dee protested.

'She never sets foot in this house again. She's not my daughter.'

Dee turned to her father.

'I don't know,' he said helplessly. 'Perhaps your mother knows best. Sylvia has put us out of her life.'

'But maybe she'll need our help.'

'She's dead to me,' Helen said stonily. She rose and kissed

Dee's cheek. 'You are my only daughter now. Remember that.'

She stalked out of the room, followed by Joe.

'I'm going out,' Mark said. 'I need to get drunk.'

'Let me come with you. We'll get drunk together.'

She had no intention of drinking, but she wasn't going to turn him loose upon the world in his present state. Taking him firmly by the hand, she led him out of the house. She, too, was in shock, but she'd had time to think about things on the way home. Mark was still stunned. When he spoke, it was in short, jerky sentences.

'How long has it been going on?' he asked.

'I...can't say,' she said, not entirely truthfully.

'Tell me,' he said violently. 'Don't spare my feelings. I want to know the truth, however bad.'

The truth was that Sylvia had been playing them off against each other for at least two months, perhaps longer. Dee had encountered Philip Mason once, a burly man in his thirties, pleasant enough but uninspiring. How Sylvia could have preferred him to the dashing Mark baffled her.

'It was a few weeks,' she said vaguely.

'And I thought she loved me. I respected her, do you know that? I thought she was a decent girl and I didn't...well, anyway, I respected her. And all the time she was...well...'

They walked on in silence for a while. Dee had tucked her hand into the crook of his arm and kept it there determinedly, lest he escape and do something that might harm him.

'Don't brood about it,' she begged. 'It can't do any good now.'

'It might teach me to be more wary of girls another time. How everyone will laugh at me.'

To comfort him, she denied it, but her words were hollow. Their performance at the party would help only for a short time. The truth would soon seep out.

'They don't matter,' she said urgently. 'You must thumb

your nose at them. All they need to know is that you and Sylvia have split up—'

'Because she preferred someone else.'

'No, she pretended to prefer someone else because she knew you'd lost interest.'

'Who'll believe that?'

This was what Dee had been preparing for, when she must risk everything on one throw of the dice. To the last moment she wasn't sure if she had the nerve, but then she took a deep breath and threw her fate to the winds.

'Everyone will believe it,' she said, 'if you're seen with another girl.'

'But how can I do that to any girl—deceive her into thinking I'm interested when I'm just playing a part?'

'But if she already knew the truth, you wouldn't have to deceive her,' Dee pointed out.

'But who would—?' He stopped as her meaning started to get through to him. 'Are you saying that you'd be willing to—?'

'It can't be anyone but me,' she said. 'You said once I was your best friend. Well, friends help each other out. One day I'll ask you to do something for me.'

'Is that a promise?' he demanded harshly. 'Because I must give you something back.'

'It's a promise.'

'I still don't understand. How do we go about this?'

'Look down that road,' she said, pointing. 'Those three people coming this way were at the party. Now they're turning into The Dancing Duck, so we'll go there, too.'

'They'll be our first audience,' he said, catching her mood.

'That's right. They're looking at us. Put your arm around my shoulders—that's it! Are you ready?'

'Quite ready. Sound the bugles! Forward march!'

Defiantly, they raised their heads and walked on into battle.

Eyes turned towards them as they went into the public house. Apparently unaware, they found a corner table and sat talking quietly while he sipped a beer and she an orange juice.

She knew, because Sylvia had told her, that they had often come here together, sometimes alone, sometimes in a group of their friends, the very ones who were glancing at them now, while trying to seem as if they weren't.

'Come to think of it, there was always something slightly wrong between us,' Mark brooded. 'She was so beautiful and I wanted her like mad, but we never seemed to talk about much. Not that we needed much talking, but when we did—I don't know—there was nothing there. I kept meaning to back away, but then she'd give me that look and I'd melt.'

'I know,' she said softly.

'You do?'

'I saw you melt.'

'Yes, you don't say much, but you see a lot more than most people, don't you? You saw what a fool I was.'

'You weren't a fool,' she insisted. 'Everyone gets carried away by their feelings sometimes.'

'Not you, I'll bet,' he said with a faint friendly grin.

'I'm just eighteen; there hasn't been time,' she said with an air of primness.

'That's not the reason. You've got your feet on the ground, not like the rest of us.'

My feet aren't on the ground, she thought. *I'm floating on air because I'm with you. If only I could risk telling you, but I can't because you'd run a mile.*

Instead, she spoke brightly, sounding confident. 'All right, I'm sensible and I know what I'm doing, so you listen and take my advice.'

'Yes, ma'am.'

'Stretch your arm a little way across the table so that your hand's close to mine, but not touching.'

He did so.

'Inch your fingers just a little bit further.'

'As though I was longing to touch you but didn't dare,' he suggested.

'That's right. You've got the idea.'

He did it perfectly, fingers almost brushing hers, drawing back quickly, then venturing forth again. She wondered how often he'd done this for real, teasing a girl into thinking that he was her humble suppliant, and involuntarily gave a small choke of laughter.

'What's so funny?' he asked. 'Aren't I doing it right?'

'Perfectly. In fact, too perfectly. This is how you get the girls to like you, isn't it? Make them think you're meek and hesitant, and they're in control.'

'You *are* in control,' he pointed out.

'But you're not trying to win my heart. I mean the others. I'll bet it works with them.'

He grinned. 'Sometimes. Some like it that way, some like a man to seem more dominant. I have to vary it.'

'You're a cheeky so-and-so,' she said.

'That's another approach that pays dividends,' he admitted. 'All right, all right, I know we're only play-acting. I'm not aiming to win dividends from you, I promise. I wouldn't dare.'

'Just don't forget that,' she said, trying to sound stern.

At the same moment they both burst out laughing. Heads turned at the sight of Mark Sellon having such a good time with Sylvia's sister, then nodded wisely. Aha! Perhaps that was the reason Sylvia had vanished.

'Permission to touch your fingers,' Mark murmured.

'Just a little.'

His fingertips brushed hers, withdrew, advanced again, paused, withdrew.

'Don't overdo the meek bit,' she advised.

'I'm nervous. I fear your rejection.'

She choked again. 'Stop it,' she said in a quivering voice. 'I can't keep a straight face. You don't do "nervous" very convincingly. It doesn't come naturally to you.'

For answer, he took her hand in his, letting them lie together on the table.

'Thank you,' he said. 'I feel happier holding your hand. I'm not sure I could cope without you. I'm just so confused by all this—'

His grip tightened suddenly. Dee didn't speak, but grasped him in return, knowing it was the only comfort that would get through to him now. He smiled and nodded to say he understood, and they stayed like that in silence until he said, 'Let's go. Getting drunk doesn't seem like such a good idea any more.'

Hand in hand, they rose and headed for the door.

'They're watching us,' she murmured.

'Then let's give them something to watch,' he said, pulling her close and laying his mouth on hers.

It was gentle, not passionate; a kiss for show, with just enough there to tell the onlookers what they wanted to know, then it was over and he escorted her out.

'You didn't mind my doing that?' he asked as they walked away.

'No, it was very clever,' she assured him breathlessly. 'Just what we needed to finish the show.' With an effort, she assumed a comically lofty tone. 'I thought we did that rather well.'

'So do I. In fact, I think I can hear applause.'

As one, they stopped and took elaborate bows to an unseen audience. People walking in the street hurried to the other side, well away from this alarming pair.

'You see that?' she said. 'They think we're mad.'

'How could anybody think that?' he demanded dramatically.

'Anyone who knows us, I imagine.'

He tightened his arm around her, not to kiss her now, but to lean sideways and let his cheek rest against her hair.

'Yes, they don't know the half of it,' he agreed.

'But at least we're mad together. We have that.'

'It's the only thing that's keeping me sane right now.'

At her doorway, he stopped, saying, 'Let me take you out somewhere tomorrow night.'

'Yes, we must be convincing.'

'No, that's not the reason. I want to thank you for everything you're doing. I don't know how you put up with me.'

'I work hard at it.'

'Good. Don't stop. Tomorrow night, then.'

'Actually, I can't,' she said with dismay. 'I'm working tomorrow night, and every night until the end of this week.'

'You're not trying to dump me already, are you? At least it took Sylvia four months to get fed up with me.'

'Don't be daft,' she chuckled. 'I'm on duty at the hospital. I'm a working woman.'

'Then I'll wait on your pleasure. Let me know the first night you can manage.'

He hesitated, and for a blissful moment she thought he would kiss her. And he did. But only on the tip of her nose. Then he walked away, fast.

Dee entered the house quietly, hoping that her parents would have gone to bed, but they were still up. To her relief, they greeted her calmly and Helen had softened towards Mark.

'I was a bit hard on him, wasn't I? It's not his fault. Is he all right?'

'He's coping. I'm trying to help him,' Dee said. 'But he needs time. I'm going to bed now. Goodnight.'

She hurried away, unable to endure any more talking. She

wanted to be alone with her memories of the evening. Mark's heart was still Sylvia's, and she knew she was a long way from the fulfilment of her dream. But for a while she'd had him to herself, enjoyed his whole attention, felt his lips on hers.

In bed she snuggled down, pulling the blankets over her head so that the world was reduced to this tiny space where she could relive his kiss again and again, and dream of the time when it would be truly meant for her.

'One day,' she whispered. 'One day soon—please—'

She was young enough to believe that if she desired something fiercely enough she could make it happen. Wasn't he already half hers? It was just a question of being patient. She was smiling as she fell asleep.

For the next few days she saw him only briefly as he arrived for work in the garage. Her hours were full as her duties increased. Although still technically a student, she was at the top of her class and often assigned to extra duties around the hospital. These were always carried out under the eagle-eye of her superiors, but she was trusted more than any of the others, due to Mr Royce's recommendation. He seldom praised her to her face. But she came to realise that he expressed a high opinion of her to others.

When she tried to thank him, he was polite but reserved.

'You must all become the best nurses in the world,' he said, 'because you'll soon be needed.'

'You really believe there'll be a war?'

'Certainly I do. And so does every thinking person. Now get to work and pass those exams in style.'

From Sylvia there was no word, but one evening, as she was leaving for work, she found a letter for her at the reception desk. It had been delivered by hand.

> I dare not write to you at home, in case Mum finds the letter first and tears it up. I know Mum will say I'm a disgrace to the family, and Dad will agree with her

because he always does. But perhaps I can explain to you, make you understand.

You're wondering how I could ever have left Mark, aren't you? You see, I know how you feel about him. It was there in your eyes when you weren't guarding them.

I did once think I was in love with him. Any girl would feel that. He's good-looking, charming and fun. They were all after him and I felt proud that he'd chosen me. But then things went wrong. He seemed to feel that he had the right to do as he liked and never mind anyone else. He didn't mean to be selfish but he's made that way. If he wanted to flirt, he flirted. If I showed that I minded, I was 'making a fuss about nothing'.

On New Year's Eve, when you saw me fooling around with other lads, I was only trying to make Mark jealous. Even back then he was too sure of me. I thought it wouldn't hurt him to know he's not the only man in the world, but it didn't really work because he's so self-confident.

Do you remember that talk we had one night, when I said that there were other men who wanted me? I think I already knew that Phil was the one. I know he's married, and it's wrong. I'm a 'bad girl'. But he's kind and gentle, and he loves me. He tries to please me because it matters to him that I'm happy. Mark never cared in that way.

There was one final paragraph that stood out starkly.

Be careful, my dear. Don't let Mark hurt you, which he could do very easily. I was lucky. I saw through him, but you might not. Love him a little, if you must, but don't give him your whole heart. He won't know what to do with it.

Dee couldn't read any more. Inside her was a storm of confused feelings. Selfish. Inconsiderate. Self-centred. That was how Sylvia saw Mark, and it wasn't true. How could she say such things? *They weren't true!*

Then the real reason came to her. Sylvia was simply trying to justify herself at Mark's expense. The relief was enormous. Of course he wasn't anything like that.

But you were, my darling. In some ways, you were like two men. One was the man who behaved so generously over the ruined bike, and was so tender and kind to Billy.

The other man was exactly as Sylvia had described. And why not? You were twenty-three and far too handsome for your own good, never mind anyone else's. You looked like a film star, people treated you like a film star, and so you acted like a film star. It's amazing that you were as kind and sweet-tempered as you were.

I didn't see it, of course. These days, a girl of eighteen can be sophisticated, but in those days you were still practically a child, under your parents' authority. I was far too immature myself to recognise immaturity in you, or I might have noticed that Sylvia's actions hurt your pride more than your heart. I thought you were perfect, and I tried to forget what she'd said about you.

But I couldn't. Now and then there'd be a moment when I saw what she'd been talking about, despite how much I loved you.

Why are you sleeping so restlessly? Are you having those troubled dreams again? You haven't had them for years, but I suppose the party tonight brought it all back. There, there! Let me make it better, like I did before. You always said there was no one like me to help you fight the nightmares.

Hush, my darling! I'm here...I'm here.

CHAPTER SIX

ONE night in March, when Mark was to take her out for supper, she arrived home from work, expecting to find him.

'He's not here,' her father said. 'I had to give him the day off.'

'But where has he gone?'

'I don't know. He wouldn't say. Very mysterious, he was. But he wants you to meet him at that new café down the road, and he says you're to wear your best dress.'

On winged feet she flew down the street, bursting into the café and looking around for him eagerly.

He wasn't there.

Never mind. Soon. Just be patient. She ordered a pot of tea and settled down to wait and plan. Between work and studying her schedule was heavy, but still she could count on an outing with him once a week, to maintain their pretence. And she would use that time to win his heart, so that gradually she would become his real girlfriend and then…perhaps…

Be sensible. You're not a lovelorn dreamer. You're Nurse Parsons, top of the class, probably Matron Parsons one day.

But who wanted to be sensible? With a little female cunning, it could all be made to happen just as she wanted. She began to feel like the scheming, adventurous women of history. Messalina, Delilah, Cleopatra; they had nothing on her. Soon Mark would sigh at her feet.

Or at least he might if he were here.

She had to wait an hour for him, but her heart soared when she saw his expression. He was lit up, brilliant with excitement. He rushed over, planted a kiss on her mouth, then settled in the seat opposite, holding her hands in his and almost shaking them in his eagerness.

She could have wept with joy to think that a meeting with her could do this to him.

'I can't tell you—' he said, almost stammering. 'If you only knew—all the way here I've been thinking what to say—'

'To say what?' she begged, inwardly singing.

'I've done it at last. It came over me suddenly that this was the perfect time. I lay awake all last night planning it, and this morning I asked your father for the day off.' He took a deep breath. 'I've done it. I've joined up.'

'You've—what?'

'I've joined the Air Force. Not the official force but the Auxiliaries.'

She knew what he meant because since the time he'd first mentioned his desire to fly, she'd done some reading on the subject. The Auxiliary Air Force was a corps of civilians who learned flying skills and were ready to be called up if war broke out.

'I'll stay here,' Mark said, 'but go for training at weekends. When the war begins, I'll become part of the official force.'

'When it begins? Not if?'

'Come on, we all know what's going to happen. They're about to start conscripting men of my age, and if I'd left it any longer I could have been drafted into the army. By acting now, I've made sure I choose the service I want to join. And it means I can learn to fly. Isn't that wonderful?'

'Wonderful,' she echoed.

And that was it. The dream of winning his love, his joyful look that she'd thought was for her—what had she been thinking of? He barely knew she existed.

Stupid, stupid girl! Sit here and listen to him, try to sound enthusiastic, don't let him guess what you're really feeling.

'It'll be easier on you, too,' he said. 'I won't be around so much so you won't have to pretend to be my girlfriend nearly as often. We'll just make an appearance now and then.'

'That's very thoughtful of you,' she said faintly.

Sylvia seemed to be there whispering, *Be careful. He's not thinking of you really. He's done what he wants.*

'You said once that you dreamed of flying,' she mused.

'Someone told me you had to have the "right background" before the Auxiliaries would look at you. But they're taking in more people now because they know what's coming. And I'm going to be part of it. I'm going to be a pilot, maybe fly a Spitfire or a Hurricane, and it'll be the best thing that ever happened to me.'

'Unless you get killed,' she murmured.

'I won't get killed. I'm indestructible.'

'But you're getting ready to fight. You could be shot down, or just crash.'

'Why are you being so gloomy?' he asked, faintly irritated. 'I've got my heart's desire and you can only look on the dark side.'

'Well, if you got hurt or killed I would find that rather gloomy,' she said, troubled by his inability to understand.

'That's very nice of you, but let's not dwell on something that isn't going to happen. Come on, let's get out of here and celebrate.'

'Is this why I'm in my best dress?'

'Yes, we're going to The Star Barn, that dance hall in Cavey Street.'

In a plush dance hall the music came from an orchestra. The poorer ones had a piano or gramophone records. The Star Barn compromised with a three-piece band that made up in volume what it lacked in skill.

She was still a little hurt at the way Mark seemed absorbed

in his own point of view and oblivious to hers. It came too close to Sylvia's warning. But the feeling vanished as he took her into his arms, and she felt the vivid joy that possessed him communicate itself to her flesh from his. Impossible to stay troubled while her body was against his, their faces so close, his eyes alight with an almost demonic energy.

One dance ran into another until the whole evening was an endless stream of movement. It had been a hard day at work and she'd been tired at the start of the evening, but mysteriously she wasn't tired now. Every moment with him invigorated her.

'You're a terrific dancer,' he said, gasping slightly. 'Let's go faster.'

'Yes, let's.'

She managed to seize the initiative, driving him on until they were both breathless, and somehow they danced out of the hall into the deserted lobby. To the end of her days she had no memory of how they'd got there.

'You shouldn't have done that,' Mark warned her.

'Why?'

'Because now I'm going to do this,' he said, taking her in his arms and kissing her firmly.

It wasn't like the other times, a skilful pretence to deceive onlookers. They were alone and it was the real thing. Now the pressure of his mouth was intense and determined, saying that he wasn't fooling any more and what was she going to do about it?

There was only one possible answer. It was she who moved her lips first, not to escape his but to caress them, revel in the sensation and drive him on further. It was something she'd never done before and she didn't understand how she knew about it. The knowledge seemed to have been part of her for ever, dormant, waiting for this moment to awake. Now it wasn't merely awake but triumphant, determined to make the most of every last thrilling moment.

She was a novice, exploring the first steps of physical love, learning fast but needing to learn more. He taught her, moving his mouth against hers with practised skill, teasing, inciting, leading her blissfully to the next lesson, and then the next. She pressed closer, every inch of her clamouring to learn.

Then, with cruel abruptness, it was over and he was pushing her away from him. When she tried to reach for him again he fended her off.

'Stop it, Dee. *We have to stop!*' His voice was harsh, almost cruel.

'I'm sorry...what—? Did I do something wrong?' She was almost in tears.

'No, you did everything right—too right. That's the problem.'

She misunderstood and her hands flew to her mouth. 'You think I'm a bad girl, that I always do this, but you're wrong, you're wrong.'

'No, I don't mean that. I know you're innocent. You must be or you'd have been more careful. Only an innocent would have pushed me to the edge like that.'

'I don't understand,' she whispered.

He sighed. 'No, you don't, do you?' He took her back into his arms, but pressing her head against his shoulder, careful to avoid her face. 'Don't cry. It's not your fault. But I had to stop when I did, or I wouldn't have been able to stop at all, and then I'd have done something that would make you hate me.'

She couldn't answer. Her heart was thundering, her whole body trembling with thwarted desire.

Hate him? What did he mean? She hated him now for leaving her like this, desperate to go on to the end and discover the secret. She pressed closer to him, hoping to remind him of what they had shared, what they might still share.

'Let's go home,' he said grimly.

They went home in silence. He didn't even hold her hand,

but kept several feet away. Dee crossed her arms over her chest as though trying to protect herself and walked with her head down, staring at the pavement, feeling alienated from the whole world, but especially from the man she loved, who was acting as though she didn't exist.

When they stopped at her front door he seemed uneasy and there was a thoughtful look on his face.

'You're full of surprises,' he said. 'I guess there's a lot more to you than meets the eye. Don't look at me like that. I can't explain right now, especially as your mother is just behind the curtains, watching us. But you...well, anyway...'

He dropped a modest peck on her cheek, said a hurried, 'Goodnight,' and walked away.

Weary and depressed, Dee let herself into the house. As Mark had observed, Helen was waiting for her, in dressing gown and curlers.

'Well?' she demanded. 'Did he behave himself?'

'Oh, yes,' Dee said softly. 'He behaved himself. Goodnight, Mum.'

She ran upstairs as fast as she could.

As Mark had predicted, conscription started the following month, and he'd been wise to get into the Air Force while he still had a choice.

Now she saw him only briefly, as his free time was taken up by the squadron, located just outside London. Joe was immensely proud of him and showed it by giving him Saturdays off so that he could devote the whole weekend to training to be a pilot.

'I couldn't be more proud if he was my own son,' he confided to his wife. 'And, after all, that may happen.' He finished with a significant look at Dee, out in the garden.

'Hmm!' Helen said. 'Hasn't he caused enough trouble in this family?'

'It wasn't his fault; I thought we agreed that.'

'I just don't like what's happening to Dee. Something's not right.'

'She's just missing him. It's happening all over the country now the men are joining up.'

He began inviting Mark in for supper on the days he knew Dee would be home, partly for his daughter's sake and partly because he was consumed with curiosity. He loved nothing better than to listen while Mark described his life as a budding pilot.

'They let me take the controls the other day,' he recalled once. 'I can't begin to tell you what it's like up there, feeling as though all the power in the world was yours, and you could do anything you wanted.'

'I remember when the war started in nineteen fourteen,' Joe said. 'Nobody thought of using planes to fight; they were so frail, just bits of wood and canvas. But then someone mounted a machine gun and that was that. Next thing, we had a Royal Air Force. I'd have loved to fly, but blokes like me just got stuck in the trenches.'

They became more absorbed in their conversation, while Dee's eyes met her mother's across the table in a silent message. *Men!*

'There's something I have to tell you,' Mark said at last. 'They've put my name down for a new course. I'm the first in my group to be assigned to it—'

'Good for you,' Joe said. 'They know you're the best. But it means you'll spend more time there and less here, doesn't it?'

'I'm afraid so. They reckon the war will be declared pretty soon, so then I'll be in the Air Force full-time. Perhaps you should start looking for another mechanic.'

Dee heard all this from a distance. It was coming, the thing she dreaded, the moment when he would walk away to the war and she might never see him again. Time was rushing by.

She had grown cautious, sensing a slight change in Mark's

manner. Since the night she'd come alive in his arms, she'd sometimes caught him giving her a curious look. She was shocked at herself, wondering if her forward behaviour had damaged his respect for her.

When they were alone, his kisses were fervent, even passionate, as though he was discovering something new about her all the time. But then he would draw back as though he'd thought better of it, leaving her in a state of confusion. With all her heart she longed to take him past that invisible barrier, and she hadn't much time left to make it happen.

After supper the three of them listened to the wireless. The official news from Europe was worrying, but what had really caught people's attention was the fact that when King George VI and Queen Elizabeth went on a visit to Canada, they were escorted by two warships.

'And there's a rumour that those ships carried thirty million pounds in gold, for safe-keeping in Canada until it's all over,' Mark had said.

Until it was all over. What would life be like then? Another universe in which he might, or might not be alive. She shivered.

She tried to speak normally, but it was hard when everything in her was focused on one thing—to be alone with Mark, in his arms, kissing him and being kissed, feeling her body burn with new life. Her heart was breaking, yet she must try to pretend all was well.

At last he rose. 'I think I'll take a breath of fresh air,' he said casually.

Eagerly, she joined him and they slipped out into the privacy of the garden. The next moment she was in his arms.

'Why must you go now?' she begged. 'It's too soon.'

'I have to. But I'm going to miss you so much,' he said hoarsely.

'Yes…yes…'

The thought of the lonely time without him lent urgency

to her movements. In the past she'd fought down the blazing desire that almost overcame her when she was in his arms, but tonight she didn't want to be controlled and virtuous. She wanted to let herself go and risk whatever the future held. If that meant being a 'bad girl', then so be it, as long as she could say that just once he'd been hers.

He lifted his head and his eyes and his breathing told her that he was in the same state. Another moment and they would become each other's and who cared for anything else?

'Mark,' she whispered, *'Mark—'*

'Do you want me?'

'Yes—'

Urgently, he drew her down onto the grass and she gave herself up to the feel of his lips on her neck, drifting lower as he opened the buttons of her blouse. High above, the spring moon beamed down on her like a blessing, and she prepared herself for what would surely be the most beautiful experience of her life.

Transported, she didn't hear the door opening behind them, only her mother's voice coming out of nowhere in an outraged cry of, *'You can stop that!'*

She felt Mark freeze on top of her, heard his muttered curse. Then he drew away, helping her to her feet.

'Mum,' she said desperately, 'it's not—'

'Don't you try to fool me, my girl. I know what it's not, and I know what it *is*. It's shameful, that's what it is. I thought you were a good girl, with more self-respect.'

'Come on, Helen,' her husband begged under his voice. 'After all, didn't we—?'

'You hush.' She turned on him furiously.

'Yes, dear.'

'You—' she turned on Mark '—you should be ashamed of yourself, acting like that in a decent home. Just what do you think my daughter is?'

'Well, I was hoping she'd become my wife,' Mark replied.

Slowly, Dee turned her head towards him as the world exploded about her, full of blazing light and riotous colours. It had happened. He'd proposed. She would be his wife. Every dream had come true. Passionate joy held her speechless.

Helen, too, was briefly dumb, but she was the first to recover. 'That puts a different face on it,' she said, cautious and not entirely yielding. 'If you mean it.'

'I was going to ask Dee tonight, only you interrupted me.'

Joe began to edge his wife away. 'Goodnight, you two,' he said with a touch of desperation as he managed to get Helen inside.

Dee's head was clearing and her sensible side reasserting itself, as it had a terrible habit of doing. She'd be a fool to believe this.

'It's all right, Mark,' she said in a low voice. 'You don't have to marry me.'

He regarded her, his head on one side. 'Maybe I want to. Have you thought of that?'

'You don't want to. You just had to divert my mother. I understand.'

'Now you've insulted me,' he said cheerfully.

'Have I?'

'There I am, learning to take to the skies and fight Hitler, and you think I'm afraid of your mother. She's formidable, I grant you, but I'm not scared of her.'

She gave a shaky laugh. 'I didn't mean that, but you know as well as I do that you weren't going to propose if we hadn't got caught.'

'Well, perhaps she did us a favour by showing us the way. Are you saying you don't want to marry me?'

'It's not that, it's just—'

He put his hands on her shoulders and spoke lightly. 'My

darling, will you give a straight answer to a straight question? Are you turning me down?'

'No, of course not, I—'

'Then are you accepting me?'

She looked up into his face, trying to read the truth behind his quizzical expression. She saw humour and good nature, but not the answer she needed.

'Yes or no?' he persisted.

'Yes,' she said with a kind of desperation. It wasn't the proposal she'd dreamed of, and in her heart she knew something about it wasn't right, but there was no way she could turn down the chance to make him hers.

'Does that mean we're engaged?'

'Yes,' she choked. *'Oh, yes!'*

This time their kiss was relatively restrained, since both knew that Helen was watching them from the kitchen window. As they returned slowly to the house, she was waiting for them. Joe produced drinks to celebrate, then Helen declared that it was late and Mark would be wanting to get home. She wore a fixed smile but both her expression and her tone said, *No hanky-panky in this house.*

Mark gave Dee a rueful smile and departed under the steely gaze of his future mother-in-law.

'Congratulations, love,' Joe said, embracing his daughter.

'Yes, you got him to the finishing post,' Helen agreed, although she couldn't resist adding, 'with a bit of help.'

'Mum!'

'He'd have taken his time proposing if I hadn't prodded him on. Never mind. We managed it. We should be proud of ourselves.'

'But that's not how it's supposed to happen,' Dee protested.

'The important thing is, it happened. You wouldn't want him going off to the Air Force without having his ring on your finger. He wasn't going to propose, just fool around with you and then on to the next. Look what he did to Sylvia.'

'Look what she did to him,' Dee said quickly.

'Does she still write to you, love?' Joe asked gently. She had told them about the first letter and read out some, but not all of its contents.

'Now and then. Doesn't she ever write to you?'

'She's tried,' Helen said. 'I tear them up.'

'Before I even see them,' Joe said sadly. 'We don't even know where she is.'

'She hasn't told me her address,' Dee said. 'But she's living with Phil and in her last letter she said she'd just discovered that she was pregnant.'

Helen stiffened. 'So as well as being a whore, she's going to have a little bastard. I want nothing to do with her. Anyway, at least we'll have one respectable marriage in this family. Get him tied to you while you can, my girl. I've done my best for you. Now it's up to you.'

If she'd thought to encourage Dee into marriage by this means, she was mistaken. Whatever Mark said, she couldn't rid herself of the shamed feeling that he'd simply taken the line of least resistance. One part of her mind urged her to rush the ceremony before he could back off, but the other part refused to do it.

These days the world seemed to be thrown into sharp relief, and everything had a sense of 'one last time before the war'. Any party or celebration, every anniversary, any piece of good fortune, must be enjoyed to the full. Just in case.

'There's a fair on Hampstead Heath,' Mark told her one evening. 'Let's go. We never know when there'll be another one.'

The Heath was a magical place, a great green park barely four miles from the centre of London. It had always been a popular venue for fairs, and especially now as the dark days approached.

As they neared the fair, they could hear the unmistakable sound of the hurdy-gurdy blaring over the distance. From far off, the giant wheel glittered as it turned against the night.

'I've always wanted to go up on one of those,' she breathed.

'We will, I promise.'

Close up, the wheel was even more dazzling.

'Ever been on one?' Mark asked.

'No. I've often wanted to, but I was always at the fair with my parents and Mum said, "You don't want to go on those dangerous things". And I didn't know how to tell her that I did want to *because* they were dangerous.'

'Right,' he said. 'Come on.' He bought the tickets and took her hand firmly. 'Those seats rock back and forth like mad, so hold onto me.'

From the moment they sat down and she felt the seat swinging beneath her, Dee felt as though she'd come home. Nothing in her life had ever been as exciting as when she was lifted high into the air, over the top of the wheel, then the descent when, for a moment, there seemed to be nothing but air between herself and the earth beneath. Then again, and again, loving it more every moment.

'Wheeeee!' she shrieked as they arrived back at the bottom for the final time. 'I want to go again.'

He took her up three times, finally saying, 'Leave it for now. There are other rides, just as exciting.'

'Lead me to them!'

Her eyes were gleaming as they approached the roller coaster, and she looked up the climb with an eagerness that anticipated the pleasure to come. She could just see a car reaching the summit and hear the shrieks as it sped down.

'Come *on!*' she begged.

He looked at her curiously. 'Aren't you afraid?'

'What of?' she asked blankly.

'You'll find out,' he said, grinning.

When they were seated he made as if to put an arm around her. 'But perhaps you're too brave to need my help?' he teased.

'I don't think I'm quite as brave as that,' she conceded, pulling his arm about her shoulders.

The cars moved off, slowly at first, climbing the long slope to the summit, then plunging down at ever increasing speed while she screamed with pleasure and huddled closer to him.

After two more rides he insisted that they get out, at least for a while.

'You may not need a rest, but I do,' he gasped. 'Where's the beer tent?'

In the tent, they sat down and sipped light ale. Every nerve throughout her body was singing with excitement, but the greatest pleasure was the look Mark was giving her, as though seeing her for the first time and admiring what he saw.

'I never guessed you enjoyed that kind of thing,' he said.

'Neither did I. If I'd known, I'd have done it sooner.'

'Most girls don't care for it,' he said, speaking more quietly than was usual with him.

And suddenly Sylvia was there with them, gasping and clinging to them in horror after her ride in the sidecar, vowing *never again*.

'I'm not most girls,' Dee said brightly. 'I'm mad. Hadn't you heard?'

'If I hadn't, I know now.'

She drained her glass and held it out. 'Can I have another one?'

'No,' he said in alarm. 'Your mother would kill me. She already disapproves of me, even though we're engaged.'

Dee nodded. Helen wanted them married for the sake of respectability, but only that morning she'd said, 'I know he can talk the hind legs off a donkey and he's got a cheeky smile, but you mark my words. He's a bad boy!'

Which was true, Dee thought. Mark's 'bad boy' aspect was seldom on display, but it was always there, just below the surface. It lived in uneasy partnership with his generous side and it made him thrilling. But she wouldn't have dared to tell her mother that. She didn't fully understand it herself. She only knew that he lived in her heart as the most exciting man in the world and she wouldn't have him any different.

CHAPTER SEVEN

WHEN they came to the dodgems she insisted on their taking a car each so that they could bash each other. Once behind the wheel, she laid into him with a will. But he gave as good as he got and when they joined up again afterwards they agreed that honours were even.

But in one thing he beat her hollow—on the rifle range his aim was perfect. He scored bullseyes with ease and was offered his pick of the prizes on display. He chose a small fluffy teddy bear and solemnly presented it to her.

She fell in love with it at once. The face was slightly lop-sided, giving it an air of cheeky humour that she instantly recognised.

'He's you,' she said.

'Me?' he asked, startled.

'Well, he's rather better-looking than you, of course,' she said, considering. 'But that cocky air is exactly you. My bruin.'

'Bruin?'

'It's an old word for bear. This isn't just an ordinary bear. He's *my* bear. He's a real bruin.' She dropped a kiss on the furry little fellow's snout.

'I'm jealous,' Mark said.

'How can you be jealous of yourself?' she demanded, tucking the toy safely into her bag.

'I'll think about that.'

He bought two ice creams and they wandered through the fair, hand in hand. Dee thought she'd never known such a happy evening.

'Will you take me on the roller coaster again?' she asked.

'Am I allowed to say no?'

'Not a chance.'

Suddenly a yell came out of the darkness.

'Look at that!' someone breathed, pointing upward, horrified and admiring at the same time.

High above them stretched what looked like a hollow pole made of metal latticework. A string of lights went up the middle, gleaming against the metal strips and illuminating the man who was climbing to the top.

'He shouldn't be doing that!'

'He's crazy!'

'Yes, but what a climber!'

The shouts filled the air, but the climbing man seemed oblivious to the sensation he was creating. Up, up he moved, never looking down, untroubled by the height, although the pole was beginning to sway.

'Is he going right to the top?'

'He won't dare. It isn't safe.'

It seemed that the man agreed, because he stopped and made a dramatic gesture to the crowd below, signifying the end of the performance. Cheers erupted as he began to descend and applause filled the air.

'What's that for?' Mark demanded indignantly. 'He got nowhere near the top.'

'He got pretty high, though,' Dee pointed out.

'Anybody can settle for second best. It's reaching the top that matters.'

'Yes, if you want to risk your neck for nothing,' she said.

As soon as the words were out she knew they were a mistake and the look on Mark's face confirmed it. To him, the risk alone was worth it. The more danger, the more fun; those had been his words.

'Mark—wait!' she cried as he turned away, resolution written in every line of his body.

He ignored her, if he even heard her. Terrified now, she seized his arm and at last he turned.

'Take your hands off me,' he said softly.

'Mark, please—'

'Let go, *now!*'

She'd never heard such a tone from him before, or seen such a look in his eyes. Where was the sweet-tempered joker that she loved? Gone, and in his place this hard-faced man who would brook no interference in his wishes.

'I told you to let me go,' he repeated coldly.

Appalled, she stepped back, her hands falling away from him as the strength drained out of them.

He was a stranger, a man she'd never met before and never wanted to meet again. In her heart she'd always known something like this was waiting for them, a moment when she would look down the road ahead and shiver.

Mark saw her withdrawn expression and misunderstood it.

'It's all right,' he said, speaking more gently. 'I know what I'm doing.'

He was gone before she could reply, striding towards the terrifying pole, leaping onto the bottom rung and climbing fast before anyone could stop him. Now there were more cheers, mingled with screams.

Dee's heart almost stopped. It was unbearable to watch him, yet impossible to look away. He was approaching the point where the first man had given up. If only he would be satisfied with going a little further and claiming victory! Surely that would be enough for him!

'Please, please,' she whispered. 'Make him stop—let him be satisfied without going to the top.'

But he wouldn't be satisfied with less, she knew that. It had to be all or nothing. That was how he was made.

The crowd roared as he reached the crucial point and climbed beyond it. On the ground, the other climber groaned and swore. 'Show-off,' he growled.

'And what were you?' Dee turned on him.

'All right, I'm a show-off too, but I knew when to stop. The metal's much thinner up there. It won't support him.'

Right on cue, a metal strut bent under Mark's foot. He hesitated, clinging on, looking down, then looking up.

'Come down,' yelled someone. 'Be sensible.'

Fatal. Be sensible! Like a red rag to a bull, Dee thought frantically.

At last he tightened his grip, raised his head to the sky and began to climb again. The pole swayed but this time the crowd didn't scream. Instead, there was silence, as though the universe had stopped until they knew what would happen.

Four more rungs, then three—two—one—and finally—

The roar was deafening as Mark reached the summit and threw up one arm in victory, waving down at them as the applause streamed up to him in waves.

'Did you see that?'
'What a hero that man must be!'
'He's not afraid of anything.'

Gradually he descended while everyone in the crowd crossed their fingers, willing him to succeed, until at last he vanished into their open arms and the roar exploded again.

'Hey, aren't you with him?'

Dee opened her eyes to see a young couple.

'We saw you talking,' the boy said. 'Are you his girlfriend?'

'I...er...yes.'

'You must be so proud of him,' the girl sighed. To her companion she said, 'You never do things like that.'

'Then you're very lucky,' Dee said with a tartness that even took herself by surprise and moved away quickly.

Mark saw her coming and threw up his arms, his eyes alight. Everything in his manner said, *How about that?*

'Are you all right?' she asked.

'Of course I'm all right. It was nothing.'

'It was reckless and stupid,' said a man who'd appeared behind him. He was middle-aged and heavily built. 'I'm the owner of this fair and I've a good mind to hand you over to the police for damage to my property.'

There were cries of indignation. 'You can't do that—we're gonna need fellows like him soon—'

'I didn't say I was going to,' the owner defended himself. 'I've never seen anything like it.' He shook Mark's hand. 'Just don't do it again.'

Roars of laughter. More applause. Congratulations. Dee watched, wondering why she couldn't join in the general delight, but she didn't want to spoil it for him so she tried to smile brightly as she approached, playing the role of the woman proud to bursting point of her man.

Clearly it was what he was expecting, for he flung his arms around her and drew her close in an exuberant embrace. The crowd loved that, clapping their hands, laughing and hooting.

She never heard them. The feel of his lips on hers almost deprived her of her senses. It wasn't the kiss she longed for, intimate, loving, personal. It was a kiss for show, but it was the best she could hope for and she would relish every moment. She kissed him back, putting her heart into it, wondering if he could ever recognise that she even had a heart.

The crowd's applause brought her back down to earth. Embarrassed, she drew back and began to walk away.

'You're very quiet,' he said as he caught up with her. 'Are you annoyed with me?'

'You're an idiot!' she told him.

'No question!' He rested his hands on her shoulders. 'I know I'm a fool, but you'll forgive me, won't you? It's just me, it's the way I am. Once a fool, always a fool.'

She pulled the toy bear out of her bag and held him up so that they could look at each other, face to face.

'You hear that?' she said. 'He admitted he's a fool. I suppose you're on his side. Mad bruins, both of you.'

He chuckled. 'Mad Bruin. I like it.'

She knew a little flare of anger at his lack of understanding. She'd suffered a thousand agonies watching him, but that had never occurred to him. He'd seen only what he wanted to do and the satisfaction it gave him. Now he was up in the clouds, bursting with delight, and no thought for her.

But then, she thought, why should he think of her? He didn't know that she was in love with him. It probably hadn't occurred to him that she suffered.

Stop complaining, she told herself. You chose to become engaged to a man who's not in love with you. Live with it!

'Wait here,' she said, rising suddenly and darting away.

In a few moments she was back at the stall where he'd won the little bear.

'He's lonely,' she said, holding Bruin up. 'He wants his mate. How much to buy her?'

'You're supposed to win her,' the stall-holder protested.

'With my aim, we'll be here all night. How much?'

He haggled briefly but gave in and sold her the little toy, identical to the other except for a frilly skirt. Then she raced back to Mark and thrust her trophy into his hand.

'There you are! Now we both have one.'

'You won this? I'm impressed.'

Briefly she was torn by temptation, but wisdom prevailed. 'No, I persuaded him to sell her to me.'

'How much?'

She grimaced. 'One shilling and sixpence.'

'*How much?* That's a fortune. You could buy several pints of beer for that.'

'I buy only the best,' she assured him. 'This is female Bruin, and she's going to keep an eye on you for me.'

'Going to nag me, eh?'

'Definitely. And spy on you, and report back to me if you get up to mischief.' But then she added in a quieter voice, 'And look after you.'

'Stop me doing stupid things?'

'Something like that.'

'Then I'd better look after her,' he said. He made as if to tuck the toy into his jacket but held her up at the last minute.

'She says it's getting late and we ought to go home,' he said.

'And she's always right.'

Hand in hand, they strolled out of the fair.

She remembered that evening long afterwards, for it was the last one of its kind. Soon after that, the lights of London went out one night, leaving the city in darkness and people groping their way home.

'It's only a trial,' Joe reassured them, holding up a candle. 'When the war starts, London will have to be blacked out for its own safety every night. This is to warn us to get ready.'

Sure enough, the lights eventually returned, but the sudden darkness had brought the truth home as nothing else could have done. Now it was real. Mark was no longer an Auxiliary but a part of the official Air Force, his skills honed to a fine edge, waiting for the formal declaration of war, and at last it came.

Now nothing would ever be the same again.

Mark managed a brief visit. Helen treated him as an honoured guest, preparing a special supper and leaving Dee only a few moments alone with him before he had to leave for the airfield where he would always be on call. As she watched him walk away, she wondered when or if she would see him again.

All around her the world was changing. Children were evacuated out of London to distant farms, men joined up or were conscripted, young women also joined up or went to work in factories or on farms, replacing the men. Dee briefly considered joining the Women's Auxiliary Air Force, an ambition that Mr Royce crushed without hesitation.

'You're a nurse—or you will be when you've passed your exams, very soon. I expect you to do well, and you'll be far more use to your country exercising your medical skills.'

It was the closest anyone had heard him come to a compliment.

By now, everyone knew that war would be declared any day, and when it finally happened on 3rd September there was almost a sense of relief in the air. Now they could get on with things. Some of the patients even cheered.

Dee kept smiling, but when she was alone she slipped away into the hospital chapel and sat there, thinking of Mark, wondering what the future held.

Her exams came and went. Later, she could barely remember taking them, but she passed well and was offered a permanent job at the hospital.

Congratulations abounded. Matron told her she'd always known it would happen. Mr Royce, no longer a distant figure of authority, approached her in the canteen and insisted on buying her a cup of tea 'to celebrate'.

Mark managed to make it back for a small family celebration, but most of the day was spent building the Anderson shelter. These shelters were made of sheets of corrugated iron, bolted together at the top, with steel plates at either end. They were set up in the garden, sunk as far as possible in the earth, for greater safety.

'I'm not sleeping in that thing,' Helen declared. 'We'll be better off in the house.'

'Not if they start to bomb this part of London,' Mark murmured.

He was reticent on the subject of his own sorties. Hitler was invading Europe, the British army had advanced in return and the Air Force was deployed to assist them. These bare facts were common knowledge, and beyond them he would say little.

The closest he came to revealing his feelings was as they were walking to the bus stop in the late afternoon. Nearby was a church, from which a couple was just emerging. The groom wore an army uniform. Instead of a wedding gown the bride wore a modest functional dress, only the flower on her shoulder suggesting that today was special.

'Is something the matter?' Mark asked, seeing her frown with concentration.

'No, I'm just trying to remember where I've seen her before. Ah, yes, she works in the bakery three streets away.'

The bride saw her and waved. Dee waved back.

'He's probably just home on leave for a few days and they won't have a honeymoon,' she reflected. 'There are so many of these quick weddings happening now.'

She didn't press it further, leaving it up to Mark whether he seized the point and pressed for a wedding of their own. He was silent for a moment and she crossed her fingers.

'Too many,' he said at last.

'What...what did you say?'

'There are too many of these mad weddings. He'll go away tomorrow and she may never see him again. If she does, he'll be changed, maybe disfigured.'

'But if she loved him she wouldn't be put off by his disfigurement.'

'She thinks she wouldn't. They all say that, but they don't know what they're talking about. The other day I met a man who was a pilot in the last war. His face had been destroyed by fire.'

Through her hand tucked under his arm, Dee felt the faint shudder that went through him.

'He hadn't seen his wife in years,' Mark continued. 'He didn't blame her. He said you couldn't expect a woman to endure looking at him day after day.'

'But he was still the same man inside,' Dee said, almost pleading.

'But he wasn't. How could he be? How could you face that fire and be the same inside?'

Again there was the shudder, stronger now, and her hand tightened in sympathy. These days she seemed to understand him better with every moment that passed, and she knew that he would die rather than admit to being afraid.

At first there had been no need to fear. Everything was beginning in sunlight and hope as the planes soared up and over Europe to tackle Hitler's invasion. But it soon became clear that the enemy had more powerful planes, and the British losses began to mount up. Mark was unscathed, but some of his friends weren't so lucky.

He hadn't told her, but she knew of two airmen whose bravery had resulted in the award of Victoria Crosses. But they never saw these tributes. They had died in action.

Now she had sensed the things that he could never put into words, and knew that secretly he dreaded fire more than anything else. More than pain. More than death. Fire.

'Maybe she won't be the same inside, either,' she said. 'Maybe she'll just be what he needs her to be.'

He gave a sharp, ironic laugh. 'If he's there at all. Suppose he dies and leaves her with a child to rear alone? Suppose she has no family left, and is really alone with a child she—is that the bus I can see in the distance?'

'Yes,' she said sadly.

'Time to go, then. Congratulations again on passing your

exams. I'll be in touch and we'll try to see each other again soon.'

The bus was there. An arm around her shoulder, a quick kiss on the mouth, and he was gone.

She didn't return home at once, but walked the streets as the light faded. Now she had her answer. There would be no early marriage, and perhaps no marriage at all. He'd expressed his refusal as consideration for her, and it sounded sensible enough, except that he didn't love her and needed a good excuse.

But then she remembered the echo from his own past, how he'd started to speak of the woman left alone with a child who she—and then he'd broken off. Who she—what? Couldn't cope with? Didn't love? What would he have said if the bus hadn't appeared at that moment? Would he tell her one day? Or would she be left to wonder all her life?

They managed a brief meeting over Christmas, but then time flashed by and it was 1940. As the months passed the prospect grew darker. Neville Chamberlain, a sick man, resigned in May to be replaced as Prime Minister by Winston Churchill.

Dee's new job was demanding. She put in as much overtime as she could, preferring to work to exhaustion rather than have too many hours to brood.

'Working long hours is praiseworthy, of course,' Mr Royce said, placing a mug of tea in front of her in the canteen. 'But if you're too exhausted you're useless to the patients.'

Dee opened her eyes and regarded him with a sleepy smile. She respected him greatly but her awe had been softened by liking. He was in his late forties, with hair already greying and a pleasant, gentle manner.

'I know,' she said, taking the mug thankfully. 'I'm leaving in a minute.'

'Do you manage to see much of your fiancé?'

'Not for a couple of weeks, although I hope he'll manage to visit us soon. The airfield isn't so far away, but of course he's mostly on call. I know I'm one of the lucky ones, because I do get to see him sometimes. The ones I feel sorry for are the women whose men are in the army, stationed in France, because they say Hitler is advancing.'

'As a matter of fact,' Mr Royce said casually, 'I can give you some news of Mark. They say he's making a name for himself, a brave and skilful pilot. You should be proud of him.'

'Thank you for telling me,' Dee said.

She didn't ask how he knew. It was common knowledge in the hospital that he had friends in high places. One rumour even said he had a cousin in the government, although nobody knew for sure. It briefly occurred to Dee to wonder how his knowledge extended as far as this one airfield, but she was too tired to think much of it.

'Mark's very pleased with himself at the moment,' she said, 'because when Winston Churchill became Prime Minister he was able to say, "I told you so".'

'He actually predicted it?'

'Not exactly, but he used to say that Churchill was the only one who knew what he was talking about.'

'That's true. Now, go home and get some sleep.'

At home she found Helen fuming, as she'd done for several weeks. There was a problem with food stocks, as ships bringing food to Britain were sunk by enemy submarines. To make supplies stretch, further ration books had been issued, directing how much could be eaten in a week.

'Four ounces of bacon,' Helen declared in disgust, 'two ounces of cheese, three pints of milk. And I have to hand over the ration book and they tear out coupons showing I've had this week's allowance and I can't have any more until I hand over next week's coupons.'

'It's to make sure everyone gets a fair share, Mum,' Dee

explained. 'Otherwise, the folk with money would buy up the lot.'

'That's all very well, but Mark's coming next weekend. How can we feed him properly?'

'I think he'll understand the problem.'

She was counting the minutes until she would see Mark, but the day before he was due to arrive the telephone rang.

'I can't come tomorrow,' he said. 'All leave has been cancelled.'

'But why?'

'I don't know, and I couldn't tell you if I did. But something big's happening, take my word.'

That was the first she heard of Dunkirk.

CHAPTER EIGHT

DUNKIRK: May 1940, a name and a date that were to become inscribed in history, but in fact few details came out at the time. It was only in hindsight that it was possible to see the story as a whole, how British and French soldiers had been driven back through France until they reached the harbour of Dunkirk, where, over nine days, more than three hundred thousand of them were rescued by a fleet of ships that had crossed the channel from England. Some were Royal Navy destroyers, but many were small vessels, merchant ships, fishing boats, lifeboats, and these were the ones that passed into legend.

Enemy planes bombarded the evacuation, and were fought off by the Royal Air Force.

'They saved thousands of lives,' Mr Royce told her, 'but their own losses were terrible, over four hundred planes. Do you have any news of Mark?'

'Yes, he called me several times to say he was all right. I'm glad I knew that before I heard about those losses. Thank goodness it's over now.'

'Dee, it's not over, it hasn't begun. Who do you think will be attacked next?'

'Us,' she said slowly. 'In this country.'

A few days later she, like many others, sat by the radio, listening to Churchill confirming their worst fears: 'The battle of France is over. I expect that the Battle of Britain is about to begin... The whole fury and might of the enemy must very soon be turned on us.'

And the front line of defence would be the Air Force.

By day she threw herself into her work, seeing Mark in every patient, finding her only solace in devoting herself to their care. At night she lay in the darkness, whispering, 'Come back to me,' and holding the little bear he'd won for her at the fair.

Now their contact was almost nil. When he could manage to telephone, the call would come when she was at work. She would arrive home to hear Helen say, 'He called. Says everything's fine and he sends his love.'

'Sends his love.' It was a neutral phrase that anyone might have used, but she treasured it nonetheless.

Mr Royce had been right in his prediction. Three weeks after Dunkirk, the Channel Islands were invaded. Two weeks later, the enemy bombers arrived over England and the Air Force was in action against them, fighting them back so ferociously that Churchill paid a public tribute that went down in history.

'Never in the field of human conflict,' he said to a packed House of Commons, 'was so much owed by so many to so few.'

The pilots were the heroes of the hour. Pictures appeared in the press showing young men, leaning casually against their planes, laughing as though danger was just something they took in their stride.

Mostly the pictures were groups, but occasionally one pilot was shown alone. That was how Dee first saw the photograph of Mark, perched on the wing of his Spitfire, relaxed and clearly exhilarated by the life he led.

'You'd think they hadn't a care in the world,' Matron observed as they studied the papers during a hurried tea break.

'Why are they all holding up their hands like that?' Dee wondered, looking at a group picture.

'That's to tell you how many enemy aircraft they've just shot down. Look at him.' She pointed to Mark, who had four fingers on display. 'You can see he's proud of himself.'

Then she gave a laugh. 'I wonder if there are any plain middle-aged pilots. If you believe the press, they're all young, handsome and dashing.'

'Some of them are,' Dee murmured.

Part of her was bursting with pride, although it was undermined by terror for his life. But she knew that this simply made her one of many, and so she was shy of speaking about it.

Even with Mr Royce she was reticent, although he'd now become a trusted confidant. If she'd had thoughts to spare for him, she might have wondered at how often they chanced to meet in the canteen, but she had no thoughts for anyone but Mark.

'How long is it since you saw him?' Mr. Royce asked one day.

'Weeks, but of course he can't get leave now.'

'But didn't you say he was at—?' He named the airfield. 'Surely there's a café nearby where you could wait for him to get a few minutes off. Let him know you're there, and that you'll wait all day if necessary.'

'But I have to be here—' she gasped.

'Leave that to me. You haven't had a day off for too long.'

By good luck, Mark chanced to call that night and she outlined the plan to him.

'That's wonderful!' he said. 'There's a little café called The Warren just outside the airfield. Wait for me there.'

Mr Royce was true to his word and for one day she was free to hurry to the airfield and settle down in the café as soon as it was open. She bought sparingly, knowing that it might be a long wait.

After a while the place began to fill up and the woman behind the counter regarded her with suspicion, even hostility. At last she approached her, glaring.

'I've got a business to run. I can't afford to have people taking up the chairs and not buying anything. You all seem to think you can use this place as a collection point.'

'All?'

'You know what I mean, and don't pretend that you don't.'

Dee did know and was half amused, half angry. 'Actually, I'm a nurse,' she said, 'and I'm waiting for my fiancé.'

The woman regarded her for a moment. 'If you're a nurse, come and take a look at my son. He's ten and very naughty. He cut himself this morning and he won't let anyone look at it.'

After that, things went well. The cut turned out to be minor and easily dressed. Her hostess visibly warmed.

'My name's Mrs Gorton. You stay here as long as you like, and I'll bring you something.'

She served Dee a lunchtime snack, on the house, and began to chat with her as the café cleared.

'Sorry about that, but you should see some of them that come in here. I suppose it can't be helped. Get a lot of young men together and the "good time girls" are going to…well… offer them a good time, if you know what I mean.'

'Yes, I know what you mean,' Dee said.

'And they do a lot of business, so I'm told. The newspapers don't tell that kind of story. Oh, no, those lads are heroes so they're all virtuous, but the two don't go together, take my word. I could tell you things well, anyway, the girls who flaunt themselves aren't the ones you have to worry about. It's the ones that look respectable, like those two near the door. What time will your fiancé be here?'

'I don't know. When he can get away. Perhaps never. No—wait—I think that's him.'

She could just see a figure in a leather jacket coming along the street. The next moment she'd leapt to her feet and hurried out to meet him. Laughing joyfully, Mark enfolded her in a bear hug and for a few minutes she forgot everything else.

'We'll have to go back inside,' he said at last. 'I can't move far.'

'I don't care where it is,' she said fervently.

As they entered she saw Mrs Gorton rise and move back to the counter. For a moment her eyes were fixed curiously on Mark and Dee realised she was conveying a warning about the two girls by the window who 'looked respectable' but clearly weren't.

It was plain what she meant. The girls were regarding Mark, wide-eyed, and in all fairness Dee couldn't blame them. In a short time he'd grown older, heavier, more adult, and a hundred times more attractive. Until now, the boy had lingered in his face, but the experience of confronting death time and again had changed him.

One of the girls seemed about to hail him, then her eyes flickered to Dee and she shrugged and turned away.

Forget it, Dee wanted to say. *He's mine.*

A young man at a corner table rose and headed for the door, passing close by. Dee frowned.

'Pete?' she queried cautiously.

He stared, then grinned when he'd recovered. 'Fancy seeing you here!' he exclaimed.

'You two know each other?' Mark asked.

'We were at school together,' Dee explained, 'although Pete was two forms above me. He saved me from bullies once.'

'Then let me shake your hand,' Mark said, doing so and giving Pete a good-natured grin.

'What are you doing here?' Dee asked him. 'Are you an airman?'

'No, I'm a mechanic,' Pete said. 'I wanted to fly, but I was useless at it. Not like him.' He indicated Mark. 'Regular mad devil, that's what they say.'

Mark grinned again, not at all troubled by this assessment.

'I'll...er...leave you alone, then,' Pete said, suddenly becoming self-conscious.

'Yes, do, there's a good chap,' Mark agreed, shepherding Dee to a table.

He sat down facing her, his hands holding hers across the table, smiling as he did in her dreams.

'I can't stay long, so let's make the most of it,' he said. 'I've missed you.'

'Has it been very bad?'

He shrugged. 'They haven't caught me yet and they're not going to.'

'But there's more to come, isn't there?'

'I'm afraid so. I worry about you, too. Are you sleeping in that Anderson shelter?'

She made a face. 'We tried it but it's so uncomfortable. Mum simply refuses to leave the house now, and we can hardly leave her there alone. To hell with Hitler!'

He touched her cheek. 'That's the spirit.'

Silence fell for a few moments and she had the strange impression that he was uneasy, which was rare with him. Then, as if coming to a sudden resolution, he said, 'I've got something for you.'

He reached into his pocket and pulled out a small box which he opened to reveal a ring.

'It's about time I gave you an engagement ring. I hope it fits.'

It fitted perfectly. It was tiny and cheap, with a small piece of glass where a diamond should have been. She wouldn't have changed it for the world.

'Hey, don't cry,' he chided, brushing her cheek. 'What happened to my sensible Dee?'

'She doesn't really exist,' she choked. 'She's just a pretence.'

'I hope not. I'll rely on her to keep me straight when this is over.'

'When it's over,' she said longingly. 'One day—but when?' To her surprise, he sighed and for a moment a bleak look came over his face. It was gone in an instant, but she knew she wasn't mistaken.

'What is it?' she asked. 'I thought you were loving it.'

'Well, some of it.'

'Being one of "the few", having your picture in the paper. After that photo appeared in the national press, the local paper used it as well. Now there's a copy hanging up in the church hall with "Our Hero" written underneath.'

'Please, Dee, you're making me blush.'

'Nonsense, I know how conceited you really are.'

'Oh, you do!'

'Yes, I do,' she said, laughing as she spoke. 'And you bask in the spotlight. Oh, Mark, what is it?' The bleak look had appeared again. 'Am I being clumsy? I'm sorry.'

'No, it's just that...well...it's not like the romantic picture they give you. When you take off, you never know what's going to happen.'

'Of course not, how stupid of me. It must be scary. Are you—?'

'Am I scared? Yes, but not in the way you think. If you get shot down it'll all be over soon. I can cope with that. It's when I shoot one of them down that it gets hard.'

His fingers tightened on her hand and she clasped him back, waiting silently.

'It's all right when they're at a distance,' he went on. 'But sometimes it happens close up and you can see them, even hear them scream over the engines as they go down to their deaths.'

'But otherwise it would be you,' she urged.

'I know. You tell yourself it's them or you but that doesn't always help. If you see their faces they've become real, and you know you've killed a man.'

'A man who was trying to kill you,' she said firmly.

'Yes. It's just a bit of a shock at first. Ah, well, never mind.'

The last words were like a barrier set up suddenly, as though he'd seen where the conversation was leading and didn't want to go there.

'Mark, please talk to me if you want to—'

'I talk too much,' he said heartily. 'I can remember when you used to say so.'

'That was in another world. If you—'

'Hey, who's that?'

There was a movement from outside the window and another airman looked in, jerking his head when he saw Mark. 'We have to get back now,' he said tensely. 'Take off in an hour.'

'Goodbye,' Mark said, rising and leaning forward to kiss her.

She had a thousand things to say. *I love you. Take care. Call me when you get back.* But she said none of them, just followed him to the door and stood watching as he walked away. The girls of easy virtue were still there and one of them tried to stop and talk to him, but he shook her off and hurried on.

Mrs Gorton came to stand beside her at the door. 'Is he your fiancé?' she asked.

'That's him,' Dee replied, her eyes on Mark's retreating figure.

She wasn't really listening to Mrs Gorton, and so missed the slight curious note in her voice. Nor did she hear the way she said, 'Hmm!' or see the pitying look the older woman gave her.

In fact she saw and heard nothing in the outside world. Now her whole universe was taken up by the feel of the ring on her finger, and joy that he'd remembered it in the middle of so much else.

There was another happiness, too. She treasured the moment when he'd come so close to confiding in her about the horrors of his job. That was what she could give him, what would draw them closer. All she needed was time. But time might yet be denied them. As night descended and she pictured him high up, making life and death decisions, she knew a return of terror and fiercely clasped the ring on her left hand.

He had said they wouldn't catch him and it seemed as if he was right. He survived that night's sortie and many others to come. Now the bombers focused all their attention on London in what became known as the Blitz. Dee and her parents took refuge in the Anderson shelter in the garden while the noise thundered around them and far off they could hear the screams of the injured and the crash of collapsing buildings. By a miracle, the Parsons' house was left standing, but when they emerged in the morning there was always devastation to be witnessed.

During that time she saw Mark once more, meeting him at the café. When he left she strolled with him as close to the airfield as possible and blew him a kiss as he vanished. The way back lay past the café. To her surprise, Mrs Gorton was waiting for her at the door.

'You've been good to me, so I thought I'd warn you,' she said. 'Are you really planning to marry that one?'

'Yes, of course.'

'Well, don't, that's all I've got to say. I told you last time how some of them carry on, but I didn't tell you he's one of the worst.'

'Nonsense!'

'Is it? Look at him. A feller like that can have any girl he wants, and don't kid yourself that he's all faithful and perfect because he isn't. He takes what's offered, like they all do.'

'Why are you trying to turn me against him?' Dee asked desperately.

'Because I like you and you deserve better. Look, my dear, I can understand that you want to grab him while you can. After all, he's a catch and you're no great beauty. No offence meant.'

'None taken,' Dee assured her quietly.

'But give him a miss. He'll break your heart.'

She could stand it no more, but fled blindly, at first not even noticing that she was heading back to the airfield. She stopped a few yards from the wire perimeter, breathing hard. In the distance she could see lights, young men coming and going, laughing. They were ready for anything but expected no call tonight. Some of the figures in shirts and trousers were actually female, taken into the Air Force to serve as mechanics. She remembered how she and Mark had shared a joke about that long ago.

And then she saw him, walking across the grass in the company of two other young men, their laughter carried on the evening air. Three young women, also in uniform, were with them, in a high state of excitement.

Suddenly Mark stopped, turned to one, took her face in his hands and delivered a smacking kiss. Then the next. Then the third, while his male companions cheered and clapped. While the girls giggled and mimed shyness.

At this distance Dee knew she couldn't be seen, but she still began to move backwards, seeking the protection of the shadows, talking sensibly to herself.

What she had seen meant nothing. Nothing at all. He hadn't kissed those girls romantically or passionately, but swiftly, one after another, in front of an audience, as if in fulfilment of a bet. Yes, that was it. A bet. Now they were all headed for the tent where the six of them would spend the evening together in innocent camaraderie.

But Mark was the last one to go into the tent, held back by a girl who grasped his hand and seemed to be pleading with him. He was arguing, laughing, refusing her something she wanted. Dee held her breath, knowing that the decision he took now was crucial.

But he made no decision. The others came out, seized him and hustled him in. The tent flap descended. Silence. Now she would never know what he would have done.

Be sensible. You've always known he was a flirt, and these are special conditions. Anything that happens now doesn't count. He didn't go with her, and he probably wouldn't have done.

But now Sylvia was there in her head, saying, *'If he wanted to flirt, he flirted. If I showed that I minded, I was "making a fuss about nothing".'*

Mrs Gorton seemed to be there as well, joining in the chorus of warning, but Dee refused to listen. She began to run in the direction of the bus stop, but when she reached it she raced on, faster and faster, as though in this way she could outrun the truth. She ran until she could run no more, then slowed to a walk and groped her way through the darkness for an hour, until she reached home.

It took a while to talk herself into calm, but she managed it. Mark was risking his life for his country, and if he was occasionally tempted to look away from his fiancée—a fiancée who he didn't love, she reminded herself—who knew the strain he was under? What right did she have to judge him?

Bit by bit, she persuaded herself that she was in the wrong. It took much effort for her sensible side kept fighting back, saying that he was selfish and immature. After a while she managed to silence common sense and send it slinking off into banishment, but it cast a grim look at her, warning that it would be back.

It tried one assault in a conversation she had with Patsy, who lived in the next street, whose husband was known as a 'bit of a lad', unable to resist temptation, but always returning home in the end with a sheepish look and the plea of, 'You know it's you I really love.'

Recently she'd heard that he'd been captured and sent to a prisoner of war camp. After sighing about how much she missed him, Patsy added wryly, 'But at least now I know where he is every night.'

Dee smiled and escaped as soon as she could, but she couldn't escape the voice that said she'd just seen her own future.

There were small incidents that might mean nothing, like the weekend he was supposed to come and stay the night with the family, but cancelled at the last moment.

Be reasonable, she told herself. He's a fighter doing his duty. He can't put you first. The phrase *even if he wanted to* floated through her mind and was finally dismissed.

It was Pete who delivered the final blow. Granted a few days leave from the airfield, he sought to earn a little extra money at the garage. Joe was glad to see him. Since Mark's departure he'd been working alone and needed help.

'He's a good mechanic,' he told Dee when she came home that night. 'And I've said he must have supper with us tonight, because I knew you'd want to talk to him about Mark.'

Delighted, she hurried out to find Pete just tidying in the garage.

'Did he give you a letter for me?' she asked, 'or a message?'

He seemed embarrassed. 'No, I don't see much of him. We'd better hurry in. I promised your dad not to keep supper waiting.'

'But you can talk to me about Mark first, can't you?'

'There's nothing to say,' he said desperately. 'He's the highest of the high and I'm the lowest of the low. We don't talk.'

She waited for the desperate feeling to settle inside her, enough for her to speak calmly.

'What is it you don't want to tell me, Pete?'

'Look, it's nothing. Something and nothing.'

'Go on.'

'They all fool around—not much else to do—and Maisie's just there for the taking—it didn't mean anything, only he was a bit late getting back and the top brass got mad at him.'

'Was this two weekends ago?' she asked, referring to the time he'd been expected but didn't come.

'Yes.'

She smiled. 'Thanks, Pete. Don't worry about it, and don't mention it to my parents.'

'Look, honestly—'

'I said it's all right. The subject's closed. Finished.'

He wasn't an imaginative man, but the sight of her face alarmed him. A woman who'd aged five years in five seconds might have looked like that.

He shivered.

CHAPTER NINE

IT WASN'T easy to set up the meeting but Dee managed it, choosing another café near the airfield, not the one where they had met before and where Mrs Gorton's presence would be all too evident.

While she waited, she took a few long breaths to calm herself. What she had to do now must be done carefully, with just the perfect air of amused calm. At the last moment she felt she'd got it just right, and when Mark appeared she was able to regard him with her head on one side and a faint smile touching her lips.

'I'm glad you could find the time for me,' she teased.

'Yes, well, my commanding officer—'

'Actually, I meant Maisie.'

Only now did she understand how much she'd longed for him to deny it, but his appalled face made any such fantasy impossible.

'How the hell did you hear about that?' he demanded violently.

'Oh, you're famous for your exploits, in and out of battle.'

'Look, it meant nothing. Don't get it out of proportion. It started with just a few drinks and—'

'And Maisie came, too,' she supplied. 'These things happen, I know. It's not important.'

He regarded her curiously. 'Not important?' he echoed, as if unable to believe his ears. 'You really mean that?'

She made a wry face. 'It's not important because it brings us to a point we've been approaching for some time.'

'What do you mean?'

'Well, let's face it, this never was a real engagement, was it? You only proposed in order to shut my mother up, and I suppose I said yes for the same reason. What else could we do, caught like that? Since then we've seen so little of each other that it's just drifted, but maybe the time has come to be realistic.'

'Meaning what?' he asked in a strange voice.

'You never really wanted to marry me any more than I... well...'

'Any more than you wanted to marry me,' he supplied.

'It was an act of desperation,' she said merrily. 'You proposed marriage to get yourself out of a hole, I've always known that.'

He was very pale. 'Meaning that you think I wouldn't have gone through with it?'

'Gone through with it,' she echoed. 'That says it all, doesn't it? You only have to go through with something if it's an effort, and I think you would have done. You'd have made the effort and done your best to be a good husband. But you wouldn't have been a good husband because your heart wouldn't be in it, and I don't want a man who has to force himself.'

She paused. He was staring at her. Slowly, she lifted her left hand and slid the ring off her finger.

'I've always known you didn't love me,' she said. 'Not enough to marry. It's better to end it now.'

She held out the ring but he seemed too dazed to move.

'You're dumping me?' he asked in disbelief.

'That's all you really care about, isn't it?' she asked with a touch of anger. 'You're afraid people will know that I broke it off. Don't worry, everything's different now. You're a hero, one of "the few" and girls are queuing up for the honour of your attention. When they know you're free, they'll throw a party. You won't remember that I exist.'

She said it lightly but he stared at her in shock. 'That's the first time I've known you to say anything cruel.'

'I'm not being cruel, Mark, I'm being realistic. You'll find another girl, like you did last time. Our marriage would have been a disaster. Here.' She held the ring closer to him. 'Take it.'

Glaring, he did so. 'If that's what you want.'

'What I want,' she murmured. 'I could never tell you what I wanted. We didn't have the chance.'

'And now we never will,' he said, looking at the ring in his palm.

'Mark, when you think about it, you'll see I've done the right thing for you. You're free, as you need to be.'

'Free,' he murmured. 'Free.'

She gave him a peck on the cheek. 'Goodbye, my dear. Take care of yourself.'

As she slipped out of the door his eyes were still fixed on the ring in his hand. She couldn't even be sure that he knew she'd gone.

That night her dreams were haunted by a little boy running through an empty house, opening door after door, calling, 'Where are you?' with mounting despair.

She awoke, shivering. After that she couldn't get back to sleep, but lay weeping in the darkness.

The Blitz lasted for eight months, officially ending in May 1941, although attacks on London continued sporadically for long after.

Somehow Dee kept going. With Mark's departure, all hope seemed to have fled from her life, but there was too much work for her to brood. The hospital was overflowing with the wounded.

Even so, there were moments when she couldn't escape her thoughts, when she would lie awake longing, with every fibre of her being, for the man she'd lost. It was useless to tell herself that he'd never really loved her, that they would have had no chance and she was better off without him. Somewhere in the depths of her misery a voice whispered that she'd been too hasty, that she could have managed things better, bound him to her and won his love.

Instead, she'd done the common sense thing because that was her way. She was wise, realistic and sensible. And her heart was breaking.

She knew that a really sensible woman would discard Mad Bruin rather than keep a constant reminder of an unrequited love, but she couldn't bring herself to go quite that far.

She knew when the planes took off for a sortie because their route lay over the city. Londoners would come out and stand looking up at the sky, not always able to see the aircraft through the clouds or the darkness, but listening until the sound faded. Hours later, they would come out again to hear the return, wondering how many planes and men had been lost.

She had no news of Mark. He never wrote. He'd accepted her rejection as final.

'How's that fiancé of yours?' Mr Royce asked one day.

'I don't know. He's not my fiancé any more.'

She described their breakup briefly and without visible emotion. He listened sympathetically and never mentioned it again, except that he always seemed well informed about the activities of that particular squadron and was able to assure her that Mark was still alive and unhurt. Otherwise, she wouldn't have known.

At work her life was filled with satisfaction, yet there was no joy. In the evenings she would travel home on a bus that crawled along at a snail's pace because the whole country was under 'the blackout'. When she got off, she felt her way carefully home in the near darkness. Curtains and blinds kept the house almost invisible from the outside. Once inside, there was the relief of a small lamp.

Joe had joined the Home Guard, a civilian 'army' consisting of men who were too old to join the regular forces, or in reserved occupations such as doctors, miners, teachers and train drivers. Their job would be to fight off an invasion, and they were equipped with uniforms and weapons. Joe was proud to bursting point and regular visits to the local church hall for training sessions helped keep his spirits up.

Helen fared less well. At first Dee had been able to bring home the letters Sylvia sent to the hospital, and in this way they learned that Sylvia had given birth to a son.

'I want to go and see her,' Helen insisted.

'You can't, Mum. She's never left a return address and she didn't have the baby in hospital.'

They kept hoping but, as time passed, Helen realised that her daughter had truly rejected her and she couldn't see her grandson. Her hair rapidly became white and her eyes grew faded.

'Things will get better,' Dee tried to tell her. 'They have to. The war will end, we'll find Sylvia and the baby and we'll all be happy again.'

Helen would smile faintly but without conviction. Her health was visibly failing and she began to have dizzy spells. She always passed these off as 'nothing' and brushed aside Dee's attempts to care for her. These days, she seemed indifferent to everything and everyone.

When the blow fell, it came with shocking suddenness.

One morning, as Dee was arriving for work, the ward sister looked up urgently.

'Ah, good, there you are. Go and see the new patient in bed five. She came in two hours ago, and she keeps saying your name.'

The woman who lay there was thin and weary, with heavy

bandages on her head. All her previous beauty had fled, yet Dee knew her at once.

'Sylvia—oh, Sylvia, wake up, please.'

Sylvia opened her eyes and a faint smile touched her mouth. 'Is that really you?' she murmured.

'Yes, I'm here. I can't believe it—after all this time! Whatever happened to you?'

Her sister was in a bad way, her face bruised, her lips swollen.

'A bomb hit the house,' Sylvia murmured. 'A wall fell in on me before I could escape. They got me out in the end but—' Her voice faded.

Dee drew up a chair and leaned forward, clasping Sylvia's hand. 'Where have you been? Why didn't you let us come to see you? Mum's been worried sick.'

'I didn't want to shame her. How would she explain me to the neighbours?'

'They don't matter. It's you that matters. What about Phil? Are you still with him?'

'He died at Dunkirk. It's just me and the baby now, but—I don't know where he is. When they rescued me they must have found him as well. But where is he—*where's my baby?*' Her voice rose in anguish.

'They'll have taken him to another ward,' Dee said reassuringly. 'I'll go and ask.'

She hurried out, seizing a phone to call an ambulance official, who promised to contact her in a few minutes. Then she called her mother, who gave a little shriek on hearing the news. *'I'm coming, I'm coming. Tell her.'*

Dee returned to the ward. Sylvia's eyes had closed again and it would be best to let her sleep, at least until there was some news. A quick glance at the notes told her the worst. Sylvia had been badly injured. Her chances were poor.

'No,' Dee said to herself. 'It can't happen.'

But it could and she knew it.

She had other patients who needed her care, but while she was tending them her eyes constantly turned to the end of the ward, watching for Sylvia to wake. Part of her didn't believe this was happening. And part of her knew that the worst was going to befall her despite her resolutions.

Hurry, she whispered inwardly to her mother, *while there's still time.*

The ward sister approached and Dee explained briefly. 'My mother will be here soon and—there she is, just coming in.'

'Take care of her,' the sister said kindly. 'The others can do your work for a while.'

'Where is she?' Helen asked, running towards her in tears.

'Mum, be ready for a shock. She's badly hurt.'

Sylvia opened her eyes as her mother approached and Dee had the satisfaction of seeing them reach out to each other.

But then she saw the sister beckoning. Her face was grave. 'I'm afraid it's bad news,' she said. 'The baby was dead when they found him. They couldn't tell her because she was unconscious.'

'Oh, no,' Dee whispered. 'How can I tell her?'

Approaching the bed, she found Helen talking feverishly. 'Just as soon as you can be moved, I'm taking you home, you and the baby, and you'll live with us and we won't care what the neighbours say. Everything's going to be all right.'

'Oh, yes, please, Mum…please…you're going to love Joey. I named him after Dad.'

'He'll like that,' Helen choked. 'We're all going to be so happy.'

Dee wondered if her mother really believed this. How much did she understand? Could she see that her daughter was dying, or was she spared that for the moment?

Sylvia's eyes were closed and she was talking wildly, her breath coming in shaky gasps that were getting worse. 'Mum…Mum…'

'Yes, darling, I'm here. Hold on.'

But Sylvia was no longer capable of holding on. Her breath faded, her hands fell away.

'No!' The cry broke from Helen as she gathered her lifeless daughter in her arms. 'No, you've got to stay with me. We're going home together and I'm going to look after you... Sylvia...*Sylvia!*'

She burst into violent sobs, clutching her daughter's body and shaking it, as though trying to infuse it with life, and crying her name over and over.

Dee felt for a pulse, although she knew it was useless. Her sister was dead.

Helen had recognised the truth and gently lay her child back on the bed.

'We haven't lost her,' she choked. 'Not really. We'll look after the baby, and it'll be like she's still with us.'

'Mum—'

Helen's voice and her eyes became desperate. 'We'll do that, won't we? We must find the baby and take him home. Yes, that's what we'll do...that's what...what we...' Her breath began to come in long gasps. She clutched her throat, then her heart while her eyes widened.

'Help me,' Dee cried, supporting Helen in her arms.

Helping hands appeared. An oxygen mask was fitted over Helen's face but it was too late. The heart attack was massive and she was dead in minutes.

'Go with them,' the ward sister said as the two women were taken away to the hospital mortuary. 'Oh, my dear, I'm so sorry.'

'It was bound to happen,' Dee whispered. 'When Sylvia went away she suffered badly, but she always nursed the hope they'd be reunited. Sylvia's death destroyed her.' Tears began to run down her face. 'Oh, heavens! How am I going to tell my father? His wife, his daughter, his grandson, all on the same day.'

Now the shock was getting to her and she began to shiver uncontrollably. She was still shivering when Joe arrived at the hospital and joined her in the mortuary. His face was so pale and grey that for a dreadful moment she feared she was about to lose him, too.

She told him what had happened, adding, 'Sylvia died in her arms.'

'Then they found each other again,' he said. 'Thank God! Sylvia was always her favourite.' Then he added gently, 'Just like you were always mine.'

Until then, she'd never appreciated her father's strength, but it was a new, tougher man who told her to leave the funeral arrangements to him because, 'You've been through enough.'

And it was true—she was reaching the end of her tether. She almost gave way entirely when she and Joe stood in the mortuary regarding Sylvia with her baby in her arms, ready to be buried together. Joe's arm was strong about her, but even he nearly yielded to terrible grief at the sight of the child.

'My grandson,' he whispered as tears streamed down his face. 'My first ever grandchild, and we meet like this. Poor Sylvia. Poor Helen.'

They supported each other through the three-way funeral, and afterwards Joe put his arms around her. 'We've both lost everyone else,' he said huskily. 'There's just us now, love.'

Like others who had suffered devastating losses, Dee and her father survived as day passed into day, week into week and month into month. He'd said they had just each other, and for now neither of them wanted anyone else. Christmas 1942 was their first alone, and they were thankful to pass it quietly, refusing all invitations.

These days she relied totally on Mr Royce for news of Mark, so that when she went in one morning in the new year to find him looking grave, she knew what had happened.

'I'm sorry,' he said.

'He's dead, isn't he?' she said bleakly.

For a moment the world went dark. She clutched the back of a chair, then felt him supporting her until she sat down.

'No,' he said. 'He isn't dead.'

'Not dead? Do you mean that?'

'I swear to you that he's alive, but he's very badly hurt. His Spitfire was hit during a battle. He just managed to limp home but, as he landed, the plane burst into flames. They brought him here. He's lucky to be alive.'

'But he is alive—and he's going to stay alive, isn't he? *Isn't he?'*

'I think so.' The words were cautious.

'But it's not certain?'

'He's been very badly burned and he needs help. It's lucky you're here. The sight of you will help him.'

'Where is he?'

'Come this way.'

As they went along the corridor he said, 'I've had him put in a separate ward. I'd better warn you that he looks pretty alarming. He was engulfed in flames. It was a miracle that his face escaped. His helmet saved him, but he has burns all over his torso, and an injury to the head where he hit it.'

She paused as they reached a door, Mr Royce pushing it open quietly and standing aside.

Dee approached slowly, and gradually the bed came into view. Then she stopped, appalled, shaking at the sight. In her worst nightmares she hadn't imagined this.

The man on the bed could have been anybody, so totally was he covered in bandages. They extended over his torso, his arms, up over his neck and around his head.

Where was the daredevil young hero who laughed in the face of danger? Gone—and in his place lay this helpless baby. She wanted to cry aloud to the heavens that it wasn't fair of life to do this to him. Why was there nobody to defend him?

But there was, she thought with sudden resolution. She was here now. She would defend him.

'Has he been unconscious all the time?' she asked softly.

'No, he's come round and muttered something, but of course most of the time we keep him heavily sedated against the pain.' Mr Royce examined a chart. 'Going by the time of his last injection, he should come round quite soon.'

'You can leave me alone with him,' Dee said. 'He'll be safe with me.'

'I'm sure he will.'

When the door had closed, Dee came closer to the bed. As a nurse, she was used to horrific sights, but nothing in her experience helped her now. This was the man she loved, lying alone and in agony.

His eyes were closed and his breathing came with a soft rasping sound that was almost like a groan. Now she could see just enough of his face to recognise him. The mouth was the one she knew, wide and made for laughter, but tense now, as though the pain reached him, even in sleep.

Dee drew a chair forward and sat down, leaning as close to him as she could get. 'Hello, darling,' she whispered.

Nothing. He didn't move or open his eyes, but lay almost like a dead man.

'It's me—Dee,' she persisted. 'I heard you'd been injured, and I had to come and see you. Even after what happened, we're still friends, aren't we? You still matter to me, and I want to see you well and strong again.'

Silence but for his soft breathing. No sign of life. Refusing to be put off, she continued, 'You really will be all right in the end, although it may take some time. They say you're pretty badly hurt, but I've nursed men with worse injuries and they come through it because they can't wait to get up there in the sky again.'

She was stretching the truth here. She knew how unlikely it was that Mark would ever return to being an airman, and how long it would be before he could live any kind of normal life, but she couldn't afford to think of that. Only one thing mattered and that was bringing him back into the land of the living. If she could do that, and even one day see him smile again, she cared for nothing else.

She went on, forcing herself to sound cheerful. 'I wish we were still engaged. Oh, don't think I'm trying to trap you. You were always too clever to be caught by any woman. But you don't seem to have anyone of your own.'

The truth of that struck her with force. The star of the squadron, the man every girl wanted to flirt with, and more. But he had nobody; no family, nobody had been allowed to get close to him. Except herself. She had crept closer than anyone, yet even she hadn't suspected his essential aloneness before now. He'd always worked so hard to conceal it.

Had he done so knowingly? she wondered. Had he really understood himself that well? Somehow she doubted it. Whatever Mark's qualities, insight wasn't one of them. That was why he had needed her. But she hadn't seen it either, and had rejected him.

'Are you glad I came to see you?' she asked him. 'I hope you are. I know you're asleep but maybe you can hear me, somewhere deep inside you, and perhaps...perhaps your heart is open to what I want to say. Oh, I do hope so because there's so much I want you to understand.

'I was clumsy before. I loved you so much that I was afraid to let you know, in case it embarrassed you. You see, I knew you didn't love me—well, maybe a little, but not as I love you. I was so happy when you asked me to marry you that I didn't let myself worry about how it happened. All I saw was that I could be your wife.

'I was fooling myself, but I wouldn't face it because you were everything to me. And when I did face it—I went a bit crazy. I blamed you for not loving me, but you can't love to order. Nobody can. You have to accept people as they are, or back off. I backed off. I thought I was doing what you wanted. Now I'm not so sure. Perhaps I still have something to give you—something that you need.'

A soft rumble came from between his lips, almost as though he was signalling agreement. Of course, that was fanciful, which she never allowed herself to be. But perhaps, just this once—

'Oh, darling, if only I could believe that you hear me and know what I'm trying to say. I came here as soon as I knew you were hurt because if there's anything I can do for you, I'll do it. It doesn't matter what it is. Do you understand that? Anything at all.'

She looked down at his hands lying on the blanket; one bandaged, the other uncovered. How fine and well shaped it was. How well she remembered it touching her, teasing softly through her thin clothes, making her want him in ways that she knew she shouldn't.

Inching her way forward cautiously, she took his free hand in hers, caressing it softly with her fingers. He neither moved nor showed any sign of a response, and her heart ached to see his power reduced to this helplessness. She would have given everything she possessed to see him restored to his old self—mischievous, disrespectful, outrageous, infuriating, magical. Even if it meant that she would lose him again, if her heart broke a thousand times over, she would accept it if, in return, she could see him happy.

'You're going to get better,' she told him, more confidently than she felt. 'You can count on that because I won't settle for anything else. I can be a bully when I set my mind to it, and that's what I'm going to do. You told me once you weren't good at taking orders, but you'll take mine. Get well! There! That's an order, do you hear?'

She struggled to keep the jokey note in her voice, but at last it was more than she could bear. Her words trembled into silence and she laid her face against his hand while the tears flowed.

'Come back to me,' she whispered. 'Come back to me. I love you with all my heart. I'll never love anyone else. You don't have to love me. Just let me care for you.'

After a while she raised her head again and looked closely at the man who lay without moving, barely breathing.

'I have to believe that somewhere, deep inside your heart, you can hear me,' she told him. 'Perhaps you're even conscious of it now, and soon you'll wake and remember. Or perhaps my words will come back to you without you even knowing how or when you heard them. Oh, my love, my love, can I creep into your heart without you even noticing, and then just stay there?'

A long sigh came from him. Summoning all her courage, she laid her lips gently against his. 'I thought I'd never kiss you again,' she murmured. 'Can you feel me? Can you feel my love reaching out to you? It's yours if you want it.'

Another sigh. She looked down on him tenderly. 'Yes, oh, yes,' she breathed. 'You're coming back to me. You are.'

Her joy soared as Mark opened his eyes. For a long moment they looked at each other.

'Who are you?' he asked.

CHAPTER TEN

FOR a long time now everything in his life had been jagged. It started with the danger that threatened whenever he took to the air, but he accepted that. It was the life he'd chosen. But then he found that the sunlight was jagged and threatening, making him reluctant to face it. Worst of all was the soft jaggedness of darkness and the insidious fear that kept him awake, all the more alarming because he didn't understand it.

It had started when she broke their engagement. He'd been cool and self-contained, as befitted a man who could have any woman, shrugging off her desertion. She'd set him free. She'd said so herself, predicting that the other women would throw a party.

'You won't remember that I exist,' she'd said.

Then the numbness that shielded him had begun to disintegrate and a spark of temper had flared. He'd accused her of cruelty, something he'd never felt from any woman before. When she'd gone the anger stayed with him, making him act unlike himself. He'd gone drinking with friends that night, casually remarking that his engagement was over. One of the others, a hearty, shallow young man called Shand, had made the mistake of congratulating him. Overwhelmed by rage, Mark had launched himself on the imbecile and might have killed him if his friends hadn't hauled him off in time.

After that, everyone regarded him differently. His friends kept watchful, protective eyes on him, lest he break out again. From Shand he received awe and respect, which disgusted him.

'Well, at least someone managed to shut the little blighter up,' Harry Franks observed once. Harry had joined the Air Force on the same day as Mark and they had immediately become friends. 'You should be proud of that.'

'He's not worth it,' Mark snapped.

'I agree. But he might have hit the nail on the head. Maybe you really are better off without this girl. You aren't in love with her, are you?'

'How the hell do I know?' Mark roared.

Harry nodded wisely, his expression suggesting that if he'd known things were like that, he wouldn't have asked.

Mark's inner fury continued, all the worse because he didn't understand it himself. Dee had broken the engagement in a way that suggested that he was really dumping her, thus preserving his dignity. So what was there to be angry about? Especially with her?

But he knew that if she were here this minute, he would explain to her exactly why she was wrong about everything, make her admit it and ask his forgiveness for misjudging him. Then he would replace the ring on her finger as a symbol of his victory. It was the only way to deal with awkward women.

'We belong together,' he rehearsed. 'We've always known what each other was thinking, and that's never happened to me with anyone else. I didn't want it before. I've tried to keep my thoughts to myself because I didn't trust anyone else, but with you I couldn't do that and I didn't mind. I even liked it. Do you realise that? You did something for me that…that… and then you abandoned me.'

No, he couldn't say these things. They sounded pathetic, and at all costs he wasn't going to be pathetic. But there were other ways of putting it so that she would see reason. If only she was here!

But she wasn't, and she didn't contact him.

He even began to jot down his thoughts, to be ready to confront her. But it was a fraught business. He slept at the base, sharing a small dormitory with five others, all ready for action at any moment in the night. It was hard to find privacy and if he heard someone coming he had to stuff his papers into a small cupboard by the bed. Once he did this so hastily that the contents of the overfull cupboard fell out and he found himself confronting a small bear in a frilly dress.

It was the one she'd given him at the fun fair, having bought it for the ludicrously expensive price of one shilling and sixpence.

Dee seemed to be there, teasing him out of the jagged darkness. 'She's going to keep an eye on you…and report back to me if you get up to mischief.' Then her voice changed, became loving, as he remembered it. 'And look after you.'

'Are you reporting back to her now?' he murmured. 'I wonder what you'll tell her.'

Then he stopped short, wondering at himself, knowing how it would have looked if any of his comrades had caught him talking to a toy.

But not her. She would have understood. Did she still talk to the Mad Bruin he'd given her? Did she still have it? He found himself hoping that she did. But of course he would never know.

The sound of the door opening made him quickly hide the bear. This was private, between Dee and himself, the one thing that still united them across the miles and the silence. In an obscure way, it was a comfort to a man who'd never admitted to himself that he needed to be comforted.

He hadn't given the toy a name, but in his mind she became 'Dee'. Incredibly, there was even a physical resemblance. Not that the little bear had Dee's features, but she had her expression—wry, teasing, unconvinced, a look that could be summed up as, *Oh, yeah?* Which was absurd if you thought about it, but he didn't think about it. He just appreciated it.

He began to keep his little friend with him, unwilling to leave her in the locker where she might be discovered. An inner pocket in his loose flying jacket made a useful hiding place and one day, almost forgetting she was there, he took her onto the plane with him.

It was a fierce and terrible sortie, a bombing raid on an enemy armaments factory in early 1943. Resistance was fierce, with Messerschmitts, the magnificent enemy bombers, attacking from all directions. At one point he would almost have sworn he'd reached his final moment, when the plane heading for him seemed to halt in mid-air before exploding in a ball of fire. He had a searingly precise view of the pilot's desperate eyes before the other plane dropped out of the sky.

When he landed he sat for a moment, arms folded across his body, feeling the little bump beneath the flying jacket that told him his tiny friend was there. To think that 'Dee' had protected him was sheer fanciful madness, and he wasn't a fanciful man, yet the thought persisted. *She* had been there, not the woman herself, but her little furry representative. It was crazy. He was a fool, a stupid, naive, delusional idiot. Yet he was also mysteriously comforted.

After that, the bear went with him on every sortie, seeing him through near-misses, escapes and the odd triumph. And it began to seem to Mark that Dee—his own true Dee, the woman who had scorned him—had nevertheless the right to know that she was influencing his life, perhaps even saving it. It was an excuse to write to her, and he badly needed an excuse.

The letter was hard. On light matters he'd always found talking easy—too easy—but now, in the depths of sincerity, he found the words eluding him. He wrote at last:

> I meant to send her back to you, but she's a nice little companion and I'd miss her. Do you still have the Mad Bruin? Do you ever look at him and think of me? I hope

so. You were right to break it off. I'm a useless character and I'd be no good for you, but let him remind you of me sometimes; even if it's only the annoying things, like how unreliable I am, no common sense, the way I make jokes about all the wrong things, don't turn up when I'm expected, stick my nose in where it's not wanted, never seem to understand when you want to be left alone. I'm sure you can think of plenty more.

The letter didn't satisfy him. It didn't even begin to convey what was in his heart, but he wasn't even sure what that was. And, even if he had been sure, he didn't think he could have said it. He put the paper away, to be finished later.

He did return to it several times, always remembering something else that it was vital for her to know. Days passed, then weeks, and somehow it was never sent.

He was afraid and he knew it. The man who faced down death a hundred times was afraid to contact the woman whose reply could damage him more than any Messerschmitt. Afraid! How she would laugh at that. And, after all, she had the right to know that she'd triumphed, just as she had the right to know that she was protecting him. Perhaps he could simply turn up and confront her with it, and watch her face as she learned exactly what she'd done to him. The temptation was so strong that he shut his thoughts off abruptly.

Another sortie was beginning, demanding his attention. He took off in the sunlight, headed out over the sea towards the continent. After that, things became confused. He knew his aircraft was hit and he was aware of himself mechanically piloting back to England and safety, frantically praying that he would arrive before the explosion.

He almost made it. As he came down the flames were beginning to take over. Another few seconds…just a few… just a few…

Then the air was rent by a terrible screaming that he didn't even recognise as his own. The jaggedness converged on him from all directions, stabbing, burning, terrifying him. Hands were tearing at the plane, pulling him out. He lay on the ground, listening to the shouting around him, waiting for his life to end. It was all over now and the only thing that really hurt was that he would never see Dee again. Then the darkness engulfed him.

But, instead of swallowing him up for ever, it lifted after a while, revealing a mist, with her voice all around him. He couldn't see her face but her words filled his heart with joy.

'...Maybe you can hear me, somewhere deep inside you... there's so much I want you to understand...'

He tried to speak but he could make no sound. Her voice continued whirling through the clouds.

'I was clumsy before. I loved you so much that I was afraid to let you know... I was so happy when you asked me to marry you... All I saw was that I could be your wife...'

My wife, he thought. You are my wife, now and always. Why can't I tell you?

'Come back to me... I love you with all my heart... Just let me care for you.'

Everything in him wanted to say yes, to find her, draw her close. He opened his eyes in desperate hope, straining to see her face, which must be full of the same emotion as her voice, an emotion that offered him hope for the first time in his life.

But his dream had been in vain. There was only a nurse in a professional uniform, the cap low over her forehead, her features frowning and severe. Disappointment tore him, making him say almost violently, *'Who are you?'*

At first the words made no impact on Dee. She couldn't understand them—*wouldn't* understand them and their terrible implication.

He stared at her, or perhaps through her. His eyes were empty of recognition, of feeling, of anything.

'Who are you?'

'I...Mark, it's me...Dee...'

But his eyes remained blank until he closed them, murmuring, 'Sorry, Nurse.'

She took a deep breath, telling herself that it meant nothing. She was in uniform, her hair covered by a nurse's cap, as he hadn't seen her before. And he was heavily sedated, not his normal self.

'Nurse—' he murmured.

'Yes, I'm here.'

He gave a long tortured sigh that ended in a groan.

Mr Royce came quietly into the room. 'He's due for more painkiller,' he said. 'Will you help me administer it?'

Together they did what was necessary, which seemed to bring Mark some ease. He opened his eyes again, murmuring, 'Thank you, Nurse.'

'Leave him to sleep,' Mr Royce said, ushering her out of the room.

'He doesn't know me,' she said flatly when they were outside.

'Given the condition he's in, that's hardly surprising, but part of his recovery will be regaining the memories of his old life and you can assist him in that as nobody else can. I'm assigning you to him full-time. Yes, I know that will be hard for you, but you must be professional about this, Nurse.'

'Of course.'

Professional, she told herself. That was what mattered. She must forget her shame at the memory of the things she'd said, the impassioned outpouring of love, the naive way she'd hoped for some flicker of love in return, only to be met with, 'Who are you?'

She took immediate charge of him, silencing all other thoughts but his need and her duty, but it was hard when her feelings were so involved. The first time she saw his burns she had to fight back tears. The whole of his chest was violently red and raw, and she could only guess at what he must be suffering. Her ministrations made him wince, despite being on such a heavy dose of painkiller that he never seemed more than vaguely awake. Now and then he would gaze at her as though trying to remember where he'd seen her before, but he always addressed her as 'Nurse'.

'Perhaps you should stay with him overnight,' Joe told her late one evening. He'd been on a training session and they had arrived home at nearly the same moment.

'What about you?' she said, looking around at the bleak, echoing house. 'I don't like leaving you alone.'

'I'm a big boy now, love. I can cope. And I'm not alone, not really. Your Mum's here with me. No, don't look like that. I'm not mad. This is the home she created, and every inch of it is what she made. If I work late in the garage, she puts her head around the door and says, "Are you coming in or are you going to be here all night?" If I'm making tea, I always fill the pot in case she wants one. I know how much she loved me, and she still does, almost as much as I love her.'

'I always wondered about that—' Dee said hesitantly. 'The way your marriage came about—'

'Oh, you mean that stuff about me making her pregnant and being forced to do the decent thing. Nah, nobody forced me. I was daft about her, but I was shy. I was even scared to kiss her in case she was offended, while as for…you know…'

'Yes, I know,' she said, lips twitching.

'All right, go on, laugh at me, but it was another age. You were supposed to behave yourself in them days. But your mum knew what she wanted, and she wanted me. Lord knows why, but she did.'

'Are you saying—?'

'She made the running. I wouldn't have dared.'

Dee stared, barely able to believe what she was hearing.

'So when you and she...she was the one who...? But I don't understand. She was always so strait-laced, saying we must be "good girls" and the way she acted when Sylvia went away with Phil—'

'People often do that,' Joe observed. 'Talk one way, act another. It was Sylvia's disappearing that she really minded, and the fact that she went off with a married man. She'd have forgiven her the other thing, because it was what she did herself. She told me later that she was determined to start a baby so that I'd have to stop dithering like a twerp and make my mind up,' Joe said with pride. 'She really loved me, you see.'

'Yes, she did,' Dee agreed.

'And when you've found the right one, do what you have to. So you get on with it, girl. And don't you worry about your mum and me. We'll be all right here together.'

Armed with Joe's encouragement, she began staying overnight at the hospital, sleeping in the Nurses' Home so that she could spend as much time with Mark as possible. She fed him, changed his dressings, soothed him when he half awoke, listened to his soft moans at night.

Gradually the amount of painkiller he needed lessened, and he began to sleep more peacefully. The bandages were removed from his head, and Dee marvelled at how little he seemed to have changed. The burns on his body were terrible, but his face was undamaged. To the outside world he would seem the same handsome young man he had always been, a little older, a little more weather-beaten, but basically the same. Yet this was an illusion. The damage might be hidden, but it was there.

She checked his pulse, wondering if he would awaken soon, and would he still ask who she was? Would she be nothing but the nurse who cared for him, without individuality, no different from any other? Would he even recognise her as that?

He stirred and she laid his hand down on the sheet, waiting until at last he opened his eyes, looking straight into hers.

'Hello,' he whispered.

'Hello.' She sat beside him, smiling and trying to seem cheerful.

'Where am I?'

She gave him the name of the hospital, wondering if he would recognise it as the one where she worked, but he said nothing. 'You've been here nearly a week,' she added.

'What happened to me?'

'You crashed. I'm afraid you're badly burned. Are you in pain now?'

'No, I just feel dizzy. I don't know anything.' He gazed at her intently. 'You've been looking after me, haven't you?'

'You remember that?'

'I know I've seen you somewhere before. You're Nurse—?'

'Nurse Parsons,' she said.

'Oh, yes—you were always there—and someone else—I'm trying to remember—did anyone come to visit me while I was unconscious?'

'Your commanding officer came, and a couple of your comrades looked in. I couldn't let them stay long. They just wanted to see for themselves that you're alive.'

'Nobody else?' he whispered, and she wondered if she only imagined that his voice was full of hope.

'Nobody else. Was there someone else you wanted to see? Can I find them for you?'

He sighed softly. 'Thanks, but no. She wouldn't want you to.'

'You don't know that,' Dee said quickly. 'If she's a good friend, who cares what happens to you—'

'A good friend,' he echoed with a wry smile. 'She was the best friend I had, but I didn't know it.'

'But if you know it now, perhaps she'd like to hear you say so.'

'I doubt it. Where she was concerned, I talked too much and said all the wrong things—did all the wrong things, too. She was glad to be rid of me.'

'You can't be sure of that.'

'I can. She despised me. She made that very clear.'

'She probably didn't mean it that way.'

'When a woman tells a man to go and jump in the lake, there's no doubt what she means.'

'She actually used those words?'

'Words that meant the same. She dressed it up, practically made it sound as though I was the one breaking it off, but that was just her way of smoothing things. The truth is, she despised me.' He gave a sigh. 'And she may have been right.'

'No, she didn't despise you.'

'You can't know that.'

Then inspiration came to her. Turning the lights out so that there was only the one small bedside lamp, she returned to sit beside him, turning so that her face was in shadow. Perhaps now she looked no more than a shadowy presence, and that might be the trigger.

'But I do know that,' she said.

He stared at her, startled. 'What do you know?'

'Everything she knows. You'll understand soon, when the drugs wear off.'

'Dee? Is that really you? I think...I'm beginning to understand now. Put the light on.'

She shook her head. 'Better not.' She didn't want him to see how shaken she was, eyes brimming in relief, that he had finally recognized her again.

'You're right,' he said after a moment. 'It's strange how I know you now that I can't see you properly.'

'You never did see me properly,' she murmured.

'What do you mean by that?'

'Nothing,' she said quickly. 'It's all in the past now. We're not really the same people that we were then. When did we last see each other? A year ago?'

'Longer,' he murmured. 'Much longer. It seems to stretch back for ever, into another life—'

'I know, it feels like that to me too, but it's just a year. So much has happened since.'

Tentatively, he stretched out his hand and she took it between hers. 'I've sometimes dreamed that it was you,' he said huskily. 'I've even tried to pretend that it was—but I told myself I was being foolish because you must still be angry with me.'

'I was never angry with you.'

'You gave me back my ring.'

'Not from anger. I just thought our paths were leading away from each other. We're still friends.'

'Are we? When I was injured, I was sure you'd come to me at once. When you didn't, I knew you hadn't forgiven me.'

'But I did come to you, as soon as I heard you were here. You were unconscious, so I sat and talked to you, praying for you to wake, but then you did wake and you didn't know me. You asked who I was. I said I was Dee but that meant nothing to you. The accident had wiped me from your memory.'

'No, nothing could do that. I've been in a dream. You were there, yet you weren't. I could hear you talking to me, saying things that—'

'Yes?'

He screwed up his eyes as though fighting an inner battle.

'I don't know,' he said desperately. 'They made me happy but when I awoke, I couldn't remember them. Was it you? Did you really say everything I heard?'

'How can I tell?' she said lightly. 'Since I don't know what you heard.'

'It was…it was…oh, dear God!' He closed his eyes desperately. 'Tell me. Say it again so that I'll know.'

'Not just now,' she said gently. 'You're going to be here for some time, and we'll take it step by step.'

'But you'll be here, too? You will, won't you?' His grip was tight enough to be painful.

'Yes, I'll be here. Hey, don't break my fingers or I'll be no use.'

He released her at once, letting his hand fall on the blanket in a way she would have called helpless if it had been any other man. Now his expression was resigned and she knew he'd accepted her words and manner as a rejection. If only she could take him into her arms and tell him of her love, which was stronger than ever. But instinct told her he wasn't strong enough to stand it right now. There would be a long road until he was ready, but they would travel that road together and discover where it led.

Now it was she who set the terms, guiding him through the days that followed as a friend and nurse, but with no hint of a lover, and had the satisfaction of seeing him relax and allow himself to be cared for. It hurt to see him so docile and unlike his old vibrant, cocky self, but it helped her take charge, which she was determined to do.

Now she was sleeping in the Nurses' Home, she could slip in to see him at night, staying with him in the semi-darkness, sometimes talking, sometimes silent. It was on one of these nights that she told him about Sylvia and Helen.

'Did that man ever marry her?' he asked.

'No, he couldn't get a divorce. In fact, I went to the street where they'd been living and spoke to some of the neighbours who'd survived the bombing, and they seemed to think he was planning to go back to his wife.'

'Poor Sylvia,' he said huskily. 'She deserved better. Did you ever see the baby?'

'Yes, he was in her arms when we buried them. She had nothing left to live for. I still find it hard to take in. When we were children she was so glorious, she was like queen of the world. She was going to have everything; we all thought so.'

Mark didn't answer directly but he looked sad, and she wondered what memories were troubling him now. But she would never ask. After a while, she bid him goodnight and crept away.

He'd been lucky in that the third-degree burns were on the front of his body where the fire had exploded. The seat had partly protected his back until he'd managed to fight his way out and collapse, which was good, Dee thought thankfully, because if his back had been in the same appalling state as his front he could never have lain down.

His chest was a mass of dark red blisters which she would anoint gently, trying not to hurt him, although she knew that there would be a certain amount of nerve damage that would save him from some of the pain. Sometimes Mr Royce would come in and stand watching before inviting her outside to discuss the case.

'He's doing well,' he told her. 'But there's only so far that his condition can improve. An Air Force doctor will be coming to see him soon.'

'They're not trying to get him back?' she asked, scandalised.

'Quite the reverse. I think they'll judge him unfit to return to the Force in any capacity.'

'Thank God!' she said fervently.

He regarded her for a moment, 'It matters that much?' he asked at last.

'I hate patching them up so that they can go and get killed,' she said defensively. 'At least he's one that will live.'

He was giving her a look she didn't understand and she escaped quickly back into Mark's room. She found him lying still, with a shadow in his eyes.

'When shall I congratulate you?' he asked.

'What do you mean? I'm not due for promotion for ages.'

'You're due for promotion to Mrs Royce, very soon.'

'Will you stop talking nonsense?'

'I know what I see. That man's in love with you.'

'Nonsense! He's a kind person who's gone out of his way to help me.'

But then she remembered Mr Royce's strange look a moment ago, the trouble he'd always taken to discover news of Mark. Did he do this for everyone? How could there be time? And if it was just for her—why?

'He must be twenty years older than me,' she protested.

'More.'

'So what? He's strong, mature, settled. He can offer you a position in the world. You were made to be a successful man's wife. He's in love with you.'

'You're making fun of me. You couldn't possibly tell.'

'I can, easily. When a man gets that look in his eyes, it means just one thing.'

'It's not like you to be fanciful.'

'It wasn't,' he sighed. 'But maybe it is now. What is "like me", Dee? You tell me, because I don't know any more. At night I lie here and listen to the things in my head, and I don't know what to make of them. Nothing is the way I thought. Everything is different, but I don't know what it all means. Can't you tell me?'

'My dear,' she said gently, 'how can I tell you when I've never been there, seen the things you've seen—?'

'Done the things I've done,' he finished for her. 'You're right. It must remain a mystery, more to me than anyone. But—' he assumed a cheerful air, as though forcing himself to rally '—I won't let you distract me from Mr Royce. Any day now, he'll propose, mark my words.'

'Will you stop talking nonsense, please?' she asked crisply. 'I want to finish your dressing.'

'But you—'

'Keep still and *keep quiet,*' she said, with a sharpness rare in her.

He did so, but continued to study her curiously. She finished the job and departed as soon as she could.

Deny it as she might, she was left with the uncomfortable feeling that Mark had seen something that had entirely escaped her. And the next time she talked with Mr Royce she felt uneasy, wondering what he was thinking. When their meeting ended she began to walk away, then looked back to say something and found him still watching her with an unguarded look.

The Air Force doctor made two visits and examined Mark thoroughly, especially his damaged hand. The verdict came by letter two days later.

'Invalided out,' Mark groaned, showing her the letter in disgust. 'Useless!'

He tried to flex his hand, whose limited movement had proved his undoing, more than the burns to his chest.

'You'd have had a hard time controlling a plane with that,' Dee said. 'They had to do this. At least they'll allow you something to live on.'

'A pension, you mean,' he said in disgust. 'That says all that needs to be said. I'm a pensioner.'

It was Joe who cheered him up slightly. He'd paid several visits, and the next day he dropped in again.

'I hate to admit it,' he said, glancing over the letter, 'but this is good news for me. I haven't been able to find a decent replacement for you in the garage. They're either useless or they leave. But now you can come back, and I'll be glad to have you. We can put you up in the house, so you won't have a journey to work.'

'But I'll be useless, too,' Mark said, holding up his damaged hand.

'You won't have to fly a plane with that, just rework the

movements so that you can do them differently. Lucky it's your left hand.'

'Joe, I can't take charity.'

'It's not charity. You'd be doing me a favour. That house is empty without Sylvia and Helen. It echoes something horrible. But if you're there, it'll be more cheerful.'

Mark was still uncertain, fearful of being pitied but eager for the chance to work. Dee slipped out, leaving them to it. When she met up with Joe later, he was triumphant.

'I told him you'd be there sometimes to keep an eye on him, so they might let him out of this place sooner. That did it. He's going potty in here.'

'You're a cunning schemer,' she told him lovingly.

'That's what your mum used to say, just like you said it. I told you once before—you have to know what you want and go for it.'

'And you think you know what I want?'

'Actually, love, I was thinking more of what *I* want. That house really is lonely, so a couple of grandchildren would suit me down to the ground, just as soon as you can get round to it.'

'Dad! You're shameless.'

'Got to be. No time to waste. There's a war on. Hadn't you heard?'

Chuckling to himself, he fled her wrath.

CHAPTER ELEVEN

MR ROYCE was understanding. 'Your father's right. It'll help him to go home and live a more normal life, and you can look after him. I don't suppose you'll be sleeping here any more?'

'No, I'll be spending my nights at home now,' she said.

He sighed and gave her a wry smile. 'Just as I thought. Well, good luck.'

For a moment it was all there in his eyes, everything he'd felt but never said over the last few years. Then the shutters came down and he was once more Mr Royce, figure of authority.

Mark came home a week later and was installed in Sylvia's old room. By now he was on his feet and able to take the bus with the assistance of Joe, who closed the garage for the afternoon to help him. They both reached home safely, followed in the evening by Dee.

Joe had even cooked the supper for her and they celebrated together, toasting each other in cups of tea. Then she ordered Mark to bed and he obeyed with comical meekness.

Over the next few weeks, things improved. Mark's burns healed slowly but steadily. He could still manage many tasks in the garage, and having something to occupy his mind did him good.

Life settled into a pattern that was so strangely comfortable it seemed predestined. There was even a kind of happiness in the situation. Often Dee would awaken in the small hours and lie reflecting comfortably that Mark was there, safe under the same roof. It wasn't the relationship she'd dreamed of, but it brought out the protective side of her nature. Whatever might happen in the future, he was here now, hers, to be looked after and kept from harm.

It was nearly five years since they had met and both of them had changed. The changes in him were clear enough, but she often wondered how she seemed to him. Surveying herself in the mirror, she saw no sign of the naive girl she'd once been. The person who looked back was a woman, settled in her successful career, in her life, and so mature that it was hard to believe she was only twenty-two.

One day, in the late afternoon, when Joe was out at a training session with the Home Guard and Mark was working in the garage, she made a cup of tea and was preparing to take it to him when a shadow appeared in the back door. It was Eileen, a young woman of her own age who lived a couple of streets away.

'I just thought I'd drop in and see how you were,' she said. 'Haven't seen you for ages.'

She was one of the crowd of girls who had sighed over Mark in the early days and, although she now devoted a respectable amount of time to chattering about nothing, Dee wasn't surprised when she brought the conversation round to him.

'I hear you've got Mark living here again. Fancy that.'

'He's working at the garage with Dad, and he boards here because it's convenient.'

'Oh, I'm longing to see him!'

'Come on, then. I'm just taking him a cup of tea.'

From outside the garage, they could hear Mark singing tunelessly. There was no sign of him as they entered, only the noise coming from under a large car. Suddenly the noise stopped and Mark slid out from underneath. Dee heard a sharp intake of breath beside her and turned to see Eileen, her eyes fixed on Mark in horror.

Because of the warm day, he'd removed his shirt and his bare chest was visible. Eileen's hands were pressed to her mouth and she was slowly shaking her head as though to say it couldn't be true. Then she turned and hurried away.

The sight of Mark's face as he understood that a young woman had fled from him in disgust, repelled by his disfigurement, made Dee want to commit murder. She slammed down the mug of tea and turned to pursue Eileen but Mark stopped her.

'Let her go,' he said wearily. 'I must have given her a shock. I'm sorry; I wasn't expecting anyone except you, and you're used to the sight. I forget how dreadful I must look to anyone else.'

'She had no right—'

'It wasn't her fault,' Mark said simply.

He pulled on his shirt, buttoning it up to the neck so that none of the scars were visible. Then he sat down and dropped his head into his hands.

'Just give me a little time to get used to it,' he groaned. 'It's not the first time. It happened one day at the hospital. You were away for a moment and a nurse looked in with some dressings. I think she was a student, and not used to confronting horrors.'

'You're not—'

'I know what I am. Don't give me false hope. I'm like this for life and the sooner I accept it the better. If you could have seen that student's face when she saw me... She went pale.'

'Why didn't you tell me about it?'

'Because there would have been no point. This is the reality. This is what I am now, a man who makes women turn from him in horror.'

Dee was still consumed by anger on his behalf, and it

drove her to do something that caution might otherwise have prevented.

'Not this woman,' she said, taking his face in her hands and laying her lips on his.

She was inexperienced. Beyond a few brief pecks, she'd known no other kisses but his and they seemed long ago. But now everything in her seemed to be alive with the awareness of his need, telling her how to move her lips against his so that he would know she cared for him, wanted him.

She tried to speak of desire so intense that his terrible scars couldn't kill it, and for a few moments she thought she'd succeeded. His hands reached for her, touched her tentatively at first, then firmly, eagerly. She could feel him trembling. But then he stiffened, putting his hands on her arms and pushing her gently away.

'No,' he said hoarsely. 'Not this.'

'I'm sorry,' she stammered, swamped by shame. 'I only—'

'You only thought you'd carry your nursing a bit further, didn't you? Pity the poor patient, don't let him suspect how disgusting he is. It's all part of the cure. Well, I don't want your pity, do you hear? I don't want anyone's pity. I don't even want my own, and that's tough because I'm drowning in self-pity and I don't know how to—' He shuddered. 'Oh, to hell with you! Why did you have to do that?'

Thrusting her aside, he stormed to the door, stopped and looked back. 'Marry that doctor. He's reliable and respectable. Not like me. And you deserve the best.'

He walked away without giving her a chance to reply and she heard the house door slam as he entered. She didn't follow him at once, knowing that he needed to be alone.

He'd given her a glimpse of the devastation inside his head, even if against his own will. She'd thought she knew the wells of despair and self-disgust that lived there, but now she knew the depths extended further than her worst nightmares. Everything he said was true. If she was wise, she would turn from him to Mr Royce, who could offer her a new life.

But Mark was still the one she wanted; now more than ever. And her resolution was growing. Once before she had lost him by giving in too easily.

She wouldn't let it happen again.

On her way to bed that night, Dee stopped outside Mark's room. Hearing only silence, she opened the door a crack and listened to his deep, even breathing. Finally satisfied, she backed away without a sound.

Inside the room, Mark lay tense until he was certain she'd gone. Only then did he relax, thankful that his breathing had been steady enough to be convincing. After the events of the day, he couldn't have endured having to face her.

He fought to attain sleep. Once it had been so easy. In his untroubled youth he had only to lay his head on the pillow to be in happy dreamland. But that had been—barely five years ago? He was still in his twenties, technically a young man, but, as with so many of his comrades, the inner and outer man no longer matched.

The feeling of being at ease with life had slipped away from him so gradually that he'd barely noticed, until he found himself lying awake at night, which now happened unbearably often. In the hospital he'd been grateful for the sedation that silenced the demons. He could have taken a pill tonight, but he stubbornly refused. He knew Dee checked them every morning to see if he'd had any, and he was damned if he was going to let her know how desperately he wanted to. She already knew too much of his weakness.

At last he felt sleep coming on, retreating, drawing closer, teasing and tormenting, finally invading him, but only to torment him further. Now he was back in the damaged plane...heading back to the airfield...wondering if he'd make it...seeing the ground coming closer...almost there...then the explosion *and the flames!*

He fought to slide back the roof of the cockpit, but it was

stuck. He couldn't get out. He was trapped there while the fire consumed him—trapped in hell. He screamed and screamed but no sound came out. Nobody could hear him—he was abandoned.

'Where are you—where are you—?'

'I'm here, I'm here. Wake up—*wake up!*'

Hands were shaking him, touching his face, offering a way out of the nightmare. He reached for her eagerly, blindly.

'Help me—help me. Where are you?'

Dee saw his eyes open, but vaguely, as though he couldn't see her. He was shivering.

'Mark—Mark, talk to me.' She shook him. 'Are you awake?'

'I don't know,' he whispered. 'The fire—the fire—'

'There's no fire. That was a long time ago.'

'No, it wasn't. It's here; I can feel it—'

'No,' she cried. 'The fire is in the past. It can't hurt you now. I'm going to keep you safe. You're safe *with me.*'

At last, recognition seemed to creep into his eyes. 'Is it you?'

'Yes, it's me. I'm here and I'll always be here.'

She felt him sag in her arms as though the life had gone out of him, replaced by black despair. She tightened her embrace, full of fierce protectiveness.

She'd gone to bed, sad at his rejection of the comfort she had to offer, but, just as she was fading into sleep, the air had been rent by terrifying sounds from the next room. She'd dashed next door to find him sitting up in bed, screaming violently into the darkness. She'd sat beside him, taking him in her arms, but that didn't help. He'd seemed unaware of her, screaming on and on, caught in some terrifying other world where there was only fear and darkness.

She had switched on the bedside lamp, hoping that its light might bring him back to reality, but even when he looked at her she could tell he was still reliving his most ghastly moments, and she was torn by pity and frustration that she couldn't help him except, perhaps, by being there, letting him feel her presence and draw from it what solace he could. If any.

'I'm all right now,' he said bleakly.

Gently, she laid him back on the bed and came closer, propping herself up on one elbow to look down on him.

'Did I wake you?' he asked.

'I heard you being a bit disturbed. It's not the first time but you sounded more troubled tonight than ever before. Were you dreaming about the fire?'

'Not dreaming. Living. It was there all around me and I couldn't escape. I was so scared, I screamed. Isn't that funny?'

'I don't think it's funny at all,' she said tenderly.

'But it is. It's the biggest laugh of all time. I used to think I was so strong. I was a cocky, conceited so-and-so, but I know better now. Just a coward, screaming with fear.'

'You're not a coward,' she said fiercely. 'Any man would have nightmares after what you've been through.'

'I told myself that at first, but they go on and on and I don't know what to do. I'll tell you something that will really make you despise me—' He checked himself.

'Don't say anything you don't want to,' she told him.

'No, you're entitled to know the worst of me. When they said I couldn't go back to the Air Force...I was...I was glad. Do you hear that? I was glad. Oh, I said all the right things about being sorry I couldn't serve my country, but part of me was full of relief.'

'So I should hope,' she said crisply. 'That merely shows you have common sense.'

He stared. 'You're not ashamed of me.'

'No,' she said, almost in tears. 'There's nothing to be ashamed of. Oh, please, Mark, forget all this. You did your bit. You served your country and it nearly killed you. You should be proud, not ashamed. You have a life ahead of you and when you're fully recovered you'll find a way to live it.'

He glanced down at his disfigured chest. 'That will be hard when women can't bear to look at me,' he said.

'That silly girl this afternoon doesn't count. A woman who cared about you wouldn't be troubled by this.'

Suddenly she became aware of a new tension in his manner, and the way his eyes flickered away from her. Looking down, she saw why. She was wearing pyjamas, and in her agitation she'd forgotten to check that the front was properly buttoned up. It had fallen open, revealing her naked breasts.

He was still averting his gaze. She took a quick decision.

'Perhaps it's *you* that can't bear to look at *me*,' she said. 'Am I so ugly?'

'You know better than that.'

'But I don't,' she said softly. 'How could I know?'

Slowly, he turned his gaze back to linger over her breasts, shadowed by the soft lamplight. Then he lay without moving and for a horrible moment she wondered if he was shocked by her forwardness, but at last he reached up to her.

At the soft touch of his fingertips on her breast she felt a blazing excitement go through her, unlike anything she had ever known before. It was the merest whispering caress, but it brought her to life in a way she'd never dreamed of. She heard a long gasp and only dimly realised that it came from herself.

She didn't know how or where the pyjama jacket went, but suddenly he was touching her with both hands, taking her to another world where all the virtuous precepts of her rearing vanished without trace, and there was only this man and her desire for him.

Now all the textbooks were useless. Only her instincts could guide her, and they told her that he was coming to life, pulling away the rest of her pyjamas, then his own, infused with some feeling that made him forget caution, reticence, fear—forget everything except that he wanted and needed her.

For just one second reality seemed to pierce his dream, making him tense as he became conscious again of his scarred chest. Her answer was to lay her lips tenderly against it. She doubted if he could feel the gesture as his burns would have destroyed the nerves, but he would see it, and know that she was glad to reach out to him. When she looked up at his face again, she saw in it a look of wonder.

Then he was pressing her gently back on the bed, moving over her, parting her legs. She gasped at the moment of his entry, clutching him to her, silently saying that the infusion of new life was for him and only him. The moment when they became one was staggering, alarming, like being carried in a roller coaster, higher and higher, up to the heavens, until the devastating peak, and then the giddying descent, holding on to him for safety.

But there was no safety in this new world. There would never be safety again as long as she lived. And with all her soul she rejoiced at it.

She looked up at him, her chest heaving with pleasure, but, to her surprise and disappointment, he seemed troubled.

'I'm sorry,' he groaned.

'But why? Why should you be sorry?'

'It was your first time, wasn't it? Oh, Lord, what have I done? I didn't mean to…I never thought…'

'Neither did I,' she said. 'And I'm glad I never thought. Thought has no place here. Mark, I'm happy. I wanted this. Don't spoil it.'

'Do you mean that?' he asked cautiously.

She gave a smile full of delicious memory. 'Yes, I mean it. Oh, yes, I mean it.'

'Dee, I—' He stopped, choking. Words had always come easily to him, but that was for trivialities, jokes, chatter. Now he longed to tell her of his fear that his skills as a lover had died in the fire and his passionate gratitude to her for helping him rediscover them, and he was suddenly dumbfounded.

'Tell me,' she said.

'It's nothing—nothing—as long as you're all right.'

'Yes, I'm all right,' she assured him seriously. 'I'm more than all right.'

'You weren't just—being a good nurse?'

'Oh, Mark, stop it! You're talking nonsense. As though I would.'

He managed a pale smile. 'I don't know. You take such good care of me, better than anyone else has ever done, ever, in all my life.' He said the last words with an air of wondrous discovery.

'Just the same, there are lengths even a good nurse won't go,' she assured him. Her physical sensations had come swiftly down to earth, but her emotions were still up there, dazed with the joy of being in his arms, feeling at one with him.

Perhaps he felt the same for he suddenly grinned. There was happiness in his smile, but also relief.

Suddenly, Dee chuckled. 'You'll have to marry me now,' she teased.

At once his smile faded and he shook his head. 'Oh, no, I can't do that. I couldn't do you such harm.'

'Harm?'

'Look, I understand that you were only joking, but we both know that I'd be a useless husband. Bottom of the class. The last resort. I only have a job now because of your father's charity, and you'd have to nurse me for ever. I'd be a burden on you, and I can't do that. Just don't make jokes like that any more. All right?'

'All right,' she said with a little sigh that he didn't hear. 'Now, perhaps I'd better go back to my room. The patient has had too much excitement for one night.'

She scrambled back into her pyjamas and was gone without giving him the chance to say anything. After that, there was nothing to do but dive into her bed, hide as far as possible under the covers and curse her own clumsiness.

Why on earth did you have to say that about getting married? What happened to your common sense?

At last she pushed the clothes aside and sat up, eyes blazing into the darkness as she came to a decision.

This was no time for common sense! She had loved him hopelessly for five years, and it was now or never. And if it meant being a 'bad girl', so what? Hadn't her own mother shown the way?

In the corridor outside, Joe stood tentatively glancing back and forth between the doors of Mark's bedroom and Dee's, both of which he'd heard open and close. He hesitated, as though uncertain what a good father would do at this point. When it finally became clear to him, he crept back into his own room and quietly closed the door.

Dee was late home the next evening, to find Mark at the bus stop.

'Have you been there long?' she asked. 'You shouldn't. It's bad for you to stand about.'

'Joe and I were concerned, even after you called to say you had extra duty. He's got the kettle on.'

'Mmm,' she said blissfully, taking the arm he offered. 'How lovely to be pampered!'

'You can't always be the one doing the looking after,' he observed.

'I'm not complaining,' she assured him.

At home, she ate the egg Joe had boiled for her while they all discussed their day. Then they listened to the radio together. In some ways the news was heartening. The Allies had gone on to the attack, taking the airborne fight to the enemy and beginning to land forces in the occupied countries. But this carried a terrible cost.

'How many aircraft have they lost?' Joe murmured sympathetically.

'Over a thousand,' Dee sighed.

Mark cocked an eyebrow at her. 'Did Mr Royce tell you that?'

'I hear things from the patients.'

'Ah, yes, of course.' Mark said no more but his mood became a little glum.

Soon after that, she went to bed and lay listening. She heard the two men climbing the stairs, saying goodnight, going their different ways. After a while she heard Joe cross the landing to the bathroom, then the clank of pipes as he turned on the taps for a quick wash and finally the return to his room. A few minutes later the sounds were repeated with Mark.

Timing was everything. She waited until he'd left the bathroom and was just passing her door before going, 'Ow!'

'Dee?' His voice came through the door.

'Ooh!' she moaned.

'I'm coming in,' he said, opening the door.

She was sitting on the bed, clutching an ankle which rested on her knee. 'I twisted it,' she said feebly.

'How?'

'I couldn't say,' she told him truthfully. 'Rub it for me,' she said weakly. 'That's it! Ah, that's lovely.'

Something in her voice made Mark look at her more closely and see what she'd always meant him to see, that her jacket was open again and her nakedness was a blazing reminder of what they had briefly shared.

'Dee—'

But it was too late. She let herself fall back on the bed so that the edges of material fell apart, exposing all the beauty he'd been trying not to think of since the night before.

'Stop wasting time,' she said, laughing up at him.

Nothing could have stopped him then. When her arms opened in welcome, he went into them like a man coming home, seeking something outside all his previous experience, something he could never have described in words, but which only she could give.

This time she had some idea what to expect and was ready for him, or thought she was. But he still surprised her, taking her to new heights while he looked into her eyes in a way that was new and wonderful, and which made her heart soar.

Afterwards, he didn't draw away so quickly but lingered as though more certain of his welcome.

'What are you thinking?' he asked.

Dee had been wondering how she'd lived so many years without discovering this particular pleasure, but she judged it not the right moment to say so.

'I've been thinking how nice it is to have my Mad Bruin back,' she said. 'Just as mad as ever.'

'Madder,' he assured her. 'Much madder.'

She opened the drawer by the bed and took out the toy.

'You hear that?' she asked sternly. 'You're much madder. He says so, and he ought to know.' She held the little bear to her ear, then said to Mark, 'He wants to know what happened to his friend.'

'I'm afraid I don't know. Things got very confused.'

'Of course,' she said quickly. 'And I suppose you could hardly keep her at the base in case anyone saw her.'

'Right.'

Dee sensed Mark had become suddenly uneasy and made haste to yawn significantly.

'You're tired, I'll go,' he said and hurried away, pausing only long enough to drop a quick peck on her cheek.

When he'd gone, she gave herself a lecture about how foolish it would be to be disappointed. She was no romantic girl, but a warrior converging on her prey. Tonight had gone well. He'd come to her bed and done exactly as she wished. What more was there to want?

A good deal, she thought, *but it'll have to wait. Patience is the quality of great commanders, and I'm going to be the greatest of them all.*

That thought made her feel so optimistic that she fell asleep at once.

One night she came home to find the house quiet. Mark was in the back room, kneeling on the floor, holding Billy in his arms.

'Thank goodness you're here,' he said, his voice cracking in relief. 'Billy's going. The vet came this afternoon and he wanted to put him to sleep, but Joe and I said not until you came home.'

One look told Dee that she'd arrived just in time. Billy was lying patiently, eyes half open, but alert when she appeared, as though he, too, had been waiting for her. Mark handed him gently to her and retreated a little way, staying just close enough to keep a hand on Billy's fur.

'Goodbye, darling,' she choked, holding his head and looking into the old eyes as they faded. 'Thank you for everything. I love you so much—I'll always love you.'

As though he'd been hanging on only to hear that, Billy's eyes closed and his breathing faded to nothing as he fell asleep for the last time.

'Billy,' Dee pleaded. 'Billy, please—just one more minute.'

But he was heavy in her arms and there was nothing to do but lay him quietly on the floor while sobs shook her and Mark took gentle hold of her.

'We were lucky he lived so long,' he said huskily. 'Remember how he nearly hurled himself under my bike?'

'Yes, but for you swerving we'd have lost him long ago. Oh, Billy, Billy!'

Mark held her close, resting his head against hers. She could feel him trembling and for a moment she wondered if he, too, was weeping, having loved the old dog so much. Then he seemed to have a coughing fit and turned hurriedly away.

'Thank you for waiting for me,' she said brokenly. 'I couldn't have borne not to say goodbye to him.'

'Neither could I. Joe said his goodbye before he went out to training, then Billy and I had an hour together. I kept promising him you'd be home in time, but I was becoming afraid you wouldn't. I'm so glad.'

He drew her closer still, for now she was weeping without restraint.

'I'm sorry, I don't mean to—'

'Cry all you want,' he said gently. 'He earned it, didn't he?'

'Yes, he did. He was my best friend. I'm going to miss him so much.'

'You've got me. Of course, I know I'm no substitute for Billy—'

That made her smile, even through her tears. It felt so good to be here with Mark, taking comfort from his kindness, feeling close in a way that was rare. Their shared passion had brought them close but in a different way, one that lacked the sweet contentment that pervaded her now. If only it could always be like this. If only she didn't have to tell him something that would change everything, either for better or for worse. But not yet. For the moment, she would treasure the feeling of being at one with him.

The sound of the clock striking made them draw apart, surprised at how much time had passed.

'I'll take Billy outside,' he said, 'and we'll bury him tomorrow, when it's light.'

He carried the dog out to the shed. As they returned, he said, 'The house is going to be very quiet without him charging around.'

'Not as quiet as all that,' she murmured. 'Mark, I've got something to tell you.'

'Yes? What?'

Absorbed in her thoughts, she missed the hint of eagerness in his voice.

'Well...after the way we've spent the last few weeks...how often we've been together in your room or mine...'

'Dee, will you please come to the point?' he asked tensely.

'I'm pregnant.'

She waited for shock, dismay, she wasn't sure what, but all she saw in his face was frowning concentration.

'It's very soon,' he said. 'How can you be sure?'

'Most women couldn't, but I'm a nurse, so—'

'Of course, you'd know. Dee, I'm sorry.'

'Sorry?' she faltered.

'I took advantage of your kindness. I should have behaved better, but...well, it's done now and...'

'And what?' she asked, almost fearful.

'You once joked that we'd have to get married. How do you feel about it now?'

'Mark, for pity's sake! Is that a proposal?'

'I suppose it had better be. If you think you can stand being married to a bad character. I warn you, I'm no catch.'

'Well, I've always known that,' she said, exasperated almost beyond endurance. 'I'll just have to put up with you, won't I?'

'It's a deal.'

Then there was a pause, during which neither of them knew what to say.

'I can hear Joe coming home.' Mark sounded relieved. 'We'd better go and tell him.'

'Yes, let's.'

That was their betrothal.

CHAPTER TWELVE

THEY married a month later in the church where the others were buried. Joe, bursting with pride and triumph, gave the bride away, and afterwards Dee laid her bouquet of buttercups on her mother's grave.

A few of Mark's comrades from the Air Force were guests at the tiny reception held at home. These days, there were constant air offensives, taking the battle to the enemy, and hope for victory was daily growing.

Dee fell into conversation with Harry, a pleasant man who'd been a good friend of Mark's and was his best man today.

'Dashed if I ever thought Mark would find a woman who could tolerate him,' he confided, laughing.

'I come from a family whose women are renowned for being long-suffering,' she assured him in the same tone.

'Good for you! I say, look at that.' He pointed to a small toy high on a shelf. It was the Mad Bruin, brought out to enjoy the occasion.

'Mark won it for me at a funfair,' she said.

'It's very like his, except that his had a frilly skirt.'

'You've seen his?' she asked, startled.

'I used to. Not recently of course, because it went down with his plane.'

'Mark took it with him when he flew into battle?' she asked, scarcely able to breathe.

'Yes, but don't tell him I told you that. He smuggled it in

secret and none of us were supposed to know, but I think it was his good luck charm, and it really did seem as though he had a charmed life. But in the end they got him, too.'

Someone called him and he turned away, leaving her free to think. Now she was a mass of confusion. Mark had treasured her gift so much that he'd taken it with him while he'd risked his life, and had continued to do so even after she'd broken their engagement. That knowledge caused a glow of happiness to go through her.

But he'd concealed it from her. So many times he could have told her; when they became engaged, when they were making love. Yet he'd chosen not to, showing that there was still a distance between them. Emotionally, he still hadn't turned to her as much as she'd hoped.

And had their encounters really been love-making? On her side, yes, but on his? Hadn't he yielded to desire because he needed to know whether his skills as a lover had survived? And hadn't he married her because, although not exactly what he wanted, it was the best option now available in a devastated life?

But surely she'd always known this? She, too, was settling for what she could get because anything was better than life without him. She would be his wife and the mother of his children. He would never be romantically 'in love' with her. It was too late for that. But his affection would deepen and they would grow close.

She must simply hope for that.

But she refused to be discouraged. She had once promised to love him to the end, no matter what happened, and it was time to keep that promise.

She was taking a risk but it was one she had to take, otherwise her vow of love was meaningless. True love meant keeping on even when the actual emotion was hard to feel.

'Hey, where are you? Dee?'

It was Mark, looking unbelievably handsome, just as she'd once dreamed he would look on their wedding day.

'What's the idea of wandering off alone?' he chided. 'They're ready for the speeches.'

'I'm coming.'

'You're all right, aren't you?' He looked worriedly into her face.

'Yes, I'm fine,' she said brightly.

'Not sorry you married me?'

'Of course not.'

'No regrets? Sure about that?'

She touched his face. 'I'll never regret marrying you, as long as I live. Now, let's go and join the others.'

The rest of the reception went splendidly. There were toasts and speeches, cheers and laughter. That night they made love gently, then lay contentedly together. It was a happiness she'd once thought she would never know.

But she had dreamed of how, on their wedding night, she could finally tell him that she was deeply, passionately, romantically in love with him. Now she knew that she couldn't do it. She would have to wait longer for the right moment. It might be years in coming. Or it might never come.

His pride in his approaching fatherhood was immense. He was home every evening, something that made her an object of envy among her friends, and his whole attitude towards his wife, and marriage generally, exuded contentment. Dee knew that she was lucky, and that it was sheer perversity that made her long for some sign that she was more to him than just the mother of his baby, that he'd married her for more than the refuge she offered.

At last it was time for her to leave her job. On the last day there was a small party in the early evening, with speeches from Sister, Matron and even Mr Royce, who'd found the time to drop in. While he was toasting her, Dee looked up to see Mark standing in the door, a glowering expression on his face that she'd never seen before.

Now she recalled how he'd said that Mr Royce was in love with her, even advised her to catch him and make a 'good' marriage. But that was nonsense, wasn't it? Surely Mark had abandoned that fantasy?

But his scowling face said otherwise.

'I see that your husband has come to collect you,' Mr Royce said genially. 'Take her home, sir, and take the best possible care of her, because she means the world to all of us.'

Mark's smile seemed fixed on by rivets. 'I don't need to be told to take care of my wife,' he said in a soft voice that only Dee and Mr Royce could hear. 'Are you ready to go?'

'Yes, quite ready.'

He drove her home in the battered second-hand car that he'd bought to celebrate her pregnancy.

'You should go to bed now,' he said as they entered the house.

'I'd like some supper first.'

'All right, but then you go to bed. You need all the rest you can get.'

'Excuse me, are you instructing me in a medical matter?' she asked indignantly.

'This isn't medical, it's husband and wife,' he said illogically.

Joe was out that evening, which was just as well, she thought, considering Mark's temper.

'You're not still making a fuss about Mr Royce, surely?' she demanded, annoyed in her turn, and perfectly ready to have a row if that was what he wanted.

'Shouldn't I be? Do you really think he's over you?'

'I'm not sure there was ever anything for him to get over. It was just in your imagination.'

'Like hell it was! Do you think I've forgotten that he's the man you ought to have married?'

'Who says?'

'We both know it's true.'

'Then why didn't I marry him?'

'Because I forced you to marry me.'

Astonishment held her silent. After a moment he turned to see her properly.

'We both know it's true,' he said. 'Once I'd made you pregnant you didn't have a choice. That's what I was counting on.'

'You were...counting...?' She was groping for answers, trying to come to terms with this.

'Why do you think I came to you night after night—?' he growled.

'Or I came to you.'

'I was trying to make you pregnant, so that I could marry you.'

It took a moment for the full glorious truth of this to burst on her.

'You wanted to—you actually wanted to marry me?'

'Don't pretend you didn't know.'

'I've never known. Why didn't you just propose?'

'Because I had no right. What kind of prospect was I? Nothing to offer you beyond a damaged body and a load of nightmares. I didn't have the nerve to ask. But if you were pregnant it would be my duty to marry you, and I could square it with my conscience that way.'

Dee listened to this with mounting disbelief.

'Don't glare at me,' he said. 'Are you angry?'

'Angry? Mark, have you *never* understood? I wanted to marry you, and you were determined not to ask me, so I became pregnant on purpose.'

'What?'

'I had to do it, to force your hand.'

'Do you mean that you…that while I was trying to force… that all the time you were…is that what you're saying?'

'Yes,' she said through twitching lips. 'That's exactly what I'm saying. At least, I think it is. Oh, darling, it's crazy. We each wanted to get married, and we forced each other. And all this time—'

The last words were almost drowned by his shout of laughter. 'Come here,' he cried. 'Come here.'

Crowing with delight, she threw herself into his arms, kissing his face madly, fumbling for his buttons.

'Let's go upstairs,' she urged. 'We have to celebrate this in the proper way.'

But the words acted like a douche of cold water on him, making him freeze in mid-gesture and step back from her.

'What am I doing?' he groaned. 'I must be out of my mind to even think of…I'm sorry—forgive me.'

'Darling, it's all right. We can go ahead.'

'You're pregnant. It could harm you—or our baby.'

'Trust me to know about that. There's a little time left before we have to stop, I promise you.'

She thought she'd swayed him. He reached for her with desperate hands, then snatched them back, groaning.

'No, you're just indulging me, but I won't risk your health. Stay away. Don't tempt me.'

He ran, and a few moments later she heard him in the garage.

She wanted to scream her frustration to the heavens. They had taken one more step along the road, potentially a happy step. He wanted her. He'd wanted to marry her.

True, he hadn't actually said he loved her, but that would come, surely, the first time she could tempt him back into her arms? But he'd made it clear that the baby meant more to him than she did, so for the moment she would have to be patient again.

But she was so tired of being patient.

* * *

After her busy life, it was pleasant to have time for herself and to be cared for by two concerned men. In the afternoons she began putting her feet up, regarding her growing bump with placid contentment.

She was half dozing like this one day when there was a knock on the door. Opening it, she found Harry, the airman who'd been a guest at the wedding.

'I'm afraid Mark's not here,' she told him. 'He's working on a car at the owner's home.'

'It doesn't matter. I just wanted to deliver this.' He held out a large envelope. 'It seems that all Mark's things weren't cleared out when he left and they found this recently. Very sorry. Can't stop, I'm in a hurry.'

He blew her a friendly kiss and departed.

The envelope wasn't sealed and she tipped the contents out onto the table. There were a couple of stray socks and a few papers concerned with his time in the service. It was while sorting through these that she came across the letter he'd written her and never sent:

...You were right to break it off. I'm a useless character and I'd be no good for you...

The touch of humility took her breath away. He'd spoken like that once before, after his injury, but this had been written before. Had he felt like this even back then? Surely in those days he'd been different, more at ease behind the mask of bonhomie?

From the garage came the sound of clanking as Joe worked away. Mark would be back soon. Gathering everything together, she hurried up to her room and shut the door. Safely alone, she resumed reading the letter.

...Do you still have the Mad Bruin?...let him remind you of me sometimes; even if it's only the annoying things…never seem to understand when you want to be left alone…

But I never wanted you to leave me alone, she thought sadly. I wanted more of you, not less.

The letter became disjointed, suggesting that he'd returned to it often, while never finishing it.

Dee threw herself back on the bed, trying to come to terms with the discovery. Her heart was touched by the man she found here, a vulnerable man, not the cockily self-confident loudmouth he tried to present to the world. But someone who was secretly waiting for love to let him down—as it always had done, going back to his earliest days.

This was the true Mark, the lovable Mark, but still the one he concealed from her. The letter had never been sent. She closed her eyes, conjuring him up in the darkness, trying to see him as he must have looked when he was writing. Had he murmured her name?

'Dee—Dee—'

She opened her eyes to find him sitting on the bed beside her, frowning in concern.

'I was just dozing,' she said, looking up at him from the pillow. She saw him looking at the letter in her hand. 'Harry brought some of your things that weren't returned before, and this was among them.'

'So that's what happened to it. So many things vanished, including my little bear.'

'Harry said you had her in the cockpit with you when you went down. He told me that at the wedding. I wish you'd told me yourself.'

He took the letter and she watched his face. He looked sad and strangely older than only a few hours ago.

'Perhaps I shouldn't have read it,' she said. 'You never wanted me to see it, did you?'

'Not then. I didn't know how to face you. There was so

much I wanted to say but I couldn't find the words.' He gave a wry smile. 'I was angry. You dumped me and it was a shock. My pride was hurt. This—' he indicated the letter '—was me trying to say so and making a mess of it. It's probably just as well I didn't send it to you.'

'Or maybe it's a pity. Who knows what might have happened? I might have come to visit you.' There was just a hint of hope in her voice.

'Or you could have had an attack of common sense and stayed well clear of me.'

'Does that mean you're sorry we're together, Mark?'

He frowned, as though not understanding the question. 'How can you say that?' he asked, laying a hand on her stomach. 'Everything that's worthwhile in my life, in the whole world, is here. All hope is here, all love is here, all life.'

He laid his face against her for a moment, then raised it and said gently, 'I'll make you a cup of tea.'

He hurried away, taking the letter with him and leaving her smiling. There was joy to be found in his words, his all-embracing acceptance of her as the hope of his life. She tried to ignore a faint niggling disappointment that his affection seemed to lack the other dimension that would have meant so much. He'd turned to her as a refuge from horrors, something she knew was common to many men who'd been involved in fighting. It was more than she might have expected and if it wasn't what she'd hoped for, so what? With the years stretching out ahead of them, it was time to be realistic.

Wasn't it?

Gradually the war news became more hopeful. Mark was still in touch with many of his pilot friends, and they passed on information not yet available to the rest of the world. In September 1943, allied troops had landed in southern Italy. In January 1944, more troops reached Italy in what became known as the Anzio landings. Their progress was slowed down by fierce resistance, but they overcame it. Hope was in the air.

Then came February, when a few days became known as 'Big Week' as the allied air forces stormed across Europe. The three of them listened to the nightly radio bulletins and Dee tried to read Mark's face, wondering if he felt excluded from what was turning into a triumph. But the smile he turned on her was always warm and tender, and his hand would reach out to touch her stomach gently.

Both Joe and Mark watched Dee like guard dogs. If there was a job to be done away from home it was always Joe who took it, and even he announced that he would soon refuse them.

'This is the last one until it's all over,' he announced one morning, buttoning up his jacket.

'Dad,' she protested, laughing, 'nothing's going to happen for a few weeks.'

'And I'm going to be here when it does. 'Bye darling. Take care.'

She settled down for a pleasant day's sewing, but within an hour she knew she'd been wrong about nothing happening. Pain started tearing through her, growing greater and greater. She screamed and Mark came hurrying in from the garage.

All the way to the hospital she tried to stay hopeful. Her moment was coming. A few hours of suffering and she would see Mark hold their child in his arms, their eyes would meet in a moment of perfect understanding and the bond between them would be sealed as never before.

But, as they reached the hospital and she was wheeled away, she knew that something was badly wrong. The pain was agonising in the wrong way; blood was flowing out of her body in a terrifying river.

'He's dead,' she whispered. 'My baby is dead.'

'We're giving you a blood transfusion,' the sister said. 'Don't give up hope yet.'

But Dee was a nurse. She knew the truth.

'No,' she moaned. 'Oh, dear God, *no!*'

Mark had married her for this baby, hoping to find a haven for his tormented heart. Now she was letting him down.

'No,' she whispered. 'No—please, save my baby.'

Then everything was dark.

For Mark, waiting in a corridor, time dragged with painful slowness. At last a middle-aged nurse emerged, sympathetic when she saw him.

'It's gone wrong, hasn't it?' he asked in a shaking voice. He wasn't sure how he knew, but he'd picked something up from Dee's tension, without understanding it.

'I'm afraid the baby was born dead,' the nurse said.

He closed his eyes, leaning back against the wall, his heart aching for his wife. She was suffering so much, with nothing to show for it.

'But she's going to be all right, isn't she?' he asked huskily.

In the silence that followed he felt terror rise in him. *'She's going to be all right!'* he almost shouted.

'Mr Sellon, I have to be honest with you. Your wife has lost a lot of blood. We're doing our best, but things may not go well. I think you should be prepared.'

'No!' he said fiercely. 'That's not going to happen. I won't let it. You don't understand. She won't go away—because she never does—when I need her—she's always there—' He was breathing hard, as though he'd been running. 'I want to see her.'

'Of course.' The nurse stood back to let him pass.

At first he couldn't believe that the woman lying on the bed was Dee. His Dee was always full of life and vitality, but this woman lay as still as death, her breathing coming so faintly that it was almost noiseless.

'Darling, wake up,' he said urgently. 'Look at me, talk to me.'

There was no response, no sound, no movement, and that frightened him more than anything. In all the time they had known each other, never had she refused him anything, save the time when she'd broken their engagement. And that had been the greatest misfortune of his life. Now she was refusing him again, and the spectre of the future made him recoil in dread.

'You've got to listen,' he said urgently. 'I know you can hear me because—' He stopped as he heard himself saying words he didn't understand. How did he know this? And yet he did know. Somewhere, far back in his mind, he could hear a voice saying, 'I know you're asleep but maybe you can hear me, somewhere deep inside you... I do hope so because there's so much I want you to understand.'

Once he'd heard those words and they had summoned him back from a dark place. Now they were his only hope.

'Can you hear me?' he asked, echoing the words in his memory. 'Can my voice reach deep inside you? Please hear me. There's so much I want you to understand.

'I've never told you of my love because I didn't know how, but I must tell you now because it may be my last chance. I think I loved you from the start. Remember how easily we could talk? That's why I couldn't commit to Sylvia. She was beautiful but you had something special about you, although I didn't properly understand.

'I was a young idiot, full of self-importance, thinking I was entitled to everything I wanted, especially girls. And all the time this feeling was growing in me but I couldn't let myself admit the truth. It mattered too much. *You* mattered.

'I was glad when we decided to pretend to be a couple because I wanted you to be my girl. So why didn't I ask you? Because I was shy, and that's the truth. There, laugh at me. I deserve it. I was a fool. If I hadn't been, I'd never have lost you. I went out on the town to convince myself that I was still in charge, free of you, when the truth was I could never be free. And you threw my stupidity back in my face, as you had every right to do.'

Mark laid his head down on Dee's breast. 'Speak to me,' he begged. 'Come back to me. I love you with all my heart. I'll never love anyone else.'

As he spoke, a door opened inside his mind and he knew that these words, too, were not his own, but had been said to him, long ago. He hadn't recognised her love until this moment, but it was as true now as then, deeper with the depth of suffering, and his own love reached out in response.

Everything that mattered to him had come from the woman who lay in his arms, who would slip away if he couldn't prevent it. He did the only thing that was in his power, laying his lips on hers, sending her a silent message of warmth and love.

'Can you feel my love reaching out to you?' he murmured, repeating what he now knew to be her words to him long ago. 'It's yours if you want it.'

For a long moment he held his breath, letting it out slowly as her eyes opened.

'It was you, wasn't it?' he whispered. 'You came to me in the hospital when I was dying, and you turned me back. Now I'm here to do the same for you.'

'Is it true?' she murmured. 'Is it really true?'

'It's true, my darling, more true than I can ever say. You're the one, the only one. You always have been. Do you remember how you ordered me to get well, saying you were a bully? Well, so am I.' He gave a shaky smile. 'Woman, your husband is ordering you to get well and love him for ever.'

'Then I must,' she said.

'Is that a promise?'

'It's a promise.'

'I'll hold you to it.'

Suddenly her smile was stronger. 'Did I ever break a promise to you yet?'

He shook his head and spoke sombrely. 'I love you, my wife. It took me too long to say it, but now I'll be saying it every moment of all the years ahead. I love you. I love you.'

The months that followed were a mixture of grief and joy—grief for our dead child, joy that we had found each other at last. Everything was sweet and familiar, my darling, yet everything was new.

You became a little more possessive, always checking to see that I was all right. People used to say to me, 'Doesn't he suffocate you? Isn't it annoying?' But it wasn't annoying. It was lovely being needed.

I remember 6th June which became known as D-Day, the start of the Normandy landings, when the allied army invaded the Continent again, this time in France. Now the final victory was in view. The war didn't end officially until the following year but D-Day was the beginning of the end, and people sensed it, pouring into the streets to sing and hold hands, looking to the future with glad hearts.

We were there, too, standing with our arms about each other, trying to rejoice with the others. I was determined to put a brave face on it for your sake, but when I glanced up I found you looking down at me with an expression of such love and concern that I felt closer to you than ever before. That night my happiness had nothing to do with the looming end of the war. It came from knowing that I came first with you.

For a while we feared that I couldn't have another baby, and I'll never forget how tenderly you assured me that you didn't care about that, as long as you had me. But then we found I was pregnant again, and before long we had Lilian. The following year Terry joined us. You wouldn't admit how proud you were to have a son. People were just beginning to talk about women's lib and you didn't want to appear old-fashioned. So you tried to seem casual, but I knew you were bursting with pride and I had a little laugh—secretly, of course.

But no happiness is ever untroubled. The following year Polly was born and it seemed we could ask for no more. She was your favourite. According to Dad, it was because she looked like me. When she died suddenly, just before her first birthday, I thought you, too, would die. I believe you wanted to, although you never said so. We didn't talk about it, just held each other in silence, night after night.

Your health improved. You got much of your strength back and Dad made you a partner in the garage. As he got older he eased off a bit, doing less mechanical work and helping to look after the children so that I was able to go back to work at the hospital. You didn't like my working. In those days a wife and mother was supposed to stay at home, but you said I must do whatever I thought right.

I think it helped that Mr Royce had got married to a beautiful girl twenty years his junior.

Once I'd started work you never mentioned it, never complained, even helped in the house to make my life easier. People who'd known you before the war were astonished. 'You should have seen him back then,' they'd say. 'You'd never have thought he'd turn out like this.'

If you had a fault it was that you were always losing things. How many times did I hear you cry, 'Dee, where's my—?' Heavens, but you were the untidiest man in the world! Still are, come to that.

For a while there were five of us in that little house and it was very crowded, but we were happy, and when Dad died we really missed him. We watched our children grow up and make their own lives, and then we were alone for the first time.

Some parents are devastated when their young fly the nest, but you said it was like being newlyweds. We were in our fifties by then, but you were right.

What a time we had! We got quite exhausted. We thought of having a honeymoon, because we hadn't had one the first time, but in the end we just locked the doors and had a honeymoon at home.

Then, in a strange way, we became parents again. Lilian gave birth to Pippa just when she was getting ready to go back to work, and she was glad when we offered to help out. We cared for Pippa part-time until she started school. And when she was a teenager we took her in because she and Lilian couldn't live in the same house without squabbling. And now it's a joy to have her here, our extra 'daughter', caring for us and understanding us better than anyone else.

I told her about having our 'honeymoon' at home, and she was scandalised. She thinks it's not a honeymoon unless you go away and we should have taken that trip to Brighton that we once talked about. Perhaps she's right. Is it too late? We've done everything else, could we still manage that, too? Oh, yes, let's do it. Let's have one last wonderful fling!

'Are you crazy?' Lilian demanded.

'No, they're crazy,' Pippa laughed. 'And why shouldn't they be?'

'Brighton? At their age?'

'They won't do anything energetic, just sit in the sun. I'll be there to take care of them, and I'll bring them home safely. Promise.'

A week later she drove Mark and Dee to the seaside resort in a trip that was planned to be as similar as possible to the one they would have taken years before. They stayed in a tiny bed and breakfast near the seafront and spent each day strolling gently along the promenade, or sitting in deckchairs on the beach. At these times Pippa moved away far enough to give them privacy, but always kept them in sight in case they needed her.

'I really envy you two,' she said once, when she'd just

finished making them comfortable. 'The way you are together—it's wonderful.'

'And one day it will be wonderful for you,' Dee promised. 'With the right man.'

'No.' Pippa shook her head. 'Not now. I'm finished with all that.'

'And you're going to spend the rest of your life like this?' Dee demanded. 'Doing dead-end jobs and turning your back on love? I'm not going to let that happen. I've got plans for you, my girl. I've left you some money in my will, but only on condition you train for a proper career. No, don't argue.'

'But Gran, I—'

'Listen my darling; Grandpa and I planned this together. We've had a wonderful marriage and we can't bear to think of you losing out, when we want you to be as complete and fulfilled as we've been. Let us have the peace of knowing that we did our best to help you, and then we'll always be part of your life.'

'You'll always be part of it anyway. You know that.'

'You obey your Gran,' Mark said contentedly. 'I always have.'

'I'll—think about it.'

'You'll do as you're told,' Dee said. 'Be off with you, now.'

'Thank you,' she said softly.

She kissed them both and strolled away to the water's edge, where she could paddle, yet still look up the beach and keep a protective eye on them as they sat in contented silence, eyes closed, faces raised to the sun, their hands entwined, like their hearts. This was how love ought to be.

I don't think it will ever be like that for me, Gran, whatever you say, she thought. *But you're so convinced that you make me think I might be wrong. If, one day, a man comes along who helps me forget the past, maybe it will work out between us, because I'll have my memories of you and Grandpa to remind me to hope and believe. I'll never forget what you and he have taught me, and I thank you both with all my heart.*

Turn the page for a sneak peek at

Wealthy Australian, Secret Son,

the exhilarating new novel from international bestselling author Margaret Way available this month from all-new Mills & Boon® Cherish™.

CHAPTER ONE

The present

IT WAS an idyllic day for a garden party. The sky was a deep blue; sparkling sunshine flooded the Valley; a cooling breeze lowered the spring into summer heat. A veritable explosion of flowering trees and foaming blossom had turned the rich rural area into one breathtakingly beautiful garden that leapt at the eye and caught at the throat. It was so perfect a world the inhabitants of Silver Valley felt privileged to live in it.

Only Charlotte Prescott, a widow at twenty-six, with a seven-year-old child, stood in front of the bank of mirrors in her dressing room, staring blindly at her own reflection. The end of an era had finally arrived, but there was no joy in it for her, for her father, or for Christopher, her clever, thoughtful child. They were the dispossessed, and nothing in the world could soothe the pain of loss.

For the past month, since the invitations had begun to arrive, Silver Valley had been eagerly anticipating the Open Day: a get-to-know-you garden party to be held in the grounds of the grandest colonial mansion in the valley, Riverbend. Such a lovely name, Riverbend! A private house, its grandeur reflected the wealth and community standing of the man who had built it in the 1880s, Charles

Randall Marsdon, a young man of means who had migrated from England to a country that didn't have a splendid *past*, like his homeland, but in his opinion had a glowing *future*. He'd meant to be part of that future. He'd meant to get to the top!

There might have been a certain amount of bravado in that young man's goal, but Charles Marsdon had turned out not only to be a visionary, but a hard-headed businessman who had moved to the highest echelons of colonial life with enviable speed.

Riverbend was a wonderfully romantic two-storey mansion, with a fine Georgian façade and soaring white columns, its classic architecture adapted to climatic needs with large-scale open-arched verandahs providing deep shading for the house. It had been in the Marsdon family—*her* family—for six generations, but sadly it would never pass to her adored son. For the simple reason that Riverbend was no longer theirs. The mansion, its surrounding vineyards and olive groves, badly neglected since the Tragedy, had been sold to a company called Vortex. Little was known about Vortex, except that it had met the stiff price her father had put on the estate. Not that he could have afforded to take a lofty attitude. Marsdon money had all but run out. But Vivian Marsdon was an immensely proud man who never for a moment underestimated his important position in the Valley. It was *everything* to him to keep face. In any event, the asking price, exorbitantly high, had been paid swiftly—and oddly enough without a single quibble.

Now, months later, the CEO of the company was finally coming to town. Naturally she and her father had been invited, although neither of them had met any Vortex representative. The sale had been handled to her father's satisfaction by their family solicitors, Dunnett & Banfield. Part of the deal was that her father was to have tenure of the Lodge—originally an old coach house—during his lifetime, after which it would be returned to the estate. The coach house had been converted and greatly enlarged by her grandfather into a beautiful and comfortable guest house that had enjoyed a good deal of use in the old days, when her grandparents had entertained on a grand scale, and it was at the Lodge they were living now. Just the three of them: father, daughter, grandson.

Her former in-laws—Martyn's parents and his sister Nicole—barely acknowledged them these days. The estrangement had become entrenched in the eighteen months since Martyn's death. Her husband, three years older than she, had been killed when he'd lost control of his high-powered sports car on a notorious black spot in the Valley and smashed into a tree. A young woman had been with him. Mercifully she'd been thrown clear of the car, suffering only minor injuries. It had later transpired she had been Martyn's mistress for close on six months. Of course Martyn hadn't been getting what he'd needed at home. If Charlotte had been a loving wife the tragedy would never have happened. The *second* major tragedy in her lifetime. It seemed very much as if Charlotte Prescott was a jinx.

Poor old you! Charlotte spoke silently to her image. *What a mess you've made of your life!*

She really didn't need anyone to tell her that. The irony was that her father had made just as much a mess of his own life—even before the Tragedy. The *first* tragedy. The only one that mattered to her parents. Her father had had little time for Martyn, yet he himself was a man without insight into his own limitations. Perhaps the defining one was unloading responsibility. Vivian Marsdon was constitutionally incapable of accepting the blame for anything. Anything that went wrong was always someone else's fault, or due to some circumstance beyond his control. The start of the Marsdon freefall from grace had begun when her highly respected grandfather, Sir Richard Marsdon, had died. His only son and heir had not been able to pick up the reins. It was as simple as that. The theory of three. One man made the money, the next enlarged on it, the third lost it. No better cushion than piles of money. Not every generation produced an heir with the Midas touch, let alone the necessary drive to manage and significantly enlarge the family fortune.

Her father, born to wealth and prestige, lacked Sir Richard's strong character as well as his formidable business brain. Marsdon money had begun to disappear early, like water down a drain. Failed pie-in-the-sky schemes had been approached with enthusiasm. Her father had turned a deaf ear to cautioning counsel from accountants and solicitors alike. He knew best. Sadly, his lack of judgement had put a discernible dent in the family fortunes. And that was even before the Tragedy that had blighted their family life.

With a sigh of regret, Charlotte picked up her lovely hat with its wide floppy brim, settling it on her head. She rarely wore her long hair loose these days, preferring to pull it back from her face and arrange it in various knots. In any case, the straw picture hat demanded she pull her hair back off her face. Her dress was Hermes silk, in chartreuse, strapless except for a wide silk band over one shoulder that flowed down the bodice and short skirt. The hat was a perfect colour match, adorned with organdie peonies in masterly deep pinks that complemented the unique shade of golden lime-green.

The outfit wasn't new, but she had only worn it once, at Melbourne Cup day when Martyn was alive. Martyn had taken great pride in how she looked. She'd always had to look her best. In those days she had been every inch a *fashionista*, such had been their extravagant and, it had to be said, *empty* lifestyle. Martyn had been a man much like her father—an inheritor of wealth who could do what he liked, when he liked, if he so chose. Martyn had made his choice. He had always expected to marry her, right from childhood, bringing about the union of two long-established rural families. And once he'd had her—he had always been mad about her—he had set about making their lifestyle a whirl of pleasure up until his untimely death.

From time to time she had consoled herself with the thought that perhaps Martyn, as he matured, would cease taking up endless defensive positions against his highly effective father, Gordon, come to recognise his family responsibilities and then pursue them with some skill and determination.

Sadly, all her hopes—and Gordon Prescott's—had been killed off one by one. And she'd had to face some hard facts herself. Hadn't she been left with a legacy of guilt? She had never loved Martyn. Bonded to him from earliest childhood, she had always regarded him with great affection. But *romantic* love? Never! The heart wasn't obedient to the expectations of others. She *knew* what romantic love was. She *knew* about passion—dangerous passion and its infinite temptations—but she hadn't steered away from it in the interests of safety. She had totally succumbed.

All these years later her heart still pumped his name. *Rohan*.

She heard her son's voice clearly. He sounded anxious. "Mummy, are you ready? Grandpa wants to leave."

A moment later, Christopher, a strikingly handsome little boy, dressed in a bright blue shirt with mother-of-pearl buttons and grey cargo pants, tore into the room.

"Come on, come on," he urged, holding out his hand to

her. "He's stomping around the hall and going red in the face. That means his blood pressure is going up, doesn't it?"

"Nothing for you to worry about, sweetheart," Charlotte answered calmly. "Grandpa's health is excellent. Stomping is a way to get our attention. Anyway, we're not late," she pointed out.

It had been after Martyn's death, on her father's urging, that she and Christopher had moved into the Lodge. Her father was sad and lonely, finding it hard getting over the big reversals in his life. She knew at some point she *had* to make a life for herself and her son. But where? She couldn't escape the Valley. Christopher loved it here. It was his home. He loved his friends, his school, his beautiful environment and his bond with his grandfather. It made a move away from the Valley extremely difficult, and there were other crucial considerations for a single mother with a young child.

Martyn had left her little money. They had lived with his parents at their huge High Grove estate. They had wanted for nothing, all expenses paid, but Martyn's father—knowing his son's proclivities—had kept his son on a fairly tight leash. His widow, so all members of the Prescott family had come to believe, was undeserving.

"Grandpa runs to a timetable of his own," Christopher was saying, shaking his golden-blond head. She too was blonde, with green eyes. Martyn had been fair as well, with greyish-blue eyes. Christopher's eyes were as brilliant as blue-fire diamonds. "You look lovely in that dress, Mummy," he added, full of love and pride in his beautiful mother. "Please don't be sad today. I just wish I was seventeen instead of seven," he lamented. "I'm just a kid. But I'll grow up and become a great big success. You'll have *me* to look after you."

"My knight in shining armour!" She bent to give him a

big hug, then took his outstretched hand, shaking it back and forth as if beginning a march. "Onward, Christian soldiers!"

"What's that?" He looked up at her with interest.

"It's an English hymn," she explained. Her father wouldn't have included hymns in the curriculum. Her father wasn't big on hymns. Not since the Tragedy. "It means we have to go forth and do our best. *Endure*. It was a favourite hymn of Sir Winston Churchill. You know who he was?"

"Of course!" Christopher scoffed. "He was the great English World War II Prime Minister. The country gave him a *huge* amount of money for his services to the nation, then they took most of it back in tax. Grandpa told me."

Charlotte laughed. Very well read himself, her father had taken it upon himself to "educate" Christopher. Christopher had attended the best school in the Valley for a few years now, but her father took his grandson's education much further, taking pride and delight it setting streams of general, historical and geographical questions for which Christopher had to find the answers. Christopher was already computer literate but her father wasn't—something that infuriated him—and insisted he find the answers in the books in the well-stocked library. Christopher never cheated. He always came up trumps. Christopher was a very clever little boy.

Like his father.

The garden party was well underway by the time they finished their stroll along the curving driveway. Riverbend had never looked more beautiful, Charlotte thought, pierced by the same sense of loss she knew her father was experiencing—though one would never have known it from his confident Lord of the Manor bearing. Her father was a handsome man, but alas not a lot of people in the Valley liked him. The mansion, since they had moved, had undergone very necessary repairs. These days it was superbly maintained, and staffed by a housekeeper, her husband—a sort of major-domo—and several ground staff to bring the once-famous gardens back to their best. A good-looking young woman came out from Sydney from time to time, to check on what was being done. Charlotte had met her once, purely by accident…

© Margaret Way, PTY., LTD 2011

VA_INTRO

&RIVA™

Live life to the full - give in to temptation

Four new sparkling and sassy romances every month!

Be the first to read this fabulous new series from 1st December 2010 at **millsandboon.co.uk**
In shops from 1st January 2011

Tell us what you think!
Facebook.com/romancehq
Twitter.com/millsandboonuk

Don't miss out!

Available at WHSmith, Tesco, ASDA, Eason and all good bookshops
www.millsandboon.co.uk

**On sale from 21st January 2011
Don't miss out!**

Available at WHSmith, Tesco, ASDA, Eason
and all good bookshops

www.millsandboon.co.uk

BEAUTY AND THE BROODING BOSS *by Barbara Wallace*

Working for author Alex sounds like Kelsey's dream job until she meets her new, rude, unwelcoming boss. Yet beneath his gruff façade could Alex be her Prince Charming?

FRIENDS TO FOREVER *by Nikki Logan*

Marc and Beth were best friends—until a heated kiss exposed secrets and ruined everything. Ten years later, are they ready to forgive the sins of the past?

CROWN PRINCE, PREGNANT BRIDE! *by Raye Morgan*

Monte believed love had no place in his world, until courageous Pellea made him reconsider. Although she's promised to another, he's now determined to fight for her.

VALENTINE BRIDE *by Christine Rimmer*

Reserved Irina was the perfect housekeeper for playboy Caleb. Then she found out she was being deported. So Caleb came up with the ideal solution: marry him!

THE NANNY AND THE CEO *by Rebecca Winters*

CEO Nick can handle billion-dollar business deals with his eyes closed —but a baby? Driven Reese is the perfect nanny, yet could she be something more?

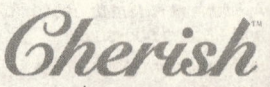

Cherish

On sale from 4th February 2011
Don't miss out!

Available at WHSmith, Tesco, ASDA, Eason and all good bookshops

www.millsandboon.co.uk

THE FAMILY THEY CHOSE
by Nancy Robards Thompson

Struggling to have a baby is shaking Olivia's marriage to the core. Despite the heartache, Jamison's intent on bringing back his wife's happiness—one kiss at a time.

PRIVATE PARTNERS
by Gina Wilkins

No one knew about the secret wedding vows Anne had exchanged with Liam. But now her irresistible husband is back and ready to claim her all over again.

A COLD CREEK SECRET
by RaeAnne Thayne

Brant is hoping to put the past behind him and find some measure of solitude and peace at his ranch—but those hopes are dashed when spoiled heiress Mimi arrives!

Cherish

MILLS & BOON

are proud to present our...

Book of the Month

Prince Voronov's Virgin
by Lynn Raye Harris

from Mills & Boon® Modern™

Paige Barnes is rescued from the dark streets of Moscow by Prince Alexei Voronov—her boss's deadliest rival. Now he has Paige unexpectedly in his sights, Alexei will play emotional Russian roulette to keep her close…

Available 17th December

Something to say about our Book of the Month?
Tell us what you think!

millsandboon.co.uk/community
facebook.com/romancehq
twitter.com/millsandboonuk

Discover Pure Reading Pleasure with

MILLS & BOON

Visit the Mills & Boon website for all the latest in romance

- **Buy** all the latest releases, backlist and eBooks
- **Find out** more about our authors and their books
- **Join** our community and chat to authors and other readers
- **Free** online reads from your favourite authors
- **Win** with our fantastic online competitions
- **Sign** up for our free monthly eNewsletter
- **Tell us** what you think by signing up to our reader panel
- **Rate** and review books with our star system

www.millsandboon.co.uk

Follow us at twitter.com/millsandboonuk

Become a fan at facebook.com/romancehq

0111_S1ZED

2 FREE BOOKS
AND A SURPRISE GIFT

We would like to take this opportunity to thank you for reading this Mills & Boon® book by offering you the chance to take TWO more specially selected books from the Cherish™ series absolutely FREE! We're also making this offer to introduce you to the benefits of the Mills & Boon® Book Club™—

- **FREE home delivery**
- **FREE gifts and competitions**
- **FREE monthly Newsletter**
- **Exclusive Mills & Boon Book Club offers**
- **Books available before they're in the shops**

Accepting these FREE books and gift places you under no obligation to buy, you may cancel at any time, even after receiving your free books. Simply complete your details below and return the entire page to the address below. You don't even need a stamp!

YES Please send me 2 free Cherish books and a surprise gift. I understand that unless you hear from me, I will receive 5 superb new stories every month, including two 2-in-1 books priced at £5.30 each, and a single book priced at £3.30, postage and packing free. I am under no obligation to purchase any books and may cancel my subscription at any time. The free books and gift will be mine to keep in any case.

Ms/Mrs/Miss/Mr _____ Initials _____

Surname _____

Address _____

_____ Postcode _____

E-mail _____

Send this whole page to: Mills & Boon Book Club, Free Book Offer, FREEPOST NAT 10298, Richmond, TW9 1BR

Offer valid in UK only and is not available to current Mills & Boon Book Club subscribers to this series. Overseas and Eire please write for details.. We reserve the right to refuse an application and applicants must be aged 18 years or over. Only one application per household. Terms and prices subject to change without notice. Offer expires 31st March 2011. As a result of this application, you may receive offers from Harlequin Mills & Boon and other carefully selected companies. If you would prefer not to share in this opportunity please write to The Data Manager, PO Box 676, Richmond, TW9 1WU.

Mills & Boon® is a registered trademark owned by Harlequin Mills & Boon Limited.
Cherish™ is being used as a trademark.
The Mills & Boon® Book Club™ is being used as a trademark.